The Widening

> *"Turning and turning in the widening gyre*
> *The falcon cannot hear the falconer;*
> *Things fall apart; the centre cannot hold;*
> *Mere anarchy is loosed upon the world..."*
>
> -William Butler Yeats
> *The Second Coming*

For my friend Dave Ramsden, without whom this work would not have been possible.

Refuge 4
A Life in Ashes...4
The Mother of Intrigue 17
The Voluntary Exile 21
A Fortress of Shadows 26
Echoes of the Past 30
Eye in the Banlieue...33
Road to Nowhere..39

Restitution 51
Born of Two Worlds 51
Gateway to Disappearance 59
Cracks in the Foundation..73
Focusing the Microscope..82
Dust to Dust..87
Threads of the Past 92
Crossroads of Purpose...102
The Weight of Survival 119
Roots of Resistance 130
Vita Procedit 143
Blueprint for Chaos...150
Lines of Fire..153
Convergence 156
A Nation on the Edge 160
The Unbroken Chain 169
Unmasking the Shadow..175
Baited and Trapped 188
Cage of Secrets..195
The Price of Freedom...207

Retribution 221
A Shoulder for the Burden 221
The Final Gambit 244
Epilogue: Echoes Across the Desert .. 256
Bonus Feature 259
Dartford Interlude 259

Refuge

A Life in Ashes

Platform two at Dartford station faces the rear balconies of newly built apartment towers overlooking a manmade pond with a central fountain. The fountain sprays individual jets arranged in a circle, with a single jet in the centre spraying straight up. Water from the central jet reaches its apex, runs out of energy and falls straight back down, while the circle of jets is angled so there is a series of parabolas of water. The image on the surface is that of concentric circles of constant perturbation, with ripples emanating out across the pond. At this time of the year the sunrise corresponds to the commute rush hour, and the rising sun catches the flecks of water in flight and shows like glints of broken glass against the mist of a tiny rainbow, imprisoned by the fountain.

Harry's eye was drawn to the fountain and his ear had latched onto the sound of falling and splashing water, like a quiet but heavy rain ever-present below the symphony of the morning commute. While his gaze was fixed on the fountain his ear tuned out the tannoy announcements, car horns and one-sided, mother tongue conversations shouted into cell phones on the platform. His mind had set out to wander but as always it had found and followed a path. It constructed a scenario and considered and rejected alternatives from his present or his past until he was living this counterfactual exercise, entirely in his head. He knew the paths his mind wandered became theme parks once he had fully descended the rabbit-hole, and he could inhabit them entirely to the ignorance of the world around him. He was aware his overthinking that had started as a means to assuage worry and regret now had the capacity to warp his perception of reality. He sometimes lost himself completely in reliving episodes where outcomes could never change, no matter the intent. Lately, losing himself in thought felt more like wandering through a vast mental landscape. He was starting to recognize when such episodes were about to take hold. He would be lost in thought considering something he could have done or should do, some reaction he should have had, and he would get an epiphany that would change the dynamics of the scenario and he would find comfort in it and follow new lines of reasoning to the bottom of the well.

For months now these agonisingly self-recriminating Sisyphean purges were focused entirely on his divorce and the breakup of his family. There was no catharsis or resolution; the more he focused on the things that drove his wife away, the more likely he was to land on his own shortcomings as an uncircumventable root cause. This deepened his guilt, eroded his dwindling self-esteem, and spiraled him into a state of mental and spiritual depletion. It was, after all, his poor mental health that began the end of his family. He had made his wife feel unsafe around him and he had undeniably endangered her physically. His son's screaming and hair-pulling brought him out of an episode where his hands were around her throat, and though she was fighting with all she had to get free, she could not. If his son hadn't brought him out of it then he might have killed her.

That first flash of a return to clarity was like rushing to the surface, gasping for the ballast of the immediate and the extant, a comfort, a relief. But with clarity came the realisation that the loss of control and the disassociation was complete. With clarity came the reckoning with what had been wrought in his succumbency.

"Mate!" the man directly in his eyeline had fairly shouted, as if he had been trying to get his attention and had arrived at this shout only after escalation. Harry returned to clarity and looked him full in the face.

"Are you alright mate?" the man asked, gesturing toward Harry's extended but as yet unfurled umbrella. The man was wearing a waterproof windbreaker with the hood up and it was clear that it had started to rain. Harry realised he was sitting on the bench seats away from the covered part of the platform and that he was getting rained on, even while he sat with an umbrella in his hand.

Harry thanked the man and muttered something inconsequential about deciding on the 7:24 or the 7:39, because the later train was semi-fast but the earlier train would get him out of the rain sooner. He was a little too bewildered to be embarrassed. He pushed the framework so the umbrella was taut, and then he put it up. The intermittent, heavy raindrops hitting the dome sounded like sporadic gunfire from a Sahelian village in the middle distance. The man nodded and moved a few steps down the platform.

Harry engaged in destructive rumination for the entire journey to Cannon Street station. He and his wife Elena have been separated for four months before the divorce was finalised. It was a no-fault divorce and the separation of assets followed the lines of responsibility, per the law. Harry did not contest any of the claims and Elena did not ask for more than was reasonable. Caring for the children financially was the playing field for their case, and the burden of care fell to Elena and the burden of support fell to Harry. Herve, eight, and Leni, six had been the centre of Harry's world. Sports, tutors, dancing school – never mind the regular school load or the seemingly endless doctor's visits – ate up all of the time he had outside the pursuit of a career to fund it all. She kept the two-bedroom house in Welling and lived there to minimise the impact of the change for the children. Harry was renting a one-bedroom flat further out in Dartford, trying to keep the costs as low as possible so the children's lifestyle wasn't noticeably impacted. One of the balconies he had been staring at from the station platform was his own. He was excluded from family life now and he lived like a pauper with nothing to distract him from his situation or his obligations. He was aggrieved and bereft of purpose. He was deprived of the love and support that helped him to cope at all, and now he could only be present as a paycheck. He had sacrificed so much to get the life that he had, and now it had all come to naught. He felt like there was a death in the family, and that it was of the family father. As he carried on in just close enough proximity to maximise his personal anguish, Elena and the kids carried on. For them, they could just stay on the rails and stay the course and accept the condolences of their acquaintances. He was wrenched out of his life and set in a petty apologetic and impoverished orbit around the family.

He got to London Bridge and changed to a train for Cannon Street. The closer he got to the office the more his mind was focused on his career regrets. Harry was a senior manager in the compliance department for Universal Banking and Insurance, one of the largest multinational financial institutions headquartered in London. He was a knowledge worker, and he had to know his onions, but he was at best a middle manager in the bigger picture. He made enough money to keep his family afloat but not enough to save for a future. He had to move out of the family home with almost no warning and he was still in his emergency digs – it was draining his savings fast, and there was no Plan B.

He got a late start in his career so he was a step or two lower on the corporate ladder than he expected he could be. He had made it through university but he had been too restless to settle and spent much of his youth in the search for adventure. By the time he settled in, he was the oldest on his rung of the corporate ladder.

His main job was to advise a policy sales unit on detecting and reporting fraud and money laundering, but lately they have seen how the divorce was affecting him, so they put him on lower-level duties. Today he was heading into the city to begin a review of the security of the computer system, and its emergency backup plan. He would be spending the day looking over the shoulders of guys on computers, watching them try fake passwords and checking the dates on logs of recent tests of the emergency plan.

He switched trains at London Bridge, bumping through the crowd on autopilot, trying not to be an obstacle to his fellow commuters. He was a very large person, but he was quite nimble on his feet and he picked his way through the crowd deftly. About the only thing that kept him on the rails during the week was obliterating himself in the gym. He did a two hour routine every day, alternating the weightlifting with different muscle groups and doing fast cardio. He hadn't slept well in years and he found that fully exhausting his body was the only way to get it to shut down from time to time. He did well cutting through crowds, but when there was a question of whom was to pass, he usually got the right of way.

From Cannon St. it was about a fifteen minute walk towards the Bank of England, a pivot toward Moorgate and he was at the office. It was a fairly large building made from white stone quarried in Kent. It was one of the grand old buildings but still large enough to hold over a thousand office workers. It had been fully retrofitted with environmentally friendly glazing, new elevators and revolving doors but the entrance had a massively high ceiling and the foyer was the size of a ballroom. It was rush hour so the entire public space was abuzz with activity. A steady stream of 'suited and booted' professionals made their way to the turnstile bottleneck of the elevator lobby. Harry plodded through and got into a makeshift queue outside one of the elevators that served his floor. When his turn came he shuffled on and made his way as far to the back as he could, as his was a higher floor. He was always amazed by those who ignored basic manners, shoving onto an already crowded elevator. And it never failed to happen.

On his floor the elevator lobby was enclosed by glass walls, with restrooms on either side. Because he worked in Compliance the entryways required a card swipe to get through. Through the glass walls he could see the rows of workstations, no longer in cubicles, and the few offices and meeting rooms along the external wall with the iconic London view. He came through, greeted the administrative assistant, and made his way to his desk.

His colleagues on either side of him on the row were already there, already had their coffee and were working through their new inbox messages before jumping on the carousel of meetings. There was Liam on his left, who had gone to St. Andrews' and Fatima on his right, a Briton of east African descent who had a neuroscience degree from Cambridge.

"Off to the salt mine for you today, Harry?" she asked before even offering a good morning.

"Good morning Harry," Liam said.

"Morning," he returned. *"Down to be among the freaks and geeks, I'm afraid,"* he said.

"Don't worry, luv," Fatima said, grabbing her coffee cup. She stood close enough to have to look up at him—he was six foot three, and she was five foot six. *"If they give you a hard time, I'll come and save you."*

"Sometimes the cure is worse than the disease, innit?" he shot back.

Though it was understood that he had drawn light duty to focus on his personal issues, neither one of them would want the job he had today. Harry put down his laptop and followed Fatima to the coffee machine. He got a double espresso, his fourth caffeinated drink of the day. They carried on light banter and he appreciated how it kept him focused on something other than himself. Back at his desk he picked up his commuter backpack without thinking and headed down to the second floor where the data centre was.

The elevator lobby on the second floor was highly secure, with barred deadbolts on every door, all restricted and no glass anywhere. Because so few badges granted access, there was a telephone mounted to the wall next to the main entrance. Harry knew that his badge wouldn't allow him entry, so he picked up the phone and it automatically started to ring with a long buzz. The data centre executive assistant picked up, and Harry told him the particulars of the meetings he had there. The executive assistant told him that his contact, the deputy Chief Information Officer, would meet him in the lobby and bring him through. They hung up but then Harry stood waiting for what seemed an interminably long time. Just as he was considering picking the phone back up, he heard the bolt and the heavy latch of the security door release, and it swung slowly open. The deputy CIO stuck out his head rather than coming all of the way out and bid Harry to follow him through the door. He was a tall grey-haired man of south Asian descent. He had started talking as soon as he had opened the door and was a full step ahead of Harry and striding quickly into the labyrinth of floor to ceiling servers and business machines. The machines were making a surprising amount of noise, and Harry at first strained to hear what his host was saying, but then gave up when he realised its futility. If it were important, Harry thought, then he would not be speaking it in the opposite direction at an inaudible volume.

They came to a row of desks set at workbench height, and there were devices and electronic components strewn about the desktops. There were six workstations in the row and half of them were occupied by employees in fully casual clothes. It was quiet enough here for people to talk, and the Deputy CIO introduced the team. Harry put down the laptop bag and the lanyard he had in his hand, knowing that the fourth drink was the one too many, and that he had to excuse himself to the gents immediately.

"It's good to see you, gentlemen, but I've got to excuse myself for a moment before we get stuck in," he said, and he started walking toward the grey, industrial stairwell door. The data centre was on the second story up from the ground and the closest bathroom was just at the end of the short set of stairs just one story down. He hit the armbar on the door and stepped quickly through it and in two steps he was halfway down the flight of stairs when he realised that his ID card was at the end of the lanyard on the desk. Just as he came to an abrupt and complete halt he heard the heavy click of the locking door. He would need that ID to get through the similar door at the bottom of the stairs.

He only hesitated a second and carried on to the bottom of the stairs. He had to go badly now, and hopefully there would be someone just behind the doors who would let him in. It was a gamble - as a compliance officer he knew employees were instructed not to open the access doors, and with good reason. Still, he had to hope that there was someone nearby who would be sympathetic enough to let him in. As an act of futility he tried the handle. He knocked insistently but without aggression on the metal, asking through the doorframe if there were anyone there. There was silence from the other side. Harry waited the expected time before knocking again. Still there was no response. Harry knocked loudly and asked again in a raised voice if anyone were there. He now had to urgently seek a solution and he was contemplating ascending the stairs again to get one of the tech guys to open the door.

Months from now, when he could put some of the pieces together he would remember it beginning with a very distinct hiss, like the short inhaled vocalisation of a lion's growl. There followed a set of percussive sounds occurring simultaneously. The most deafening was the full throated roar of the blast from the data centre, only a set of stairs and a steel door away. Harry was briefly insensate. All he knew was that smoke and darkness commanded his environment. He had been plucked from the continuum of time and tossed into this unknowable scene as a set of nerves, its receptor organs and the apparatus of muscle and bone to carry out the actions the moment required. There was no continuity, only reaction.

'Luckily' for him this was a familiar space. Emotion was shut off and it was: (1) ingest information, and (2) act. Applying logic and reason in the moment was the best way to survive from one to the next. It could lead to things which appear rash or dangerous at the time, though they were the best option for survival.

He had been blown against the wall and knocked briefly unconscious, and his body dropped like a rag doll, hard on his side against the first couple of stairs. He felt as though he had been momentarily turned to liquid and he was entirely deaf. He found 'up' and struggled to his feet leaning against the steel railing. There were now blinking lights that revealed the curl of the smoke in red strobe. Doors opened above and below in the vertical tunnel that the stairwell had become, allowing in light in jagged rays blunted against the smoke. There was no light near Harry and he could sense activity around the doors above and below. He began walking slowly down the stairs with the help of the railing and at the next landing down he saw a stream of people coming out of the steel door.

Some people were trying to maintain some sort of order and dutifully file out like they had for hundreds of drills, but some were just overtaken by fear and were trying to dodge around others and were shoving the people in front until the bottleneck around the door became a crush. Harry stumbled down into the torrent of people, joining at the newel of the railing from the floor above, where he was the only person joining the exodus. He stumbled into the hard crush of bodies and used his feet only to balance, because the pressure from packed bodies above kept him upright. He assumed people were screaming or there were alarms and sirens but he right now he couldn't hear anything at all. He could see terror on the faces around him though, appearing in the red strobe of the emergency light. It was like being on the dancefloor of a disco in hell. It felt like an interminably long time to make it down the few stairs to the street.

People were jettisoned out onto the pavement and into what felt like the blinding light of the morning. Many people lost their footing and there were visibly upset people frantically stepping around in no particular direction, and in the unnatural silence Harry could see people running their hands through their hair, shaking their fingers against the air and in many cases unselfconsciously crying. Some people wore the hi-viz vests and they looked like they were trying in vain to corral people. He could see people talking to each other, so they must have been able to hear. A growing cloud of smoke and debris was casting a haze over the street, emanating from the part of the building where Harry was standing not five minutes ago. Small groups and clots of people had congregated wherever there was space.

Harry found his feet and carried on directly to the edge of the sidewalk. Just as he reached the street a group of people on his left wandered into it, to cross to be with a group of their colleagues. This caused a black taxi that was speeding by to have to brake hard, bringing the taxi to an abrupt halt right in front of Harry. The door of the taxi flew open and a young woman in business attire with a look of sheer terror on her face jumped out in panic. Harry stopped the door from closing and immediately fell inside the taxi's back seat, closing the door with his left hand. The taxi driver had begun to drive again before Harry was situated and the vehicle was stopped for mere seconds. Harry was immediately tossed around inside the car because he had no seat belt and the driver had the vehicle all over the road.

Harry sat up properly and braced himself into the corner. He could see the driver's face attempting to get his attention in the rearview mirror, clearly shouting and intermittently turning his head to try to get confirmation that Harry had heard him. Harry shouted that he couldn't hear anything and that the man should please just keep driving. The driver must have understood because he had a clear response, which visibly looked like an apoplectic fit, but he could not afford to focus away from the road and he kept the taxi moving.

After only a few seconds of the driver focusing on the road exclusively Harry understood why the woman staggered out of the taxi in terror. It appeared as if the driver had taken leave of his senses and had become entirely reckless. From his perch braced in the far corner of the back, and because of the configuration of passenger seats in the back of a black taxi, Harry could see what the driver was contending with. Harry recognised escape manoeuvres and breaching techniques taught in security training courses. The driver was avoiding major roads and was consistently popping bollards off of their bases to access pedestrian only walkways. Right now there were emergency vehicles and what appeared to be refugees filling the roadways and blocking normal routes of traffic.

After some time Harry began to faintly hear the sirens and honking horns. They were everywhere. There was debris and smoke coming from other areas too, and hordes of frightened pedestrians flooded the streets far from the office. There must have been other explosions elsewhere in the city. Eventually, miraculously, the taxi made it out of the crush of the city centre and Harry could tell they were headed east toward Dagenham and Ilford. He began to hear the soft whoosh of the vehicle speeding along the motorway and he thought that he could hear well enough to communicate. He leaned forward to speak through the glass, even though the intercom was on.

'You've driven in combat before,' he said to the driver.

'You don't have to shout, mate,' the driver said, *'Can you hear again?'*

'I can hear you now, but my ears are ringing' he said touching his ribs where he landed on the stairs, *'and I got the wind knocked out of me.'*

'Baghdad, early two thousands,' the driver said, *'but the other car was a lot bigger.'*

'Where are we going?' Harry asked. They were in Essex now, heading toward the Dartford Tunnel.

'I told you to get the hell out of my taxi or you would be coming home to Kent with me. I'm not stopping for anything. God knows what's happening or how far it will reach,' the driver said.

'Kent is fine,' Harry said, *'Whereabout do you stay?'*

'All the way down in Folkstone,' the driver replied. *'Do you want to hear this?'* The driver was looking at Harry in the rearview and he pointed to the radio. Harry nodded that he would and the driver hit some buttons and the radio came on in the back. They listened in silence as the miles flew by and Harry's mind started to push options out of the new information.

Several of the financial powerhouses had been hit, with the attacks focused on the data centres. There were explosions outside of the city as well, and the speculation was that these were focused on the business recovery sites for those financial institutions. Most horrifically, though, there were reports coming in of explosions in the tube stations at Bank and Charing Cross, where mass casualties were reportedly caused by trampling.

Harry thought that he was lucky to be alive, considering how close he was to the blast site. The deputy CIO and his direct reports were almost certainly dead as were everyone else on that floor and in that area. It boggled and numbed the mind, those men just gone in an instant. If he hadn't been locked in the stairwell things might have been very different. Then he remembered leaving his ID on the desk in the data centre. The record of his movements would show that he swiped to get into the data centre and that he hadn't left. As far as anyone would know, he was with those men when the blast occurred. There would be no identifying who was or was not there by way of remains. He had been so much lower to the ground than his workmates, since he was one level up from the street. He didn't try to report to his designated recovery area and he didn't hang about on the street and none of his workmates saw him. In the confusion no stranger would remember him even being there.

It's not that I could be dead, Harry thought to himself, *I **can** be dead.* His mind automatically started to work on the details. If he were to simply disappear right now, never to be heard from again, then he would be counted as another casualty of the terror attack. He would be considered to have been killed at work in the performance of his duties and the company would pay out the maximum of his policy. Elena would never want for anything again and the children would be well taken care of. It was an elegant solution to the financial problem but it meant that he would not see his children again. He wondered if he could bear it, but he had already all but lost his mind anyway. He had thought of his living situation as characteristic of a death in the family; why couldn't he consummate that circumstance and try to live out his life differently?

He was at this very moment in a vehicle speeding toward a coastal town where elicit waterborne transportation was known to be available. If he could make it to Calais then he could do the migrant route in reverse, living on the land and staying off camera and out of the public eye. If he could make it back to Africa then he could disappear more easily than people would expect. He knew an old comrade from the Legion who was currently in Marseilles who could make it easy for him. Was this mad?

He took the battery out of his phone and threw it out of the window onto the highway. Then he took out the sim card and snapped it in quarters and threw it out too.

The intercom jumped to life. *'Ayop!'* the driver said, *'whatcha doing back there?'*

Harry had more clarity and conviction than he had since the day he joined the British army.

'You were in Baghdad in oh-four? That's the year I joined two para,' he said through the intercom. The driver raised his eyebrows and looked more intently through the reflection, sizing up Harry in a different light now. *'Today brought too much of my young life back to me just now. The world is too much with me, as the saying goes, and I need to spend a couple days at the seaside with no ringing phones. Can you understand that?'*

The driver looked back at the road to drive safely and said through the intercom, *'Yeah. I get that. I even know a place you can stay, but you'll have to pay cash.'*

The Mother of Intrigue

Five years before the major action of the story.

Three men sat around an ornate table under an awning on the roof of a mansion in Jeddah, in the Kingdom of Saudi Arabia. The flat roof mirrored the building's expansive footprint, and was entirely paved with ornate tiles. The mansion was just across the road from the corniche, and though it was just before daybreak they could see a group of itinerant Bedouins who had stopped there long enough to put their feet in the Red Sea, five floors below. It was quite cool before sunrise and the nearness of the sea provided a constant gentle breeze. They were in one of the homes owned by the family of Abdul Aziz Al Sudeiri, the blond blue eyed man at the table. The other men were the same age but they had dark hair and darker skin. One, Hani Nesralla, was a Lebanese tech billionaire and Ahmed Tahlawi, the other, was from an Omani oil family. They had met fifteen years earlier while studying at Balliol College, Oxford. There were short glasses and long spoons next to small steel teapots in front of each man, and they poured and sipped strong black tea intermittently throughout their conversation.

"Finally, Hani," Al Sudeiri asked, *"what was so important that it couldn't even be spoken through an encrypted line?"*

"For fifteen years now, Zuz, we have been plotting without serious direction on how to achieve our ends," Nesralla said, *"but now we finally have it."*

"Have what?" Tahlawi asked.

Nesralla tapped on his tablet for a few seconds and then propped it on its base so its screen faced the other two. The tablet displayed charts and graphs so busy, and text so small that it was completely illegible in the hard angled glare of the Arabian morning.

"What are we looking at?" asked Al Sudeiri, whose friends called him 'Zuz', which was pronounced the same as the English 'zoos'.

"This wonderful gift from Allah is the playbook for the independence of the Islamic world," he said.

During their time at school they had vowed to do whatever they could to drive the Islamic and the western worlds apart, but not so one would destroy the other. Rather, they wanted the Islamic world to be left alone to perfect its society, unsullied by the influences of globalisation and westernisation. They believed there was a path of modernisation and social evolution that should be allowed to thrive without neo-colonial mores creeping in through globalist influences. For a decade and a half they had been building networks of connections, establishing safe houses and cultivating relationships with key players in multiple overt and covert organisations. They had groomed human assets and placed them within government, scientific and supranational organisations, placing religious zealots where they expected the most extreme action might be required. And they were not averse to the use of violence to achieve their ends.

They were intelligent, well-educated realists who were expert at running projects and building enterprises, but they lacked a real plan that gave any level of certainty that their outcomes would be achieved. As luck and the grace of God would have it, Nesralla had been asked to contribute to the construction of a suite of scenarios for a set of tabletop exercises for Millenium Horizon, a Washington based think tank. They believed they had created the most instructive counterfactual exercises that had ever been launched, because they had access to big data and AI in ways that no one in history ever had. They had the best-informed models and they had the best roster of political, industry, defence and sociological experts ever assembled. They had assigned each expert a role in control of an organisation or an aspect of society and asked them to respond in scenarios using policy, determinations on public mood, market actions and military activity.

Nesralla was contacted by the lead developer and the sponsor of the project. It was a man he'd known well when he was pursuing his master's in information technology from MIT. Nesralla said he was flattered to be invited and he put other projects aside to attend to this one. He was involved for months, contributing both data and expertise to the calibration of the models and construction of the scenarios. During that entire time though, he had been building a dossier of opposition research on his old friend. He had hired detectives and committed spies working to turn over every stone in his old friend's life. By the time they could run the scenarios Nesralla had human intelligence and data-based insights that pointed to unexplained losses in his friend's accounts and knowledge of some proclivities the friend would prefer remain private. Nesralla approached him as Hani, his old friend from their days together in Boston and asked if they could do each other a favour. He offered to cover any 'short positions' in his friend's personal accounts and to protect his professional reputation. In return he just asked that his friend keep the lights on an hour or two longer and run a quick scenario for him, quietly. Nesralla was pleasantly surprised when his friend readily agreed. His friend didn't see any harm in it, so why not get a leg up?

Nesralla asked his friend to retrieve several scenarios previously dismissed as too extreme or unlikely. Together, they altered the parameters so the desired outcome was predetermined, allowing the model to generate the policies and actions required to achieve it. When it was all over he was astounded. In his hands, he now held a precise set of instructions for his cabal. Nesralla felt that things were falling together by the will of God.

The model called for an overt act of terrorism in the U.K. designed to disrupt financial markets. Then, an act of domestic violence in the U.S. which would lead to each camp vilifying the other. Then, and from then on, a sustained increase in the flow of migrants would be timed against the upcoming U.S. election to ratchet up the sense of fear and clannishness. They needed to undermine public faith in the strength of the U.S. border. They knew these objectives were achievable with their available resources and their readiness to make sacrifices. The final act needed to be so heinous, devastating, and irreversible that executing it would be a formidable challenge.

Hani Nesralla made it clear that these things would need to happen in the right sequence and at the right cadence to be successful. They would need to have plans and resources in place to execute each 'project' at the right moment. They agreed that they would proceed and they talked through specific plans until the sun had risen and the day grew too hot. They concluded and went back inside to enjoy their wealth away from the pious eyes of the kingdom.

The Voluntary Exile

Folkestone is a seaside English town with a typical history. It's not wealthy like some seaside places, but it's not a down and out wharf town either. There are sandy beaches that gussy themselves up for tourists but there is still an active marina and a ferry that goes to France every day. It is a nice place to visit, but there is an underbelly if you look for it. It was nearly three hours from the time Harry got into the cab until they crossed into Folkestone town. The sun was just getting high because the attacks happened right at the outset of the workday. Harry was getting stiff, but he didn't think he had any cracked ribs. He would have a pretty good bruise, and his head was still ringing a little bit. The driver put his window down and Harry could smell the ocean. They went straight through the town centre and carried on down some side streets. Harry saw signs for Sunny Sands beach, it looked like they were headed for the ocean. The driver started to talk when they were a couple streets back from the waterfront, just as they were passing a hotel under renovation.

"I'm taking you to stay with my mate Kevin," he said. *"He did some time in the Middle East, so I know he'll understand."*

He immediately took a sharp left, down and around the hotel, and pulled into its car park.

"He's rehabbing this old hotel and it's completely empty," he said as he drove to the covered part under the building. He parked and shut off the engine and both men got out of the car. Harry's body ached, and his mind buzzed with possibilities. He resolved to stay in the moment and let things unfold. He took a few deep breaths to test out the flexibility of his ribcage and started walking behind the driver as he was headed for a door in the garage.

"What's your name?" he asked the driver. *"I'm Harry."*

"I'm Connor," the driver said.

Harry noticed that Connor hadn't called anybody to let them know they were coming, nor did he knock or anything before going through the door to the hotel's basement. Connor led the way down a short concrete corridor to a corner stairwell, and up to the lobby. The lobby resembled that of an oversized B&B more than a large hotel. There were plastic sheets duct taped over furniture and protective plywood covering the windows and some wall hangings. There were powertools, stepladders and makeshift workbenches everywhere, cementing the impression of the hotel as a work site. There was one person in the lobby, a man sitting on top of the plastic on a couch, hunched over a radio on a step stool. He looked up when Connor came in and then stood up when he saw Harry, a stranger.

Kevin was of average height, likely around 5'10", dressed in workman's hi-viz gear.

"Who's this?" Kevin asked Connor without preamble, pointing to Harry with his chin.

Harry took Kevin in. He was a person of a type Harry knew well. Wiry but lean to the point of being skinny, constantly burning whatever it was that fuelled him. He was a bantam rooster made of beef jerky. People like him were almost always more capable than they let on, and they were always working some sort of angle or other. It was telling that he was closer to forty than thirty, and he was still that way. Harry would have to put him at ease to expect to get any kind of help. He stayed quiet and still while Connor explained what was happening.

"This here's Harry, mate. He jumped into my taxi near around the Bank of England. He was in one of them buildings – " Connor pointed at the radio that was droning out grim news tensely delivered – *"and it put 'im back in the old days. Says he can't trust himself to be fit company for a day or two and he needs somewhere to lay his head. You of all people know how that goes, Kev."*

Kevin visibly loosened up and started to pace the length of the sofa.

"Jesus Christ, Con. This is a goddamn catastrophe. It's enough to do a lot to anyone. I can't imagine being right there in the middle of it."

He stopped pacing and looked at Harry. *"It's enough to bring the old days all the way out, and you might never even know it. Sit down. Have a can. You can get a breather and we can get caught up."* Kevin pointed to the armchair across from the couch, also covered in plastic, and stepped around construction detritus to grab three pint cans from the fridge. He handed the beers out and sat on the other end of the couch from Connor, across from Harry and started right in with the conversation.

Though Harry liked to think of his corporate life as a numb shadow to his former life, some required skills were quite useful. He was essentially in the criticising and bad news business, so he had experience trying to put people at ease while getting salient facts out of them. He made guarded statements and declared no incriminating facts until Kevin had, through clever nuances, intimated that Harry did something after the bombs went off that makes it necessary for him to hide. It wasn't in Harry's interest to refute it, so he left it out there. It looked like Kevin was willing to help Harry out by keeping him hidden. Harry was very grateful and he said so.

For the next two hours Harry matched them beer for beer and talked about what came over the radio. It is natural for people to seek connections, to identify common elements from each others' pasts. Harry actively avoided talking about his personal history and in very short order Kevin and Conner knew to stay away from it in conversation. But there was plenty to talk about coming over the radio. There was no discussion of who had perpetrated the acts, but they were definitely coordinated and definitely focused to damage the financial network. The attacks at Bank and Charing Cross were intended to cause casualties and early indicators were that there was a large death toll. The more beer Kevin drank the more indignant and outraged he became. The more outraged he became the more he alluded to whatever speculative act of violence Harry had committed in the moment, and the more he convinced himself that it was true. Harry neither confirmed nor denied that he had done anything as an act of retribution and allowed the legend to grow in Kevin's cloudy mind.

At the end of the second hour Harry stopped drinking, claiming his injuries were troubling him. Kevin hadn't slowed down. In fact, he had gone to the basement and replenished the beer supply from some store room. Two hours after that Kevin and Conner were in a different state of mind than Harry and it was clear that Connor was staying at the hotel too. Harry had crossed that boundary where the only sober person at a party can tell that everyone is well on. It was like instant culture shock. In the manner of someone inebriated, Kevin returned to the subject matter of Harry's anonymity. In Kevin's mind it had grown to the need to disappear and evade the authorities, and he started speaking openly about it as if it were a fact. Harry appreciated the shift in mindset and hoped that it worked out well for him.

Eventually, as the sun was setting, speculation came across the radio that the dead may number over a thousand and they began broadcasting eye-witness accounts from different sites. Kevin had made up his cloudy mind and he was going to do something about it. He leaned in, his face inches from Harry's, placing a hand on his shoulder.

"Do you know what?" he said, *"Do you know what? I have the perfect solution for you my friend, but it will take a lot of trust on my part. Should I trust you? Connor? Can I trust this man? Should I trust this man?"*

Connor said that Harry should be trusted, based on his commitment to Queen and country and the bond that men of arms have, beyond their days of service.

"Do you know what?" Kevin restated the rhetorical question, *"I am going to trust you. I've got an arrangement with ferry employees, you see? In a couple of days I'm to drive a car onto the ferry, across the channel and leave it somewhere over there. I'm going to step aside and let you drive it; you get me?"* He waited a minute to let that sink in. *"It's not a paying job like. I'll give you a couple bob out of the goodness of my heart, but this is your way to get from one country to another with no paperwork, right?"*

Harry did get it, and if sober Kevin would honour this agreement then he couldn't believe his luck. Hard to believe that only this morning he was going through the motions, feeling trapped in a world he feared would never change. Now he was once again living on the very edge of his wits, praying for luck and hoping this concoction of rage and pride in this capricious man would be enough to put him beyond the land of the living, figuratively.

Harry told Kevin that this was exactly what he needed, and he thanked him for the chance.

A Fortress of Shadows

The Caliphate of Malitania came into being around the time the French sent troops to Mali to quell the northern rebellions. Malitania declared its independence from Sankara, aligning the political borders with the ethnic and cultural connections of the northern people. Before the secession, the overwhelming majority of Sankarese were tropical farmers living in the forested areas and in the cities along the coast. The northerners were an ethnic and cultural minority which was not only underrepresented but also actively preyed upon in the fields of business and politics, and they had limited access to the wider world. Apparently it was just dumb luck that six weeks after establishing the Caliphate, they discovered oil.

Malitania was instantly weak and rich. This is a deadly combination in the Sahel and southern Sahara. The charismatic and powerful leader who took control of the fledgling country assigned the Caliph the role of monarch on the English model and made a key alliance which was widely considered to be a stroke of diplomatic genius. He proposed admittance to the UAE as a kind of 'associate' emirate. Malitania would use the dirham and receive defence assurances in return for handing over decision making over the distribution of its oil. This worked well for years, but the lack of infrastructure in Malitania made it impossible to police the expanse of open land. When the Islamist and separatist movements started spreading across the Sahel, they moved freely through the empty landscape, and it was thought they had set up permanent facilities undetected by the Malitani government.

Malitania requested assistance from the Emirates, and the Emirates contributed money and some high level administrators, but they did not help to restrict the movement of the men under the familiar black flag. Then things calmed down; if there were insurgents settling in then they weren't extorting taxes on anyone or exerting control over a known piece of land. A kind of unofficial and uneasy détente was established, with a potential parasite lurking in the shadows and Malitania unable to do anything about it. Surely though, the Leader thought, as they had done elsewhere, they would eventually try to take the oil.

It was in this Malitania that a nondescript five story administration building was built, at the very end of the trunk road where oil exploration petered out. Years ago it was intended to process samples, house administrators and act as a logistical layby for crude extraction operations. Since there was no oil it had no practical use, and the administration building and receiving yard and storage facility were auctioned off to an oil exploration consulting firm. The firm's ownership was nested in a gordian knot of legal entity relationships spanning four languages, three nation's legal regimes and a web of investors. Almost no one knew of its existence and even fewer people knew its real purpose.

It was made from concrete blocks, as is typical in the region, and its flat roof was bristling with transmitters, receivers and dishes and antennae of every description. There was a high wall around the entire compound and access was restricted to a road going straight through the receiving yard, with gates on either end. There were cameras and sensors everywhere around the compound, and it would be unwise to assume that there were no mines. There were guards in guard towers along the perimeter, overwatch for the armed vehicles clogging the yard.

The bottom two floors were open and meeting spaces, with offices on the third floor up. The fourth floor was all apartments and the top floor was an executive meeting space. More of a penthouse salon, really. It was luxuriously decorated with comfortable, low cushions of silk with north African brocade. There was a 'muffrage' area recessed into the floor in the centre of the space with service stairs in and out. Ornate comfortable chairs were placed in pairs around small tables, positioned around the perimeter behind the muffrage. Fit young women in short, form-fitting clothes ran drinks to tables and tobacco to the shishas. The women were almost exclusively southeast Asian and the men in attendance were almost exclusively Arab. A heavy dose of frankincense hung in the air to compete with the shishas. There were several televisions on in differentiated spaces, broadcasting the world's major news outlets. There was a high buzz of conversation across the entire floor.

Zuz sat at a low table with Nesralla and Tahlawi. Zuz was a major contributor to the movement and a key planner of the attack in London, three days prior. Because of this, he knew things others did not. Like the fact that the physical attack in London was only one leg of a broader, more coordinated attack. Like the fact that, while the physical attack was a wild success, the cyber-attack across the globe was far more successful. For the past three days there were no credit rating systems functioning, and credit feeds into the operational and risk management tools across the financial system had stopped.

Zuz looked at his compatriots and exhaled his rare blend before speaking in Arabic.

"Suli rests a bit easier in his grave today. Finally we have taken the first steps of our great revenge."

The other men nodded, appearing contemplative.

Zuz went on, *"Those in power in Washington, Paris and London now understand that it is their fear and mistrust that is their greatest enemy."*

A young woman approached timidly, carrying a tray of nuts and clean ashtrays. She deftly and unintrusively removed the ashtray in use and replaced it, and quickly set down the nuts. They had nothing to fear from this woman who was there of her own volition, spectacularly compensated for what she did. Still, they held their conversation until she receded, turned and left them.

Sheikh Tahlawi was the first to speak after the interruption. *"The first blow is struck. Hani's been observing the data and western countries have been keeping their new business to themselves."*

Hani Nesralla jumped in. *"They'll restore the infrastructure in about ten days. The next blow has to be struck before the psychological momentum from this one is lost."*

They all nodded in agreement and conversation dropped off while they sipped and smoked.

"Eleven were martyred in London on the day and there were unsung martyrs in America and other European capitals," Zuz said. *"They had all come from South Asia and East Africa. Authorities will be looking for men who look like them, and focus will stay on the Middle East."*

He let that hang in the air before continuing, *"Now we bring the fight behind their highest walls. This next blow will drown them in paranoia and shatter their false sense of national identity."*

"It is high time," said Nesralla, *"They have taken too much for granted for too long."*

"Yes," Tahlawi agreed, *"and they are likely to overreact and overrespond because they are strangers to hardship now."*

From across the muffrage a muscular Russian got his attention and waved him over. *"You'll excuse me, gentlemen, I have our business to attend to. Until next month, in Paris."*

Zuz took his leave and Tahlawi and Nesralla carried on discussing what they needed to do to further the cause.

Echoes of the Past

Three days had passed since the attack, and Harry hadn't shown himself in public. He stayed inside the hotel and ate whatever the guys brought in. He'd had some sober conversations with Kevin and Connor now and he had tried to tread lightly on their hospitality. Currently he was sitting across from Kevin; he was on a couch covered with a dust cloth and Kevin was on a chair covered in sheet plastic. In the intervening three days there had been no progress on the renovation, as there was no effort expended on it whatsoever.

Kevin leaned forward, resting his elbows on his knees, and he jiggled a set of keys in his hands. He looked Harry directly in the eye.

"Do you know you talk London when you're awake and Geordie when you're asleep? And once, when you were distracted, you were whistling Le Kepi Blanc*?"*

Harry didn't know what to make of the comment. He had been hyper-focused on making his disappearance convincing. And here Kevin held the key, literally, to his escape into a world where his family's security is assured. A world where he, Harry, could find a way to live out his days in relative comfort. A world where guilt and shame had been repaid in full by his sacrifice, and his family could start anew and hopefully keep only the best memories of him.

Kevin held the key to a Renault Kadjar, registered in France. Harry was to drive this onto the ferry and he would be passed through the border with no troubles. From there he was to drive the car to Bordeaux and to leave it in a parking facility that was programmed into the GPS. Once the car was parked and the key was deposited in a known location nearby, Harry was completely on his own. He had, and could keep, the one thousand pounds sterling that Kevin handed over. Kevin then told him where the car was parked in the lot near the water.

Harry knew that Kevin wasn't a person who would be able to put Harry's past together in a way that could do him any real harm. Kevin was probably just proud that he figured out that Harry had been a Legionnaire. Harry was going to play it cool and give Kevin the benefit of the doubt. He had been nothing but good to him up until this point, and Harry needed to appeal to that common sense of duty to solidify his support and his silence.

"I did some time in the para and I did some time in the desert," he said, *"Driving an automatic for a few hours isn't going to be a problem at all."*

In Harry's own estimation things were moving along well. He believed he made the right decision and it seemed that tomorrow he would have his last glimpse of his native land. The leaving was terribly difficult, and he was in a constant state of anxiety and agitation in addition to the hyperawareness. Every second felt like a 'stay or go' decision, his life reduced to a string of breaking points. Herve and Leni were his world – are his world. Before the divorce their family was his world, but that ended irrevocably and against his will. From now on he would, emotionally and psychologically, have to face their absence just like a death. They were lost to him, anyway, and this sacrifice on his part was intended to ennoble that loss and give it purpose.

This wasn't the first time Harry endured this. Harry and his sister and two brothers had lived in a Newcastle city council flat that was too small for their family. Their father drank heavily, neglecting the family and erupting into bouts of violence. Harry, as the oldest and biggest, was the natural protector. He tried to give what he could to his younger siblings and to get in the way of his father when he was on a tear. His siblings loved him for this and they grew a very strong bond – they were his world. Once Harry came back from Army training he wouldn't stand for the eruptions anymore and he told his father so. Harry had one little brother in secondary school and one even still in primary school. Harry's father still felt like the family's leader, but in the cold light of day the conversation ended with a kind of unspoken détente. Things were fine and home life was stable, for a while, until Harry's father came home drunk and kept on drinking. The father became loud and sounded both angry and wounded. He pushed Harry's mother after accusing her of something ridiculous. She fell hard, Harry got to his feet and his father went to the knife rack. Harry's father was a large and imposing man whose motor functions were dangerously impaired. He had the knife flailing around the small galley kitchen when Harry rushed him. They both fell backward, hard, over Harry's prone mother and fell in a forty-stone heap. Harry's father ended up with the knife through the side of the ribs to the hilt and was completely lifeless. They tried to revive him but they couldn't.

Harry's mother plead with him to run away and stay gone, and his siblings echoed everything she said. In the heat of the moment with his dead father on the kitchen floor Harry weighed up the options and made the decision to go. Back then it wasn't very hard to get across the channel from England to get to France. With his military ID and a fast story about a girl in Calais he was able to get across. There was a story around the paras that if you ever really needed to just disappear then you could always join the French foreign legion. The talk said that you had to physically appear and knock on their door in Marseilles and if they let you in then you were reborn. That's what Harry did, and for the next six years he was a valued and well-used asset to the Legion, across North Africa and beyond.

In the intervening years he learned that his father, through some kind of miracle, had not died that day. His father was in long term care and would never lead a 'normal' life again. Harry was still a deserter, but he was no longer guilty of patricide. Under the identity granted by the Legion, he felt safe enough to come back to England but not safe enough to reconnect with his siblings. He was able to get a job in London, and that is when he met Elena. So he stayed in Britain even though he couldn't ever see his siblings. Now again he was leaving the three people who meant the most to him on an abrupt, split-second decision.

He thought of the value of their settlement. At well over a million pounds it was more than enough to pay off the mortgage, pay for any education the children may want and establish an annuity so Elena could be a full-time carer for the children. They would have a very good life from now on, all three of them. He hoped that news of his death would let Elena move on and find the committed relationship she deserved.

He had been staring at the floor. He reached out an open palm and Kevin dropped the key in his hand. He would leave at dawn for the first ferry.

Eye in the Banlieue

She glanced over her open book, held just above her purse on her lap, seated on the RER. Three American students were returning from their poverty-tourism excursion into district ninety-three. They were three white men, aged twenty to twenty-two, audibly discussing the colonial and cultural origins of the "North African situation" in Paris and its surrounding communities. Their conversation was steeped in English academic jargon, full of references to cultural studies and post-colonial theories, making them sound nauseatingly pretentious. She could easily puncture their assumptions, like popping balloon animals at a street fair.

On this train, though, they were the exotic ones. This was the line to Montmartre, packed almost exclusively with brown-skinned commuters heading into the city to work jobs that native French citizens avoided. She, too, was just a few years older than them, but her mixed-race heritage and North African features meant she could never assume the same carefree confidence that came with their privilege. They moved through the world as if they were always right, buoyed by a society that rarely challenged them.

She was jealous—not of their wealth or their time, but of the unshakable security they carried. While she had earned her master's degree from George Washington University, she had long ago given up on trying to educate others about their privilege. Experience had taught her that the act of explaining its existence only reinforced the dynamic. Instead, she had learned to navigate the currents of privilege and manipulate them to her advantage in any role she chose to play.

Throughout the ride, they glanced at her occasionally, and she made a point to look engrossed in her book. When they reached Montmartre, she waited until they had left the train and disappeared into the crowd before stepping off herself.

By any measure Paris is a magnificent city. She loved Paris but she rarely got the chance to experience it fully. When work brought her here, like now, she mostly stayed in the less desirable suburbs, because the *banlieues* were where her subjects stayed. Last night she was in Seine-Saint-Denis attending a poetry reading. The Algerian bookstore was just crowded enough for her to spot and follow Hani Nesralla's movements, but not crowded enough for her to follow him undetected after the event. She found the poetry unartistic, with the focus on changing languages mid-poem. The idea was that certain things could not be expressed in French, so the author had to revert to Arabic and sometimes Hausa. As a person educated in the politics and culture of the post-colonial francophone world, her authentic self saw trite references and constructs strung together to exclude anyone who was not a speaker of these three languages and who could not identify with the historical references of the Sahel. This was a collective trauma response, not art. The bohemian émigré student she was pretending to be was rapt, though. She snapped her fingers at the appropriate times and ululated at the appropriate times. She deftly deflected both the barbs at her mixed-race status and advances from the confused young men around her. She was there for the poetry, and to browse the bookshop's wares and to make connections with like-minded devout Muslim women. Or so it appeared to anyone who might be watching.

She watched Nesralla for close to three hours. The bookstore was in the ground floor with a large shopfront window to the busy high street outside. There was a retail area that was furnished with comfortable seating and some small, low tables, as one would expect from a bookstore. There was a small stockroom that was not much bigger than a typical closet, but there was also a small galley style kitchen with a bathroom. From outside on the high street there was a step built outside the external door that went up to the flat above the shop. This was where the owner lived, though there was no direct access to the shop from the flat.

The event drew in a larger crowd than the shop could accommodate, and patrons took up every logical standing room only space. People congregated outside on the high street pavement. They had gathered some boxes and random outdoor furniture and had propped the door open to hear the reading. Between readers and poems the buzz of conversation rose people and moved around freely. Many came and went to purchase drinks and snacks from vendors on the street or got tea from the bookstore's kitchen. The shopkeeper and his inner circle made several trips to the flat through the door on the high street. Nesralla had started the night inside the shop, where he made the rounds greeting people. He was a well known contributor to many faith-based charities and foundations in Paris and about a third of those in attendance were familiar to him. He moved around and got tea between readers and congratulated or thanked the readers themselves. She noticed there were two men who stayed keenly aware of Nesralla's movement and position at the venue – he had security. At one point he abruptly stood and went out onto the pavement beyond her hearing and field of vision. She waited until his security made their adjustments – one stepped out while the other shifted his field of vision – and tried to get up as casually as she could while taking what appeared to be a vape pen out of her pocket. As she stood to make her way to the front door, Nesralla stepped back in and lifted his hand and nodded to someone behind her. Pretending to be caught off guard, as if he were gesturing to her, she turned to see who it was. She saw the shopkeeper holding up one finger in a 'just a second' gesture. She turned back toward the door and saw that Nesralla had already turned to go back outside. She went outside around ten feet behind him and came out front and looked around, as if trying to spot the best place for a smoke. She saw Nesralla standing on the far edge of the clot of people outside, talking to a well dressed older man. She tried as casually as possible to stand on the edge as well. She ended up about five feet away from him facing the other way. She took a couple draws on the vape pen and checked her phone, all the while listening carefully to try to discern Nesralla's voice above the buzz of conversation and ambient street noise. She thought she picked out enough to know that he was meeting someone called Zuz at the Little Frog for lunch tomorrow. Then the shopkeeper came out and Nesralla followed him through the door to the flat. A new reader came on and she stayed outside, just another listener on the sidewalk. She was unsure exactly what became of him after that and she lost him for the night.

She verified that the Little Frog was a café in Montmartre and went home. That was why she was on this RER train this morning. She was going to be at the Little Frog before it opened and apply for a job. She used the map on her phone and it took her a while to find the place but when she did she liked what she saw. This was an urban neighbourhood but set back from any major through-roads. Three streets came together to form a kind of small, open public space. The Little Frog took up one of the sharp corners and had mostly open air seating. The door was unlocked so she followed the sounds of clanking plates until she came to the kitchen. There were three people in the kitchen preparing to open. She asked if they were looking for servers and she was told that the owner wouldn't be back for a week. She thanked them and asked if it would be OK to have a look around, which they said would be fine. There were very few people around at that early hour and as she moped around admiring the café she placed microcameras and listening devices. She also took one of the server aprons which have the embroidered café logo and hid it in a nearby mailbox. Then she sent a text saying that it was all set up. A minute later she got a text back saying, *"I'll let you know when I hear from him."* This meant that she should wait until she got a text informing her that Nesralla had turned up at the Little Frog, and then show up.

She went to the Square Louise Michel and took in the sights, then sat for a leisurely coffee. It was four hours before the next text came in. It said, *"He said to swing on by."* She checked and prepared her equipment and made her way back to the Little Frog. When she approached the trisection she immediately saw Nesralla at one of the central tables outside of the Little frog. He was sitting with a blond man who appeared to be in his late forties but in good physical condition. She took a seat at an open table nearest the mailbox with the apron in it. She knew what Paris cafes could be like in high season; she wasn't in any danger of being approached by waitstaff. She put on her glasses and stared at her phone, trying to appear as nondescript and casual as she could. She was checking the video from the camera feeds and the signal strength from the microphones. There was a good view of both men, but she was unable to get anything of what they were saying. A text came in saying, *"Your new friend is cool."*

She sat and checked the feeds and tried to figure out if there was anything useful in there. If we didn't have trilingual lip readers then there wasn't much here to go on. She would have to get more, somehow. Just as she was ruminating on this, Nesralla got up and walked into the café. She assumed he was on his way to the men's room and decided to do something. There would be a chance that Nesralla would recognise her from the poetry reading, so she had to act while he was away. She kept staring at her phone, but with her free hand she took the apron out of the mailbox and put it on the table. Then she stretched, put her phone in her pocket and laboriously unfurled and donned the apron. Letting out a disappointed sigh, she picked up all of the dishes and glasses from a nearby table and headed toward the café. On her chosen trajectory she would come right up behind the blond man.

When she did, she stopped blatantly behind him and fixed her glasses on the device in his hand. Jackpot. He had a split screen with side-by-side invoices or some kind of payment document, with a stock price crawl across the top. She stood and stared until he took notice and clumsily turned on hundred eighty degrees to confront her.

"Are you finished with the cup, sir?" she asked blandly, and left it at that. Though she needed this information, she wanted to be as forgettable as possible.

"Ah, no," he said, apparently perturbed. She moved on into the café building and saw Nesralla coming out of the men's room. She ignored him and headed for the kitchen with the dirty glassware. He passed behind her and appeared to take no notice. Once in the kitchen she put the things down at the sink station and made a show of removing the apron. One or two of the brigade stopped to see who this was. She found one of the three who were there in the morning, when she made her application. She spoke directly to him, throwing the apron in a bin of soiled napkins and aprons.

"I apologise, but this really just won't work for me. I'm sorry, and thank you for your time," she said.

He was bewildered but she left no time for anyone to detain her. She was back on the Metro before they knew what happened, but honestly they weren't bothered and no one followed.

Road to Nowhere

The Kadjar was a left-hand drive and Harry wasn't used to shifting with the other hand; it wasn't an automatic after all. Fortunately, he didn't have far to go. In fact, it wasn't long before the road markings were painted with large letters and arrows pointing to FRANCE. It resembled a motorway toll booth, with broad white lines guiding vehicles to a gated checkpoint. On a motorway, this would be the toll station, but here at the ferry yard, it was where French immigration checked tickets and papers before granting entry into the EU. There was already a line of six vehicles waiting at each booth.

Harry put the car in gear and crept forward at two minute intervals, like clockwork. Eventually he came up to the booth.

The car's French license plate bore an EU panel, with an upside-down 'F' oval inexplicably added beside it. He assumed this was how the French border control officer would recognise the car. The checkpoint resembled an oversized tollbooth, manned by an officer in a signature blue polo. There was a small sliding window open just enough for documents to be passed through. A disinterested young man said in English, *"Pass me documents, please."* Harry retrieved a small plastic folio from the glove compartment and handed it over. He could hear a soccer game being broadcast on the radio at very low volume through the glass. It was in French. From here on out, he suspected, everything would be in French. He hoped it wouldn't take long for his mind to adjust to speaking and thinking in French again.

He also heard the crinkling of an envelope before the thump of a stamp, and the folio was handed back out through the window. The entire transaction took exactly the same amount of time as all of the others, and Harry drove away. All of the road markings carried on funnelling traffic to the ferries. There was an expansive parking lot with a shop and restrooms at its centre. Harry's ferry wasn't scheduled to depart for some time, so he parked near the shop and took out the cash he had. It was an envelope of twenty pound notes that looked like they had been gathered by a builder, one by one. Not crisp, not sequentially numbered, these were just pocket-worn bills that were frequently exchanged. Kevin had given him his own money. Harry wasn't under the impression that Kevin was a saint. If he had given Harry a grand then he was probably getting very, very much more for this delivery. Harry put the whole envelope in his pocket and went into the shop.

He only needed a few essentials to see him through to the stop. Kevin and Connor had brought him some things to wear, since he had pissed in Connor's taxi and he had no possessions. Now he had a light backpack with a change of clothes, a water bottle and a motorist's map of France. In the shop he picked up two litres of still water, some high calorie, portable candy and two ham and cheese baguettes. He reckoned it would be about ten hours from now when he would be driving into Bordeaux; he added a toilet roll to the basket just in case. The shop was nearly empty, staffed by a single older employee at the counter. The counter took up the length of the shop and behind a designated section there were tobacco products and lottery tickets for sale, behind the next was a money exchange terminal. Harry put his purchases on the counter and asked the employee if he could help him with money exchange. The shopkeeper took payment in pounds and nodded at Harry to move down the counter.

"How much do you want to exchange?" the older employee asked.

Harry took out the envelope and pulled out the small stack of wrinkled twenties.

"This is my driving tour through France money. It took me forever to save up, but here I am cashing it in now. I really need this holiday," Harry said. *"Should be near to a grand there. Could you please change it into Euro for me?"*

Harry knew the shopkeeper would be obliged to ask him the source of the funds, and he would reply that it was construction wages, offering no further explanation. The man did ask, and seemed to be waiting for more of an explanation, but then moved on with the transaction when he realised Harry was done talking. Harry took the Euros and his purchases and went back to the car. He turned it on and checked everything before pulling out. The GPS turned on and displayed the route once more. It showed the red line going through Paris and directly down to Bordeaux. Harry had no intention of taking that route—or going anywhere near the capital. He was going to take the western motorway that ran through Rouen and Tours. It would take a little longer, but it was bound to be less crowded and it brought him through a couple of scenic woodlands and down into the wine country of Aquitaine. It was a beautiful day, and despite the uncertainty and danger awaiting him, he looked forward to the road trip.

He uneventfully brought the Kadjar through the herding and corralling that was boarding a ferry, and in no time flat they were underway. Kevin had told Harry several times never to leave the car, under pain of death, but as soon as they got the 'all clear' Harry left the vehicle and walked briskly around the deck. It helped to get his energy level up and it gave him a look at his surroundings. In a couple of places he found spots where he could get in some chin-ups and other isometric and body-weight exercises. Then he spent about twenty minutes stretching. His bruised ribs still hurt and he knew he'd get cramped after staying in the driving position for hours. He stayed in the café on the observation deck until it was time to get back in the car. They then disembarked in the reverse of the embarkation routine. There was no border control on this side and Harry just drove off. Since the steering wheel was on the left, driving on the right was more natural and he had no problem orienting himself on the road. Before he knew it, he was on a French motorway out in the country with the window down and the radio on. The miles dropped away behind him and he was left alone with his thoughts.

Only a few days ago this prospect would have terrified him. Being trapped alone for ten hours would mean he would have had to spend every minute locked in a spiritually exhausting contest of wills against his own demon. Right now though, strangely, he wanted to think of his children and his wife. He felt as though he had the benefit of perspective from beyond the grave. He imagined that the duration of his life with them was over regardless of whether the death was real or imagined. It made him appreciate the memories more, and attach positive emotions to them, like love and pride, rather than regret. But then pangs of loneliness would punctuate the transition from memory to memory. Though he wasn't 'happy', he knew it was as it should be. He did love his family and he did miss them, and as long as he drew breath it would remain that way. The sooner he allowed his mind to align with the new paradigm the better. Breathing the country air and watching the miles tick by gave him the chance to sit with that, and to let it settle in.

By the time he stopped for gas and to grab a bite and hit the head, he felt like he was in a better place, mentally. In a relatively short time he would look up an old friend and hopefully get all the help he needed to establish himself somewhere comfortable and remain anonymous and seek pleasure in the simple things. He saw an internet café at the rest stop and he fed ten Euro notes into the machine to buy time. He sat at a carrel with a terminal and created a fictional, unverified email account on a web-based service. He composed an email to an address that appeared to be a list of random characters. It read;

'Lost myself after reeling in the years. Headed to the kingfisher next Mo-day. Can use all the help I can get.'

And he was back on the road. It had been a long time since he had been in France so he could notice some differences, even if they were subtle. He crossed some picturesque bridges and drove straight through country villages and he was particularly enjoying the temperate weather. He imagined that his near future would be somewhere very hot, with limited infrastructure. The friend he emailed was Mohammed Batu. He was an Olympic weightlifter on the Turkish team before he joined the Legion and he was the legendary strongman in Harry's unit. Mo was a very big drinker back in the old days, and he used to call Sundays, his day to recuperate, Mo-days. He and Harry had spotted a crane on the banks of the Nile and he insisted it was called a kingfisher. He adamantly stuck to his position when Harry corrected him, and it took a bet of a crate of Egyptian beer to get him to admit he was wrong. Harry used this memory as a touchpoint to let Mo know where he was going to be. In Marseilles there is a brasserie called *The Tilted Crane*, and there is an image of a construction crane leaning too far to the side on the signboard. This place was familiar to them both, and he checked that it was still there. They have rooms available above the pub and Harry planned on staying there once he got to Marseilles.

He daydreamed about the possibilities in his new life. Perhaps he could franchise a mobile phone business or something similar in a large West African city. Perhaps he could keep accounts for a medium sized business somewhere around the Med. Being in a mindset of possibility rejuvenated him.

Eventually the sun was low on his right and both the road signs and the GPS were telling him that he was approaching Bordeaux. He focused, and followed the instructions of the GPS explicitly now, though he could still see that he was entering an impressive city. He passed outstanding examples of architecture going back as far as the middle ages but he was too focused on the directions to learn anything about them. He passed St. Patrick street and could see that it was broad and alive with foot traffic, but the parking garage was just a few streets behind it and he hurried there.

Harry found it under the universal parking sign. There were double barriers at the street and Harry had to stop with the back of the Kadjar on the street while he found the parking ticket in the plastic folio. This left the upside down 'F' exposed longer than he would have liked, but he eventually got it fed into the machine and the bar went up. He had to go to the top floor. It was steep and the corners were sharp and he could only go a strange speed that wanted to wind out first gear but clunked in second. He made it to the top floor without touching anything and found the parking space reserved by his ticket.

He shut off the engine and immediately got out to stretch. He got caught in the stretch as one does in a yawn, and he was unable to cut it off. His ribs were healing, and the stretching relieved the discomfort. The top floor of the parking garage was covered, and it was dim inside. He was parked against the outside wall, midway in a line of cars that was about fifty feet long. The stairwells were on the far edge of the building while the elevator was in the centre. Kevin had made it clear that he should put the key atop the front driver's side tire and depart; there would be no meeting taking place. That suited Harry just fine.

He opened the rear door on the driver's side to get his backpack and he heard the stairwell door creak open. He ignored it and put his pack on the ground and crouched to place the key on the tire. He thought of how unsophisticated this plan was, and his confidence in its veracity waned a bit. A steady cadence of approaching footsteps followed the clunk of the closing door. He grabbed his pack, stood up and walked to the end of the vehicle, glancing briefly to his left to note the man approaching. His glance was camouflaged in the actions of adjusting his pack and orienting himself to the elevator. He did not hesitate or break his stride, and in his first couple steps toward the elevator he assessed whether or not the man was a threat. He was an average height Caucasian man with brown hair wearing heavy boots. His arms were folded and his hands were not visible under the folds of his open green fatigue jacket. He was walking too fast not to be swinging his arms while not visibly carrying anything. Harry carried on a few steps toward the elevator and heard the man's pace quicken. As he got closer to the elevator it chimed and the door opened and a tall black man wearing a balaclava got off.

Harry felt a wave of relief like a boxer does when he finally hears the bell. The resolution to this pantomime was now known. Harry abruptly stepped back and delivered a back kick, crouching to do so. His foot caught the man right in the midriff and pushed all the air out of him and sent him backward and down. The sound of a tire iron clattering to the floor echoed loudly across the open space. Harry recovered his stance and saw that the man in front of him was pulling a handgun from his belt and bringing it to bear. Not having the weapon out and ready was another amateur move. Harry hopped forward just enough to assist a long lunge. Perhaps the man thought he would brandish the weapon and secure compliance with whatever he commanded, but his reflexes weren't ready to be challenged for the gun from so far away. Harry aimed for his right sleeve with both hands, turning his trunk to present the smallest possible target. Harry had misjudged his own reflexes. He was just a beat slower than he thought he was, and he got the man's sleeve but not at the wrist as he had planned. At first the man fought to get his arm free and then tried to turn his wrist to point the gun at Harry's torso. The man on the ground had gotten to his feet. Harry spun to body check the man while running both hands down his arm to the gun; the idea was to force his wrist joint to put his hand in a shape that could not hold the weapon.

It worked, but not before setting the gun off. The report was extremely loud, followed instantly by the gun clattering to the floor. Because Harry was now facing the man who was behind him, Harry saw his face register the shock and surprise of unexpectedly being shot. Harry turned while trying to land an elbow on the man in the balaclava, but he had disengaged and Harry saw his fast-twitch response and he was in full flight toward the opposite stairwell twenty feet away. Harry let him go and picked up the gun. It was a stock automatic, functional but cheap.

Harry approached the man who had fallen on his back. The chances of being shot in a circumstance like this were very, very small. This man had incredibly bad luck. The bullet was high calibre and it must have been a hollow point or some other kind of insidious projectile. The man's feet were sliding across the polished cement in a weak motion that may have been intended to right himself. His right arm was pressed against the cement and his neck was struggling to keep his head up. The bullet had entered his body just two inches to the left of the centre of his ribcage, and just above the diaphragm. It had ejected an amount of tissue roughly the size of a cricket ball, which was trapped by the jacket, making a small mound of sticky goo that audibly squelched with his gasping struggles. Harry assumed some of that goo was lung, based on the gasping sound the man was making. He couldn't speak and Harry could see the shock and horror written on his face. He was numb and suffocating, even as he gulped all the air his mouth could find. Harry knelt down next to him, careful not to touch him, and looked him directly in the face.

"You are dying," he said in French. *"Nothing can change that now. Embrace it and carry on with your journey in peace."*

The expression on his face changed from disbelief to acceptance as he lay his head carefully back down on the cement. Harry stood and put the gun in his pack. He would calmly, as casually as possible, take the elevator down and exit the building and disappear into the Bordeaux night. He pushed the elevator button and tried to maintain his composure. By the time the elevator bell rang the gasping behind him had stopped. But the opening doors revealed something he had not expected to see. On the elevator were four men. Three were standing around the perimeter with guns drawn and the man in the balaclava in the centre had his hands clasped together in front of him. They pushed balaclava off the elevator and followed him out. They all had their faces exposed and one kept his gun drawn on balaclava while the other two pointed their guns at Harry. The shorter, swarthy man had an air of leadership and he advanced toward the body. Harry raised his hands to chest height in front of him, to indicate that he was unarmed and was not a threat.

The shorter man briefly inspected the body.

"Where is the gun?" he asked.

"It's in my pack," Harry responded.

"Hand it over," the man said, pointing with his chin to the man with his gun on him. Harry slowly slid it off his arms and to the floor, where he kicked it over to the man.

"You're not Kevin. Where the hell is Kevin?"

"He told me to make this run," Harry said, *"He paid me a grand in sterling."*

"Where is the package?" the man asked. Harry thought that he should have seen this coming.

"Kevin told me to park here and leave the key on the tire," he said, *"I don't know anything about a package."* He paused to weigh up whether or not to say the next thing. *"But if these jokers came for something then it must still be here."*

The man said that they had to get the hell out of there. He instructed the one who had Harry's backpack to get the key and try to retrieve the package. He said that they were taking the stairs with him going first, then Harry then balaclava and finally his associates. Then he marched them off quickly but not at a run, to the stairwell and then down. The stairwell was dark and musty and the lighting was dim, but they descended the five flights at speed.

On the way down the shorter man spoke loudly over his shoulder to Harry and balaclava, *"When we get to the bottom we're going right out into an alley. We have a van running there. Get in the back of the van quickly and quietly."* He didn't say it out loud but Harry knew there was a very real 'or else' on the end of that. They got to the ground floor uninterrupted and they went through an emergency exit with a sign saying the door was alarmed; it wasn't. Through the door they were in an alley, where a running Mercedez seven-seater's side door slid open and they piled into the back. All the seats had been removed and replaced with benches along the sides. The van began driving as soon as the door slid shut.

Harry and balaclava still had guns trained on them.

"What the hell was all that?" the shorter man asked them both.

"I made the drop and I got jacked on this end," Harry said. *"They fucked with the wrong guy and that poor bastard's luck ran out."*

Balaclava didn't even try to make an opposing argument. He knew it wouldn't have made any difference.

"Are you English?" the shorter swarthy man asked Harry.

"Not anymore," he replied. *"I'm on my way to Marseilles to connect with old friends and begin my new contract."* Although that wasn't technically true he didn't want it to appear as if no one would miss him if he didn't make it to Marseilles. The swarthy man said something to his crew in a language Harry didn't understand, and the two in the back restrained balaclava's hands and feet in zip ties. They drove in silence for five minutes until the van pulled over and stopped on a fairly busy street. The shorter man motioned Harry to the door with his chin as he put his gun under his coat, *"Get out,"* he said.

Harry got out of the van and the man followed him, slamming the door shut behind him. The now-dark city street was backlit with neon and artificial light and the hum of human and vehicular traffic. Standing up fully, Harry could see that the man was holding his backpack out to him.

"This is the bus station. Get on an overnight bus to Marseilles right now. Don't stay in Bordeaux one minute more than you have to," he said.

Harry took his pack and slung it over his shoulder.

"There's one more thing," the man said, *"You owe me a favour now. I'm Gino, from Corsica, and one day when I ask you for a favour in return you have to repay it."*

Harry thought that was a bit dramatic. Still, Gino had the power to keep Harry in the same boat as balaclava and probably Kevin, but he let him go.

"My name is Harry," he said, *"You got it."*

Gino got back in the van and drove off and Harry went into the bus station. Gino seemed more professional than the thugs that jumped him, but there was no way in hell Harry was going to get on a public bus directly after being present at the scene of a murder in a low-crime city in France. From the entrance to the bus station, he went directly to the exit and left. He was now on the side of the building at a taxi rank. He looked back out front and nothing looked out of place. He approached the first taxi in line and the driver waved him in. He took a seat inside and the driver asked where he was going. Harry told him that he was going to Marseilles. The driver said that there was no way in hell he was going to spend the whole night driving to Marseilles and back, especially since there was no way he would get a return fare. Harry took out his envelope of cash and made a show of counting out twenty notes, making four hundred Euros in cash, and putting it to the side and counting out another twenty.

"I'll pay you this four hundred for the ride. And this four hundred I will tip for the quiet. The ride will be quiet and you will be quiet about the ride. Does that work for you?" Harry asked.

The driver kept complaining but said for that money at least he could get some decent coffee, and reluctantly put his hand out to the small opening in the partition between front and back seat. Harry gave him four hundred Euros and slid back to position himself for sleep. He was in for about another six hours in a vehicle and his body needed to shut down. By the time they hit the motorway he was snoring.

Restitution

Born of Two Worlds

When she told her colleagues at the office that she was going to Boston they all started reminiscing about their college days there. Most had gone to Harvard and MIT but others had gone to Brown and Dartmouth. They all had stories about hockey games at the Garden, working fens along the banks of the Charles, or doing mushrooms and wandering the streets of the city. Every one of them had opinions on the best food in Boston but the only place they all seemed to agree on was the Barking Crab. Getting a lobster roll at the Crab seemed to be a Boston tradition, and everyone told her that she simply must go. After this talk she looked up restaurants in Boston and found there was a very vibrant food scene with some very well credentialed and well recommended restaurants. She would try several, but she definitely would be going to the Barking Crab.

The Barking Crab is the last bit of real waterfront hanging onto the financial district at the end of Seaport Boulevard, built atop wooden pilings sunk into the harbour. This gives it a broad deck on three sides overlooking the water, but a table facing the city sees the beige towers of Lafayette Place and the hunched low-rises where accounts were managed and trades were made. She got there half an hour before they opened, to have a good look and get the best table.

She had booked a room at the Holiday Inn in Brighton, and this is what she would run through expenses when she got back. She had gotten into Boston three days early, though, and had been staying in a suite at the Boston Harbor Hotel. This was an iconic Boston hotel right on the water. High society events were held here and only clientele who required luxury stayed there. It was the kind of place where a new money tech billionaire would stay.

On American soil she was not allowed to surveille or gather intelligence on American citizens, and she would not. As a private citizen she was able to stay where she chose, and whatever she happened to observe was hers to know. It didn't matter too much though, as she was in Boston to establish a connection with Curtis Chase, a high-flying tech entrepreneur and to try to get him to do some work for the government. If he did agree then there would be a rigorous vetting process undertaken. She was doing her own diligence because she wanted to know that she herself would be safe. He had been in town for a week conducting business talks with a global custody bank that wanted to use his tech for identifying very specific investments and acquiring their rights in an automated way. He had private security which was very discreet and his comings and goings were quite routine. He left the hotel in the morning after breakfast, stayed in meetings at the bank's headquarters most of the day and returned to the hotel for dinner and a spate of calls. All was very much as one would expect.

All appeared normal at the Crab as well. Someone came to unlock the large glass doors and the quiet hubbub of preparing a restaurant for opening could be heard inside. She stepped inside and took in the scene of the empty restaurant. It was very clean and utilitarian. There were muted brown and black colours of wood and wrought iron brightly exposed by the midday sun. It was immediately familiar and the strong smell of freshly brewed coffee was invigorating. The weather was good, so she would sit at a table on the deck, with the city behind her so he would have more to look at than just her. Conversations would be more private there. She took a menu from one of the workers and asked that a coffee be brought to her table on the deck. She took that seat and scanned to see what was in her natural eyeline. From her seat she could see most of what was going on inside and she could see everyone approaching in any direction from the deck. There was a railing behind her with the water of the harbour just a five-foot drop below.

Her coffee arrived after a very short wait. Now she had probably half an hour to just sit. While her coffee cooled she took out her copy of the Boston Globe and set it on the table without opening it. She listened to the sounds around her. She heard the water lapping at the pylons, seabirds settling some kind of dispute and the ambient hum of a large city just a few blocks away. A two-inch blurb at the bottom of the newspaper referred to a story about a refugee from Myanmar who had won a scholarship to MIT and had subsequently made a significant engineering discovery. It made her think of her own journey to becoming an American.

Her story would seem unbelievable to most westerners, but there were many, many unbelievable stories that were true. Every person who has sought asylum or who has been displaced by the need for refuge has such a story, which they prefer to keep quiet. She had met hundreds of people whose stories were more harrowing than hers, and she had met many whose endings were not nearly as happy. She herself had been on the back foot from the time before her life even began.

During the second Tuareg rebellion in northern Mali a detachment of Legionnaires from the 2e REP, the elite parachute regiment, were dispatched to gather intelligence and to assess the likelihood of the Tuaregs breaking with the Islamists. At the time it wasn't clear that president Toure could hold the country together, and France needed to formulate her policy. The breakaway group of Tuareg invited the Legionnaires to stay with them and to move with them on their operations, because they wanted to impress them and win the support of the former colonial power.

From stories she'd heard from her mother, the paratroopers were generally young and wild, and whenever they were not on operations they were drinking hard or finding ways to get to a city with available women. But there was one young man who never touched alcohol and who was largely left alone when his comrades went sowing wild oats. He would stay in the semi-permanent Tuareg camp and try to learn the language and learn how to survive in the desert as the Tuareg did. Her mother was the one who was tasked with cleaning the foreigners' lodgings while they were away, and she started bringing the straggler tea and then later his evening meal. Without going into any detail her mother told her that they had fallen in love and had married each other in their hearts. Shortly thereafter the 2e REP soldiers were abruptly called away to a hot war somewhere else in Africa, and she never saw him again.

Once her mother realised she was pregnant she knew there would be no life with her people. She fled in the night and made a harrowing journey to Tombouctou where she found transport to Bamako. She was taken in as a domestic worker by a fairly high-ranking civil servant in Bamako, explaining that she was raped by a foreign mercenary. This was a much more likely story than the truth and it explained why she would have to flee her people. She immediately began to learn Arabic. When the baby was born she was allowed to keep her in the servants' quarters. The baby's shocking eye colour and light skin made her an exotic standout, but her insatiable curiosity and loving demeanour made her the favourite of the staff and of the family. Her mother gave the baby the name of her father's mother as a constant homage to the man that she had loved so dearly, even if it was impossible to pronounce – Betty Holloway.

When Betty reached the age of five the civil servant exercised some influence an got her accepted at an international boarding school run by a Catholic charity. It was agony for her mother to be separated overnight, but they visited together and spent every weekend together.

Here her own memory picked up. The French Catholic fathers called her Fanta, because it was not an uncommon name for a Tuareg girl and because they found her overly sweet just like the drink of the same spelling. She fell in love with education and became addicted to the praise for her academic accolades. As her education progressed through the years it became clear that she had a photographic memory. Because the Catholic education values memory so much, she became not only the top student in her school but also something of a national prodigy in Malian education circles. When the opportunity for her to attend an elite Parisian high school arose, both she and her mother knew that this was the best thing for her. Though it gave her great pain to do it, she left her mother and her native Bamako and went to live and study in the city of light at the age of only thirteen.

As the only light skinned person in her school aside from the priests, she had always been made to know that she was different. There were taunts and jeers and exclusion, but she assumed these were caused as much by jealousy of her academic prowess as by anything else. In Paris, though, she encountered true racism. She was put in a homestay with the only family in the programme who were Tamahaq speakers, in the banlieue of Sarcelles. Though the family did their very best to protect her from the world around her, they could not change the France in which they lived. Her daily commutes to and from the school reinforced her impression that France had a clear idea of who she was and how far she would be allowed to progress in society. She was supposed to become an excellent engineer and contribute to the social security of the nation, but to stay out in the cultural hinterlands where she belonged.

Instead, she became keenly interested in the civil rights movement for people of colour in Paris and as a teenager she began joining the marches. With the mind of an engineer she began to unpick how the society had become this way, and she applied her significant academic skills to unravelling the circumstances and historical events that brought Paris to the brink of chaos time and time again. When she was finally offered a 'full ride' scholarship to study cutting edge sociology at George Washington University in D.C., she jumped at the chance.

She loved D.C. and she loved America, even though it was still living its history with race relations. She loved being independent, finally with no one hovering over her trying to protect her from the world. Most of all, she loved that her academic pursuits of the nature and causes of both racism and radicalisation were not only tolerated but also encouraged. She quickly became a star at the university and in four years' time she was writing her master's thesis in 'intersectionality and influence in radicalisation and de-radicalisation in large out-groups'. She was thinking about Mali and Islamist groups, but the only ones available for study in Virginia were homegrown, far-right militias. Her paper was genius, a true masterwork, and that is what got the attention of the agency.

Now here she was, waiting to meet with Curtis Chase. With the right data he could model an environment where radicalisation could be predicted. She wanted to talk to him about that, and maybe one day she would get the chance, but this conversation was to get him onboard to combat Russian influence in the cyber war that was definitely underway.

Patrons began to arrive. One of the workers assumed the post of the hostess and began seating people for lunch. Someone inside went behind the bar and turned the television on to what looked like a sports channel. Chase arrived alone, and spoke with the hostess, pointing over to Betty. He must have recognised her from the description.

He saw the young woman with the curly ponytail sitting alone by the water, wearing a crimson Harvard sweatshirt. The office of a sitting Massachusetts senator had contacted him and put him on the line with the senator. They had known each other at college, here in Boston, and the senator knew Chase would be in Boston for a while. He asked if he wouldn't mind meeting a representative to discuss a way in which his tech could be put to use in the service of the nation. When he agreed, the senator gave him this time and place, and described whom he would meet. When he got closer he could see that her eyes were the colour of pale hay, which was a stark contrast to her complexion. She stood to greet him and then tucked her right leg under her as she sat down; very casual, very unconcerned. Almost immediately a server came with water and took their drink order. Once the server left, he dove straight into conversation.

"I have to say, I'm intrigued to hear what this is about. I thought a pitch from the government would be much more...official," he said.

"I get that," she said, *"but the thing about this is that it isn't official. That's kind of the point."*

She had a very subtle but distinct accent. He tried to place it but he couldn't.

"Is it the kind of thing that is secret?" he asked.

"Not secret," she replied, *"but the kind of thing we want to talk to just you about."*

She was speaking more loudly than she had intended. She had to talk over the wind and the seabirds.

He nodded. *"Fire away,"* he said.

"We want to ask you to volunteer to help your country. We know there's nothing you need or want, so we are appealing to your sense of altruism and patriotism."

"I see," he said. *"I'm as patriotic an American as Indiana has ever produced. How can I be of service?"*

He saw that she had become distracted, and then engrossed, and had not at all heard his response. He turned his head to see what she was staring at behind him. It was the T.V. in the bar. It was showing some major breaking news and there appeared to be fire and flashing lights.

"What the hell?" he said as he took out and unfolded his phone into a flat screen tablet. He tapped a few things until the screen in his hand was displaying the same feed as the screen behind the bar. He propped it up on the table and turned the volume up, pulling his chair to her side of the table so they could watch together. A reporter was shouting into a microphone to be heard over the background of sirens and the impromptu lighting set up for the broadcast was interrupted with the strobe effect of flashing lights from scores of emergency vehicles. The reporter herself appeared flustered and kept looking down at a notebook in her hand then back at the camera, blurting out several disturbing but disconnected facts between stammering out 'um' and 'ah' a frustrating amount of times. They passed back to the newsroom where a

talking head broke down what they knew in as coherent a way as possible. Apparently there was some kind of a gun battle at the Hoover Dam, followed by a series of major explosions. From what they could tell, a known Eco terror group attempted to destroy critical infrastructure and they were interrupted and attacked by a radical militia. Following the explosions there was no sound coming from the dam, but emergency workers were unable to enter until the soundness of the dam was verified.

Betty and Curtis looked at each other, shocked by this unexpected news. Betty spoke, *"I was going to stay in Boston as long as you were, and try to win you over, but I think I will have to go back to D.C. and get back to work now. I think this proves how badly your country needs you – can I tell them you will help?"*

Chase carried on looking at the screen, obviously shocked at the armed conflict emerging in America.

"You can tell them that I'll help in any way I can."

Gateway to Disappearance

"Wake up and welcome to Marseilles, Englishman," the taxi driver shouted into the back seat. The *Tilted Crane* was in the fourteenth arrondissement in Marseilles, about a mile inland. This was an area of the city that was always known to be rough, but in the last few years it had become both a commercial boomtown for the drug trade and the venue for the gambol of disaffected frustration. Harry sat up in the back seat and felt around in the dark for his pack and his belongings. He had been in a deep sleep and it took him a minute to come to. Out the window he could see that it was still mostly dark, though the eastern sky offered an ominous glow. The *Tilted Crane* was right there across the street, and it was as he remembered it, mostly. This was an older part of the city, with the newer towers of the housing estates, which

had virtually become a battleground, further inland. The brasserie was a large unit of a three-story terraced building that took up the entire block. There was a broad pavement in front of it and there were sets of stairs from the pavement to the businesses at each door. The taxi driver gave Harry one last bit of advice as he was counting out the remaining four hundred euros.

"I have no idea why you wanted to come here so badly, English, and I don't want to know. But you should know that you are in an unsafe area in an unsafe city at an unsafe time of night. Stay off the street until the sun comes up. I'm going to take your money and turn around and leave Marseilles as fast as I can and I won't even stop for petrol until I'm out of the city limits." And then, as he was taking the small stack of twenty-euro notes, *"Bon chance and au revoir, English."*

Harry unfolded his six-foot three-inch frame from the back seat of the taxi with the small pack in his left hand. He raised his arms in a full body stretch and got locked in a yawn as he did so. The taxi pulled far over to the left and did a u-turn around Harry, its passenger-side wheels going over the pavement's kerb as it did so. The tires whined in the sharp turn and then chirped as the driver hit a higher gear and gassed it to speed away hastily. So much for remaining incognito. Harry stayed in the middle of the street and completed his yawn and then started toward the entrance of the *Crane*.

He hadn't had time to prepare his mind for re-entry into this region of his past, and his memories poured out, stumbling over each other and clamouring for his attention. Their depth and richness unnerved him, and he felt like he was visiting with an erratic and dangerous old friend. This was the city he would return to in his youth when an operation concluded. Being in Marseilles meant that he was safe, though no one was ever truly safe in Marseilles. This is where his fear and anxiety would slowly leach out, in the same way he could feel the heat of the previous day still leaching out of the pavement and the concrete of the buildings. Eons of trauma from the tribulations of European history percolated still from the city's marrow, now joining with the rage and violence born of the inequity and injustice in which the contemporary city's psyche was steeped. There were few streetlights in operation but the one directly in front of the *Crane* was on. Harry walked directly through the pool of light and sat on the ground beside the staircase to the leeward side, in shadow. It had been swept and he leaned back against the side of the staircase, and let his memories in. His mates back then were all fit and dangerous young men, disciplined in the field but having disdain and even contempt for routine civilian life when returned. They were members of an elite unit of an elite army and they felt entitled to rambunctious release when they were back in the Republic. Very often they drank themselves completely into oblivion, where a three-day bender with varying degrees of lucidity was not uncommon. Harry himself did not drink, because of his experience of his father, and he remembered how his friends would hit a certain stage where they would become maudlin and become consumed with past injustices or unrequited love. Harry enjoyed this aspect of their liberty; bravado and machismo were drowned in the alcohol and the eternal child emerged. Harry remembered one liberty in Marseilles after a particularly dangerous operation in Chad, when, under the influence of hallucinogens, he decided that monogamous sex was a sacrament where the participants connected with the numinous. In this religion only that which is eternal is important, and god is agnostic to the telic, egoistic portion of man and only guides the id. He hadn't considered real belief without evidence before because he didn't really know what faith meant. Since that night though, he felt that this was as good a guess as any.

Harry's memory had always been his own and he never knew it to be unusual, but over the years of conversation with friends and schoolmates he came to know that his way of remembering was not the same as his peers'. Harry would live in the moment and later when he remembered a noteworthy point the details around that would fill in, accurately and completely. These moments would eventually connect, and he could remember some episodes of his life as if he were watching a film. Now, remembering back to the London attack, he could hear the telltale sound before the explosion, he could smell the acrid smoke in the stairwell and he could precisely retrace the route of the black taxi from the city to Folkestone. As far as he could tell, his memory gave him facts while the memories of others were much more subjective. People's memories were not nearly as reliable as they expected. If someone were telling a story in a pub then embellishment was fair enough, but when someone was recounting fact as accurately as possible, say briefing an officer on enemy strength and location, there was up to a thirty percent skew from Harry's point of view. With this amazing memory he could easily relive being blown against the stairwell wall and pissing himself when his ribs landed unguarded on the sharp stairs. He knew this one would join the cavalcade of memories that intruded on him unbidden, as sharp as the crack of human vertebrae.

Headlights were approaching and they slowed as they neared the *Crane*. A white four-door sedan stopped directly under the working streetlight so it was easy to see. Harry had no idea what to make of it so he didn't move. He was fairly hidden in shadow so he decided just to stay quiet and see what happened. Harry saw three men in the car, but only the driver got out. He was average height, wearing jeans and a sweatshirt, and he locked the car with the fob on the key and put it in his pocket. He held nothing else. He crossed the street and when he went through the pool of light Harry could see that he was Caucasian and probably in his mid-thirties. He walked slowly as if approaching Harry, and he stopped about ten feet away. Harry was alert, but did not want to incite trouble if it was not necessary, so he remained hunched but coiled for action.

"Are you Harry Holloway?" the man asked in English.

Harry was quite surprised. He kept his eyes on the man's face and put a palm flat on the ground and rose to his feet slowly, in readiness.

"Mohammed Batu sent me to let you into your room and get you set up with toiletries and towels," he said.

Harry was both relieved and bewildered.

"How did you know I'd be here?" he asked.

"Mohammed has been expecting you," he said, *"we've been watching the video feed."*

The man reached into a pocket of his sweatshirt, very slowly and deliberately, and pulled out an overfilled key ring. It was about two inches in diameter but the keys were packed so tightly on it that they were held against each other and could not dangle.

"My name is Limier," he said, *"and I'm Mo's brother."* He started up the steps focusing on searching through the keys. *"Please come with me,"* he said.

Harry knew that Mohammed had family but there was no way this man was Mo's biological brother. He wondered what affiliations Mo had made that allowed this man to call himself Mo's brother. Perhaps he was also a former Legionnaire. In English his moniker meant Bloodhound and it sounded to Harry like a nom de guerre.

Harry followed Limier up the stairs and while he fumbled with the keys Harry surveyed the street in the growing light. The sedan sat with two men inside doing nothing. Some bins were out waiting for collection. There were several short driveways next to businesses and behind locked gates where covered skips collected the commercial refuse. It was still too dark to detect the silhouettes of surveillance cameras, but he knew they must be out there. There were places to hide, there were avenues of emergency egress, there were high spots where a sniper could be murderously effective. With the right security measures *The Tilted Crane* could be made into a fortress.

They stepped into the closed brasserie and in the dark the stools perched upside down on the tables gave Harry a start. There was a bar and a seated dining area as well as a small stage with stacks of karaoke equipment in its corner. Limier spoke to Harry but in the direction he was looking as he went about his business, and it reminded Harry of the man in the data centre. Limier went briskly to two separate stations that did not appear to be alarms and adroitly entered codes. Then he went behind the bar and flipped some switches that caused a loud clunk from somewhere behind the rear service area, and Harry assumed it was a magnetic deadbolt being thrown to release a heavy door.

"Mo said your wit hasn't dulled since you last met," he said. *"He said to tell you that he will come in mid-afternoon tomorrow, to give you a chance to get caught up on sleep and to wash off the road. He didn't tell me to say this, but you are completely safe here,"* he said.

He picked the keyring off the bar and tilted his head towards the back, as instruction for Harry to follow him.

"Get meals and beverages from the brasserie below at any time. Laundry and amenities are provided in your room, and if there's anything specific you need or want right now then you should tell me."

They had walked through the kitchen to a heavy metal door that looked like the entrance to a walk-in freezer, but when

Limier opened the door there were stairs behind it. They had ascended the stairs and arrived at a landing to an interior hall with two electronically locking doors on the far side and one on the stairwell side, so it looked like the interior of a hotel. Limier took a key card out of his pocket and walked to the far door in the opposite corner, beeping it and turning the handle when the small light went green. They stepped into a room that would be a good-sized hotel room, with a full bedroom set, a closet, a T.V. and an ensuite bath.

Once they were inside Limier handed Harry the key card and said, *"Here. You can put your bag anywhere. Welcome home."*

"There are clothes in the drawers, sheets and towels in the wardrobe," he went on, *"and the equipment in the nightstand is for you."*

He nodded to the open top drawer of the bedside table. Harry took a few steps over and looked down. The lamp on the table perfectly lit a tableau of a pistol, a cell phone and a stack of twenty-euro notes.

"That magazine is full and there is nothing in the chamber and the safety is on. There's a box of fifty in the drawer underneath." He stopped his tour-guide persona and said in a more conspiratorial tone, *"Mo said you wouldn't need any education in how to use it or where to point it. Maybe before long you will be my brother too."*

Harry dropped his small bag on the bed and immediately kicked off his shoes.

"If you could ask someone to bring up a meal then you will be saving my life. After that I'm going to sit in that bath until I'm pruned from head to toe."

"Done," Limier said. *"The two guys in the car are going to come inside and start prep for breakfast. They'll bring you something first, so wait until after your meal to bathe."*

He nodded to the bedside table again. *"There's a three o'clock alarm set on that phone. Mo will be here no later than four."*

Limier stopped as he was closing the door and said, *"It was good to meet you. I look forward to getting to know you over the coming months."*

"Thank you again," Harry said in reply.

Once Limier was gone Harry had a closer look around the room. There were two changes of casual clothes in the drawer that would fit him. There was at least a week's worth of toilet goods and brand-new toiletries in the bathroom. There was stack of towels and an extra blanket in the wardrobe. He really didn't need anything more.

He turned the T.V. to a twenty-four-hour international news station and sat on the edge of the bed and picked up the pistol. It was a Glock 17, French army issue. He touched the release button and removed the magazine. Hollow points. He racked the slide and saw that there was nothing in the chamber. He could smell cleaning solvent and gun oil. This was a well maintained and highly reliable piece of equipment – he liked it. Then he picked up the cell phone. There was no lock on it. The clock did have an alarm set. It was already connected to Wi-Fi and apparently it was loaded with an extreme amount of data. The only applications loaded were typical, publicly available and useful applications. The envelope icon showed that he had a new email message.

The low-volume news feed from the T.V. was deconstructing the London attack but he was too curious about the email to pay attention to the report. He opened the email and it was from a nondescript email address. It said simply "read your

Notes". He opened the Notes app and found notes describing each of the men who were now downstairs bringing the brasserie to life. There was a note from Mo that expressed his sympathies for all of the losses associated with the London attack. It also said that he was completely safe and that they would speak in person soon.

Just as he was putting the phone down to turn his attention to the news, there was a knock on the door and a muscular young man with a military haircut introduced himself and handed a tray through the door. He asked Harry to put the tray outside the door when he was finished. Harry thanked him and said that he would.

Harry put the tray down on the coffee table and lifted the lid. There was a full breakfast of meats, eggs and potato, with a small bowl of cut fresh fruit. There was a pot of strong coffee too, and the man had left a package of still and sparkling spring water as well. Harry set about eating slowly and deliberately. He was so hungry that he knew onboarding solids too quickly would cause sharp pains and may cause his digestion mechanism to twitch and get stuck in a clench. He sipped at the coffee and nibbled at the toast and let the pain hit and settle. Then he increased his intake until the hunger was normal hunger and then was soon feeling the promise of satiation. When he was done he saw that he had consumed every morsel of anything edible on the tray. He put it outside the door and ran the bath. He could feel his body working on the food and he swore he could feel it being absorbed. He had to get into the bath, his energy level was dropping precipitously. He took his time bathing, but wrapped up when he felt his head nodding. He barely remembered putting on the track suit before he was sound asleep.

The alarm interrupted an ordinary dream and woke him up. He shut off the alarm and lay thinking for a minute. The dream had been something completely innocuous and was immediately fleeting; he had been riding the Southeastern Rail into London on a typical commute. What was noteworthy about that was how normal it was. He had been extremely exhausted, it was true, but he hadn't gone out of his way to manufacture exhaustion to subdue his subconscious mind. He had the feeling that if it were a normal sleep then he would still not have had a sinister dream. Though there was still a lot that needed immediate attention, his mind was not in a state of constant high anxiety. When he was taking his leave from the site of the London attack appearing dead and being dead were nearly equally appealing. Now though, he felt like there was at least the possibility that he could return to his right mind.

If the alarm woke him then he had slept nearly a full twelve hours. He went to the bathroom and pissed out one of the two litres of water he had drunk and brushed his teeth. He was rested, fed, hydrated and behind strong walls and locked doors. He was as ready to face an unknown future as he would ever be. He put the cell phone, the room key and about a hundred euros into the pants pocket of the track suit and went down to the brasserie.

At the bottom of the stairs he opened the door a crack and stuck his head through. The kitchen was busy with about three people working. No one paid him any attention and he made his way back through to the front through the swinging service doors. The pub was in full operation and they were at about half occupancy with people sitting down to a late lunch and some people sitting at the bar. The décor was faux-posh with white metal and naugahyde furnishings, as an unattainable homage to the brass and leather they could never afford. There were original hand painted landscapes on the walls, favouring brooding skies and angry seas. The lighting was dim.

Harry went to the bar to occupy an empty stool. As he did, the middle aged north African woman behind the bar approached him and asked, *"Mr. Holloway?"*

"Yes," he said as he stopped and waited.

"Mr. Batu is in the office, and he asked me to see you in," she said.

"Great, thank you," he said, and followed her around the bar to a room adjacent to the back exit.

She approached, knocked, and waited for the 'come in' before opening the door and showing Harry in.

"Mr. Holloway, sir," she said, and took her leave without waiting for any further interaction.

Harry looked in around her and saw an incredibly unkempt office with stacks of notebooks and piles of loose paper on the desk and heaps of aprons and paper products piled in the corner. Mohammed Batu sat in a leather chair behind the desk and Harry could see that the seat level had been raised because Mo was so short. His feet weren't fully on the floor and he looked like a child playing at business.

Mo still had the weightlifter build, with large powerful arms and a barrel chest. Harry could tell he was a lot fuller around the middle than he remembered him. Mo was a Turkish Kurd who had dark eyes and dark hair with a pale complexion. Though he was a fearsome adversary in the field, Harry always thought that Mo had kind eyes that made people trust him. Mo hopped forward to stand and came around the desk with his hand out.

"Harry!" he called, *"So good to see you so well!"*

"And you," Harry said. Then there passed some five minutes of hand shaking, shoulder patting and congratulatory and introductory noises. When the fervour of the meeting died

down Mo pointed to a chair across the desk and said, *"Sit, please sit."*

Mo picked up the phone and asked for coffee and pastries to be brought in.

Harry waited until there was a lull and he broached the subject that he did not yet know about.

"Mo, you know I am eternally grateful for the help. I was surprised to find you in the corner office of The Tilted Crane though. Will you get me caught up on what's going on in your life or should I start?"

Mo told him that he (Mo) was too curious to know what was going on, so he asked Harry to tell his tale first. And this Harry did, starting with his divorce and then talking about the attack in London, and his decision making in the emotionally charged moment that led him to fake his own death. Then he told about Kevin and Connor in detail, and gave a clear, factual account of the exchange in Bordeaux that led to the shooting death. He told of his unbelievable release by Gino the Corsican and how he jumped in a car and immediately came to Mo.

The bartender knocked and came in with a tray of coffee and pastries, put them down and took her leave. There was a brief lull while they poured coffee and had a bit of a continental breakfast.

"That story is wild," Mo said, his Turkish accent as strong as the coffee. *"But my story is wilder by far."* Then he stopped thoughtfully and said, *"English is hurting my head, can we speak French?"*

"I'll try to keep up," Harry said.

Mo went on in French. *"You've heard of Blackwater and Wagner Group?"* Harry nodded. *"Well there is another such group operating to represent the interests of the Republic."*

Harry knew he meant France.

"Nobody was looking out for the people of the Republic's allies. The Americans are preoccupied and the Russians are the bad guys. North and West Africans have been paying a heavy toll to Wagner and the Islamists."

Harry knew that was a sad truth. The encroachment of the Islamists into the empty spaces in the Sahel was a known problem that got little attention. Wagner and tin pot leaders were extracting mined goods as fast as the Islamists were.

"The Republic sanctioned the incorporation of La Lance Fournie as an answer to this need. Do you remember the history lessons from the Legion?" Mo asked.

"The natural military unit that evolved to support the mounted medieval knight," Harry said, *"How poetic."*

"Yes," said Mo, *"a private defence and security consulting group, currently operating with broad authorities in jurisdictions across the Sahel."*

Harry poured and drank the cold coffee that was left in the pot.

"Most of our revenue is security consulting fees from Sahelian governments for the protection of interests in remote areas," Mo said. Harry let the *'notre'* sink in; so they were *our* revenues, were they?

Harry's recent compliance experience had him constantly thinking about keeping money out of the hands of bad guys. He had to mentally anticipate what nefarious actors may do, and it gave him practice in insidious scheming.

"And all of that is funded by international aid to support defence. Particularly from France, no?" he asked.

"Harry's back," Mo said.

They talked for about a few minutes about mundane things, with Mo getting Harry settled. Then they reminisced about old times for a few minutes, with Mo staying present in the conversation but not steering it. He was waiting for Harry to want to talk about things himself. Eventually he talked about Elena, and Herve and Leni. He talked about leaving the Legion and going back to England under his assumed identity, Herve Du Bois. No one in England seemed to care that Herve Du Bois, a French national, had a Geordie accent. He wasn't in London long when he met Elena, from Italy, and for the first time in his life he was happy to sit still and focus on her. Before he knew it he had a 'normal' job and they were moving into a flat together in Woolwich. It wasn't too long before Herve came along, and when they were pregnant with Leni they started looking for a house in a suburb with good schools.

Finally, Harry had a decent job and a stable family life; exactly the kind of thing they used to daydream about in the field. Harry confessed to Mo that the adjustment was more than he could take. He said that he had flashbacks, but they weren't limited to his combat experience. He had flashbacks to the days of his father's hair-trigger rage and immediate despondent contrition, steeped in the volatility of an alcoholic haze. On the corporate ladder, the level of stress and anxiety was hugely out of proportion to the level of physical danger, presenting an antagonistic and generally toxic environment. It had gotten to the point, he told Mo, that his daydreams felt the same as his night dreams, and like a mini-seizure he would act out what he was living in his daydreams. Finally, one day, he had decided to stand up to his father and wouldn't take his hands from his throat. Except it was Elena.

Harry sat staring at the desk for a minute in complete silence. Mo waited as long as he thought was healthy, then he spoke.

"Herve Du Bois was listed among the dead in the London attack," he said. "The official form says that the remains are unrecoverable, like too many others on that day."

Again he paused, then went on.

"La Lance could use Harry Holloway, now that Herve Du Bois is gone."

Harry had already considered this as a possibility and had been thinking it over since he learned of La Lance only minutes ago.

"I've been such an old suburban dad for so long that I think I'm not fit for it anymore, really," he said.

"No, Harry," Mo said, "I would need you to coordinate logistics. You know the people, the language, you know what the 'office culture' is like. You won't be the one kicking down the doors."

He looked at Harry to gauge his reaction and then went on, "Besides, in the last few days you survived a terrorist attack, faked your own death and got away clean from a fatal shooting. I'd say you still have operating skills."

"Alright," Harry said, "it's not like I've got much else going on."

"It's settled," Mo said. "We'll get you a crypto account, send you to a very quiet private doctor outside the city for care, tests and vaccinations, and get you plugged into the machine. Right now we've been asked to keep an eye on a site in the Caliphate of Malitania. Their government thinks it may be a staging ground for a push to take their oil fields."

"Straight in then," Harry said.

Cracks in the Foundation

The FBI had a file on the Defenders of Mother Earth for a long time, just like they had a file on the Homeland Minutemen. They were extreme opposites on the political spectrum but they had one thing in common – they had a penchant for action based on their beliefs. Somehow, though, each had been radicalised to the point where they were willing to take and lay down lives for what they believed. The events at the Hoover Dam went further than any prior radical action, and this time somehow there were two independent organisations attacking each other rather than one organisation being overcome by the government.

The Defenders of Mother Earth infiltrated the Dam complex and set charges to destroy the pumps and incapacitate the machinery that sent water from Lake Mead to Los Angeles. They had arranged to have an 'Earth manifesto' released to the media while they were still on-site. The Homeland Minutemen, who usually patrolled the southern border with Mexico, were in Nevada and they assaulted the offices and workspaces of the Dam to 'rescue' them before they could be destroyed. The Homeland Minutemen's timing was too perfect – they had not only been tipped off about the attack but they had very specific intelligence about the placement of the charges and the blueprints of the Dam. Before authorities could get on the scene there were clashes between the groups which amounted to a hunting expedition by the Minutemen because the Defenders were not armed. Once both groups were intermingled in the concrete catacombs the bombs were detonated, and almost everyone within was killed. Now what remained of each group was engaged in heated sabre-rattling and the media was having an absolute field day.

Immediately following the attack Curtis Chase worked feverishly and closely with financial watchdogs to deploy AI programs to identify and cross-reference all sources of funding for each organisation. There were common sources of funding that clearly were intended to be identified; this was a signal in the audit trail that pointed directly to South Asian Islamist groups. A terror organisation was funding both sides to foment armed conflict within the United States. But the radicalisation techniques were too sophisticated for this group, and there was no way this group had the communication infrastructure inside the United States to exchange such detailed information to both domestic groups with such precision in that short a time. Even though Curtis was not in the loop, he could see the data, and he surmised that something else was clearly afoot.

A week after Betty had met with Curtis she got a call from him, asking her to meet with him in person. He said he needed to talk to her face to face but that he couldn't step away from a negotiating table. He sent her a first class ticket from Reagan International to Rome, where he was working on an acquisition. She speculated that this may be a flex on his part, and maybe a way to express romantic interest, but there was too much on the line and in the end she took the flight. She was picked up from the airport and brought to a suite in the conference centre where the negotiations were taking place. She was asked to stay in the room and she was told that Mr. Chase would be with her shortly. She turned on the T.V. and ordered room service and watched the news until the food came. Three hours later the bell on the suite rang and Curtis apologised through the door for taking so long. She looked through the peephole and saw him through a fisheye, standing with a man in a suit whom she assumed was security. She opened the door and let him in.

"I swear to God," he said, *"I'm back-to-back with this deal…"*

As if on cue the phone in his hand rang and buzzed. He glanced at it and then carried on.

"But I need to give you this physical storage personally." He handed her a big clunky fob that ended in a USB drive. She took it and his phone went off again. He silenced it and dropped it in the inside pocket of his suit coat. He poured

himself a coffee from her tray without asking and sat at the low table.

"The relationship between these accounts looks like a fractal tree with three limbs above ground and a root system that feeds the trunk. We never would have seen the roots if we didn't have the details of the oil consulting firm that you gave me. That was the key that revealed the source of funding for each of the Islamist organisations that are the limbs."

He stopped to sip the coffee but he wound up downing the whole cup at once. She didn't take the chance to interject, because he sounded like he still had more to say. She was right.

"I'm not one to tell you your business, but I could get flags on all the accounts associated with the obvious ones and I could mirror the rest. That way there would be inquiries on all the obvious ones and they would eventually be closed, forcing all of the flow through the other accounts, maybe. Then you could monitor the mirrors and know when there was a big inflow or outflow, and you could match it off to arms sales or whatever you knew about and be sure of who was doing what."

She thought about it. She wasn't one of the forensic accounting team, but she was educated and had been exposed to a lot of the world for a person her age. It sounded like a solid plan. Now she spoke.

"You should be the one to explain it to the forensic accounting team. You have a good grasp on it."

"Actually," he said, *"I'm just parroting what my financial crime expert told me. But he will be free to go meet you in D.C. and help set up the whole financial dragnet."*

"That's fantastic," she said. *"You might have just made the world a little safer."*

Two days later she was in a conference room in a nondescript office building in northern Virginia. As far as the world knew it was a shared office space where hot desks were rented to startups and small businesses. In truth, the whole thing was owned by the government and though everything about it was encrypted and jammed, its tactic was to hide in plain sight. Betty was in a room with everyone who was assigned to the new interagency task force. Representatives from the FBI were handling domestic surveillance and the U.S. aspects of following the money. There were representatives from Treasury leading a group of examiners from the Fed and the SEC, and there was an observer from the House foreign affairs committee. Mostly, though, it was an agency operation and they were coordinating, collating and analysing all the human intelligence from the network overseas, data from mechanical surveillance and insights from their own analysts' desks.

The conference room had a large oblong desk with about a dozen chairs around it and there was a large flatscreen monitor hanging on the wall behind the head of the table. There was a folding table set up along the side of the room where pitchers of cream and stainless steel containers for coffee and tea water were placed. Curtis Chase's consultant sat at the middle of the table. He had a small remote control in his hand and he was manipulating the media on the laptop that was connected to the screen. The screen displayed a graphic that showed the relationships between accounts where the size of the account number's font indicated the value of the balance. The weight of the connector lines indicated the value of transaction flows between the accounts, and the accounts were bubbles grouped by country, where the colour of the bubble indicated the expected importance of the account in enabling terror operations against the U.S. and its allies. The consultant had started by sketching out the level of confidence of the information included, noting that there was a lack of information for the most closely held accounts and that transaction reporting in many of the countries involved was not reliable. He then went on to explain that money laundering flags were placed on all of the accounts that were telegraphed through the Hoover Dam attack, clicking animations on the screen that removed them from the graphic, but leaving one on the Isle of Man. Then the set of remaining accounts in developing jurisdictions expanded and their values, flows and connections were depicted according to the legend.

"This is our best guess of the 'root system' of the flow of financing between several of the organisations the agency identified for us," he said. *"Based on the amounts and timing of transactions between these,"* he used a laser pointer to indicate some of the minor accounts, *"we believe this was the source of funding for the London attack."* He stopped to let that sink in and waited for questions. The congressional observer jumped right in.

"So the same people responsible for Hoover Dam are responsible for London?" he asked.

The consultant cleared his throat and adjusted his glasses, and said, *"Based on the flows of funding, yes, we believe they are. And this isn't the only evidence we have. Miss Holloway,"* he nodded across the table to Betty, *"is the human intelligence operational lead, and she has some observed and testamentary evidence. Miss Holloway?"* He handed the small remote control device across the table.

Betty had had at least some interaction with every person around the table, whether it was passing the coffee or holding the door on the elevator. Now she noticed the reactions of some of the attendants when they found out this black woman with a French West African accent was named Holloway. Betty took the remote, advanced the presentation and began to facilitate her portion of the discussion.

"Thank you," she said. *"To keep it brief, I'll give you the highlights."* She hit something on the remote and the monitor displayed eight separate panes, each showing a highlighted document. Several were written in Arabic and the rest were in French.

"We interrogated the documentation of every company and organisation transacting with the root accounts. We identified all of the principals and directors and we tracked incoming and outgoing cash flows to the extent possible."

She hit a button on the remote and the presentation advanced to show three faces. The pictures were taken from various press releases and public facing websites, so they were fairly flattering photographs. They were all men in early middle age, one Caucasian and two apparently middle eastern.

"These are the likely sources of funding. The blue-eyed blond is Abdul-Aziz Al Sudeiri, a Saudi national, the man in the middle is Sheikh Tahlawi, an Omani oilman, and the last man some of you may already know. He is Hani Nesralla from Lebanon, a tech mogul."

The congressional observer looked confused, and interrupted.

"So the white guy is Saudi Arabian?"

"Yes," Betty replied, *"there are more blue eyed Arabians than you might think. This may be the legacy of the crusades. More important than his skin tone, though, is the fact that he is one of the bad guys."*

She nodded back to the photos on the monitor.

"These three were friends and students together back in the nineties when they were in school at Oxford. From school records and interviews with their peers we know they faced severe hazing and discrimination. And ever since then they have been active in funding faith-based community groups in the Islamic world and in the west."

She used the laser pointer to single out the photo of Nesralla.

"I recently saw Nesralla meet with Al Sudeiri in Paris, and neither of their official diaries show a record of the meeting."

There were murmurs around the table; this was new information for most. Betty went on.

"This made us curious and we tried to reconstruct their whereabouts for the past few years. Even though they are all important executives there are blackout periods and vacations and other 'off time' that corresponds and sometimes overlaps for all three of them. So we plotted the overlapping time gaps against general trends in activity in the Islamist organisations from the account map we just looked at, and there seems to be a spike in activity following their potential meetings."

She paused again here to let the people around the table catch up.

"So we think they are probably doing more than writing checks. These three may well be the ones pulling the strings across several of these Islamist organisations."

A general question and answer followed, where Betty was asked to disclose sources and methods to support the veracity of the agency's assertions, and where she could, she did. There was a lot that she was not at liberty to disclose, though, and that rankled some of the people in the group, especially the representatives of domestic law enforcement. The arc of the conversation came to a bottleneck where several people asked what to do with this information, asking Betty what the next steps were.

"Three of these organisations own real property in areas outside the reach of the rule of law. One is in Syria and two are in North Africa."

She clicked something on the remote and then used the laptop keyboard for several minutes and then clicked something on the remote again, and an aerial image of a warehouse in Damascus displayed. After a few seconds the view changed to an aerial image of the oil consulting firm's compound in the Caliphate of Malitania, then it changed to a different building in a part of Nigeria controlled by Boko Haram.

"We have U.S. intelligence assets watching the site in Damascus. The Nigerian army will move to regain control of the entire federated area where Boko Haram operates, if they get foreign aid support. In the Caliphate of Malitania the French version of Blackwater, La Lance Fournie, is launching a covert operation to observe and monitor the site on behalf of the local government."

Again there was a spate of question and answer about where and who. Eventually she continued.

"Based on the patterns in chatter and the flows of funding, and following their successes in disabling the credit monitoring capabilities after London, and in getting armed conflict to occur in America, we believe they are set to meet again. This becomes three separate, covert locate and capture missions."

There were nods of agreement and assent around the table.

"The agency will take over from here, and we expect you to maintain your level of cooperation as we move into active operations to capture or thwart these terrorists."

The meeting broke up and there were several smaller conversations that persisted as people drifted away from the conference room and out of the building. Betty packed up her workspace right away and hurried home. She had to catch a commercial flight to Niamey, Niger later in the day. She would be the team lead on the ground in the Caliphate of Malitania and she had to get the lay of the land before her people arrived.

Focusing the Microscope

Abdul Aziz Al Sudeiri stood on the beach and watched the waves come in. The beach was shaped like an almost perfect crescent and the offshore underwater topography gave a long gradual rise toward sea level. A coral reef presented a natural break a quarter of a mile out, like the string of a bow, and waves that had travelled the expanse of the Pacific rose up over it and rolled into the crescent shaped beach, creating a 'bowl' phenomenon where both ends of the wave curled in toward the centre. The wave threw a lip early and the face rose to roughly two feet, which is measured off the back of the wave, so there was a distance of four feet from the nexus of power where a surfer would stand to the white spray blowing back out to sea. This geological, geographical and hydrological circumstance was extremely rare, and on days like today where everything had fallen into synch just so, an incessant set of perfect waves advanced, crashed and receded. It was as if the earth were meditating, focused on her breathing.

The smell of the ocean was in the air and the powdered sand under his feet was bright white. Coconut trees ringed the crescent beach behind him, and gave way to lower, leafier palms where the volcanic soil took over from the beach sand. It was as though someone had drawn a green curtain around this small piece of paradise. He was reminded of the times at the Ala Moana Bowl in Honolulu, where he had learned to surf during vacations in his youth. He would often go and watch the sun set over the ocean there. The dark would chase the crowd of surfers off the set and they would come in to rinse off and find their way to their cars. They'd take the folding chairs and coolers out of the trunks and relax with some drinks before ending their day. A lot of them, including the girls, would make some comment as they passed him so he would know he was not wanted. *"Better be no haoles after dark,"* was a common phrase.

They assumed he was a whiteboy from the mainland. He was not like those other haoles, but that didn't matter to the locals. He would break his reverie and pack up his rented Benz in a parking lot full of old beaters. He focused less on the 'othering' by the locals and more on their assumption that he was a WASP because of the colour of his skin and the quality of his possessions. He did not disabuse them of this notion. In fact, in his youth, he often would go along with people's assumption of his identity. At first, whenever he did this, he felt that he was 'passing for Western' and it gave him an unfiltered view into the mind of the white Westerner. On vacations in the U.S., the U.K. and in Europe he had heard sickeningly racist remarks when they were confident they were sharing with a like mind. It was far more common than he expected. Whatever simmering miasma of vitriol caused these outbursts, it had to be Western culture, logically.

So there in Hawaii, as a very young man, he thought he knew the mind of the West and he knew he was 'other' and excluded if he presented his authentic self. And he knew he would never be like them, not in manner of thought and not in spirit. Zuz got quite good at surfing and he could consistently catch waves and was adept enough to ride smaller waves others would find unrideable. When he first felt the feeling of being lifted and propelled forward by the ocean herself he was more than exhilarated. The sound was all encompassing and the hyperfocus heightened every sensory receptor in and on the body. The first time he caught a very long wave and rode for nearly a minute he had an epiphany. He was in a state of absolute euphoria and something that was unknown stepped into his knowledge without needing to be processed as thought. And it was this –Western civilisation and Islamic civilisation don't have to be in constant existential competition. They can co-exist but they must forever remain separate.
This he truly felt to have been received from wherever Allah

resides and he believed it as a true fact, without any proof. This, he felt, must be what faith really is.

It was the very next year that he started at Oxford. He found it even more insular and privileged than anything or anywhere, and exclusion of the out-group was a much more subtle art form. Here he met Hani Nesralla, Mohammed Suleiman and Ahmed Tahlawi who were going through the same thing. They spent a lot of time together and Hani and Tahlawi got caught up in Zuz's enthusiasm for his revelation. Over time they all came to understand that the world they talked about had to be made real. They made a plan. They would use the existing Islamist organisations and direct their activity through funding. They would work to cause and inflame fundamentalist reaction in the West, with the aim of tipping them into isolationism. Now, twenty years later, they finally thought the time was right to take a more active role. The attack in London nearly felled the financial system and several of the very same people who mocked them at Oxford had died in the attack. The real point, though, had been to deny them of their electronic trust machines, so the mighty financial powers were forced to lean back and take stock of their partners and counterparties in a more human way. According to the studies this would prepare them to take sides in a domestic struggle. Then the spark of division in the U.S. had been nurtured into a flame at the Hoover Dam. Everything seemed to be going to plan. They found out there were a flurry of account closures and intelligence leads being followed for the organisations they had telegraphed as being involved. That was part of the plan too, to let them know their own division had been incited by a deservedly feared enemy. This was supposed to give them a familiar scapegoat and get them to raise their walls.

Unfortunately, Zuz also got warnings that some of the other accounts, the accounts closer to home, were also being observed, though there was no flagging of these accounts.

Could they somehow have let on more than they intended? Now Zuz was experiencing a new kind of fear that he hadn't known before. It was the feeling that everything he ever was or did would come crumbling down and come to naught. It wasn't just an existential crisis for him as an individual, it was a crisis for the vision that, honestly, was received from Allah. They could not allow that to happen, even if worse came to worst.

Here on this remote island of the Indonesian archipelago his money bought him anonymity and anonymity bought him safety. From here he would get on a secure device that could only connect to two other devices in the world, encrypted by Hani Nesralla's personal lab in Dubai, and propose to his friends that they select one of the most secure sites to serve as an option of last resort, an 'Alamo'. He was confident they would go along and he was confident they would agree with his choice of the site in the Caliphate of Malitania. It was the most remote and defensible, and it had the most abundant water source. He thought they could build a usable runway that could accommodate a private jet in short order and they could resupply rapidly by air.

Anonymity wasn't all his money had bought him. He rented the whole island for the week, along with its twenty-eight-year-old surf instructor. He could see her at the cabana now, getting breakfast ready and setting out beach chairs. Worldly matters would just have to wait while he pursued euphoria.

On the call they held later that day Zuz told his friends everything he knew. He proposed setting up the hideout and they agreed, as he expected they would. He was the one with the most knowledge of financial transactions, although they all were wealthy, capable businessmen. Zuz was suspicious that the authorities may have mirrored the accounts they didn't flag, and he suggested they stop using all of the accounts altogether. They held significant positions in crypto and in physical precious metals to which they still had access. Tahlawi suggested they work through their proxies and intermediaries to get what they needed from the dark web and to begin moving gold to the Sahel. Tahlawi reassured his comrades that they had prepared for this, and just as with a large business project, they would just follow the plan until it was completed. Now they would hunker down and become invisible. They would enter the long operational phase of their plan that involved continuing to split the societies of the West and drive them toward reactionary isolationism by inciting violence between their liberal and conservative camps, and by doubling the flow of asylum seekers over the next year. Their very expensive model told them this was the scenario with the greatest likelihood of reaching their desired future. By the end of the call they each had a list of things to do and they agreed to meet in the Caliphate of Malitania in no more than a month's time.

On the following day, as Zuz 'surfed' to his heart's content, Nesralla got a message that Interpol had warrants for his arrest for his role in purposefully spreading misinformation through his social media application. They alleged that he himself was responsible for spreading misinformation that resulted in violence and civil unrest, and they called for his extradition to the United States to stand trial. He learned that they had teams of agents assisted by local police at all of his residences as well as at all airports servicing those residences, waiting to snatch him up. The authorities were a lot closer than he thought and he had to make a life-changing decision while he was still in the air. He made contact with Hezbollah and they secured a sanctuary agreement with Tehran. There was no fanfare or public welcome when his plane touched down but he was met by representatives of the government and shown to his apartment in the city. He was now a guest of the republic, not free to communicate with the outside world and essentially under house arrest, but free to carry on trying to destabilise the West. He still had his encrypted device and when he told his colleagues what was going on they were shocked and unnerved. They all realised that they were a lot closer to the business end of this thing than they had thought, but they steeled their resolve and carried on with the plan.

Dust to Dust

Harry sat at a table near the bar in *The Tilted Crane* staring at his phone while the news played on the T.V. on the wall. He had been using a fake social media account to view Elena and the kids' posts and to see where they were tagged as present at different events. Elena and the kids were more heavily impacted by his death than he thought they would be. They appeared at all the memorial events, they changed their backgrounds to the memorial motif, and Elena's posts became more religious. Harry felt an unearned sense of pride, but it was nothing compared to the sadness. To see their pictures and videos made him enormously sad, and to see his family so sad for no reason broke his heart. This was not what he envisioned when he made that hurried decision after the attack. Harry hadn't forgotten everything though; their lives were hard and his was unbearable. He knew that after a number of months there would be new posts showing football games or Christmas trees, but this is what it had to be for now. He wondered if the same held true for his divorce. If he gave it enough time would things have normalised, with the potential for a happy future in London? He thought not. He felt not. He felt that, in London, he would have always been as distant from his children as he is now.

The T.V. announced a breaking news story and Harry looked up. Apparently the tech billionaire, Hani Nesralla, had a warrant for his arrest for misuse of his social media business. Police were dispatched to several of his properties simultaneously to bring him in, but they failed to locate him and he is assumed to be on the run. The reporter then explained the connection between the social media campaign and the Hoover Dam incident. Harry listened with interest, like much of the audience, but he was unaware of what was behind it. There were some crackpot conspiracy theorists who tied Hoover Dam to the London attacks, but they were howling in the wilderness.

Harry had to snap out of his funk because he had work to do. Mo had given him the portfolio for In-Country Logistics to 'own', and he didn't really know what that meant. Mo had given him a rolodex and a shopping list and told him to get to work.

Harry was not involved in any of the planning, but Mo said they would have to start in Sombokto, the capital city of the Caliphate of Malitania and assess available options from there. Harry got on the internet and researched all the names in the rolodex. He knew there may be nothing at all, but he did it anyway. Then he picked up the phone and started dialing. He spoke with whomever answered the phone, though they didn't always have a common language. He followed a script where he politely introduced himself and asked what business they were in. Then he would engage with them as a representative of an archaeology project and ask for quotes on a per-person or per-item basis. He took notes on each conversation and made note of whom he spoke to, the length of the call, what they spoke about and any agreed terms. Then he started to get a picture of what the commercial landscape looked like in Sombokto. Mo had given him contacts for food, lodging, materials shipment around the country, and local purchasers and providers for heavy equipment and a local workforce. Later in the day he and Mo would be leaving for Sombokto. They were supposed to meet different people and get things rolling so they could eventually sustain an operation in the field upcountry.

He packed his laptop and enough things to sustain him in a foreign city for a few days, which was pretty much all he owned. It all fit in a medium sized, rolling hard-sided suitcase, in flat black of course. He threw it into the back of the van and jumped into the backseat with Mo for their trip to the airport.

"Take a look at this," Mo said, handing over his phone that was showing a news story, *"and tell me what you make of it."*

Harry took Mo's phone and spent ten bumpy minutes in poor van light, reading the whole story. Apparently there was a humanitarian assistance group that had vowed to stop the unnecessary deaths of migrants in the sea. Rescue efforts were too ineffective, they said, and they provided more seaworthy vessels so the migrants would survive, at a bare minimum. Every small and medium private vessel in the region had been purchased and put to task escorting migrants from shore to shore safely. The video reminded Harry of the newsreels following Dunkirk. Across Greece, Italy and France the spigot of migrants was suddenly opened all the way, and all of southern Europe was instantly embroiled in a humanitarian crisis. Three months' worth of recent, record high migration levels were reached in a single day, and the reporter speculated that the momentum was building rather than slowing.

Harry handed the phone back to Mo and asked him, *"What do you make of it? You think it's part of something?"*

"I don't really know, and I'm not paid to think about these things," Mohammed Batu said, *"but there's too much happening at once for it all to be coincidence."*

"Okay," Harry said, *"What am I supposed to do with that?"*

"I'm just saying," Mo replied, *"stay alert in the Caliphate. And not just the kind of fast reaction on your feet alert. Back in the old days you used to read people and know how they would react in some situations. Well here you'll have to read the*

people but more, and figure out what they're after. And you can pick your way through the defence once you know who wants what you want, and who wants what you can offer."

"You sound like officer candidate training," Harry said through a grin, *"Should I be sure to keep my wallet in my front pocket, too?"*

They arrived at the airport and they took their leave from the driver, went inside the building and went straight to departures because they had checked in on-line and they only had carry on baggage. This was the first time Harry was using his new French passport. Here there were waist-high barriers with biometric readers on the glass tops to their right. Harry waited his turn, placed his passport face down on the reader and was relieved when the light turned green and the barrier retracted. They went through the security check without incident; they even kept their shoes on. They were travelling at night and they had a short hop to Casablanca where they changed planes but stayed with the same airline and carried on to Sombokto, where they arrived just as the sun was rising.

Just like that Harry was back in Africa. The airport, and the entire country around it, Harry speculated, had its own not unpleasant but particular smell. There was a dusty earthiness to it, with a note of industrial cleaner. The rest of the passengers from the plane were returning home from Europe and they all had checked luggage that they went to retrieve. Mohammed and Harry marched along to the customs checks and arrivals exit straightaway. When they got to the line of booths that made up passport control there was a uniformed officer and a Malitanian man in a suit standing to the side, apparently waiting. Mohammed stopped on his way to a booth and Harry bumped into him and stopped very close to him while they both looked up at the officials approaching. The man in the suit greeted them both warmly with handshakes and introduced himself as a home office attache sent to get them settled. He asked them both for their passports and her personally brought them both to the nearest booth and instructed the border officer to stamp them, then he returned and gave them back. Both Mohammed and Harry put them away without looking at them. The man, who was called Rene, led them through the arrivals lobby and out to the sidewalk where a van was waiting. Rene would escort them to their hotel and see them settled before taking his leave for the night. They all got into the van and drove into the city. Though Harry had never been to this city it seemed familiar. It was a typical Sahelian city that sprung up around a river and the arable land surrounding it. It was brown and dry and dusty in the dim after-dark intermittent street lighting.

This city was a little different though. This city had clearly marked streets defined by the new gutters on either side and the bright painted lines providing drivers direction and instruction. Many of the buildings looked new or newly refurbished and they passed pedestrian areas where urban planning provided for lighted, safe social spaces at night. This city looked more like the Emirates than sub-Saharan Africa. This city looked like a lot more of the oil money made it down to the infrastructure than other places he'd been in west Africa. They pulled up in front of the City Hotel, which was a five-star property, and they went in, checked in, and were shown to their rooms by hotel staff. Rene took his leave in the lobby and said he would be by at 9:00 the next morning to collect them and bring them to the conference centre where they would hold a series of meetings. They each tipped their bellboys and Mo asked Harry if he would join him in the bar for a quick meal and to watch him drink. Harry declined, saying he would order room service, and that they would catch up at breakfast. They wished each other a good night and parted ways.

Threads of the Past

The UAE and the U.S. had a memorandum of understanding in place that covered the sharing of intelligence resources. Betty had been in Sombokto for a week and she had established a working relationship with the Emirati intelligence services. While she waited for her team to arrive she had been preparing logistics and she had been comparing notes with the Emiratis on who was coming and going in Sombokto and when. Though there was facial recognition software running on all arrivals and departures through the airport, she had taken to watching the video feeds of arrivals because the Russians had ways of evading detection. She had the flight schedules and she was mostly watching after flights arrived. She had a learning program identify those flights that had the best chance of carrying Europeans based on the connection schedules through north African airports. She was watching a feed from the customs and border control booths when two men approached while the rest of their flight was still retrieving their luggage. They stopped abruptly and, standing oddly close, looked up at the camera at the same time. She spoke Arabic to her Emirati counterpart and asked him to pause and freeze the frame just where those two men were looking up at the camera, and the agent did so. She kept staring at it so intently that the agent didn't say anything so as not to disturb her. There was something about those two men in that pose. The swarthy one was built like a fireplug, they would say in Virginia, and the difference in their height was almost comical. But the pose, the way the taller man was almost leaning over his colleague. There was something about this tableau that was agonisingly familiar.

Then it finally came to her, and when it did it took the atmosphere out of the viewing room. Suddenly she had no breath and no feeling, and the universe was pulled inside out and connected back to the most challenging part of her youth. She had seen that pose in a faded polaroid that her mother set up next to their bed when they finally got their own flat in Bamako. It was a polaroid of five western soldiers in uniform, posing together with the empty land behind them and Tuareg guides crouched in the foreground setting up a radio. Not only were those two men affecting the same pose as the two men in the photo, but after staring long enough for her eidetic memory to fully recall the photo, she was also convinced that these two men were the actual men from that same photograph. She could also precisely recall her mother's voice telling her that, if she insisted on knowing, then yes, the Englishman in the picture was her father. *"That one,"* she said, putting her finger on the picture of the tall one. Touching and not releasing, staring herself, and allowing the moment of memory to linger. Betty reached up and touched the image of the tall man on the screen. Unbelievable.

After a second she asked the agent to run the video and she saw they were looking up because the local official had gotten their attention. She asked the agent if he knew who the official was and, as their interaction played out on the screen, if he was aware of these men's arrival. The agent told her that these were the representatives of La Lance Fournie, and that she would be meeting with them tomorrow to begin coordinating their joint operation.
▪▪

After breakfast Mo and Harry found the meeting room. It was a typical comfortable meeting room that one would expect to find in any conference venue anywhere in the world. The door was stopped open and a coffee service had been set up on a side table next to a bowl of fruit. The placard slid into the holder next to the door said, 'Digital Digs', and as they got coffee and sat down they discussed what that could mean. After only a minute, and exactly on time for the meeting start time, a group of seven arrived, all wearing business casual and all carrying laptops. There was a general bustle as they came in and Mo and Harry stood. Mo began with good morning greetings to the two people he knew. One of these men was Carl Horton, who had introduced himself as the Head of the North Africa Desk for the American foreign service. After Carl greeted Mo he introduced the other members of the contingent, giving their names and roles, and as they were introduced they took seats. Rene, who had met them at the airport, was there. Halfway through the introductions a young woman in traditional business wear stepped up and leaned in to shake hands.

Just before Carl could say her name she interjected, *"You can call me Fanta. I'll be running things on the ground here, so you'll be seeing a lot of me."*

Harry had a look at her as he leaned over to shake her hand. He was certain that he had never seen this woman before in his life, but there was something about her that he knew. He realised he had been looking her straight in the face trying to discern what was familiar, which is rude in a first time business introduction. But she was looking at him in the same way. She was nearly six feet tall and the lightness of her eyes was an attention getter. Her long curly hair was pulled back tight across her head and there was a pony tail that expanded past shoulder length.

Once the noise of settling in died down Carl cleared this throat and connected his laptop to the screen through the connector ports set into the middle of the table. Carl was a Caucasian in his mid-fifties, of average height and build. He had hair that remained sandy-coloured even though he now had to wear horn-rimmed glasses. He wore a very expensive full Western business suit and he looked comfortable because of the air conditioning. The monitor came to life showing his computer's desktop display, which was a completely back background and only a single dialogue box for a password.

"I'll jump right into it because we have so much to cover," he began. *"The Caliphate of Malitania believes that a nefarious*

organisation has established a stronghold in its empty quarter in the far north-east."

He nodded toward Rene.

"Malitania wants to find out if that's true and do something about it if it is," Carl stated plainly. He went on.

"Intelligence we already possess indicates that it's likely. We've already identified the compound and we think there may be some high value adversaries either in situ or enroute."

Though this was all new, it was nothing that Harry and Mo couldn't expect in some way.

"In particular," Carl said, *"We think we're onto the very individuals who are responsible for the London attack."*

Harry gripped the edge of the table with both hands and flexed his quadriceps to push the small of his back against the chair. This was an unexpected turn and he was unpleasantly surprised that he wasn't able to stop the physical reaction that came with it. Over the past week he had seen that there were thirty-three dead from Universal Banking and Insurance. Horror stories from Bank and Charing Cross tube stations had gotten out on the internet. Talk show news chatter had changed focus from grief to vengeance and as an Englishman he found it hard not to get caught up in it. He could not deny that he himself wanted revenge.

"Our information leads us to believe that they are acting fast and effectively," Carl continued, *"We'll need to pool resources and work together to match their speed."*

He gestured toward Mo with an upturned hand and said, *"Mo, could you please let us know our operating parameters, timeline and next steps?"*

Mo looked at each person and then jumped in. *"Sure thing. Our logistics officer, Harry here,"* he nodded at Harry, *"had* been establishing initial contact posing as an archaeology project. We thought that was a good idea and we're sticking with it as the cover. As an archaeology project we'll set up a base as close as we can get it to the compound, where we can have a fully effective listening post and stage for an assault if the Malitanian military opts to eject them by force."

Rene took the opportunity to let them know of Malitania's position. *"I want to be clear that using the Malitanian military is the least preferred option. For reasons unknown to me the Emirates do not want to be seen as violently hostile to the black flag just now. And we, in our own neighbourhood, can't be seen to be massing troops so near the border."*

Mo began again when he was finished. *"We intend to start by gathering information. We need to know everything we can to figure out what's going on."* He looked at Carl and said, *"Carl, you had some ideas on how to go about that, right?"*

"We talked it through back in Virginia and we think we can help a lot," Carl said. *"Fanta is across this, so I'll let her explain."*

Everyone in the room looked at Fanta and out of habit she pointed to the screen on the wall that still displayed the black background and password field.

"Basically, the premise is that we are a tech company that has developed new imaging tools for archaeology. AI models have predicted an intersection of ancient trade routes that would have required a market and a fortified site just near the compound. We've gotten the permission from the government of the Caliphate to road-test the equipment on the ground and in the airspace."

Rene reached into a folder and took out some official looking forms.

"Here are the permits and documents," she said.

"We have all the numbers crunched for the budget and all that in the files. We even have a project plan of proposed actions broken down sequentially that could convincingly nest in the project plan of an archaeology project."

She paused and sighed just a little too heavily.

"What we don't have," she went on, *"is a network of capable, effective operators on the ground. America hasn't kept current with its friendships around here."* Here she switched from French to Arabic and said, *"But we have uncles and cousins who must help with the hardest work."*

She knew Carl hated when she conducted business in a language he did not understand, but she felt that articulating this point in Arabic was part of the message. She was reminded of how pretentious she thought this was in the poetry reading in Paris, and she wondered if she should go back and read any of that poetry.

Harry was impressed that Fanta, who had introduced herself in English but was conducting the meeting in French, could so fluently switch to Arabic and back. He was also impressed with how well she commanded the attention of the room and articulated the plan. She was a formidable young woman. To be in her position at such a young age she must have shown other kinds of impressive skills as well.

Fanta kept directing the meeting for about another fifteen minutes, during that time mostly laying out the major milestones in the plan; establish a secure perimeter, construct the base, gather intelligence. Harry was a bit surprised to learn that the plan included deploying real imaging equipment, which could supposedly look into the compound through the walls and reveal critical information. They would employ a project workforce who would, in truth, be members of La Lance Fournie and a local workforce who would be Emirati agents who were Malitani locals. Key counterparts were assigned and the practical discussion ended.

While wrapping up Carl said, *"I don't think I have to remind you all how to treat confidential information or of the consequences of breaches of operational security. Godspeed and good luck."*

The room began to clear out and Mo and Harry engaged in light discussion as they too packed up and drifted toward the door. Mo told Harry that he would have to arrange digs in Sombokto for about thirty men to begin with, and to find a place to discreetly store equipment in the capital for starters. Rene had been lingering near the open door and as Mo rounded the corner of the table Rene handed him the folder of documents. *"Here are the permits and lading permissions you'll need to start getting your people and materiel in place,"* he said. Mo took the folder and stepped out into the hall.

Fanta had been lingering too, taking her time getting her laptop together, even though they never opened the presentation. She stopped Harry from passing by putting a hand on his right arm.

"Could you join me now for a coffee?" she asked. *"There are some things you and I should get caught up on."*

"I guess so," he said, a bit surprised. He looked out into the hall where Mo was just taking his leave from Carl. Mo caught his eye and Harry told him that he'd see him for lunch in the hotel restaurant.

"Lead on," he said to Fanta, and followed her out.

■ ■

The tables near the hotel bar were open for a la carte breakfast, which was just finishing up because of the hour. They found a table and Harry excused himself to the loo.

When he came back he saw that she had a cocktail in front of her and there was a sparkling water with lime at his spot across the table. He sat down just as she was putting down her drink after the first sip.

"Good call," he said as he lifted his drink in salute.

"I'm not one who ever has a drink because I need one. But I also don't not have a drink when I want one. I'm still jetlagged so for me it's nearly dinner time."

"I'll buy the next one," he said.

"You know," she said in a very personal way, "the circumstances that brought me from Mali to France to America are so unlikely. Over the course of my life I have met so many people whose stories are extraordinary. The most improbable things are a lot more probable than you may imagine."

"Clearly you've had an interesting life," Harry said.

"Yes," she said, "and it's getting more interesting all the time. Which is what I need to talk to you about. My life."

"OK," Harry said. He was very curious to see how this connected to the project. "Please tell me more."

"I know who you are and I've known about you for more than ten years now," she said.

"Really?" was all Harry could muster. "How?"

"You are in a photograph that was hung up wherever we lived when I was growing up. You and Mohammed Batu are both in it, standing near each other wearing the uniform of the 2e REP."

She watched as his mind was racing not to put two and two together but to cube two and come up with eight.

Before he landed where his mind was headed, she added, *"My mother is Miriam Djiakite."*

She waited again. A stunned look came over him and he looked at her again, studying the contour of her face. He was making the connection.

"My mother swears to me there is only one man who could be my father," she said, *"though I never knew him."* She reached into a small purse she had sitting on the table with her keys and folding money. She took out her American passport and opened it to the photo page.

"I was named for my paternal grandmother, as a constant reminder," she said, and pushed the passport across the table to Harry to see. He read the name, Elizabeth Holloway. He looked back at her and tears welled up in his eyes.

"Oh my God," he said, *"I never knew."*

"I know," she said. *"There was no way for you to know."*

They sat in silence for a moment while Harry raced through his past life.

"Your mother," he said, *"Miriam. Is she…"*

"She's alive and well," Betty said. *"She lives in a house I bought for her in Bamako. She is finally comfortable and at peace, and she wants for nothing."*

"That's such a comfort to know," he said. *"I loved her so much."*

It was as Betty expected. Her mother had always spoken of their time together as the best in her life.

He broke his reverie and a broad smile came across his face. *"I know I haven't earned the right, but I've got to say I am so impressed, and proud of who you are."*

Betty was glad to hear this, but she had already had more than a day to process. She wasn't looking for approval and she had to admit to herself that she was a little angry with him for never seeking her out, though she understood that he did not know she existed. It wasn't logical, but that's how it was. There was something that she wanted from him though, and that was information. She wanted to know everything about his side of the family and how he came to be in a position to become her father. She told him that, finished her drink, and called to the waiter for another.

Harry said that he'd be more than happy to oblige, and that his memory was cruelly precise. He could tell from her face that was a trait she inherited.

They spent the next hour with Harry recounting his family and personal history, and with Betty directing the narrative with questions that seemed both well considered and pointed and specific. He told it 'warts and all' without changing any facts or masking any shortcomings of his family's or of his own.

At one point she interrupted and said, *"Wait, you said you'd never forget the sound of the knife clattering on the kitchen floor."*

"Yes," he said.

"But you said when you fell together he was stabbed at that time and accidentally."

"Yes, that's what happened."

"So how could the knife have possibly clattered on the floor?"

He didn't have an answer, and he carried on with the narrative. She seemed pleased to learn that she had a brother and a sister. She had known that was a possibility. She said that she felt bad for Harry's wife Elena and wondered if there were a way to end her grief without jeopardising

Harry's situation. Harry showed her their pictures from their social media accounts.

He knew that she was a veteran of the intelligence service so he didn't spare any details when he talked about his history in the Legion or about what had transpired recently. When he got to recent events she took notes about Kevin and Connor and the people in Bordeaux. When they were completely caught up they were both emotionally exhausted and she had had three drinks. She said that she was going to skip lunch and go back to the room and take a nap. They stood up and she came across and gave him a hug, then held him at arm's length and said that, if it was OK with him, she was glad she'd found him and that she was looking forward to getting to know him as a person on this project. He was pleasantly surprised, hugged her back and said that he could not be happier that they finally found each other.

As she made her way to the elevator Mohammed Batu came out of the lobby and up to the table. He looked at Betty just getting onto the elevator and asked Harry, *"What was all that about?"*

"She's Miriam Djiakite's daughter," Harry said.

"What, your Miriam?" Mo asked.

"Yes," Harry said, knowing that Mo was doing the same math that Harry had just done, *"…and yes."*

Crossroads of Purpose

Dawn in the Sahel was always amazing to Harry, and he wasn't going to miss the chance to experience this one after a decade away. He had set out just before sunrise, according to his weather app. He wore all dark clothing and he exited through the hotel's front door briskly, minimising the time he would be in anyone's line of sight. He had plotted a short walk of about a one-mile circle that would bring him right back to the hotel and he turned on the directions. For all his time in the region he had never been to Sombokto before.

Once he was outside the door it was immediately familiar even though it was difficult to see well in the darkness. It takes a lot of activity to get the day going in a city the size of Sombokto, and everyone goes about it as quietly as possible until it is full light. Harry set out following the road to the right, toward an A-road that served as the high street in that part of the city. He was walking through a dark neighbourhood of closed shops and flats and houses with dim lights speckled here and there. Even in the last bit of the night's cool he could feel the heat coming off the concrete structures around him. From a good distance he heard the closing of a door cause a rooster to crow. Half a block later he heard water being poured on the ground; it could have been someone disposing of cookwater or someone brushing their teeth. He reached the A-road and turned right again. There was flat, packed earth along the asphalt road but there was no sidewalk. Intermittent vehicle traffic left a haze of grey dust barely reflecting the glow of the streetlights set impossibly far apart. Aside from the gas station, the shops were more like permanent kiosks, with electric wires running to them though they had no other facilities. They had just enough room inside for the merchandise and the merchant. Even the roadside bar was such a kiosk, holding the folded tables and chairs that would be set out when it was time to open. Harry stayed to the well-trodden walkway behind the shops and out of clear view of the busy street.

A lorry loaded with goats passed on the road and in the quiet the doppler bleating hung in his ear like the aftertaste of a priceless wine. This was why he had come out in the dark. This was a unique place in the world and he didn't want to take it for granted. He had also come out at dawn to think. He found that his imagination wasn't running away with itself, and he wanted to make sure he kept it that way. He figured that being purposeful and disciplined about thinking through what faced him was the way to do it. As in the old days, walking quietly at dawn put him in the frame of mind for what he called 'productive reflection'. His phone told him to turn right again off the A-road and that put him on a long, straight secondary road that faced the rising sun.

Because the Sahel was so flat, day broke wide when the sun cracked the horizon. At first the world in front of him seemed to be magically imbued with stratified layers of orange under purple. Then new, lighter layers slowly rose and lifted the earlier layers from the horizon to the sky, where they quickly peeled away. The waking of the city was as animated as the rising of the sun, and the noises of people getting ready for work and school filled out the soundscape around him.

As he walked he remembered the conversation from the night before where he remembered the Sahelian daybreaks from his young adulthood. Betty had called him on the phone, to his pleasant surprise, and they ended up talking for over an hour. He tried to explain the broader circumstances prior to her birth and he was sure it must have sounded to her like a history lesson. He told about the Tuareg independence movement for Azawad and how they joined forces with the Islamists against the government, which was supported by France. He and his comrades were placed with a group of Tuaregs who were unhappy with the Islamists' methods. They wanted talks to gain French support for Azawadi independence in return for ejecting the Islamists from Azawad. His detachment of the 2e REP was there to assess their capacity to do that and to provide security for the French 'government man'. On a day-to-day basis it meant going out with them and tallying up men and weapons, and preparing and sending briefs over the wire. There was a lot of down time that his comrades used poorly, during which the affair with Miriam Djiakite played out in semi-secret. When the response came from Paris that Azawadi independence would not be supported, this faction of Tuareg militia had to rejoin its greater movement as though nothing had ever been wrong, and the 2e REP were considered enemy combatants. They were lifted out in helicopters almost directly to a new deployment in Chad. It wasn't long after that when the French presence supporting the government in Bamako began to feel to the Malian people like colonial occupation. This was never the desired outcome, and the French pulled out altogether, citing the responsibility of local Sahelian governments to establish and maintain the integrity of their borders.

This is where Betty picked up her tale. Miriam had run to Bamako as a refugee as soon as she knew she was pregnant. Betty told Harry how she had stability through her mother's employment and how she came to be educated in France. All the while she was excelling in school, the people of northern Mali suffered as the Islamists perpetrated an unbidden jihad against innocent and often helpless populations of non-Tuaregs. The iconography of local cultures was destroyed and policies of disfigurement and sexual violence were implemented across the north. The only thing that kept the government in power in Bamako was the Wagner mercenaries' pugnacious 'bias for action'. If Miriam had stayed among the jihadis under sharia law, young and pregnant while unwed then she may well have been stoned before she gave birth. Even now indigenous militias were making heroic stands against the Islamists in a bid for survival with no assistance from Bamako or the wider world. At this point in their conversation she shared some contemporary intelligence saying that in the region only Mauritania had launched a proper national military campaign to keep the black flag from flying in its country, and only they were having success. They speculated on why the Emirates didn't want the Caliphate army to engage directly, which she could do because she had no idea. What she could not yet share with Harry was her knowledge that America wasn't going to put boots on the ground any more than the French, but neither could they suffer another Saudi national to plan terror attacks against the U.S. from a lawless no-man's land like Bin Laden did. The Caliphate was writing a very, very big check to cover all that the Americans would do, and they would have that compound secure no matter what. If the Americans could capture Tahlawi and Al Sudeiri then that would be ideal, but if they couldn't take them alive, well, so be it.

She told him that she had to travel to London for a meeting and she asked his permission to get a look at her brother and sister. Harry had seen how confidently she moved around others and how she could steer conversations to elicit information while offering none herself and have it all appear so natural. He was certain she had training in tradecraft, and he trusted her judgment. If someone saw Harry and Betty together in the same room then they would be able to see the resemblance, but seeing them separately in different context one might not make the connection. He was beside himself with guilt about Elena's and the kids' grief, and he just wanted some way to make their pain stop. He suggested to Betty that she meet with Elena under some pretence and gauge whether or not she could be trusted with the news of his survival. If Betty thought Elena could handle it then she should swear her to secrecy and let her know that she should carry on with her life, having suffered no real loss.

And here he arrived back at the hotel. He would wake up Mohammed Batu and they would make their way back to France to prepare to put the project in motion. He was second guessing the wisdom of his request to Betty and he prayed for a good report the next time they met.

Fanta Djiakite, aka Betty Holloway, sat on a park bench, watching the river flow by in Henley-on-Thames. This was undeniably a pastoral beauty spot just a little over an hour outside of London. It was a full-fledged town, with a population somewhere between ten and twenty thousand. It was just north of, and across the fields from Reading in Oxfordshire. Henley had money, and it showed. There were no supermarkets except for the Waitrose, and the one fast food restaurant allowed within town limits had exposed posts and a faux thatch roof to match the town's architectural motif. Everything about Henley exuded the politeness and correctness that came with wealth. The riverside walking trail was well maintained and cleaned on a daily basis by town employees. The bench she sat on was wiped down daily. She was convinced that the overcast creeping over the boathouse at the riverbend just over a mile away had been purposefully curated.

She couldn't help making comparisons between here and the suburbs of Paris; they were like night and day. There were poor areas on the outskirts of London, surely – she had passed through Slough to get to Henley – but the overarching policies and the planning approaches of the two cities were very different. From what she could tell, the French made an effort to segregate marginalised populations in the volatile outer suburbs while London suburbs like Henley were bastions of tranquillity for the well to do. Some of it, she assumed, was also cultural. Though she was always acutely aware of her racial identity in London, she didn't feel that it occupied as much focus in London as it did in Paris, nor did it frame the character of interpersonal interactions as strongly. When she rose from the riverside bench and walked to the brasserie at this early evening hour she did not feel or appear out of place. She glanced over her right shoulder to take in the view of the quaint bridge before heading up the market street into the town.

Calling a business by its French name 'elevates the atmosphere', and calling Les Trois Oseilles a brasserie instead of calling it The Three Sorrels pub was supposed to impress. It was lost on Betty. She went inside, catching the door before it could swing shut after being released by the patron ahead of her. A middle-aged white man had just followed his wife through the door and noticed someone reaching out just as he was letting go. When he turned to see if he could catch it to politely hold it open, he was surprised to see such an attractive young woman stop the door, acknowledge him with a nod and come through. She was wearing contacts and she had spent quite a bit of time on her makeup and her clothing choices to look classy while not standing out. She fit in with the young professional crowd that floated in and out of Henley on the tides of its white-collar work.

The lighting was strong but indirect, so visibility was good without the lighting being harsh. The French style was reinforced with tasteful and authentic artefacts; there was a vintage bicycle pump attached to a vintage bicycle tire positioned around an umbrella barrel. Slow jazz provided a backdrop to the murmur of conversation from the patrons. The couple in front of Betty went left into the area with dining tables and Betty went straight ahead into the bar area. She followed the bar to the far corner, passing only two other patrons there, and sat tucked away at the end. The bar was panelled and furnished with dark woods and the furniture was well-padded and comfortable. The bartender waited until she had settled in and then came over and engaged in light banter and took her drink order. Betty ordered an expensive glass of red wine, French of course, and a sparkling water with lemon over ice. The bartender commented on her accent when he left her drinks, and she said that yes, she was French.

She took out her phone and played at a word game and sipped at the water for some time. It was Thursday just after work and business was picking up. Two people came and sat at the bar until their table was ready and took their leave. After a while a middle-aged man in a business suit came into the bar area and he was striding toward the corner when he noticed Betty and slowed, but still approached. He was one seat away from her when she looked up to see who was approaching her. It was the man whose picture was in the self-destructing electronic dossier she had been staring at for the better part of the week. In person he was well presented and he carried himself confidently. Late forties, successful, comfortable, unused to hearing 'no', she felt that in her twenty-something years on earth she had grown to understand men like this more than she should need to.

"Hello,", he said. *"You know you're not going to believe this, but you are in my usual Thursday night spot."*

"Oh no," she said. *"I had no idea. Let me buy your first one to make it up to you."*

She gestured to the barman who had looked up when he heard them talking.

"That's very civil of you," he said. *"And whom shall I thank?"* he held out his hand in greeting. She shook his hand and gave a common first name as an alias and asked his, which she already knew. The barman arrived and the newcomer told Betty he would have a gin and tonic, which she ordered for him.

The man in the suit asked her what she was doing in town, and she told him she was here interviewing for her first VP role with the global wealth manager who was the town's largest employer. He said he was impressed and this gave them context for ongoing conversation. She engaged with active listening and appeared enthusiastic when talking about her prospect. It turned out he was in finance too, and he may be able to get a good word in. The conversation gained natural momentum and just when they were finishing a laugh at his clever quip she hopped off her stool and grabbed onto his left forearm to steady herself.

"I have to run to the loo," she said, *"Keep an eye on my drink and keep it safe, won't you?"*

"Of course," he said, and she disappeared for a respectable amount of time and returned. During this time the man checked his phone and spoke briefly to the barman.

She was busy putting something away in her purse when she returned, and she hopped back up on the stool.

"There we are," she said, and reached out to slide the glass of wine closer to her.

"Wait a second," she said, putting on an overly inquisitive face. *"You didn't let anyone put anything in my drink, did you?"* she asked him with a mischievous grin.

"Of course not," he replied in kind. *"I've kept a very close eye."*

"So nothing got into my drink?" she asked almost comically, *"A girl can't be too careful you know."*

"Please, allow me," he said, picking up her wine and drinking off the third of it that was left in the glass, whereupon he immediately lifted it toward the bartender and pointed to it, indicating that he should pour another.

Betty laughed and again reached out and touched his arm, saying that chivalry wasn't dead. In the next few minutes while they talked, his propositional innuendos appeared, and when they were not immediately rejected, they became a bit insistent. Again, without a transition of any kind, Betty hopped off the stool, thanked the barman and said that she must be off. He said that he'd see her out, and she said that would be kind of him, thanks. She didn't wait for him then, she strode off to the exit and he had to pick up his pace uncomfortably quickly, for the scene, to catch her at the door. On the pavement in the now dark town street, she stayed ahead of him for a full step. Whatever speed he went, she went just fast enough to stay that far ahead of him. This had him walking much faster than he expected to or wanted to, because he couldn't be suave at this speed. She got to a dark narrow laneway between terraces and took a hard left into it. The man followed her, his breath ragged and fast as he asked her if she knew where she was going.

"Yes," she said back over his shoulder, *"It's just up here in the car park."* Her right hand gestured toward the dark end of the laneway. There was a fair grade heading up now, and he did see an illuminated sign for a car park. He kept after her and began to feel tingling in his extremities. His mind was getting cloudy and he spoke out to her but couldn't be sure he heard his own voice. The tingling and numbness found its way into his head.

She stopped and turned back to him, and said, *"Come on you piece of shit, keep walking."*

His left hand slapped out and rooted to the wall, jerking down on his shoulder, hard. His head lolled to the side as he tried to lift and straighten it to look at her. He was being robbed of awareness at the inverse rate of his rising fear.

"The closer you get to the boot of that car, the less I have to drag you."

He fell into the wall at a strange angle because his knees wouldn't buckle but his consciousness failed. His shoulder and head bounced off the wall and he fell to the ground. It would be a matter of several short minutes before he would be completely dead, but he was done moving or even breathing now. She took a pair of slip on trainers out of her bag and took off her heels. She got her arms under the unconscious, prone man and dragged him backwards the fifteen feet uphill to the end of the laneway. She left him in the corner, in dark shadow and retraced her steps back down the laneway to the market street, where she returned to the same park bench.

Somebody else was supposed to handle the logistics from there, and she prayed that they did their job well. From the same park bench she called a ride service and got a lift back into London's west end.

It was full dark and traffic had picked up. They hit roadworks on the way and she was in the car for nearly two hours before she got to the flat. On the way, she thought about death and killing. Her environment from her most formative years was one of unsafety and uncertainty. Until she moved to France death was never very far away. Her mother thought it probably gave her too cavalier an attitude about death, that it made her too callous, but that is not what Betty thought. Betty felt there were things that were more important than an individual life. There had been countless incidents where individuals had given their lives for country or the greater good, and willingly. She felt the greater good take shape in her own life, and she would not shy away from her responsibility to bring it to the lives of others, particularly the women of Africa. Her responsibility may also require her to take life, and this she would also stand ready to do; sometimes it was necessary to prune the garden of humanity. This was rooted in the same ethos a member of the military may have, but the cause to which she was committed went beyond country. The rights of representation and opportunity for a female seemed like foreign values in northern Mali, but to her they were no less self-evident for it. The man whose body was being removed from a Henley car park was a veteran enemy agent in deep, deep cover. He had assisted with some very high profile murders by poisoning many years ago not far from where he now lay. He never would have let himself be taken in so easily if he hadn't truly believed that he was off the radar after all this time. She wasn't a decision maker in this matter, but she speculated that it was less about meting out justice and more about sending a political message.

■■■

Elena Du Bois was nearly finished with the morning school routine. She had woken the children after making their breakfast, gotten them into their uniforms and checked at the door that their school bags had everything they needed, and that their P.E. kits were clean and ready. The short ride to the Welling Academy in the Volvo estate car was stop and go, as always, and it felt like it would have been faster to walk. There was no planned drop off area and there was surely no parking near the school so getting the children from inside the car to inside the school was an endeavour that smudged the regulations of the highway code across conventions of social grace. She often found herself stopped at a green light while the car in front of her jettisoned school children, infuriating businessmen on their way to stations that would bring them into the city. At this speed they showed their annoyance in the most British way possible, pulling a face showing impatience and a level of disgust commensurate with the parent's lack of consideration. Some days Elena was the one fully stopped at the green light. When she first arrived in London years ago her Italian point of view filtered out the nuance, so she was unaware of and unaffected by British micro responses to such transgressions. As the years drew on she became more sensitive to such things, and her morning stress level continued to rise. Since she stopped working she formed a habit of pulling into the on-street parking in town, which was almost always available because of the exorbitant cost, and stopping in at the high end coffee shop for a breather and a well crafted brew. At this hour she could expect a queue of men in suits and women already wearing makeup waiting for their orders. Today, the queue encroached on the swing of the entry door and she had to open it very slightly at first, to catch the attention of the nearest people so they could shuffle around and she could sneak in apologetically. She had to shove the door a bit to get it moving and when she did the small bell attached to the top at the inside rang, but the sound was lost against the noise of the busy shop. The warm smell of strong fresh coffee rolled over her and she heard her name being shouted over the din of customer conversation by the barista. The aproned employee at the far end of the counter was holding up a large cup at his own eye level and reading her name from the side.

"Elena!" the young barista shouted and then scanned the crowd with his eyes, *"Large soy chai latte for Elena!"*

She was quite puzzled but she skipped the queue to order and started apologising her way through the crowd to collect her usual. Perhaps they had become so used to her that they prepared it ahead of time, knowing she would be there at the same time of the morning as always. She got near the barista and nodded and raised an index finger when she caught his eye. He moved to hand the drink over just as a tall young black woman in business attire stepped forward and deftly but gently took it out of his hand. Before Elena could react further the young woman addressed her.

"I got your usual hot drink for you, I hope you don't mind." She took one step back and, holding up the beverage, swept and angled her shoulders toward a 'two top' high table by the window, as a matador might do when passing a charging bull.

"Please join me, if you would," she went on.

Elena was on her guard. This was very unusual, but it seemed harmless enough. She went to the table, which had a ceramic 'for here' coffee cup and a small handbag on it. Since the settlement she had been getting clever cold calls from wealth managers, and she figured this must be the best researched of the lot.

Elena took the seat with her back to the door and Betty put her tea down in front of her.

"I apologise for the bit of theatre here," Betty said, *"but I need a few minutes of your time and I knew you would be stopping in."*

Betty wasn't prepared for how short Elena was. Harry had told her Elena's height, five foot five inches tall, but she had grown up with centimetres and she hadn't bothered to do the conversion. In her mind's eye she placed Harry next to her and found it just the slightest bit amusing. Elena was beautiful, and dignified in middle age, and Betty thought she must have been stunning when Harry first met her. Betty felt a small lift of pride in this woman, even though, again, it was unearned.

"Thank you for the tea," she said, *"but all of our assets have been deployed. I'm afraid there is no point in a sales call now."*

She had retained her north Italian accent but her diction and enunciation in English were precise. The accent added an engaging charm and did not detract from understanding.

"Yes, well," Betty started, *"I'm here on a personal matter."* She paused while Elena tilted her cup above eye level. *"A very personal matter in fact."*

"Blimey," Elena said, arching her eyebrows in an exaggerated manner, *"what can this be about?"*

"I'd like to talk to you about your husband," Betty said. *"and about your relationship just before the attacks that ended his life."*

Now Elena was offended. She didn't know what this young lady was after, but digging into a very painful and very recent past was no way to get it.

"I'm quite sure it's not your business," Elena said, and she was about to go on when Betty spoke over her.

"I understand, and I apologise," she said, *"but I represent someone who had as much invested in that relationship as*

you, and who has an imperative need now that only you can assist with." Betty rehearsed this line profusely since getting back from Henley.

Elena considered getting up and walking away but she was also intrigued. She stayed in her chair and finished the latte.

"How well did you know your husband's past?" Betty asked.

"I knew my husband had a past," Elena said without inflection.

"And what name did you call him? Was it Harry?" Betty leaned in. She was now genuinely engaged and she reminded herself to be more of an observer.

Elena looked at this young woman more closely. What did she know, and who did she say she represented?

"His alias was earned through service to the Republic," she said. Bringing up Harry's service to France made her think of Africa, and a realisation dawned on her when she connected Africa with this woman's ethnicity and France with her accent.

"What do you know of my husband's past life?" Elena asked insistently, leaning in herself now, *"And what do you want from us?"*

"I know that he served bravely and honourably," Betty said. *"I know that he loved you and he loved his family."*

Elena believed the former and knew the latter, and she had heard much of it before, straight from Harry himself.

"If you knew he were going through continuing pain, even now, then wouldn't you do whatever you could to stop it?"

Elena thought this sounded odd. Could this woman be a sham medium, out to scam recently bereaved widows?

What are you asking for, exactly?" Elena asked plainly.

Betty knew that she had crossed a threshold with Elena. She trusted that she could confide in her to help stop her father's pain. If she would accept the knowledge about Harry and not rock the boat then everything would be much better. Harry could stop worrying about his family's mental and emotional well being and focus on his mission. Elena could stop grieving and move on with her life. The family would be well looked after.

"Are you comfortable speaking personally here or would you prefer to go somewhere else?" Betty asked.

"I don't think anybody here is paying any attention. I think we can talk," Elena said.

"Herve Du Bois died during the London attack," Betty said, *"but Harry Holloway did not."*

Elena tapped her empty cardboard cup against the table, hard.

"Are you saying that Harry is alive?" she asked, quite a bit louder than she had intended or expected.

Betty sat quietly for a moment to allow any glances or other notice to subside.

"Your relationship was completely over and it had no chance of being fixed. He knew he had lost you and the family."

Elena bit back tears and looked out the window and across the street at the family car.

"That wasn't my choice," she said.

"I know. He knew. But it's true, isn't it? You felt that too?"

"Yes," Elena answered, *"There's no way we'd have been safe living in the same house with his ghosts."*

"Of course," Betty said. *"Still, it kills him to know that you are grieving for him."*

"So you're saying he is alive," Elena stated as fact.

"Harry Holloway is back in the service of the good guys," Betty said, giving no specifics. *"He is alive and quite well."* She waited a second before going on, *"Unfortunately, for*

everyone's safety, you can no longer have direct contact with him."

Here Betty paused again and Elena cut in.

"So you're saying he's out there and we should know that, and that's it? What the hell do you – does he – expect me to tell the kids? For Christ's sake!"

"He said you should tell them whatever you think hurts them the least. He said that your judgment should not be questioned."

Elena thought that had to have come from him. That was a personal, inside joke between her and him, in those very words – my judgment should not be questioned.

"He wanted you to have this," Betty said as she placed a wedding ring on the table in front of Elena. Elena picked it up and read the inscription inside.

"He wants you to be happy and find love again. He thinks it would be good for the kids to have a good man in their lives."

Elena put the ring in her pocket and dabbed her eyes with a handkerchief.

"You said direct contact," Elena said to Betty. *"What other kind of contact is there?"*

"Well," Betty said, *"You can send messages with me. Periodically, whenever I'm in London, you and I can catch up, if you like."*

"You'll just drop by for tea and a catch up from time to time, is it?" Elena's word choice and inflection sounded very English to Betty's ear.

"If you'd allow me then yes," Betty said, *"There is nothing I'd like more than the chance to watch my brother and sister grow up."*

Elena was embarrassed for having missed it even as it came crashing in on her. The bone structure, the age, the location.

Instinctively she reached across the table with her left hand and gave Betty's right hand a squeeze.

"And what should I call you?" Elena asked Betty.

"For now please call me Fanta. I'm leaving London tomorrow morning but until then I'm at your disposal."

The Weight of Survival

In Marseilles, Harry got a text message from an anonymous French number that was a link to a local Kentish news outlet. It was an article about a hotel under renovation in Folkstone that had burnt down some time ago. Apparently the contractor was heavily under the influence of alcohol and had mishandled a petrol fuelled generator. Sadly, two bodies were recovered at the scene.

Harry thought about Kevin and Connor and searched his feelings about them. Kevin had likely sent him into a trap where Gino and his goons would find Harry dead at the wheel of the Kadjar and whatever 'package' the delivery was, missing. Maybe Kevin thought staging a robbery would protect him from suspicion, and the presence of a body would reinforce his innocence. Did Kevin not think that making a last-minute change in the driver would raise questions? No, Harry thought, Kevin hadn't thought it through.

Harry had spent years as a compliance officer at a giant bank and insurer. His last job was all about money laundering but he had also held roles that focused on fraud and professional malfeasance. There were many reasons something would come to the attention of the compliance department and there were different ways compliance would be made aware. Sometimes internal audits would flag something fishy, sometimes data analysis, limit flags or transaction alerts would raise something that required a compliance officer's attention. Most often though, it was complaints. A lot of people knew when they were wronged or when something was off.

However these things came into his queue, Harry was supposed to open an item on the tracking system and put it through steps to either clear it as resolved or open a full investigation. Over the course of the four years when he held such a role he had cleared thousands of items, but he had to conduct and complete investigations only about twenty or so times. About half of these were cases where the local insurance broker or financial advisor suffered from substance addiction, had a gambling habit or was embroiled in some kind of affair. These were almost always open and shut cases where Harry pulled together the documentation and his colleagues in Legal took it from there. About half of the remaining investigations were insurance fraud, where adjusters needed compliance to sign off that there was nothing more that could have been done internally to detect or prevent the fraud. But then there were the others that stuck with him. Like the one where he had to tell the elderly couple that their nest egg was gone and only a small portion of it could be replaced. Like the one where the executive assistant who had been with the broker for thirty years had been stealing the same amount each month for decades, characterising it as a routine adjustment. The one that stuck with him the most though was the case where a trust officer had been assigned as the guardian for a young woman with limited mental capacity. The trust officer's duties were to manage her financial affairs and look out for her best interests as a fiduciary and as parentis in loco. He had set up grocery deliveries for her and paid the bills when they came in, for example. If she wanted something that was not considered an 'incidental' then she had to ask him for it; like if she wanted a top of the line appliance or a frivolous spend on a spa day. He cultivated a relationship of dependence with her, taking the time to curate her reliance on him and establish behavioural conditioning routines that he knew would embed, due to the challenges with her intellectual and emotional development. He eventually convinced her that sex was a required part of the transaction for special requests, and he abused her for a number of years before Harry got onto the investigation. During the investigation while the facts were still coming to light, Harry and a representative from the legal department had a meeting with the trust officer at his private office in

Great Yarmouth. The lawyer was the one maintaining the dossier, and he had put all of the evidence together and invited a public prosecutor to review it. It looked like the trust officer was guilty and Harry had made up his mind that he was, even though he hadn't yet had the benefit of a fair trial. Harry's whole purpose as a young person had been to protect his siblings and later his mother from a capricious, violent man. To know that someone even more vulnerable had been so heinously victimised, and that the person specifically appointed by the powers that be as a protector had done it out of exploitative, perverse malice was more than Harry could let go. Harry remembered that he spoke sternly to the trust officer and that he strongly insisted that the trust officer tell the truth. What the lawyer remembered, though, and documented in his debrief minutes for Harry's file, was very different. The lawyer saw Harry become very calm and almost detached as they discussed the new information that disclosed the criminal nature of the activity. Harry carried on in his normal demeanour as they approached the office, but he changed drastically just as they were entering the office. The trust officer had a comfortable, well appointed office in the corner of the top floor of a newer shared building. He was there alone. The lawyer said that Harry's gaze turned to a menacing glower and remained that way until the interaction was complete. He said that Harry's whole frame was flexing and relaxing incessantly and that his nose flared like that of a bull about to charge. The lawyer led the discussion and the trust officer kept glancing at Harry and quickly looking away. Harry said very few words and when he did they were admonitions to divulge all of the relevant facts and to be truthful. The lawyer knew that writing those words and leaving them on a blank white page to be read without any other context would render them clinical and passionless, and well within the conventions of such interviews. The lawyer wondered why there were no words to convey the anxiety, agitation and fear the trust officer experienced. A clinical reliving of this interaction would show that the relevant procedures were followed and investigation practices were appropriate, but there was no way to recreate the primal intimidation that filled that room on that day. The encounter ended with a good result and no questions were raised, but the lawyer recommended Harry work on something based in the back office from then.

So no, after his musing, Harry wasn't out of sorts because Kevin found justice. He felt bad for Connor, if that were him, because he was largely collateral damage. Harry wasn't so naïve to think that someone would hand him the exact remedy to his extremely dire circumstances without there being a catch, but Harry still took it. He fairly well knew that he was rolling the dice and he did it anyway. Was that the same for Connor? Harry had the fatalistic view that some things just happened, even if you made them happen yourself, and things shook out one way or another. When you're out there, part of events as an operator, you're nudging things to shake out your way.

Harry was doing that in a new way now, as a logistics manager. He had gamed out and budgeted the needs for a project that established a camp in the wilderness to sustain thirty people for at least thirty days. He had identified and vetted purchasing partners, mostly using contacts that were given him through the French embassy and leads from Betty. Everything was expected to be purchased or arriving in Sombokto over the next month, where it would stay in a warehouse until the personnel arrived and staged in Sombokto too. Mohammed Batu had asked for volunteers for this project from within La Lance Fournie and they had nearly three candidates for every available space. Mo convened a panel to assist in interviews and he wanted Harry and Limier on it. They had a list of questions and an interview script but Mo told them that he was looking for "guys with balls who weren't complete idiots". They had taken their time going through the process and they constructed six teams of five, comprised of operators with unique skills. This way the teams could operate independently if required and deliver the gamut of required capabilities, like La Lance Fournie of medieval times. In the end, six of the "guys with balls" were women.

Most of the thirty volunteers were from Asia and Africa, with the rest originating in Latin and South America and Eastern Europe. Harry liked the international diversity and their common sense of duty; if you fought for the Republic then you belonged to it. Because he had been on the panel Harry got introduced to each of the volunteers and he would know them by sight from now on.

Harry had all of their applications for sponsored project visas for the Caliphate of Malitania in a folio and Limier had driven him to their consulate near city hall. They parked in a parking deck near the port and made their way north and east on foot through dense cityscape, eventually arriving at the three-story stone building that held the consulate's offices. They ascended the steps, entered the lobby and were directed to the second story to a meeting room behind transparent doors you had to be buzzed through. It reminded Harry of his former corporate life. When they approached the conference room they could see that Rene was there waiting for them. He had made the journey from Sombokto rather than videoconference. They greeted each other and Harry and Limier sat across the table from him. His laptop was plugged into the media feed and the monitor showed his home screen.

Harry started the business part of the discussion, saying, *"Here are the applications for all of the staff on our project who will need visas."* He slid the folder across the table.

"We'll have a look and vet them all on our end," Rene said, *"and we'll let you know if we have any questions or challenges."*

"Are we still on track for being in-country in two weeks?" Harry asked.

"Yes," Rene said, *"barring any unexpected circumstances in the vetting. We have space for all of you to land and to accept briefings and get underway. We've arranged for you and Fanta to stay in a village near the compound so you can scout the ground and decide where to set up. I think all of your bills*

of lading have cleared and the matériel has been stored in the city."

"Sounds good," Harry said. "Call me when I can pick up the visas."

They said their goodbyes and took their leave. It was all a very mundane errand in a normal business day for a logistics officer.

Harry and Limier decided to stay in the city centre for lunch since they had already paid for parking. Harry thought it would also be a good opportunity to get to know Limier, since they would be working together in the Caliphate. Harry hadn't been in Marseilles for a long time, so Limier chose the venue. Limier said he knew a place that had recently opened, which was a small kitchen that served tables set up along the seawall. He said the food was great but the place was still relatively unknown. Harry was game to try it and they decided to walk the whole way because the weather was good.

On the walk Limier told Harry about his history. His family had been Spanish pied noirs who sought refuge in France when Algeria gained independence. They found that, hypocritically, they were ostracised as bigots in France and they could not find a peaceful and happy life. They emigrated to Tahiti, which was still under French control, and established businesses in export-import and opened shops. Limier was born there and raised as a privileged son of a tiny country. His education was French but provided locally in private schools and he travelled to Europe several times during his young life. He joined the police force in Tahiti and rose to the rank of detective at a young age, hence the moniker 'bloodhound'. He grew restless though and Tahiti was too small a box for his capabilities and oversized ambitions. He transferred to the Parisian police force, where he finally had a venue in which to shine. He showed real talent in locating and tracking wanted criminals and fugitives, and he became a young star as a liaison with Interpol. His meteoric rise in the force was not only derailed but stopped entirely when he, as he explained to Harry, *'got into a spot of bother, as you English say'*.

"*Well, this sounds like it's going to be a good story,*" Harry replied.

They were walking along the seawall on the wide pedestrian thoroughfare, which provided a kind of public square by the sea. The seawall was thirty or forty feet above the rocks and crashing waves below, which is not uncommon on that part of the Mediterranean. Just ahead of them a man was leaning against the seawall, whose banister was about four feet above the pedestrian walkway, and turned to face them as they approached, removing his sunglasses. Harry was unpleasantly surprised to see that it was Gino the Corsican.

"*Hello again, Harry,*" he said, "*how nice to run into you on such a glorious day.*" He extended his forearms from the elbows, palms up, to indicate the sun and cloudless sky. And it was a glorious day. The sun was bright, the Mediterranean was aquamarine and the seabirds were at play above. Harry looked at Gino to get a read on him. He was wearing boat shoes, belted pleated trousers that were not jeans, a polo shirt and he held a casual blazer draped over his arm. He was apparently alone and he wasn't armed, as far as Harry could tell. Harry and Limier had stopped walking and Limier stood by, waiting for Harry to engage with Gino.

"*But not entirely a surprise, though, is it?*" Harry asked. "*You couldn't have called? You couldn't have bought me a coffee somewhere? Just showing up out of the blue like this might make some people nervous.*"

"*I can tell you're not the nervous type,*" Gino said. "*And you're hard to pin down. You know how long I've been staring at the sea?*"

"*Did you want to set an appointment, or is there something you needed right now?*"

"*Yeah. Right now I'm going to tell you where **you** start reporting to **me**. Every week I want to see you…*"

He didn't get to finish that thought. Harry had taken a half step closer and turned his hips and shoulders together and thrown his left hand hard and short. The index and middle knuckles landed right across the bridge of Gino's nose, breaking it. Gino's head and neck had initially jerked back but had returned to their place above his shoulders as his body began to drop, straight down from his centre of gravity. The blazer fell to the cement with a metallic clatter as the gun landed before the fabric.

Harry stepped forward into Gino and leaned against him to take his bodyweight. Gino's nose dripped blood onto Harry's shoulder and Harry used both hands to grasp Gino's belt firmly.

They hadn't yet really attracted attention as no one was very close by, and Limier deftly picked up the gun and threw it over the seawall far enough for it to land in the water far below. Limier didn't know what Harry was up to, but he assumed Gino must be a very dangerous man.

Harry took another full step in and lifted with both hands, using his hip to hoist Gino over the side of the seawall just as he was returning to full consciousness. Pain and anger were eradicated as soon as he realised he was dangling forty feet in the air over unforgiving jagged rocks below, and the instinct for survival was all that remained. He began to struggle and flail, making it harder for Harry to hold him steady. Harry shouted at him to stop moving, but Gino tried to position himself so he could get a grip on the edge of the banister. As he did, Harry moved along the seawall, dropping and raising the belt to prevent Gino from obtaining purchase.

"Stop struggling or I let go," Harry shouted at him. Limier picked up the jacket and went through the pockets.

Gino calmed down enough to hold his hands up to Harry, showing him that he was not fighting back.

"What the hell do you think you're doing, man?" Gino shouted. He was hurt, embarrassed and angry. He wanted to lash out

and teach Harry a lesson, but there was no way to do that in this position.

"I'm making my goddamn point," Harry said. *"You did me a favour that could have saved my life. Now I'm doing you a favour that will definitely save yours."*

A couple who had been walking in a direction to pass them showed interest as they grew nearer, and as they approached Limier moved to intercept them, talking as he got nearer. *"My friend just caught his husband cheating on him. Pay them no mind, they do this every other month really."*

Gino had let loose a stream of invective punctuating threats in several languages. Harry let his shoulders drop to the level of the banister, dropping Gino a foot abruptly. That got his attention and he quieted again. Harry left him that low. Gino had been clenching his core to keep his body level because he was so much heavier above the waist and now he relaxed and let his head hang.

"I'm going to pull you up," Harry said, *"and save your life. And we'll be even and you won't feel like I owe you anything anymore. Isn't that right?"*

Gino didn't answer right away and Harry waited. When no answer came after a few seconds more, he repeated, *"Isn't that right?"*

"OK," Gino said, *"OK. Pick me up for Christ's sake."*

Harry lifted him and Limier helped to pull him back over the seawall banister. When he was back on his feet he produced a handkerchief from a pocket and held it tight against his nose.

"What the fuck," he said to Harry, *"I came here with a proposition."*

"Bullshit," Harry said. *"You came here with a gun and started giving orders. I don't work for you and you don't threaten me."*

Both men were breathing hard and both stayed on the balls of their feet, staring each other down.

"Well it looks like I owe you one now, and you can be damned sure I'm going to pay up," Gino said as he grabbed his jacket from the ground and stalked off holding the cloth to his nose.

Limier tugged on Harry's sleeve to get him walking again and he scanned the thoroughfare checking for cameras. The whole thing had happened so suddenly and was over so fast that the pedestrians he intercepted were the only people who appeared to have taken any interest. There wasn't much foot traffic besides them and the only places he could think may have cameras were the businesses all the way across the walkway. As a former policeman he knew how well covered mainland France was by cameras and he knew how often anonymous reports came in. He knew there was a chance this would come to the attention of the police and he would have to get Mo caught up just in case he needed to put out any fires.

To Limier, Harry didn't look like a man who had just been in a fight. He was back to complete calm as they walked along. Limier had seen many types of villainy in his career and Harry's sudden and brief actions just now made Limier think that Harry may be a bit detached from his emotions when it came to violence and that he may be operating in a different framework of reasoning than most people. With La Lance Limier had seen men like this in the field; men of action who needed high stakes results fast. There was a dire need for men like this in the service of the Republic, but they often wound up incarcerated in civilian life.

Harry caught Limier's look and thought he needed an explanation. Harry told Limier what had transpired after he took the ferry and drove to Bordeaux. He didn't spare any details and he didn't withhold any information. Limier listened as they walked along and again he took note of how little emotion Harry displayed when he talked about the unfortunate shooting death. When Harry finished his story Limier stopped on the sidewalk and reached into his pocket. They were a long way from the seawall now, and there weren't many people on the street. Limier took out Gino's wallet and took out the driver's licence.

"The licence has his picture on it. The name is Maurizio Luongo, but it's French," he said, wondering if any of that meant anything to Harry.

"I have no idea who that is," Harry said, *"but I'm pretty sure he's connected to a fair-sized criminal organisation. He was comfortable with command when he had his guys around him."*

"I'll take this info to my former colleagues on the police force. If you don't mind me filling in a few details for them then they will reciprocate with anything we don't know, but may need to," he said.

"That's fine," Harry said.

"And you may want to keep your head on a swivel, at least until we get out of France," Limier said.

Back at the Crane, Limier made a point to catch up with Mo and get him up to speed on what happened with him and Harry. Mo started with the same thought as when Harry figured out who was paying La Lance, *Harry's back,* but he had to hear Limier out and get him familiar with his new colleagues for this mission. Limier asked Mo if he had any reservations about putting Harry in sensitive situations. Mo explained that the Legion's paratroopers are professionals but they are not diplomats. When an objective requires an active response, an operator has to rely on his own judgment. And sometimes to make an omelette you had to break a few eggs. Mo asked Limier how it would have played out if Gino got the drop on them and started making demands. Limier had to admit that in the near term the outcome would have been worse. Limier told Mo that he would keep him up to date on what he learned about who Gino was and who he worked for.

Roots of Resistance

Carl Horton met Betty at the office in northern Virginia. This was a scheduled meeting about getting this project underway. The relevant select committee had signed off on the budget and significant assets were being positioned in a non-aligned country under a tenuous Memorandum of Understanding and there could be significant political consequences if things went as wrong as they could go. He wanted Betty to understand the gravity of the situation, but he also wanted her to understand how important it was to catch these guys if they really were the ones responsible for both London and Hoover Dam. In this session they were reviewing the 'mosaic' analysis from the terrorist finance and terrorist activity desks. This was essentially when they spit-balled ideas on who may or may not be involved.

This latest surge of activity looked different from other terror campaigns to Carl. There were some tenuous connections to other organisations for local logistical support but the terrorist dead from the London attack weren't currently associated with any known groups. It was a bit puzzling. They had to be a very sophisticated and well-coordinated organisation to nudge the two extremist groups in the U.S. to armed conflict during an act of sabotage. They must have had a lot of resources deployed in the right places to make it work. The psyops know-how required rivalled that of any state actor that Carl had ever worked with.

So far, their monitoring of the three sites had come up short. The Nigerian government hadn't made any progress in stabilising the area under the control of Boko Haram and the warehouse in Damascus didn't seem to have any activity at all. Betty had spent a couple weeks in Sombokto getting the logistics together to establish a camp close enough to the compound. So they had no new information on the ground yet, although the satellite images did show increased activity. Most of what came and went as supplies, they assumed, came in on the covered trucks. The analysts estimated, based on their load capacity, that they could carry enough provisions to sustain a garrison of two hundred men indefinitely on the current flow of vehicles. They couldn't be sure of where the remaining two bankrollers were and they desperately needed more information. If they waited to launch these two separate but somehow related operations until now then they likely had a plan that had been set in motion. They needed to be alert to anything, and Carl had one last nagging thought he needed to cover off. He brought it up to Betty.

"So the logistics officer from La Lance. You said he was on-site in London. That he brought a bag down to the data centre, made an abrupt exit and then deftly escaped both the city and the country, winding up at a murder scene in Bordeaux in just about a week," he said.

"Yes," Betty said, *"all of that. That's what Batu told me anyway."*

"You don't think that's all a little too coincidental?" he asked. *"And what about the counterfeiting software he was supposed to have delivered? Did he get anything from that?"*

"Maybe," she said, *"maybe not."* She did not want to believe that her father was one of the bad guys.

"How did he make out in all of this, in the end?" he asked. *"We already said how capable this adversary is. Would they have the foresight to put a fox in among us hens?"*

Betty had given it some thought. She could understand the mechanics of it, and she could understand how Carl could line it up in his mind like that too. Carl was too far removed from it, and he couldn't see how things would have worked out for this person in this way, organically. Obviously Carl was unaware of her relationship to Harry or he would never have asked this question.

"I'll stay on my toes and let you know what I learn," she said.

"Good," he said, *"Now let's focus on this group of friends from Oxford."*

Balliol College Oxford, twenty years before the major action of this story.

Abdul-Aziz Al Sudeiri had been at university for only about two weeks and he was already feeling down. He was convinced that he was experiencing more than just homesickness. He felt an anxious depression that seemed to hurt everywhere and nowhere. To him, it felt like the first time he kicked off the wall in the deep end of the pool when he was learning to swim, not sure what was going to happen but paddling for his life, literally. More than that, it already felt like an existential crisis of non-becoming. He 'passed' for European easily, and he didn't have to choose to be so different; there were only about six Arab and South Asian kids in the Fresher intake this year. He could see how they were treated and he really did not want to be a part of that. They were ignored and condescended to by not only the posh whiteboys who ruled the halls, but also by the tutors, professors and administration that was supposed to look out for them. Their meals were tampered with if they left them unattended. During lectures and tutorials students made blatantly prejudicial comments and the tutors and professors never refuted them or chastised or even corrected the students. The people were as cold as their drizzly wet weather. They had no sun driving the rhythm of their day and they had no sun in their character or in their disposition. It was dark as an Arabian night at five p.m. Freshers were required to live in the halls, and regardless of the university's reputation the accommodation was cold and damp and approximated a Middle Ages living experience. Even the food seemed to want to disappear, with absent textures and no spice. Abdul-Aziz, who went by Zuz, needed to make connections with his people, to take comfort in salaat and eat kebabs of grilled meat with pickle and spice.

He attended a private lecture on the role of Islam in post-Soviet central Asia with the hope of running into some of the Arab students he had seen about on the college's quads. He forced himself out of the safety bubble of his room and he walked to the lecture venue. He was surprised how busy the small city of Oxford was, jumping up out of nowhere in the English countryside, with people having to step out into the street to get around each other on the pavements even after dark. Many of the people were at the task of going somewhere, focused on their purpose and not paying attention to the people around them. There were also bands of young students out for the sake of being out, flexing their newfound liberty and testing the boundaries of their privilege. When Zuz passed them he simply stepped around and carried on his night.

Zuz hopped up the couple stairs and went quickly through the door of the venue. The lecture was given in a university building but it was presented by a private organisation, so there was a sideboard with 'drinks and nibbles' as the English said. A group of about twenty people were milling around the aisles surrounding the square configuration of chairs facing the podium. Zuz saw a familiar looking Arab standing at the sideboard so he approached him and looked where the young man was looking. He could see bacon wrapped sausages and gin and tonics set out among the refreshments.

"Why would they even put these out?" Zuz asked the other student, speaking in Arabic.

The other student looked at him, surprised because his Arabic was so fluent.

"Are you an Arab?" he asked. Zuz said he was, and introduced himself as coming from Riyadh, turning the 'dh' to a 'z' in the dialect of the Saudi capital. The student introduced himself as Ahmed Tahlawi from Muscat. They shook hands and almost immediately Zuz felt less alone in the world. They grabbed some incongruous snacks which were the only ones that were not haram and sat next to each other as the lecturer began to ask listeners to take their seats. While everyone was settling in two other young men who looked like Middle Easterners came to the row where Zuz and Tahlawi sat, shaking hands with Ahmed and sitting just as the lecture began.

The focus of the lecture wasn't familiar to any of them. The lecturer showed how the Afghanistan War had rallied the Islamic world into a jihad against the Soviet Union, and this included devout Muslims from inside the Soviet Union. Now that the Soviet Union had no influence over places like Turkmenistan Uzbekistan and Azerbaijan, how would Islam be utilised in nation building, and where would the sympathies of the new countries lie?

Despite the lack of cultural sensitivity and an obvious western point of view on the subject, the lecturer was expert in the field and the lecture raised some very good points for consideration. At the intermission Tahlawi introduced Zuz to Hani Nesralla and Mohammed Suleiman, the two Freshers who sat with them. They stood in the back and carried on the line of inquiry raised during the lecture, and no one approached them to join the discussion. Zuz noticed that all of the Caucasian students were gladhanding, networking and talking about other things; they were there for the event, not for the lecture. Zuz wondered at the optics of all the Caucasians moving around the clump of Middle Easterners and he was legitimately surprised that the organisers wouldn't at least try to get them involved in a broader conversation. He wondered too, then, if the other students saw him as the 'token' Caucasian speaking to the Middle Eastern group, so they were covered?

They returned to their seats and the lecture concluded. At the end, a sign-up sheet went around for the Balliol Middle Eastern Studies Society and they all decided to join. This way they could at least convene with each other once a week in a scheduled and purposeful way. They soon learned that of the twenty or so other students in the society many of them came from families that had significant oil interests and who had spent at least a year of their youth somewhere in the Middle East while their fathers were on a lucrative expatriate post with an oil company. They were an exclusive tribe unto themselves; rich, white, and with the same superficial experience that gave them the echo chamber to feel like experts. At first they tolerated the Middle Eastern contingent and treated them like an exotic diorama to talk over. The white kids drank during the society meetings, and it wasn't long before they were explaining Middle Eastern culture (just the one, you see) to the Middle Eastern students who tired of it quickly. During one session six or seven Caucasian students were more than mildly inebriated and were talking over Tahlawi and Suleiman to force a point that wasn't going to change anyone's mind. Suleiman said that he had enough of the conversation and that they would have to agree to disagree and he tried to break from the circle and get to the door. The boys surrounding him began to point their fingers into his chest while punctuating their points, not allowing him to make a dignified exit. Suleiman looked to Tahlawi and he commented how rude and perhaps even dangerous these boys were, but he said it in Arabic. Tahlawi agreed and added more commentary in Arabic and they were soon having a side conversation in Arabic about the boys right in front of them. Though the boys generally bragged about having spent time in the Middle East none of them had learned enough Arabic to understand what was being said and they took umbrage, loudly insisting that they speak English. The volume and the confrontational aspect of the conversation got the attention of Zuz and the others who broke into the circle and walked Tahlawi and Suleiman out by the arms, ending the night.

The Caucasian members of the society reconvened the next day, hungover and in foul moods, to accuse the Arabic speakers of openly supporting terrorism by conferring in Arabic and keeping their conversation secret. They agreed that the society would not be a vehicle for these kinds of anti-democratic activities which, as far as they knew, could include plots to undermine human rights themselves. They would teach the Arabic speakers a lesson that would put them in their right place. The week came and went, and the secretary had put some particularly incendiary points on the agenda to ensure the Arabic speakers would attend. Every member of the society showed up for the next meeting and the agenda included a twenty-minute opportunity for like minds to confer in preparation for the debate of several academic points of Middle East policy. The Arabic speakers took one side and a cadre of other boys took the opposite side. During the preparation period none of the Caucasians ate anything but pork-based appetisers and drank nothing but cans of lager and ale. The meeting was scheduled over the beginning of the dinner hour at the dining halls, and almost all of what was on offer was consumed by the time the debate began. The opposite team made some ridiculous claims that were not intended to promote a real debate, and they watched the Arabic speakers closely as they badgered them about nothing.

Suleiman went to Zuz and said that he wasn't feeling right. Zuz felt the same way, like his body was shutting down to unconsciousness though he was not at all drowsy. He turned to Nesralla to ask after him, but Zuz felt like he was moving in thick gelatine. He looked back to Suleiman and said that they'd been drugged, but he didn't know if he even made any sound.

Suleiman was the first to regain consciousness. He had no idea where he was or even that he had been unconscious; he was coming to as if he'd just entered the world for the very first time. He was shocked to find that he was wearing his Balliol gown and his cap was nearby, but his pants were around his ankles and he was bare from his midriff to his feet. He sat up and swooned, regained his focus and realised he was on the floor of the junior common room. His compatriots were strewn about him on the floor and in the very same state. He was horrified to hear movement in the corridor beyond and he rushed to put himself back in order enough to get to the door and lock it. He hurried to rouse his compatriots and get them cognisant of their surroundings and their circumstance. Some lay in puddles of urine. They found indecent props about them on the floor which could easily have been used to stage the most profoundly indecent acts, if not perform them. They were horrified and filled with rage. They wanted to know what had happened but they also wanted revenge. Suleiman was immediately concerned that they could be expelled, and Zuz reassured him that they were victims and that none of them were in any state to agree to or to consummate any 'unnatural' acts. He told them that it was imperative that they stick together and told the same, truthful version of events. He checked the time and said that the faculty sponsor for the society was right then holding office hours. He asked if they had the energy and the will to march over and address this right away; their indignation dictated that they do just that.

The front quadrangle of Balliol College is surrounded by long stone buildings that are about three floors high. These buildings are separated into vertical groups of offices, like a terraced house. The offices are grouped by discipline and identified by which staircase accessed the office. The group of boys entered the quadrangle from a corner and walked briskly aside the lawn toward the professor's staircase. When they were about forty feet away they saw Oliver Bean, one of the students in the society, exit the staircase and turn away from them and walk on as if he hadn't noticed them. The group didn't break its stride, it carried on to Professor Reeves' office without stopping.

Professor Reeves' office was on the second floor, so they had to come up two flights of stairs. Four sets of heavy shoes made an ominous march in an otherwise silent staircase, and everyone in this part of the building knew they were coming. Halfway up the first flight Suleiman said that it wasn't too late to turn around, and that they should, but they kept on marching up the stairs without responding. They reached the landing and took a second to gather outside of the office door. Zuz knocked and then put his hand on the knob before Professor Reeves said to come in. Nesralla was last to enter the small office and he closed the door behind him. Professor Reeves was sitting behind his desk, wearing his gown and closing a book. The boys filed in behind the two chairs facing the desk because no one would sit.

Professor Reeves had a short conservative haircut that was rapidly greying. He had lines in his face and neck, but they weren't so pronounced as to be his dominant feature. Zuz thought he looked as though he was going through elderly puberty. His blue eyes were expressionless. He addressed them as he stood to open the window.

"Gentlemen," he said, *"What can I do for you?"* His accent was upper class English.

Zuz spoke for them. *"We're here to lodge a complaint with you, before we go to the police,"* he said.

"Oh dear," Reeves stated blandly, *"What in the devil has happened that was so terrible?"*

Zuz thought that was too specific to be an uninformed, spontaneous response. So Bean had come to run interference.

"We were drugged and attacked by the students of the Middle Eastern Studies Society and we want to report it."

Reeves sat back in his chair, leaned his weight on his elbows at the back of the chair's arms and made a steeple of his palms facing each other.

"Well, boys," he said, *"one man's attack is another man's prank. What exactly happened?"*

Zuz told Reeves what happened. Throughout his short narrative he checked details with his compatriots and got them to agree to key facts, like who was there and what was offered to eat and drink. All of them felt shame and embarrassment and rage while it was all being recounted. They were just boys of eighteen, expecting some kind of justice from this virtuous institution. They had enough experience to know what was right, but not enough experience to know what was real. They were shocked when Reeves immediately attacked the credibility of their story.

"Well it sounds very like you're unsure of what happened," he said. His circuitous speech put the boys on the alert. *"You said you were all drinking…"* Here several of the boys started talking over him, correcting that they hadn't drunk anything.

"You'll forgive me boys, but you smell strongly of spirits and something else godawful. If it came to testimony I'm not sure I, or anyone else for that matter, should believe you."

He levelled his blank blue eyes on them and saw their amazed looks. He continued.

"You're all away from home for the first time and you may not yet know how to handle your newfound freedoms," he said. The boys immediately protested that this was not true.

"You all got a little too tight and the horseplay may have turned into a prank that was a touch over the line, that's all." Again, a hubbub of refutation.

"Being involved in this kind of thing can result in expulsion," he said, *"regardless of the role played."* He looked at each of them in turn. They were burning with rage and indignation but they were also at the height of anxiety and fear, and embarrassment and shame.

Zuz spoke for the group again. *"We are the victims of a number of crimes, Professor. What those boys did requires severe punishment and we are going to the police to report these crimes."*

"Why don't you stay in your rooms tonight and think it over," Reeves stated. *"You need to take some time for your own wellbeing. Either see the nurse or stay in your rooms to collect yourselves. Take the night to consider what's best for you, and we can reconvene tomorrow if you like."*

"We'll be going to the police straight away," Zuz said. *"Good day!"*

They marched out of the office and into the city. The further they got from Balliol the more their resolve waned. Mohammed Suleiman slowed his pace until he was standing still beside a wrought iron railing to a public park. There was space on the pavement to stand in a circle, so they did.

"What is it?" Zuz asked Suleiman.

"I'm not like you boys," he said. *"My parents don't have money. I'm here as a scholar funded by a bursary."* The others already knew that.

"I can't do anything to jeopardize my position here. I couldn't go back, there's just no way," he went on.

"Look," Zuz said, *"we can't just let them do this to us and get away scott free. Of course we have to go to the police."* He looked from one face to the next, judging their conviction to see this through. Nesralla and Tahlawi understood Mohammed's position. They liked him and they didn't want to blow up his life, but they also felt that justice should be done. Their body language showed a noncommittal response.

Zuz Al-Sudeiri tried a new approach.

"Guys," he said, *"what do you want to do here? Are you coming to the police station or not?"*

Hani Nesralla spoke as if for the three. *"How about we take the night to think about it? Maybe tomorrow we talk to Reeves again and see what concessions we can get from the uni? Maybe we go to the police. We might have a clearer answer in the morning."*

Mohammed Suleiman readily agreed with that. Tahlawi shrugged and remained neutral. He had taken to almost always following Zuz's lead, so this meant that he was behind the other two.

Zuz was livid.

"You know what? Fine. Take the night but know this – if we let them get away with this then we can't show our faces on campus. I'll meet you right here at eight a.m. tomorrow and we'll do whatever it is we agree. But it has to be going either to the police or to the Prefect. Otherwise I'll have to drop out myself."

A double-decker bus passed within four feet of them, with the draft blowing leaves around the tines of the wrought-iron fence and the noise forcing a few seconds of contemplation. Without taking leave, Zuz stalked off into the city where he hid out in a basement coffee shop drinking one strong espresso after another until his nerves vibrated in harmony with his emotions. He stayed there in the sumptuous décor of the rich, dark underground until the sun dropped like a stone and the darkness reached into every corner of this unlovable country. Eventually he went back to his residence hall, passing the very spot he left his friends and of course they were no longer there. All through his walk back the winds rose and fell, and leaves blew against the kerbs and into the corners of doorways until every eddy had collected the matted detritus of decay.

Back at his room he found the photograph slid under his door. It was vile, and it was only an example of what they had available if they wanted to make this uglier and uglier. He sat by his window reliving the incident in his mind until the sun came up. He continued to sit there as the room grew from black to grey. Eventually his numb mind stopped the replay and cast itself forward to think about the fallout. His father had told him explicitly to make connections with established, old money families and to learn how business really gets done in the West. Abdul-Aziz the son was intended to take the business empire into the future and make the family enterprises diversified and global. His father told him, clearly, that his job would be to get some of the eggs out of the petrochemical basket and to do that safely he would need the kinds of connections that could be made in one of the most exclusive of Oxford's colleges. Just being there and being rich were his two objectives. He would never need a real education, but he would need the context that these years at the top of the English food chain would provide.

At 7:45 he started the ten-minute walk to the corner near the park, but he didn't make it that far. Once he got outside of his residence hall he could see an ambulance parked on the quad just a few staircases down, immobile with its lights flashing at the top setting. There were several first responders running between the vehicle and the door to the staircase and there was a small contingent of students gathering to stand by and spectate. Zuz hurried down there. Mohammed lived in that staircase.

None of the first responders were physically present at the ambulance when he got there so he asked several of the students what was going on. They only knew that someone inside needed emergency care. Tahlawi stepped out of the small clot of people in the grey morning and tapped Zuz on the arm, pointing to Nesralla coming across the quad to keep their appointment. They raised their arms as he scanned the small crowd and focused back on the door when he had seen them. The industrial steel door with a stainless-steel bar and small peephole window was propped open by a doorstop and they could hear loud and crisp instructions and commands coming from the ambulance service above. The sound of incidental activity increased in pace and volume and in short order they heard counting getting louder as it got closer. Nesralla joined the other two just in time to see two first responders carrying Mohammed Suleiman on a patient board while a paramedic administered CPR compressions. They brought him into the back and placed him on the built in stretcher while the paramedic continued compressions but did not punctuate them with breaths. One of the stretcher bearers withdrew, closed the back doors and got into the driver's seat. The ambulance started again and drove off with the lights still flashing but it left the siren off.

"He'll be pronounced dead at the hospital," Hani Nesralla said. *"They need a doctor to declare death. They weren't giving breaths and they didn't run the siren. They're in no hurry. Oh my God, Mohammed is gone."*

Years later they would recall to each other how they felt in this moment. They had this additional shock on top of everything else that had happened. Just when they thought they could be no more horrified and saddened, they learned that they could be. In the future they would consider these few minutes, standing together on the quad in the emptiness of the driven-off ambulance and the wandered off crowd, to be the first true meeting of their cabal. The Tahlawi family paid for transportation of Mohammed Suleiman's body back to Egypt. Each of the boys got compassionate leave from the university and they all went to Alexandria for the funeral, where the real planning began in earnest. By the time they had launched the London attacks they had already murdered two of the five boys who were responsible for Suleiman's death. Serendipitously, Oliver Bean was crushed to death on the day of the attacks, trampled to rags on a stairwell in Charing Cross station.

Vita Procedit

In the northeast section of the Caliphate of Malitania is a town called Mai Zurfi, which means 'deep well' in Hausa. The town is on the northeastern extreme of the Hausa speaking part of the Sahel. It is so named because it has access to the last significant aquifer in the Caliphate before entering the Sahara. Traditional trade routes go through Mai Zurfi because of this, so a small town has always been there. After the Caliphate gained independence from Sankara and, some would argue, ceded independence to the UAE, there was an oil boom across the country. Because of its abundance of water and its size and permanence, Mai Zurfi became the supply depot for wildcatters in the Caliphate's 'empty quarter'. The town grew to about twenty thousand residents in size and the government built a state-run hotel there. The town receives fuel deliveries via tanker so there is consistent vehicle traffic on roads that are comparatively well maintained.

Even though there were several buildings just as tall and impressive as the hotel, Mai Zurfi had a frontier feel to it. The town was overwhelmingly brown and small herders still drove their goats and sheep to the market through the streets. Someone was always passing through and several languages were spoken on the main street everyday. Outfitting companies still provided for projects in the empty quarter.

In the hotel's business centre, a meeting was scheduled to launch a major local project. It was for a fairly large archaeological project sponsored by a British museum and an American TV network. The project entailed underground imaging using new technologies, carrying out a live dig based on the findings and filming the whole thing for a documentary. The local traditional leader, the assemblyman, prominent supply firms and the project representatives were all in attendance. The crew were filming the meeting for the documentary and it was a very official event intended to cover both traditional and government responsibilities. There were three representatives from the project in attendance, a French woman of mixed north African descent who represented the TV network, a British man who represented the museum and their Hausa interpreter who was provided by the government. The long conference room had a person in every seat and the shot through the camera's lens looked like the painting of the last supper, with the project team out of the frame. The chief and the assemblyman, at the centre of the table, were both middle aged local men wearing 'up and down' local print suits with their matching hats folded like napkins next to their place at the table.

The assemblyman invited the project to present its credentials and the young French woman leaned in and spread out a tabloid sized document at the centre of the table. Her face was not visible but the camera could see that she wore local garments covering shoulder to ankle with a separate covering for her hair. She spoke in French, saying that these documents established the commercial project and allowed them to do business with local vendors. She kept her place, slightly bowed after having spread out the document, and did not return to her seat until the Hausa translation was complete. The assemblyman offered the chief the floor and the chief spoke in French supporting the discovery of their lost history and wishing them much success. The assemblyman then took the floor and spoke in French also, pointing out the good branding that could come of a successful documentary and hoping for a boost to the local economy. The representative from the British museum then said a few words of thanks to the local leaders for allowing them the opportunity to work in their land. The chief then led a short prayer and the meeting concluded for the camera. Half an hour after packing the camera they were still engaged in leave-taking. Individual conversations in small clots carried on while some vendors drifted away. Eventually, everyone retired to refresh before the dinner with vendors in the hotel restaurant scheduled for early evening.

Harry and Betty went to the covered café on the hotel's roof to get away from everyone and to have a public spot to talk, to maintain adherence with the local custom. The Hausa interpreter went with them. They took an elevator to the roof, where they found the café and bar. It was covered with a tent roof and there was a pergola just beyond the canvas. There was a bar with a workspace for the barista and bartender behind it, where the refrigerator and other machines were kept. There were no employees or patrons on the roof. The three of them ambled to the sides of the roof individually, taking in the views from within the town and beyond. The sounds of traffic and commerce rose from the streets below and the smells of daily life rose on the heated convection currents. The sun was brilliant at the high heat of the afternoon and the horizon in the distance was blurred by refraction and rising heat. The conditions were right for mirage.

Harry had to get out of the sun so he went to the covered part and sat at a small table with four chairs around it. Betty joined him and so did Khadija, the interpreter who was almost certainly an Emirati spy. She wore the traditional cloths of the locals and was similarly covered.

Harry started right in with the practical part of the conversation.

"So here we are," he said, looking at each of the young women in turn, *"Can we speak freely as equally interested parties?"*

"We can indeed," Betty said. *"Rene introduced me to Khadija while you were abroad. We can all know the same things."*

Khadija spoke up then, saying, *"I speak Hausa and the local dialect, as well as French, and I know some of the people who want to be your suppliers. You tell me how I can help."*

"Let's talk about the suppliers for a minute," said Betty. *"At tonight's dinner I'm going to press them for information about what they can produce in what quantities and what is available for us to buy. In reality we can bring in whatever we need, but I want to know how much of what they are delivering to the compound."*

"I just heard from our men at the depot here. Everything that we've asked to be staged here is ready to deploy," Harry added.

"Still," Betty replied, *"We'll both need to work them to get a picture of their full capacity."*

Betty looked at Khadija. *"Also, I'll need to make contact with lower level people who provide for the compound. I need eyes in their crews and we need to get one of our people inside the compound on a delivery as fast as we can. Can you work that angle for us and come up with a list of people who may be susceptible to monetary or other persuasion?"*

"I'll get on it tonight," Khadija nodded.

"OK," Harry said, *"the teams are coming from the training camp in Morocco in two weeks' time. We have to have the camp set up by then. Khadija should mention the construction crews she 'hired' from the capital, so all our stories stay in line."*

"Got it," Khadija said.

Betty summed up. *"Tonight we spread some money around and get promises for more contact soon. We ask to tour their facilities and verify that they're making deliveries to the compound. Then we start to figure out who and what is inside those walls."*

The heat was getting to Harry, and he figured they were away long enough. They all agreed to stay together during and after the dinner so they could fully understand what was said in any language and they could compare notes to get a full, clear picture. Harry went down to his room first, to break up the grouping.

Harry was in a corner room near the stairwell on the second story up from ground level. If he needed to he could sprint down the stairs and access secondary roads to get him clear of the hotel in roughly three minutes. It was a good sized room that had an air conditioning unit, but the electricity had been off in the city for some time. The room had two large windows that had louvres, which were a series of rectangular plates of glass the size of elongated tiles set into metal brackets, attached to a lever built into the housing of the window. To open the louvres one pushed down on the lever and each of the twenty or so louvres tilted to a full ninety degrees, leaving them perpendicular to the ground and allowing in any slight movement of air. Harry had jumped in and out of the shower to cool down and he hadn't fully redressed. He lay on the bed trying not to move in order to battle the oppressive heat. There were only intermittent animal sounds from the street below, as the city had gone into siesta mode. He thought of the picture he made, lying motionless and completely silent. There were many, many days in his past where this was the tableau he presented, and it always reminded him of the opening scene to *Apocolypse Now*. There wasn't much to do at times like these except think.

Not so long ago Harry's anxiety level would have risen just knowing he would be trapped with his thoughts like this. Now, though, he looked forward to a few minutes of respite. He remembered a social science course where happiness was measured for people at different stages of their lives, and people in their fifties found a spike in happiness because, as the researchers postulated, 'the burden of the future was lifted'. They then applied the same concept to people in the developing world and found that extreme poverty with no possibility of improvement had a similar effect. Ambition was a vestige of social evolution that went numb. More people lived for the day and as a result focused on the daily lives they were living more than their counterparts in the developed world. Harry felt this in his own life now.

Though his old life was irrevocably over, his family was well seen after. The residual guilt and pain of missing his children were new facts of life, but he was stepping through a breakpoint. The burden of the future was lifted and true purpose was reintroduced because the outcome of this project mattered. His professionalism and expertise would be the very cogs of the wheels of justice and public safety. He was connected, engaged. He was living more in the moment and 'for the day' than he had in many years. He felt like someone different. In fact, when he thought about it, the few years longer than a decade of so-called normalcy seemed inauthentic compared to how he felt now. He was forged in uncertainty and hardened through violence, and riding the train and herding into office buildings felt somehow incorrect.

These days he found himself thinking about Mariam Djiakite nearly as much as he thought about Elena. He wondered more and more of what might have been if she told him about Fanta. Would he have dropped everything and moved heaven and earth to build a family? He honestly didn't know, but he felt angry about being left out of her upbringing. He missed her whole life up to now and he wanted to see pictures from her infancy and childhood. Apparently he would have had endless opportunities to be proud of his daughter and to give her encouragement and praise like he did with Eleni. Somewhere along the line she entered the conflict between the Islamists and the west, and Harry would have liked the opportunity to prevent that.

He heard the very slight creaking of the stairwell door in the hallway and he listened very carefully. He sat up as quietly as he could and put his feet on the floor. A light knocking was followed by a quiet call of, *"Hello, sir?"* in English.

There was no eyehole in the hotel room door, so he could not look out and see who it was. He quickly replied, *"Just a moment."*

He stood up and threw on a t-shirt and opened the door just wide enough to see out. Khadija stood in the hallway holding a tray that had a small ceramic teapot and two clear teacups that looked like large shot glasses, with portions of dates and nuts next to them.

"I thought you could use a visit," she said. *"May I come in?"*

Harry knew immediately what this meant. She had presented herself to an unattached man in his hotel room and asked to be allowed in unsupervised. In the locally practiced version of Islam the intent carried as much guilt as the act. She was taking a very real risk here.

Harry stepped aside and opened the door and closed it when she was inside. He didn't know what to say, so he didn't say anything at all. She put down the tray and removed her headscarf, looking at him and holding it halfway on and halfway off, asking, *"You don't mind, do you?"*

"Not at all," he replied.

She removed it revealing shoulder length straight hair that was arranged in a fetching hairdo, and she hung the scarf on the bedpost. She had a beautiful face. She must easily have been a decade older than Betty but she was clearly younger than Harry.

"You're catching me quite a bit unprepared," he said, using both hands to indicate his attire, which was a pair of shorts and a t-shirt.

"And you're letting me," she replied. She unhooked and removed her covering gown, under which she wore a tailor-fitted but conservative, Western style business suit with a

knee-length pencil skirt. She looked like she was ready for a meeting in a London boardroom but Harry felt like she had just stripped naked. She approached him and reached out to touch his cheek and when Harry didn't turn away she put her hands on him, whereafter he felt he could reciprocate.

To Harry this was a very strange experience. He had never been approached so brazenly in the Sahel; when he had connected with Mariam it had been just them two left at the camp for days getting to know each other. But Harry couldn't think of a reason to reject her advance, and his body had been lonely for a long time now. Though Khadija was experienced, Harry didn't think she had ever been with a westerner. She seemed quite surprised, pleasantly he would like to think, at his focus on intimacy rather than simply release. Well into their interaction she began to return intimacy in such a way as to make him wonder if he had created a monster. But their leave-taking was focused on her covert exit, carrying the still full tray, with him helping her to make her way quietly into the stairwell.

Blueprint for Chaos

Zuz, Tahlawi and Nesralla all joined the call on the encrypted devices, which they still believed secure. The picture was clear and the audio crisp. They each had their background blurred. They took quite a bit of time catching up before they got down to business because it was the first time they spoke since Hani had run to Tehran. They were all in safe places and though it was likely they had been linked to some nefarious activity, it was highly unlikely that anyone had connected enough dots to put their plan off course before it set.

So far, things had come to pass largely as they were gamed out, and indicators in the markets and opinion polls were heading in the exact directions that they should. Now it was one year until the U.S. election and there was one thing left to do, according to the model, to tip the U.S. into either isolationism or chaos. After that there was one thing left to do on mainland Europe and their mission should be complete.

In the U.S. they needed to make the most volatile people's worst fears become reality. They needed an armed incursion across the U.S. border by armed desperadoes leading hundreds of dangerous illegals across, complete with the murder of red-blooded, patriotic American citizens. Over the last three years they had bribed and trained an entire unit of Salvadoran special forces to carry out the deed. They had retained the free market Russians to oversee funding and provisioning, and they used a string of political contacts along the route to make the passage frictionless. They even went to the trouble of staging coordinated prison breaks in San Salvador and in Honduras two days before they set out on their journey. That attack was ready to be launched now, and they expected it to occur over the next few days. They agreed on spending, on contingencies and on further communication relating to the attack, and they were about to conclude the call.

"There's other, seemingly unrelated, business I have to tell you about," Nesralla said. His friends paid close attention and bid him go on.

"Hamas told Tehran that they are launching a major attack into Israel's undefended kibbutz area bordering on northern Gaza," he said. *"This is designed to shock and frighten them and to draw them into the tunnels under Gaza."*

Zuz gasped. *"They certainly have reason enough, but there's no way they can endure the reprisals, surely."*

"They are counting on the Arab world to support them, but outside of Tehran I don't know who could help, in practical terms," Nesralla said.

Tahlawi thought about it from the point of view of the Arabs on the peninsula. *"There's no chequebook diplomacy option here. Nobody in the Middle East can stand up to Israel *militarily right now, and there's no chance of a meaningful alliance doing anything but clutching its pearls."*

"What does this mean for us?" Zuz asked.

Nesralla let out a sigh. *"Well,"* he said, *"there's no way to run new scenarios and take this into account, but I think it could go one of two ways."*

He took a second to think again.

"It will play into public opinion in our favour, as long as Israel wants to keep the apartheid system they have in place. Timed like it will be with the attack in Arizona it could just strengthen the view that the wolf is at the door. But if it goes too far and triggers a military response from the west then we could be two steps back."

"In truth," Zuz offered, *"it's too late to do anything about it. Let's see how it plays out in the newspapers and parliaments and take it from there."*

They agreed not to take any different action than was planned.

"There's another point I'd like to discuss," Tahlawi said. They let him speak.

"I'll be taking the precious cargo to the compound soon, by air, as you'll remember, from Bamako."

"That's right – we remember," Zuz responded. He knew Ahmed was talking about the gold. They had staged their working capital in precious metals under heavy guard in Bamako and he would be taking it to the compound by helicopter over the next couple days.

"There's been some activity in Sombokto. There's an archaeological dig, of all things, that's just gotten licences and permits to film a dig right near the compound. They say it's at the crossroads of an ancient trade route, and it might be, but that could be more attention than we want in the neighbourhood just now."

"I didn't know that," Nesralla said, *"Can I share that with Tehran? They don't have a lot of friends in the Sahel, but they might know something."*

"I think that's a good idea," Zuz said, *"and let's learn as much as we can about the people putting this expedition on the ground."*

"Right. Will do. I'll keep you posted," Tahlawi said.

They took some time saying their goodbyes and wishing each other well and ended the call.

Lines of Fire

Outside of Nogales, Sonora (Mexico) and Nogales, Arizona there are several border ranches owned by Americans with a wide range of political views. Some ranchers have taken action against illegal migrants crossing on their land and there have been incidents of violence. A private paramilitary militia made up of U.S. veterans, law enforcement officers on leave-of-absence and other volunteers had established a presence there and began patrolling the border each day. They discovered there were some ranchers who took no measures to either prevent or detect illegal crossings. It was on one of these ranches that the militia decided to take a stand and make a point by constructing a makeshift barrier there. The family that owned the land demanded they leave, but they refused, making a claim in both state and federal courts that the border is the border for every American, and as such they had a right to enforce the laws of entry. Of course, there was no legal merit to this claim, but they stalled their eventual removal.

Normally the militia's people go back after dark, but because of the case media stayed on the scene, making the most of the optics ahead of the deeply divisive election. As long as there were cameras the militia were going to stay on site, hammering home their xenophobic message.

This was the exact spot the Salvadorans attacked. They opened by firing several rocket propelled grenades into the makeshift barrier. The barrier was just junk piled against an abandoned bus that had been dragged into position, and the barrier itself was no more than fifty feet long, including the bus, and it was not connected to any kind of fencing on either side. Three of the RPGs hit and the loud explosions shattered the dull night. Another RPG with an incendiary payload landed right after, and the bus and all the flammable junk caught fire, with the flickering light illuminating dozens of figures running right past, some carrying long guns. There were only six armed militia men there that night and two were killed outright when the attack began. It would be reasonable to expect that the remaining four would be aghast and overwhelmed, but they were all combat veterans. They took time to throw on body armour and unsling and ready their weapons. One fired a flare into the sky to provide visibility. They took defensive positions and complemented each other's fields of fire, as they had practiced.

There were far too many opponents though, and they were outflanked and outgunned. The media had nowhere to run and they kept filming. The light on the camera attracted attention and fire, and the video clip the next day would go down in the annals of broadcasting history, falling over halfway through and showing the demise of the Americans from a sideways position. The firing went on for a very long time before it stopped off camera because the body armour kept two of the militia men alive until the Salvadorans were right on top of them. Once the firing stopped, what appeared to be hundreds of illegal migrants went sprinting by. They were still streaming by when the light of the dying flare quenched and the camera kept recording the sound of their running feet, only catching glimpses of shadows of their bodies in the light of the burning bus. The only people who survived on the American side were the family of ranchers, who stayed inside their house the whole time.

By daybreak the Arizona national guard had established a cordon around the site and the state police had marked out the entire area as if it were a massive murder investigation. Along with the bodies of the six militia men and the three journalists they found two bodies of armed central Americans who had mara salvatrucha tattoos. The Democratic administration sent federal law enforcement and put all border patrol on high alert but they did not send any military assets to the area. By nine a.m. local time the video clip was playing on repeat on most of the major news networks and the far right media outlets were having a field day not just criticising but outright threatening the administration and specific people within the administration. The far right Republican candidate fairly ran to the border and basked in the grotesque photo ops. By midday members of militias across the southwest had arrived to eulogise their comrades and drink to excess while brandishing loaded assault weapons, working themselves into higher and higher states of agitation. By the time the sun was waning the militias had devolved into roving bands 'searching' through local communities on the American side of the border, harassing and threatening locals who had lived there their whole lives, but looked exactly the same as the Mexicans on the other side of the border.

Zuz and the others knew that the people who had filed past that dead cameraman had immediately returned to the Mexican side and took their payment and disbanded. The fact that no illegal migrants were captured or even located played into the Republican narrative of the ineffectiveness of the Democratic administration. Private militias continued to arrive on the border across the southwest and harassment and intimidation began to creep onto the Mexican side.

The following day, according to the plan, there were coordinated murders of average border patrol employees all along the border from California to Arizona. The Democratic administration called on state national guards to restore order over the armed private militias. A nationwide vigilante manhunt for the illegals caused thousands of violations of civil and human rights across the United States, and the Mexican government called for the demilitarisation of the border immediately as it called its own troops north. Half of American society was at the other half's throat and the political climate boiled over as protests in every major city became violent.

The following day Hamas attacked kibbutzim across northern Gaza and attacked a music festival in full swing. Hundreds of hostages were kidnapped and the most heinous inhumane acts were carried out in the name of generational rage. Zuz, Tahlawi and Nesralla were horrified.

Convergence

The vendor dinner at the hotel in Mai Zurfi was held in the only function room. It was a large room with access to service doors and three large, round tables set for ten guests each. The electricity was working so the low hum of the air conditioner complemented the piped in Malian music. The guests were all seated and hotel staff ran plates to and from the tables. Conversation was kept to a murmur while they ate the quarter chicken, small mound of fried rice and cabbage salad with bottled still water. After dinner the three representatives went from table to table, speaking with each vendor. They had worked out a patter so they would get as much information as they could and still leave no gaps in their story for when the vendors compared notes. Betty would introduce them, wait for Khadija to translate, and give a short spiel asking them to describe what they had to sell, tell how much they could produce and give prices and timelines for delivery. At the end of the night they estimated that these providers were supporting about a hundred and fifty men. They also consummated three contracts for material and local services.

They asked select vendors if they would be interested in other opportunities with the project. They would need assistance communicating and coordinating with the locals and they wanted contractors for that. They held three separate and private discussions and came away with a 'commercial understanding' for ad hoc services with one provider. He said his name was Mr. Bell, and he was one of those older men of indeterminate age. His hair was almost all white and his age lines followed the rounded features of his face. They stayed sitting at one of the large tables while guests wandered away. Betty felt she could speak plainly now.

"Mr. Bell, we may need to 'dramatize' some scenes to enhance the realism. We may need to put some of our people in local situations, but candidly, to ensure people's reactions are genuine."

Khadija translated from French to Hausa.

"I see," he said. *"Candour is a rare commodity around here. A combination of candour and authenticity is even more rare. I can provide both of those things."*

He drank from the glass of still water on the table, *"For the right price, of course."*

"I like the way you think," Betty said. *"To begin with, we'll need your help getting three people to appear as guides on our imaging tour, for the first show."*

She pushed a fat, sealed envelope across the table.

"I'm sure you'll find that this is the right price," she said. After Khadija translated, Mr. Bell smiled and nodded, covering the envelope with his hand and dragging it back across to him.

Betty told him that Khadija would be his liaison. Earlier it had been agreed with Khadija that she would communicate directly with the locals and run operations that relied on Hausa speakers. Khadija knew the objectives were to get local, Emirati agents placed as local guides and cleaners and delivery men. Once the right local counterpart was identified she was to pursue it aggressively, first placing people in innocuous filming sessions to see how it all works in practice and how well accepted they are. Then, she would try to get eyes inside the compound, either by placing one of their own people or by bribing a staff member to share what they know.

By the end of the night of the vendor dinner it looked like she was on her way to being successful.
■■■

Ahmed Tahlawi came from oil money, so he had ridden in helicopters as part of his upbringing. The secret he never shared with anyone is that he hates helicopters. The noise and the uncertain flight path kept him on edge and he had never enjoyed a flight in a helicopter. This time was worse. They had two fully armed men with full sets of body armour and a box that weighed just over two tons on board. Because of the weight of the payload they had to take a large helicopter, which was very bad on fuel. They had enough fuel on board to make the return trip if needed, but just barely.

Everyone had boarded at the airfield outside Bamako and put on their headphones and buckled in. The engine fired up perfectly and the pilot ran the rotors up to speed smoothly. In no time they had their instruments calibrated and they were rising into the hot, still air. Even with a calm takeoff Tahlawi could tell the machine was labouring under the weight of the cargo. Through his headphones he could hear the pilot's communication with the tower and he could still hear the loud thrumming of the motor. He'd be a lot happier when they were once again on the ground.

Once they had risen up and marched into the sky they could see the Sahel laid out below them. It was a characteristically bright and sunny day, and the greens in the landscape attracted the eye out of the ocean of brown. Signs of human habitation were sparse, which was fine with Tahlawi. Out here there were still local tribal militias that were fighting against the Islamists, and they had weapons capable of severely damaging the aircraft and possibly taking it down. On today of all days, the fewer encounters the better.

They had droned on through the empty sky before the pilot said into the headphones that they were approaching the border with the Caliphate of Malitania. Then about five minutes later he said that they had crossed into the Caliphate and they were in Emirati airspace. It was only a couple of minutes after that when they heard an external transmission come over their channel.

"Unmarked unscheduled helicopter," the voice said in French, *"You are violating Emirati airspace. Identify yourself and your destination immediately."*

They had agreed before the flight that they would simply turn back if challenged, claiming that there was a mechanical error with the navigational system. The pilot didn't say anything, though. He kept flying without responding. Tahlawi knew that as the passenger his mic was turned off. He wondered what the pilot was playing at.

"Unmarked helicopter, the Emirati air force is enroute. Identify yourself or be forced to the ground," the voice warned.

Still, the pilot didn't respond. Tahlawi leaned forward against his straps and tried to tap the pilot on the shoulder. The copilot pointed to a display where their radar had detected an incoming aircraft. It was closing on their position as fast as a jet. Tahlawi took off his shoe to extend his reach and hit the pilot's shoulder with it. Both Tahlawi and the pilot knew the depth of the insult of touching the bottom of your shoe to someone. The pilot looked at Tahlawi's shoe through the mirrored visor and appeared to be frozen with disgust. The copilot's voice raised in alarm, jabbing at the radar display and a modern fighter jet flew directly above them at less than a hundred feet. The rotors wobbled and the body of the helicopter swung a hundred and fifty degrees under the plane of the rotating blades. The weight prevented the craft from correcting its attitude and it continued to swing as it carried along through the air.

At this point the pilot spoke into the hot mic and followed the agreed upon script. The copilot showed the fighter jet on a new intercept trajectory. The helicopter pilot said that they had reoriented and were on their correct flight path. The pilot made adjustments as he could and pointed back toward Bamako. The fighter jet established a perimeter circling the helicopter and stayed with it until it was well into Malian airspace. Tahlawi had just about wet himself. He felt thrown around the sky as if he were tied to a bucking bronco. He swore he looked out both side windows and saw the approaching earth. They carried on for the next hour shouting invectives at each other and levelling accusations of madness. They found a flat enough place to land that looked suitably deserted and descended to refuel. While they were on the ground they were vulnerable to marauding bandits or tribal militias, but they were able to refuel and take to the air unmolested. They made the rest of the journey in silence.

A Nation on the Edge

Carl Horton had grown up in the reddest of the red states in America's Midwest. He did ROTC in college, so he had to do a full hitch in the air force once he got his degree. He tested into intelligence and worked closely with the DIA for his whole hitch. He found that he had a gift for analysing operating environments and he stayed in intelligence after leaving the military so he could further his career and continue to serve his country. On one of his holidays back in his hometown he reconnected with a girl from his high school, and they hit it off. Carl's father was a Protestant pastor and his upbringing was quite strict. Carl was soon married and he moved his new bride into his apartment in northern Virginia. They bought a house the very next year when their first child was born. His wife stayed home with the baby and they found a community of relocated Midwesterners and likeminded church people.

Carl's wife, Sandy, stayed very much rooted in Midwestern culture, but Carl started to see some things in a different light after living in D.C. for a few years. His work put him in direct contact with people whose circumstances were dire, and Carl had learned to use that to his advantage. There were blatant injustices in the world that a clear-eyed Jesus would know exactly how to handle. But Carl didn't have the luxury of asking himself 'what would Jesus do?'. There were hard decisions to be made that would lead to truths that were difficult to live with. Sandy never saw life in that way. She had a very black and white view of the world where right and wrong were clear and a single step off the virtuous path was unforgivable. By the time their third child started kindergarten he felt that Sandy had missed out on some intellectual and emotional development and chose to stay in this childlike state of naivete, cocooned in her bubble on the cul-de-sac and echo chamber of right-wing media.

He had begun to push back on some of her views and it caused an increasing number of little spats. They loved each other and his commitment to the vow was enduring, but his job kept him away for long stretches. When he had to be away without a spat resolved, it ate at him. He hated that he had to steer her back into a good place without conceding to an irrational stance. This was one of those times. The attack at the border had everyone on edge and he had heard her telling their kids to cross the street if they ran into anyone who looked like they could be those fugitives. In private he asked her not to say things like that and she accused him of not wanting to look after the safety of his own family, never mind the safety of the country. He rubbed the bridge of his nose and listened to her call him one of the government elite.

The American military had faced down homegrown militias to keep them from accessing the border. As a result, many of them had carried on vigilante actions to 'locate fugitives' on the American side. Violation of civil rights of Latinx Americans was rife and there had been several kidnappings carried out as 'citizens' arrests'. A particularly large militia stopped in southern California on its way back to Utah and decided to hold a 'right to residency' check in LA. The minute they detained young Latin men they were challenged. Gunplay escalated to open exchanges of automatic weapons fire in running gun battles across much of the city. Authorities stayed out of it until it was largely resolved, with a much-chastised militia fleeing north and calling for an alliance of all West Coast militias to occupy LA to restore order.

So there was civil unrest and civil disorder, and now platoon-size pitched battles in the streets. If the parties battling each other got more organised then there could be a real challenge to the political and social order of the country. Carl knew the growing division could lead not only to consequences nobody would want but it could also lead to circumstances from which no party could reasonably extricate themselves. The slow motion car crash that was American politics was playing itself out in the dynamics of his family and probably many others like it around the country.

This was the America he had left behind to be here in West Africa, and he didn't like leaving his family there alone in it. If the family went to the in-laws back in the Midwest then they would be further from potential trouble, even if they were well entrenched in the ruby red states. He just wanted them safe and he couldn't focus. The news from around the world wasn't much better on the migration front. In the same news reports of what was being called the 'American Troubles' they showed the Greek and Italian navies turning back overloaded and dangerous boats from Aegean and Mediterranean ports. They also showed Bulgarian border guards firing live ammunition at large groups of migrants rushing the border. Small boats were sinking in the English Channel every day now. The major powers were not simply allowing their borders to be overrun. Either their borders or their values had to be compromised and their choice was clear. On top of all that Carl Horton had checked the value of his 401(K)'s after the market sank, and it had pushed back his retirement by three years. He pinched his nose again and breathed out sharply to expel the scent of goat faeces.

They left Mai Zurfi at sunrise and travelled until they arrived at their site in the heat of the day. This was where they had selected to establish their camp, about two and a half hours travel from the compound, driving. They drove a train of lorries that carried everything they needed to set up the shelters, drive the borehole, and start doing archaeology right away. When they came to a stop out on the Sahel they parked around a designated area for ease of access to the material and for defence if necessary; it looked like they had literally circled the wagons. By three p.m. most of the shelters were set up and the office, canteen and lab, made from shipping containers, were brought on-line. At sundown the sound of generators underscored the hum of activity of setting up the camp, and work carried on. When the borehole hit the water level at eight-thirty they called it a day. They had all of the structures set up, and the water, electricity and data and communications systems functioning. It had been a major logistical effort, executed deftly by professionals.

The sun descended fast out there and Carl was impressed with the vivid colours of the sky as the sun met the level horizon. He made one last round checking on the placement of the antennae and checking that the security devices were functioning properly. This took him to every part of the camp and he ran into almost everyone. While on his round he saw Harry and Khadija interacting in two different parts of the camp. In both instances Carl was too far away to hear them, but he could observe their nonverbal cues. First, they were among other people and they interacted in a businesslike fashion. In the second they were on the outer edge of the camp, speaking next to a lorry with the open desert in front of them. They looked to be speaking into each other's ear, to stay quiet. Carl wasn't entirely convinced that Harry's story was vetted as energetically as it should have been, and he wasn't convinced that Harry was as one-dimensional as he wanted to appear. Carl completed his rounds and went back to his shelter for the night. He'd have to tell Betty to keep an eye out for any unusual behaviour, just in case.

The next morning the camp was ready for operation. The mess tent had breakfast ready and briefings were scheduled within each team. According to their project plan each team had a route to cover in a vehicle that had a machine on board for imaging underground. They also had LIDAR to fully image the landscape. They set out to do that, with film crews embedded with some of the teams. The team members and support staff were in and out of the office container but Carl, Rene, Mohammed Batu and Betty all had permanent desks there. Here, at the start of day two, they all sat. They had set up their computers and calibrated the settings on the machines in the office as well as their mobile devices. They pinged everybody they needed to ping, and now they sat with cups of coffee and tea, just talking for a minute.

The desks were in the far corners of the container, facing the outer wall to make the best use of open space. Betty and Carl sat across from each other and so did Mohammed and Rene. Right now they all had turned their chairs inward and it looked like they sat in a circle. At one point Mohammed Batu, out of genuine concern, asked Carl if he was affected by the 'American Troubles'.

"Well," Carl started, *"every family is affected in some way."*

"We're not strangers to unrest in our home countries," Batu said, *"but none of us ever thought it would come to the U.S."*

"Well," Carl Horton said again, *"things just spiralled out of control. People got so angry and vengeful that they started shooting each other, and as a result…"*

A thought came to Carl and crowded out all the other thoughts. It took his focus for a second and he trailed off. Then he blinked and finished his sentence.

"…and as a result we have a militarised border and a significant portion of the population under military control."

"It can't be as bad as all that," Rene contributed. *"Ten of the states responded to the President's request and they are overseeing their own state's national guard units. Restoring public order and providing for public safety is what we pay them for, no?"*

Carl thought Rene was being kind and trying to minimise it for his benefit, but Carl knew how bad it was. He also, as of just now, knew that some other party knew exactly what was going on. If Carl was right then they may have a better chance of unravelling this whole mess.

As soon as he could naturally take his leave, Carl did. He went straight back to his bunk at his shelter, leaving the people in the office wondering at how badly his family was really affected. He opened his sat-phone and dialled a number. The phone rang and rang. Carl let it ring for what seemed an eternity, and it was eventually picked up.

"Service for Mr. Curtis Chase," the voice on the other side said.

"I apologise for the hour," Carl said. *"I understand it is hours until morning for you. But I need to speak with Mr. Chase immediately please."*

"If you have this number then I'm sure that Mr. Chase appreciates your call and will get right back to you first thing at start of business. Please do call this number at that time."

"Don't hang up," Carl said. *"Tell Mr. Chase that his dear old uncle is gravely ill. Please use those words and tell him now. I'll wait on the line, thank you."*

There was a complete lack of sound for a few seconds, as though the line on the other end had been muted. Then the open line sound returned and the voice said, *"Please hold for Mr. Chase."*

There were some clicks on the line and Carl sat on the edge of his bed and kicked off his shoes. Eventually he heard a receiver being picked up and a throat clear.

"Curtis Chase," a gruff and annoyed sounding voice stated.

"Curtis. This is Carl Horton with the agency. Apologies for the hour, but I need to clarify something. We may need to get to work on this urgently and we'll need every day we can get."

"Carl. Right. I remember you. We did the um, thing, together. That thing."

"Exactly, the tabletop exercise we did for the think tank. That's what I wanted to talk to you about."

"And it couldn't have waited until after breakfast, for Christ's sake?"

"No, sir, not today. A little while ago I was explaining the situation in the States to some overseas colleagues."

"Yes?"

"And I said something like, 'as a result the border is militarised and a significant portion of the population is under military control' to describe what's going on. That reminded me that these conditions were negative outcomes from that scenario test."

"You're losing me. What are you trying to say?"

"What we're seeing today was modelled in that exercise."

"What? That's a bit far-fetched, don't you think? We were trying for the best results, remember?"

"Sure, but stay with me. Have some more coffee or something. We played that thing tons of times. One of those times I screwed up everything for my desk. Everything. I screwed it up and the thing blew up in my face, and the message was that the border was militarised and the population blah blah blah."

"Interesting. I guess you could use the model to solve for different shit. Let me take this away and think about it and ask some engineers some very pointed questions."

"OK."

"In the meantime can you go to the agency and get a complete who's who that worked on the thing?"

"Yeah, that should still be an open file. I can do that."

"OK. I'll call you no later than dinner time in D.C. Keep this phone on."

"Thanks Curtis."

They hung up. Carl had never had a hunch this strong and been wrong about it. He hoped it led somewhere, because they could use all the good news they could get.

Carl made a call to the agency and asked for a list of everyone who worked on Millenium Horizon's model and project. He asked them to cross reference the list against all persons of interest in Hoover Dam, London and the project he was currently on. The analyst he spoke with said that he'd have it on his secure phone in three hours or less. Carl thanked him, hung up and went back to the office.

The office people got up and went to the mess tent together and had a long lunch. The heat in Mai Zurfi had been bad, but out here exposed on the plain it was much worse. They were in the field now, there was no denying it. They used sun protection but mostly they stayed out of the sun if they could. After lunch they all piled back into the office, which had a solar powered air conditioner going full blast.

Eventually the teams came back in. They had been in radio contact which had been fairly constant. They had discovered several areas where signals were apparently being jammed and they adjusted by going to secondary and tertiary bandwidths. Team leaders came in and out of the office to soak up the cool and finally Limier opened the office door and called everyone to the mess tent for a debrief of the day's findings.

They filed over to the mess tent and when Carl Horton got back out into the blinding heat he felt like he'd never get used to it. In the Aleutians it was the wetness of the numbing cold, in Finland it was the bitterness of the cold, in Central America it was the humidity and heat but here, in the Sahel, it was the relentless, baking heat. There were jobs in the agency that brought people to comfortable, temperate places, but Carl had never had any of those jobs.

Inside the tent the folding tables and bench chairs were arranged so most people could see the table in front. There were three monitors set up side by side on it and Mohammed

Batu sat at the side of the table with the laptop plugged in. Batu was explaining what they were looking at, which was their real imaging target for the day. They now had a map of the hollow spaces in the compound. Further enrichment and enhancement of the data would be done by their colleagues in offices following the sun, and by tomorrow morning they could expect soundings and images that would be as good as a blueprint from the compound. For right now, though, they could tell that there were a lot of walls in most floors except for the second one from the top and that there was definitely a network of tunnels dug below and around the basement.

Carl's phone buzzed and lit up his pocket and he stood and made for the door as he reached into his pocket to fish it out. He punched the numbers to receive the call just as he stepped out into the end of the Sahelian day.

"Carl Horton," he said into the phone as the heat once again, and insistently, reintroduced itself.

"Carl it's Curtis Chase. I only have a minute so I'll talk fast. There are a lot of similarities to the scenarios in Millenium Horizon's exercise and we're going to keep looking into it."

"Jesus, I knew it."

"That's not the shocking part though," Curtis said. *"Hani Nesralla played a big part in that too. I hadn't thought about it when you woke me up in the middle of the night, but he was all over that. The sponsor was his roommate from MIT or something like that."*

"That can't be a coincidence," Carl said.

"And it may be nothing, but that's not all," Curtis went on. *"Your friend Betty Holloway interned as an analyst on that project while she was working on her thesis."*

"I'll be damned," Carl said. "Well I'll be damned."

The Unbroken Chain

The three friends were preparing for another call. Hani Nesralla was in his flat in Tehran with two babysitters in the room. The Iranians were unable to crack the encryption so they put people right in the room with him. He hadn't been left unattended during daylight hours for a few days now. Nesralla could assume they could both speak Arabic but as far as he could tell they couldn't speak English. He opened his computer and typed a few things, making it look like he was busy at some other task and he asked if one of them wouldn't mind making some tea. While one of them stood to go to the kitchen Nesralla surreptitiously sent a text over encrypted handheld device. It said, being watched by minders, let's do the call in English please.

Ahmed Tahlawi read the message in the business centre of his hotel in Bamako and texted OK back. Tahlawi was still shaken up from his helicopter being intercepted, and he was happy to be on firm ground. He had rented out the entire business centre to ensure privacy, and he was pacing around the large room gathering his robe tightly around him against the frigid air conditioning, intermittently snacking from the platter of cut fruit and waiting for the green icon to appear and start the call. He hadn't spoken to his friends since the incident and he had been feeling very alone in Mali.

Abdul-Aziz Al Sudeiri was back in Saudi Arabia. He had flown in from Jordan on a chartered private flight in the dead of night to avoid generating records of his arrival. He was waved through a checkpoint manned by one of his cousins and he was met in an employees only area by his personal driver who had been with him for over a decade. From the airport they drove straight through to Jeddah, which took nine hours. The custom luxury SUV was fitted with a first class air carrel, and Zuz configured it as a bed and slept most of the way. In Jeddah they pulled into the compound of a mansion on the corniche that had fifty foot tall walls surrounding it and no yard or garden. They parked two levels underground and Zuz used the elevator to get to the ground floor. He was sure there was no way anyone could know his whereabouts. He was in the lounge with the device set up on a stand when the green icon showed that the meeting was starting.

Each of them accepted and let the video feeds arrange their faces on each other's screens. Zuz and Tahlawi were surprised to see that Nesralla was growing a beard. They greeted each other in English and kept to English throughout the call.

Tahlawi started right in on Zuz.

"Why in hell were the Emirati air force sent to intercept me?" he asked.

"They have radar and they patrol their borders. It must have just been a routine encounter. They keep two jets in the Caliphate and they are constantly testing Sankara's airspace. It must be nothing more than that."

"We're glad you're well, my friend," Nesralla said, adding, "but now is the time we are all being asked to make sacrifices for our future." He panned the device to show the flat where he was kept, and to include the burly armed men who sat drinking tea and listening to a conversation they couldn't understand.

"Well," Zuz said, "we have to get those metals situated in Malitania. We are on the brink of playing out our final act. Initiating our last plan will drain our coffers of any remaining fungible assets and these metals will be all we have left."

He drank some tea and waited for them to interject. Once again they were taking their lead from him and they left him to finish his thought.

"By the time our final act is over we'll all be hunkered down there, hidden from the world and unknown to anybody around us. Once that final thing is done then we have fulfilled our purpose on earth and we spend through that gold, living like kings and watching a world of our making materialise before our very eyes."

He was rapt by his own speech, drinking his own kool aid. Tahlawi thought of the many times Zuz ridiculed religious zealots, saying how little their zeal mattered to the movement. Now here he was, bought into their plan that had taken on magical power somehow. Tahlawi was a critical thinker, even if he was a bit of a natural follower, but even he was starting to think there may be a divine hand at work in their machinations. America was embroiled in civil unrest that was disrupting commerce, provision of essential services and the functioning of government. European navies were destroying migrant vessels all along the coast of Africa and the eastern borders of the union were blatantly militarised. Traditional European populations were highly suspicious of foreigners and a reactionary movement was gaining momentum across western Europe. Israel had started a full scale war in the Palestinian lands and the Arab world appeared to be having an identity crisis. It was not difficult to imagine the final act separating Islamic and Judeo-Christian societies completely. Tahlawi knew exactly what Zuz meant when he alluded to the 'final plan'; Zuz was being cryptic on the slim chance that someone who could understand was listening, after all. The final plan still made Tahlawi's skin crawl. Was it something they absolutely had to do? It was truly biblical in scope, and this event would separate historical memory the way the plague defined the Middle Ages. Tahlawi wasn't a very religious man, in truth, but he did pause to wonder what would become of his eternal soul after they consummated the 'final plan'.

"We'll all be there soon enough," Zuz went on, "so we have to get the metals out there now. Our own people can only go as far as the Caliphate border. We've arranged for the mercenary unit from the compound to come to the border and escort you in."

"Those people I met when I was last there? The unit made up of only white Christians?" Tahlawi asked with raised eyebrows.

"Yes," Zuz said, "They don't know what your cargo is and they've been well paid to complete a job and not ask what is being transported. Their reputation has been tested for over a decade in the Sahel now, and they are a lot more trustworthy than the mob of foreign fighters who are drugging and whoring themselves into a frenzy."

"OK," Tahlawi said. "I'll meet the Russians." He became pensive and then said, "We can't think too badly of the brothers we've assembled to complete our work. We have promised them paradise for what they have agreed to do, and our Imams offered them spiritual liberty to begin enjoying the fruits of martyr's heaven here now."

They all agreed that the fighters assembled at the compound deserved forbearance and gratitude for the sacrifice they would make. They were difficult to be around, though, with their caprice with violence and their emphatic disregard for Islamic law and conventions of decency. They had reports that the men in Damascus and northern Nigeria were exactly the same.

The three spent the next fifteen minutes arranging the logistics of the meeting and transfer. The convoy traveling to the border would be heavily armed, but all local parties between the city and the border were made aware that there was a convoy passing through under the black flag. Each of them had been impressed and coerced, and then paid handsomely to ignore them. There would be no transfer of metal in the desert; the vehicles carrying the cargo would be refuelled, maintained and would carry on with the Russians back to the compound.

When that discussion was concluded Nesralla said that there was other business to catch up on.

"My friends here have given me an update on what they know of the project going on out there. They call it 'Digital Digs' and it is supposed to use new technology to spot and map ancient sites. According to their project plan, an AI program has identified that spot as a likely site for an ancient fortification."

They had a brief discussion of the likely technologies used and the kind of coding and models that might be available. They concluded that it was possible that it was a legitimate dig.

"They have a film crew with them," Nesralla said. "My contact at the British Museum said that the guy heading the project is a real archaeologist and the size of the presence matches what he'd expect."

He wasn't sure how the next piece of information would be received by his two friends. He was about to tell them that the Iranians helped him to split Digital Digs communications as well as providing the photos of the staff. Ever since he was 'hosted' by the Iranians they were getting more deeply entwined in the operations of the group. Zuz was bound to get his hackles up.

"My friends here have helped me to split data off one of their routers," he said. "They have been sending reports to the British Museum, the production company and the government of the Caliphate's ministry of antiquities. They found an ancient river that flowed right through Mai Zurfi. Now they're estimating the siltification trends or something to identify where the trading site and fortification would have been."

"Fascinating," Zuz said, "but who are they and what do we do about them being so close? Anything?"

Nesralla said, "This is what we could put together, from public info and intel in Sambokto."

He changed the meeting setting and they could all see rows of four passport sized photos displayed. He began to scroll and said that there were around eighty in all, and that only about ten of them were Caucasians. They needed to pass a fitness test to be allowed on the expedition and they all looked like they could have done it easily. He was just picking up speed on the scroll when Zuz interrupted.

"Stop right there. On that one. Wait, now go back up a couple. There. Wait."

Nesralla stopped scrolling when he saw what Zuz saw. Nesralla had looked at the pictures before the call but none stood out. Now that Zuz saw something, Nesralla thought he saw it too. It was a light skinned young woman with curly hair tied back, wearing no makeup. The photo was passport sized but it wasn't a passport photo. She was photographed secretly, and this one showed a three-quarter profile.

"Right," Nesralla said.

Tahlawi joked, "Is that your yoga teacher or your surf instructor or something?"

"I don't know who she is," Zuz said, "but she does look familiar."

"Now that you mention it," Nesralla said, "something about her rings a bell."

Tahlawi had no idea what they were talking about.

"I don't know," Zuz said, "I can't place her right now, but let's find out more about her."

"Will do."

They scrolled through the rest of the photos and none of them jumped out as odd. Nesralla showed where the camp was on the map, in relation to the compound and debriefed them on the count of staff and vehicles present. His opinion was that the camp was unusual but it wasn't necessarily dangerous. He said they'd keep an eye on it and they concluded the call.

Unmasking the Shadow

Harry and Khadija had been sneaking around the base for over two weeks now finding places to be alone. They were in their most comfortable hiding spot now, it was the opaque oxygen tent in the medical unit, where they had rolled down the privacy blinds. Aside from the attraction, they found that they enjoyed each other's company immensely. They lay quietly whispering to each other, talking about the base and the mission, since neither of them was a 'sweet nothings' kind of person.

"You know I've been out there twice," Khadija said.

"Out there?" he asked. *"Like out to the contractor's compound?"*

"Yes," she said, *"I went out with the local cleaners. I am a local, and I'm covered from head to toe. If I'm brought in as one of them then who is to know the difference?"* she said.

"Were you in danger?" he felt compelled to ask. They were all of them in danger all the time. What was he expecting for an answer?

"I'm never in danger," she said. *"I'm always in complete control."*

"Can you tell me about it?" Harry asked.

After a couple of weeks in the field, Harry's duties as logistics officer slowed down quite a bit. Mohammed Batu had been as good as his word. He was mostly overseeing shipments and making deals with local businessmen. Harry was included in all of the briefings, and he walked around armed, but he wasn't on one of the six teams and he wasn't expected to do any of that heavy lifting. To fill the empty time he stayed up to speed on the briefings and trained on all the gear until he could use every piece of lethal and nonlethal equipment to good effect. He had lost considerable muscle mass since leaving London. He was more agile and just as strong, but he had stopped lifting weights just to feel something hurt. Now his exercise focused on balance, resistance and muscle locks; he had traded in imposing for deadly.

"I could," she said, *"but you'll get it all in the briefing."*

"OK," he said, *"Just be sure to stay alert when you're out on operations."* As soon as he said it, he thought it sounded out of place.

A few hours later the leads and the core team met in the office container for the nightly briefing. Limier was there as Operations lead, and Horton, Rene, Mohammed Batu and Khadija were there. Batu took the lead, as usual, and said there were some developments and breakthroughs since their last briefing. The biggest thing was that the results of their scans were fully analysed and they had an almost perfect map of the compound. He put a picture up on the computer and it was a rendering of the compound as a blueprint. The images showed walls and tunnels. Each space within the building had a blurred shape of a specific size with either a red or blue hue of varying brightness. Batu explained that red was for expected combatants and blue was for expected noncombatants, and the brightness of the colour and size of the shape showed how many were there. They estimated around a hundred and ten fighting men, of whom roughly fifty were expected to be Russian mercenaries, according to the locals who did the cleaning. They found that the main kitchen was in the first level below ground, and there was unexpected egress from the kitchen and larder to the outside through a bulkhead in the external wall. It must have been for deliveries directly to the kitchen, and it was the only internal part of the building that touched the outside world that wasn't within a heavy machine-gun's field of fire. The defences they had seen from above and that they had photographed with drones appeared to still be in place.

They spent the next hour talking in hypotheticals, putting forth strategies and tactics to defeat a heavily defended position in the worst case. Carl Horton said that, contrary to popular belief, the U.S. wouldn't just drop bombs where innocents were unless they could definitively identify the two remaining targets, Al Sudeiri and Tahlawi. Batu explained that they had first person accounts of what was inside, and he began asking Khadija questions. The locals said that there were about fifty white mercenaries, who they confirmed were Russians, and the remainder were foreign fighters who could not speak Hausa but could speak Arabic. The Russians were preparing for an expedition somewhere deep in the wilderness, but the locals couldn't tell where. She said that the foreign fighters weren't disciplined, and they didn't form up or train like fighting units would. She said that, according to the locals, the foreign fighters were taking hard drugs and had to be separated from the women who served the VIPs upstairs. She also said that the white mercenaries and the foreign fighters had to stay far away from each other, because they were so recently on opposite sides of the battles, with the Russians working for the local governments against the black flag. The picture she painted wasn't one of a happy family all singing from the same hymn sheet.

Carl Horton listened as the British mercenary, the logistics officer, asked what they could be doing if not training and preparing for operations. Carl already had an idea. Intel from the other sites indicated that volunteers for martyrdom were beginning to receive their heavenly reward on earth. This tracked with the sex and drug use and the sense of supernatural entitlement reported in all sites. Carl knew more, too, of what they may be getting up to, because he had a direct call from Curtis Chase, personally. Curtis was a tech billionaire who didn't have time to make personal calls to operations contacts in the agency, but since they had met in Washington they seemed to have formed a connection that went beyond the typical office colleague dynamic. Chase and Horton were both products of the Christian Midwest. Chase had a typical Methodist upbringing where bringing the values of the church into your everyday life was emphasised. The democratisation of access to God was something he connected with at a young age, though he lived a largely secular lifestyle. He expected intelligent people who had access to a thorough moral education to live the golden rule. Horton was born and raised in Michigan. Most people's first associations with Michigan are with Detroit and Flint as rust belt bellwethers where the symptoms of America's decrepitude are on display. Rural Michigan is still very much the heartland, though, and Horton was raised in Gaylord in an evangelical household where his father was a part-time pastor. Horton's religious upbringing was focused on the personal relationship with God, but particularly with God's incarnation as Jesus. Horton was raised to believe it was his personal mission to connect everyone on earth to Jesus as a personal saviour, without whom no one could ascend to paradise. At a young age he married a woman whose beliefs were deeply evangelical. Horton pursued degrees to improve his earning potential and worked for the government to serve his nation, and as he was exposed to more diverse beliefs and points of view he was surprised to learn that people outside of the evangelical community could live their own truths and still be good people. Rather than this being a pleasant surprise for him, it sparked a sort of identity crisis. His wife and other evangelicals in their circle reinforced the belief that evangelicals were who they were because they were right, and that they were right because they were who they were. This self-fulfilling self-actuation put them in an iterative spiral that built their walls ever taller, their moats ever deeper and drove all 'others' ever further from their metaphorical promised land.

Curtis told Carl what was happening on the ground in their beloved Midwest. There was a reactionary movement of the far right that was gaining popularity and was emboldened to act publicly against all things foreign. Long and well established communities of immigrants were coming under physical threat, and there were marches and protests by the Heartland God and Country movement, which was made up almost exclusively of white supremacists who were now constantly and overtly armed. Heartland God and Country had mobilised militias for operations to locate and remove immigrants who the Republican presidential candidate said were 'poisoning the blood of the nation'. Some Asian-American communities reverted to the self-reliance which had allowed them to become established within a hostile white population to begin with, and armed for self-protection. There were strikes and widespread work stoppages and the apparatus of administering civil society was breaking down rapidly. The Republican presidential candidate declared falsely that there was overwhelming support for his candidacy and that the situation in the country required new leadership now, and that the country could not wait for an election. He called for a referendum to allocate executive powers to him so he could deal with the crises until power could be officially transitioned. Governors in states where the National Guard had already been called out deployed them to immigrant areas to separate the opposing parties, but many of the military leaders were white supremacists themselves and they placed their thumbs firmly and deftly on the far-right side of the scale.

Curtis Chase confided to Carl Horton that the Midwest they grew up in was gone, and he feared it may never return. Carl told Curtis, in candour, that there was now a full court press of foreign actors interfering in American politics and social discourse, and that those American people responsible for the covert and overt defence of the Constitution were no longer sure who could be trusted. Carl was so disheartened by what Curtis told him that he considered taking his family back to Michigan and hunkering down and protecting them until it all blew over. But that was when Curtis got to the real point of his call. In the model runs by Millenium Horizon every outcome was recorded and retained for posterity. Curtis had his people match out the model outcomes against scenarios observed in the real world and a few runs could be close enough matches. The ultimate outcomes of all of these were American isolationism and a militarised, fortress Europe. All of these runs had one final sequential event missing, and in the most-likely matched case to reality it was the meltdown of a civilian reactor or a military nuclear accident somewhere in Europe or America.

Carl Horton had gone cold. The cabal who met at Oxford were out there utilising and playing religious and secular organisations and movements like pieces on a chessboard. They had embedded assets for as long as decades before activating them for very specific nefarious ends, and they had an enormous cache of resources. They prosecuted successful operations once in London and twice in the United States. They appeared to have set the stage very purposefully and Carl could easily imagine several scenarios where a warhead could be detonated or a reactor made to meltdown. While they were still talking Carl could think of several very soft civilian power generation targets in the Midwest alone. There was no burying your head in the sand from this one. While they could strike anywhere in the western world, they may just render his homeland uninhabitable for a millennium, and they could kill his entire family in the process. Now, more than ever, it was imperative that they be stopped.

Dissemination of this information at the agency was above Carl's paygrade, and Curtis would be taking care of that. But Carl knew they had as good a chance as anyone of getting their quarry here in the Caliphate empty quarter and stopping them before they could hatch any more serious plots. Imagine if the horse soldiers had caught Bin Laden right after 9-11. Carl would keep this close to the vest and use what resources he had on hand to get into that compound and take them alive. They had thirty highly trained and well equipped professional soldiers with specific areas of expertise. They had some of the newest technology developed by the soldier centre in Needham and by Curtis Chase's new projects. They had the element of surprise, as far as he knew, and they had very detailed electronic and human intel. The compound was highly defensible, with heavy machine gun positions and battle tested veteran mercenaries planning its defence. If La Lance made it inside they would then need to contend with zealots who had little regard for their own lives, far outnumbering the entirety of La Lance. Storming the compound was out of the question, but they did have options. The Russians going out on an expedition was fortuitous. They could ambush them and pare their numbers down. If they could get eyes-on confirmation that Tahlawi and Al Sudeiri were inside then they could call in an airstrike and eliminate every living thing in the compound, regardless of what the Emiratis said.

Carl stopped his rumination and his attention returned to the room, and he answered the British mercenary.

"They may well be keeping their human assets under close watch, keeping them ready to sacrifice themselves when the time comes. That means those Russian mercenaries are the fighting force. We need to remove their capability to defend the compound."

He looked from person to person in the room. Clearly, he was proposing something they hadn't yet fully considered. He went on, to push his point.

"It's imperative that we capture Tahlawi and Al Sudeiri," he said. *"New intelligence shows they're raising the stakes. Not only do we have to take them alive, but we have to do it fast, too."*

Mohammed Batu spoke up. *"Do we know when they're heading out?"*

At this point Carl, as the most senior person from the agency, had buy-in from the group for his providing direction. This whole operation was led by the Emirates since this was Caliphate territory and the removal of the Islamists was the objective, but Carl was exercising America's soft power to usurp leadership. If everything worked out then all objectives would be achieved anyway, and he didn't feel bad about it.

Others chimed in and they had a very public discussion about how to lay an ambush for up to fifty well equipped mercenaries. Khadija's firsthand information was very useful. On several occasions Carl had to stop the conversation to remind people that the human wave attacks in Ukraine were not done by the same people, and that the units within the walls of the compound were smart and brave to the point of recklessness. They would be a formidable opponent.

Mohammed Batu took the La Lance Fournie leaders to the mess to plan the ambush and they left the intelligence people in the office. Harry went with Batu to contribute to the planning, even though he was a support person and wouldn't be on the mission. They laid a topographical map of the area on the table and took out the photographs they had of the vehicles and weaponry that had from drones and from Khadija. The compound had been resupplying from trucks that came out of the Badlands and through low hills that were occupied by the local indigenous tribe. To call the topography low hills was not precise enough. The low rises in land were scarps and mesas where the faces of the rise may be entirely sheer. The compound obviously had a deal with the tribe that the Islamists didn't have, because their vehicles came through unmolested. They would set up the ambush along the normal supply route, with each team acting as a set 'pounce' point and then as mobile units that could be repositioned as needed. Since they may well be outnumbered, they needed to be able to outflank the convoy and fight on ground of their choosing as the encounter developed. It was a good plan, and their shoulder fired rockets and mobile machine guns they would have a good chance of incapacitating the vehicles on the first volley.

After the broader plan was agreed, team leaders met with their teams to brief them on the mission and to start preparations. Betty came into the mess and asked Harry if he was free to join the intel team back in the office, and Harry followed her there. They went in and he saw that Rene, Horton, and Khadija were already there.

"Is the gang all here?" Horton asked. Betty nodded in reply.

"Thanks for joining us," Horton said to Harry. *"We want to ask for your help with something. Batu said you would be free to help and Betty tells me that you are a capable person."*

"Alright," Harry said, *"what do you need?"*

"We want to test some equipment that's straight out of the workshop. We have these new guns that are set up on automatic response, and we want to see if they work," Horton said.

"What does 'automatic response' mean?" Harry asked, his curiosity piqued.

"Well," Horton said, *"these are supposed to act as an unmanned machine gun nest. They use motion detection, gyroscopes, laser sighting and AI to acquire and eliminate targets without human intervention."*

"Well that hardly seems sporting," Harry said in as droll a manner as he could. So this was the product launch for the fighting robot. *"Are they mobile?"* he asked.

"They're not mobile. I have a picture of one here, and there are three of them waiting to be put together in one of the supply tents," Horton said, pointing to the cleared-off desk under the wall map.

Harry stepped over and had a look. There was a blueprint with several system-specific schematics and there was a CGI rendering of one of the units completely assembled. It looked to be the size of an oil drum suspended within a globe shaped set of metal rails, and it had as much mass in electronics as it had in gun. Harry immediately thought that it would be too fickle to work in the hot, sandy Sahel. In his experience anything with small moving parts that needed to be lubricated and grit free were functional less than half the time, really. He said so, and Horton told him that it had already been tested in similar conditions in Arizona and that it held up well. It was built to be as durable as possible, with hardened, closed flexible tubes and armoured casings protecting sensitive machinery.

"Once this gun starts to kick, this thing will roll all over the desert," Harry said.

"Look at this rendering on the next page," Horton said as he turned the page on the blueprint packet. There was a rendering of the gun deployed in a CGI landscape. It was mounted atop a large square bag that was made up of high strength nylon strands, just like the 'builder's bags' back home.

"You need to dig a hole to store the ammunition below the level of the unit, and you put that dug earth into the bag that serves as its anchor," Horton pointed out the individual details with his index finger.

Horton took out his phone and turned on a short video, showing it to Harry. *"This is it in action in Arizona."*

Harry watched the video. It was the middle of the day in a desert, and the globe was set up atop the bag of dirt, next to a hole in the ground into which the belt of ammunition disappeared. A narrator with an American accent pointed out four remote controlled vehicles at various distances in the foreground. The narrator explained that the gun should detect motion and laser sight on the source of the motion, and that they would test it at increasing distances. Then, the closest vehicle activated and advanced toward the gun. The gun whirred, pointed to the vehicle and let out a burst of gunfire that destroyed it. There was a pause, a discussion of the points of functionality, and the subsequent test at greater distance. The gun worked for each test with the furthest being roughly one hundred and fifty yards away. Harry was impressed, and a little scared if he was honest with himself. People could be the most horrific monsters, but not everybody was. Sometimes humanity could show itself on the battlefield, but there could be no mercy or compassion from a machine. This was the inevitable future, but was it really progress?

The video then reset, with new remote controlled vehicles positioned among the detritus of their predecessors. The voice explained that a simultaneous attack test would be done by sending all of the vehicles at once. After a brief pause all of the vehicles advanced on the gun and they were destroyed in turn, beginning with the nearest. Harry noticed that the gun stopped between acquiring targets, that it appeared to be able to lead a target, and the average time between detection and destruction was no longer than a few seconds, even in the open landscape. After a brief discussion of the result the video switched to drone footage and the voice explained there would be a test of the gun with movement in 360 degrees. Twelve targets advanced on the gun from twelve spots around the midpoint at varying distances from the gun. They were all activated at once but they were given erratic stop and start times and varying paths to the gun. The gun swung at top speed and the whirring motors made nearly as much noise as the gun itself. Twice during this portion of the demonstration the gun ceased firing to allow for the barrel to cool. After no longer than three minutes the targets were all neutralised.

"What do you call this?" Harry asked.

"We're calling it 'the trebuchet'," Horton answered.

"And you want us to do what with it, exactly?" Harry prodded.

"We want to take it out in a live environment to see how usable it is and how it performs. There's a lot of setup; we want to know if the juice is worth the squeeze," Horton responded.

"On the ambush with the guys?" Harry needed to know what the ask was. He looked from Khadija to Betty and back again. Neither had any real reaction during all of this, which made Harry think they had already seen the demonstration and they knew the plan. Rene had been nodding along in agreement, reinforcing the feeling that Harry was being read in.

"No," Horton said, "we're going to set up somewhere different. Have a look at this map."

Horton stepped behind the table and pointed at the map on the wall above it. Harry noticed that it was the same topographical map being used in the mess by La Lance.

"Supplies have been coming out of the Badlands in the east via the border with Mali. This area of low hills is occupied, by a local tribe. Convoys go through here with no problems, so that's where your buddies are going to set up the trap," Horton said.

"Right," Harry said, "we were just talking about that before you called me in."

"Yes," Horton said. "Only, this isn't a supply run. It's happening at a strange time and it is being purposefully planned and they're sending ten times as many armed men, and we think up to four vehicles."

Harry nodded and actively listened.

"Whatever they are carrying this time, it must be important. If they didn't want to go through ambush country then they'd have to come around the hills to the north here," Horton indicated the area on the map. "Then they'd come down this caravan route southwest to the compound."

Horton waved his fingers from point to point.

"We'll set up a trebuchet on either side of the caravan route and position some mines to drive them right into them," Horton concluded.

"And you want us to be out there with up to fifty men with just these two little machines," Harry said.

"Uh huh," came the reply, *"three, actually."*

"You know if we get caught out there and one of those machines fails then we're dead," Harry said. *"Just dead."*

"If we needed to then we could pull some smoke and mirrors and bug out pretty clean, I think. But it won't come to that," Horton said. *"So are you in?"*

Harry had to think about it for a minute. Rene probably wasn't going along, but both of the ladies would need to be there to run the guns. That didn't seem like putting the right skill set to the right job.

"Who is going to be there, exactly?" Harry asked.

"Good question," Horton said. *"We have some muscle from Sombokto to help out on this."* Horton nodded at Rene in thanks. *"Each of you three will be in charge of a position run by you and an Emirati gunner. I'll be here coordinating on a satellite frequency they can't jam. If need be, there's egress through a secured landing zone that you should be able to reach."*

Harry weighed the pros and cons even though he knew what the answer would be. As long as his daughter, his own flesh and blood, was going to be out in a hole in the desert setting a trap for battle-tested, professional mercenaries then he was going to be there too.

"Alright," Harry said, *"I'm in."*

Harry had to cross the camp to get to his quarters to prepare for the outing. Each of the barrack tents had a six-man team inside making preparations for the night's operation. Harry could hear the banter in French and the noises of gear being hoisted and jostled. He had a moment of real nostalgia for his days in the Legion. The Legion, like the British army, gave him an escape from dire circumstances and had saved him, as a person. But the Legion demanded that every soldier relinquish his individuality to strengthen the unit. Paradoxically, the person he became was very much the person of the corps. Though the men in those tents were preparing for imminent danger, he envied them. There were no liabilities in any of the teams, no one who would need to be babysat. Each was a competent and credible professional and each would commit to the objectives of the mission even above their personal safety. With the test that they had ahead of them, they would have to rely on their comrades with their very lives; none would have such a night as this again. Harry arrived at his bunk and sat heavily on it. He gave himself five minutes with his thoughts before he started to gear up.

Baited and Trapped

Sheikh Ahmed Tahlawi waited with an armed convoy of four vehicles at a temporary camp near the border between Mali and the Caliphate of Malitania. He was escorted by two armed men loyal only to him and his two friends as well as an armed contingent of men under the black flag. The sun was just going down, and they had refuelled the two vehicles that would be continuing the journey out into the emptiness. They kept pinging the frequency their escorts would appear on and waited for them to arrive. Tahlawi was expecting three vehicles carrying twenty armed Russian mercenaries. They would make contact, refuel the Russians' vehicles, coordinate procedures for movement through the dark and set off for the compound taking the Tuareg caravan route around the foothills, heading southwest. The Russians would be coming through the foothills as if they were on a supply run, but once they arrived at the rendezvous they would take the new direction back, to confuse any would-be attackers. Also, the weight of the vehicles carrying the gold would be too great to make it through some of the moonscape terrain of the low mesas.

Tahlawi hated to wait, generally, and waiting out in the open surrounded by murderous zealots was worse. No one was told their cargo, but they knew it wasn't a scheduled supply run and the vehicles were heavily burdened with such a small load in size. He didn't want them to have the chance to explore their curiosity. When the sun began to set the ping came in that the Russians were thirty minutes out. They pinged back and in only a few minutes they could see the pinpoints of the headlights bouncing along the horizon. The three vehicles pulled up and Tahlawi saw that they were hard sided vehicles but they weren't armoured. These were transports rather than armoured vehicles. He hoped that would be sufficient. The Russians got out long enough to stretch, relieve themselves and refuel the trucks. They stayed close to their vehicles because they didn't want to interact with the Islamists who they were fighting a mere two months ago. Tahlawi spoke with their leader, in English, and it was decided that two of the Russians' vehicles would lead, followed by the two trucks that were continuing on with Tahlawi, then the final Russian vehicle carrying mercenaries. They set out, following their satellite navigation systems and their augmented lighting to travel through the desert in the dead of night. As ominous as the undertaking appeared, the caravan route was not difficult to follow and the road was discernible, passable and flat as far as they travelled. Though their pace was slow, progress was consistent into the night.

The convoy had rounded the hills and was headed southwest when they were first picked up. Betty had control of the drones and they were following the caravan track north to the end of their range, turning around and returning to recharge. Before one set of drones would turn back the other would be enroute. Betty had sent four sets of drones after sunset from her dugout below her trebuchet. She had Harry and Khadija on the headsets locally and she had a satphone link to Horton back at the base. They had been talking fairly regularly and reporting on the challenges with setup and the performance of the trebuchet system in sandy conditions thusfar. No one expected they would be getting any real contact, and they talked about turning them on to test the motion detection against movement of any wildlife. Betty explained again that they were set to a master switch that activated the roadside bomb and the array of claymore mines. Switching them on would be very, very loud and destructive. They were unpleasantly surprised when the fifth sortie of drones detected headlights and movement.

"Shit," Betty said into the headset, *"they're really coming this way!"*

"We see them," Harry said. *"Let them come. It looks like they are walking right into the trap."*

Harry was beside himself with the surrealistic nature of his situation. He was in a hole in the ground in the desert in West Africa, tending to a death machine above him, fed from an oil drum filled with one continuous ammunition belt of thirty calibre rounds. His new girlfriend was in a hole on the other side of the road and his daughter was in a hole in the middle of the road behind him. While the unlikelihood and absurdity of it could get the mind trapped in an introspection loop, there was no time to focus on anything except trying to stay alive.

"Insh'Allah this contraption works," Khadija said into her set.

They kept close watch as the convoy crept closer. It was going much slower than they expected.

"They're going so slowly," Betty said. *"It's going to be a while until they reach the explosives. I'm going to send up the thermal imaging drones to see if we can learn anything new."*

She put her head out of the hole and told her Emirati partner to send the first sortie of three thermal imaging drones, and he did.

Time passed interminably slowly as the convoy crept closer. Through their devices they could see the lead vehicle come into focus and the vehicles behind came into view. The first thermal images also came onto their devices. There had been hours since sundown, and the day's heat had drained out of the big rocks, making the heat signature for a human being stand out distinctly. After the drones made their pass, they could see that the first two and the last vehicles were filled with fighters, and the middle two only had drivers and two passengers.

"They can't hear the drones over the sound of their own engines," Betty said.

Sitting in the third vehicle laden down with gold, Sheikh Ahmed Tahlawi was unaware of a trap laid for them. They had taken an unused route and were scanning the road in front with telescopic, night vision binoculars and so far there was nothing out of place. He just wanted to make it to the compound and get the gold stored in the vault before the people inside were awake and curious. He was extremely apprehensive, but he was looking forward to being secured in the compound's underground bunkers.

Through the cameras set up at ground level, Harry and Khadija could see the headlights approaching. Amazingly, they were sticking generally to the known road. Then with their own eyes and ears they could see the lightening of the area caused by the headlights and they heard the labouring of the engines in a low gear. They were well within range for deadly effect of the rebuchets.

"The last vehicle is nearing the starting gun. We're going to put every kamikaze drone in the sky. Stay in your holes and get ready for the fireworks," Betty said into the headset.

Betty pressed the big red button on the circuit board and when it went flat the one adjacent to it turned red, meaning the circuit was enabled. She pressed the other flat and the button on the other side of the board showed green light. When she pressed that one all of the explosives detonated and all three of the trebuchets snapped into immediate action. The sound of the roadside bomb drowned out everything else at first, and when that reverberation travelled out across the desert the reports of the claymore mines were cast as echoes. The guns were firing so rapidly that they sounded like enormous sewing machines, and inside the dugouts below them a monsoon of hot metal casings rained down a percussive soprano. Under this metal rain Betty piloted the drones onto the vehicles one after another. The low crumping of their detonations was now accompanied by the screams of the survivors. From inside their holes they could tell that vehicles were on fire. The guns fell silent and they heard people shouting to each other in Russian. Then, intermittently, one of the trebuchets would send a rapid spray of fire somewhere into the night. Then there was no sound for a long time.

"I'm sending up a thermal imaging drone to survey the area," Betty said. From within her position she sent one up and used it to make low sweeps. Most of the useful views were washed out in the heat of the fires. *"These heat signatures are illegible,"* she said.

Then, unexpectedly, a burst of automatic weapons fire rang out in the night and Harry heard impacts around his position. His trebuchet came to life with a response. Silence.

"How long do you think we should wait before we take any action?" Khadija asked into her headset.

"We have about two hours until sunrise," Betty responded, *"let's wait until then."*

"Roger that."

"Copy"

Then they sat listening to the anguish of dying men until the sun came up. At daybreak Betty sent the thermal imaging drone again, and by then the fires had died down. The bodies laying out on the field had grown cold. As far as they could tell there was only one strong heat signature in the wreck of the vehicle that had been third in line.

Horton, who had been on the line with Betty throughout the night, advised them to put on full body armour and carry assault weapons to inspect the scene. Betty turned off the trebuchets, threw a can outside to verify that they were inactive, and climbed out of the hole. Khadija and Harry also came out of their positions, as did their Emirati counterparts.

They emerged to a scene of absolute devastation and carnage. The Sahelian sunrise, framing the ghastly scene, was magnificent as always. Harry thought that this was a very fitting end for a warrior who lived the code.

The front vehicle was raked by machine gun fire from both sides and it appeared that no one within had survived. After the effects of the trebuchets and the bombing by the kamikaze drone, it was hard to tell where one combatant ended and another began. As horrible as the gore was, they could at least be sure that there were no survivors in that vehicle. In the second vehicle the driver was dead behind the wheel and there were three bodies around it at differing distances, indicating that some had made it further than others. They all wore full body armour and two had fatal wounds in places not covered, such as the face and neck. The third appeared to have taken a full burst to the chest, and while the body armour was not catastrophically compromised, its wearer had expired. Human bodies were not made to withstand that much trauma and his heart could have stopped, his back could have broken, his vital organs could have split. Betty verified that he was dead and moved on. There appeared to be bodies around the furthest vehicle to the back, which was bombed, and there was an unarmoured body on the far side of the fourth vehicle, which still had small flames licking from the flammable material not yet consumed.

Harry was the first to approach the third vehicle. It had been raked by fire from a trebuchet, and while the vehicle was disabled, there was heavy plating around the cab. There was a conscious man in the back seat and the doors had been misshapen by the blast of the kamikaze drone, warping two permanently closed and leaving the front passenger's side and rear driver's side swinging on their hinges and banging against a chassis they no longer fit. Harry swung the door open with the muzzle of his assault rifle and kept it trained on Tahlawi. A heavy strongbox in the middle of the cab had come apart and there were bars of glinting gold strewn about the floor and seats. This man with the ash smudged face and the bleeding ears sat atop a fortune like a dragon on his hoard.

In his ear, Harry heard Betty's voice say, *"That's Ahmed Tahlawi. From the briefings."* Harry assumed she was addressing him because he was the one facing the survivor, but there was no response from anyone. Betty explained further, *"Mastermind of London and Hoover Dam, etc."* Then Harry made the connection. Out loud he said, *"Goddamn. It is you."*

Tahlawi had been shocked and surprised when the attack happened. They were not expecting an attack of this sort and they were unprepared for it. Although he knew there was danger in what he was involved in, he was not a jihadist or a warrior so he had no training to fall back on, no muscle memory for crises. He froze in shock and was really surprised when he survived the onslaught. He could see muzzle flashes from guns somewhere in the near distance, and there were beams of laser light but there were no tracer rounds. Whenever one of the mercenaries moved to flank or made a run for it he drew fire. Tahlawi figured out that there were no humans targeting the guns, and he decided to stay stock still and survive. After the nearby impact of the drone he didn't think he could move anyway. He sat in shock, resigned to the fact that he had been caught and that Zuz and Nesralla would have to continue the fight while he rotted away in Guantanamo Bay. When the sun finally rose he could see the devices set up to wreak the havoc on the convoy. Finally he could see the enemy combatants emerge from their defensive trenches and work their way through the carnage on the ground. He stayed stock still until an enemy soldier approached and held him at gunpoint. He could see that he was Caucasian and that he wasn't a particularly young man, so he assumed he must be an officer. Now was the time for Tahlawi to give himself up. The soldier's face registered shock and rage and he said something Tahlawi couldn't hear because his ears were still ringing. Tahlawi said that he couldn't hear anything in both English and French, and he adjusted his position to begin to descend from the wrecked vehicle.

Once Betty told Harry that Tahlawi was one of the ones responsible for the London attack he recognised the face. Once he recognised the face the rage burned through him in an instant. He relived all of the emotions of dragging himself out of the wreck of the UBI office and fleeing with his life and leaving his family behind once more. He was again, instantly consumed with rage and with shame, and here in front of him was one of the people directly responsible. Harry had said out loud, *"Goddamn. It is you,"* and the terrorist said something back and shifted his weight and pushed his hand down next to him on the seat. Harry pulled the trigger and let out a burst of automatic fire that tore his unarmoured body into large chunks that spattered red drops onto the glimmering ingots of gold.

"No!" Betty and Khadija both cried in unison.

Cage of Secrets

Harry sat on the edge of his cot in his unit at the camp. It was a large tent with rigid elements rooted to steel foundations sunk in the earth, and the walls were a woven canvas material that was pliable. He had rolled up the walls so only screens separated him from the camp behind him and the open savannah ahead of him. The heat of the day had arrived, and though the air was dry the baking heat was a heavy weight pressing down on everything he did. The dressing down he received from the American weighed heavy on his mind, and the anger it induced kept his body in a state of agitation. Horton was livid that he'd killed Tahlawi and he laid into Harry for having made such a boneheaded mistake. Harry explained that they were on a dangerous operation in which they were purposefully opposing a much greater force, and that his pulling the trigger was a reaction to the terrorist's reaching for a weapon, or so he thought. Horton didn't listen, and went on ranting invective with no point to make. When he crossed into insulting Harry personally, Harry stepped close enough to look down on him and raise his own voice to make it clear that interpersonal issues would be dealt with on a personal basis, and that Horton should consider carefully if he really wanted to go down that route. Mohammed Batu got between them and asked Harry to wait in the mess until the debrief was completed, which he did. When Batu came in he was visibly angry, but not with Harry. Apparently Batu stood up for Harry, and made it clear that Horton's actions were unprofessional. Unfortunately though, the Americans were in a position of significant influence with the Emirati government, and they were pulling the strings even if the Emiratis were paying for it. Horton had insisted that Harry be reassigned with immediate effect, and Batu had to comply. Batu told Harry that he had to go back to Marseilles and do the required mental health sessions following an active operation. Batu told him that he could keep whatever gold he had carried away from the wrecks, even though there had been no mention of gold before. And so here Harry was, loading his rucksack sitting open-topped on his bed, baking listlessly in the African heat while his restless mind couldn't keep still. It was closing in on midday and the adrenaline from the dawn action wouldn't subside, so he was symbolically packing even though there was no transport for forty-eight hours.

Khadija, Rene, Betty and Carl Horton were inside the office container completing the debrief from the action. Betty could tell that Carl was in a heightened emotional state. Her training in Virginia told her people in this state may make rash or unadvisable decisions. She could also tell from his line of questioning and frequent and visible distraction that he was in crisis management mode. Betty and Khadija just came out of a significant action out on the plain and they thought the crisis was over. Horton's behaviour wasn't filling them with confidence.

In Carl Horton's head he was calculating the time it would take for word of the ambush to make it back to the compound. Then he was calculating the available vehicles and their top speeds in this terrain. Then he was estimating combat effectiveness of the remaining La Lance personnel against that of a man willing to sacrifice himself for his cause. No, he thought, they couldn't expect to take the compound in a full assault, and he wouldn't try. He had to know who was inside there, and he expected that Al Sudeiri was already there. If he could get verification that Al Sudeiri was there then he could call in an aerial bombing to completely destroy the compound and probably everyone in it. That would be the best outcome. But to achieve it somebody had to get inside the compound and get visual confirmation, because nobody was moving around the compound and they couldn't get photographic evidence.

The two women in the room with him were the only assets on hand, so they would have to do it. They already had an 'in' because Khadija had been going in regularly with the local cleaning crew; a bit of baksheesh and Betty could go along. He knew they were likely to be very tightly wound after the dawn action, but they were both professionals. Carl calculated the likelihood of solving the final terrorist plot if they didn't have Al Sudeiri to provide any information. He didn't like the odds, but he had to weigh them against the likelihood of their plot succeeding if Al Sudeiri escaped the compound. He couldn't let that happen. He had to trust that they could figure it out after Al Sudeiri was taken off the board.

"Listen," he said to them, *"somebody has to go into the compound to get visual confirmation of who is in there."*

It was a lot to hang on them. They were silent for a few seconds. Betty spoke first.

"Khadija has only ever been in the kitchen and service are. How are we supposed to gain access to areas where VIPs are holed up?"

"I can't tell you that on this one," he said. *"We can't miss the window to get in there before news of the ambush breaks. Once you're inside you'll have to think on your feet. We need to know who is in there. It's key to avoiding a new, bigger threat."* He knew what he just said sounded odd, but he knew they would follow.

"I just got an idea," Khadija said, *"We get Betty on the cleaning crew. We clean normally until we get to the quarters of the women entertainers. Betty changes into one of their costumes and just makes one pass through the floor. That is all she could get and expect to still get away without causing any upset."*

"Jesus Christ," Carl said. *"I know what this is. But, Betty, can you do it?"*

"If it's as important as you say it is, then yes."

"Alright," he said, *"let's get this planned,"* and he opened his laptop and they crowded around.

∎∎∎

A Hiace van had been converted to carry a cleaning crew and their supplies, but it was still decorated with hanging baubles and 'Insh'Allah' was painted brightly across the strip above the windshield. The road to the compound was straight but largely untended, and the van rattled against washboard ruts of potholes the whole way. The windows were down and what breeze there was didn't compensate for the full coverage that Khadija and Betty had to wear, including masks of net for the eyes. The sound of the winding engine poured in through the windows while the shudder of the bouncing chassis surrounded them from below. They each had short wave headsets under their headgear on a frequency they knew would not be jammed. They practiced communicating through the microphones as they drove. They could send and receive loud and clear.

Eventually they approached the compound and Betty found it rose ominously out of the horizon. It wasn't an enormous building but it was bigger than anything else around it, so it appeared huge. There was the main building and one or two small outbuildings, and an eight foot high block wall surrounded the whole compound with closed gates on either end. As they approached the walled compound itself she could see there was razor wire across the top of the wall and out front there were guard towers flanking the front driveway. But they weren't going to the front. They approached from an angle and turned right round the rear corner of the building and pulled up next to the bulkhead that led to the kitchen, one floor below ground. The driver said something into the walkie talkie in a language Betty did not understand and the bulkhead made the sound of heavy locks disengaging. The cleaning crew got out of the van and unloaded their supplies. After the bulkhead swung open heavily, two armed men came out and talked to the man who led the cleaning crew, speaking the local language. There was some back and forth and Betty was aware that something was being resolved. Khadija must have read her mind because she whispered into the headset, *"They're not happy with the constant switching of workers."*

Betty could see that their weapons were shouldered on straps, pointing down. There was no attitude of alertness here, so she stayed quiet like the rest of the women and waited. Eventually the two men waved the crew down into the bulkhead to the level below ground. Khadija had told Betty what to expect, so she wasn't surprised, but stepping out of the bright openness down into dark containment felt claustrophobic. The women put all of the cleaning supplies in the centre of the kitchen floor and stood to the side. While their eyes adjusted the men walked by poking at the supplies as a show of vigilance. Betty found it ironic because they just knowingly admitted two poorly vetted strangers. Again she was amazed how the right incentive provided to the right cog could divert an entire operation.

Once her eyes adjusted she could see institutional block walls lit by institutional neon tube lighting, appliances where you would expect them, doors on the far walls. The crew leader barked some orders in the local language and the two armed men exited through a far door. To Betty, this was mistake number two. Common security protocol required armed escort of strangers. Okay, this mosaic was coming into focus. The people inside the walls may be highly trained professional soldiers but the people responsible for security of the site itself were not. She just might have a chance at this.

Khadija explained through the headset that they were supposed to start there, in the kitchen and then break up into groups of two and take different rooms. Khadija said that this was the routine, so there was nothing to worry about. Khadija stayed with Betty and steered her to the right tasks and they worked together on everything. Khadija felt good about it until Betty had to reach to dust something high and her sleeve fell to her shoulder, revealing the lightness of her skin. She immediately dropped her arms so the abaya covered to her wrist again, hoping no one had seen. Khadija saw a woman take notice, but she didn't make any comment or change what she was doing. They waited for the head of the cleaning crew to give his approval that the kitchen was clean, and they moved to different rooms. Khadija took hold of Betty's abaya sleeve and led her quickly to the serving women's quarters. The whole basement level had an institutional feel throughout. There were grey block walls with neon tube lighting, and to Betty it looked like it was probably built by a foreign contractor. Wiring and lighting looked European, and the doors were thin wood, for privacy and not protection. Through a door to the left they found a short hall with stairs up, and a door in the near wall at the far end of the hall. Khadija went up the stairs and straight through a door at a small landing and Betty followed. They found themselves in another dimly lit institutional room with three sets of bunk beds along the far wall. There were temporary closets made from tubing and canvas and there were metal storage chests at the foot of each bed. It looked like a dozen young women lived there.

"There's a bathroom through that door in the far corner. Grab something that you can make fit and I'll stand watch."

They both started going through the tubing closets and the chests until they found the largest of what Khadija had described as the servers' uniform. It was form-fitting yoga pants looking thing with a cropped blouse of similar material. It was the opposite of modest and she remarked that the Islam she knew was not held within these walls. Khadija hurried her to the bathroom, where she stood at the mirror and removed her abaya hood to see her made-up face and hairdo to match the servers' tight bun. She got into someone else's dirty uniform and tried not to think about the laundry. When she came back out she looked like one of the serving women, but there were only twelve of them and Betty was an ethnic match for maybe only one or two.

"Alright, just like we planned," Khadija said. *"Through that door,"* she nodded at a door at the interior corner, *"and you'll come into the drinks kitchen. Grab something that looks like it gives you a reason the be there and go out the opposite door."*

Betty was listening intently and nodding along. This was the plan they had hatched and agreed. She had it committed to her impeccable memory but this last deep breath standing face to face with a comrade was valuable. Betty needed to settle her nerves because she needed to put on the performance of a lifetime. Khadija went on.

"Now, when you come out of the drinks kitchen you'll be in the muffrage. If you cross the muffrage to the exact opposite of the door you came in then you'll find the staircase down to the main kitchen again. I'll have your abaya waiting for you there and we get back in time for cocktails on the patio."

"Right," Betty said, *"I'll see what I can find out."*

"Listen, you're not going to dawdle up there. Walk through at as fast a pace as you can without attracting attention and get out of there. That's it."

Betty lowered her chin and tilted her head to one side. The long dangling earring she wore lay against the top of her shoulder and she whispered into it, *"stay with me,"* and

Khadija heard it in her earpiece. Betty went through the door and tried to make it look like she was hurried with a task in case anybody was in the room when she entered. No one was there but she could see refrigerators and sinks and there were plenty of trays, ashtrays, glasses and tumblers. She told Khadija what she saw, knowing that Khadija could not respond.

"I'm taking this tray and going through now," she said into the earring, and pushed through the door with her hip, holding the tray of three drinks and two clean ashtrays level. The muffrage was air-conditioned and the cool air hit her. The décor and the lighting here were not at all industrial. It was carpeted and panelled and there was a long open runway to the opposite door that passed by both the entry and exit stairs to the recessed area. There were circular booths upholstered in leather scattered about the top tier. Because the floor plan was open she could see all the booths, but the booths were high-backed and she couldn't see everyone who sat around each table. From the people she could see, she recognised three who were face cards in the agency's deck. She was clear enough of other people to say that into the earring.

There were several other serving women either at or making their way around the tables, but there couldn't have been more than five or six. She had just come from both of the other places they would be. She wondered where they were and how they would collect them if they needed to evacuate innocents. She made a quick tactical plan to get a look at the people in the booths. She would approach each booth at an obvious angle to see inside, under the pretence that she was offering clean ashtrays. As she approached each booth the men inside sometimes looked up at her but no one seemed to pay her any mind. She got through four booths and had to change two ashtrays and between booths she told Khadija who was there. There were very dangerous wanted men who were nowhere on the map as far as the agency was concerned. This was already a major win, but she didn't see Al Sudeiri and she didn't see anybody in the recessed area. If she descended that stairwell then there would be at least a few seconds where she would absolutely be the centre of attention. She took a deep breath and decided she would commit to a breeze through to collect ashtrays only, glancing and leaving as quickly as she could. She said as much to Khadija through the earring. On the other end, Khadija's warnings got no further than her thoughts. This was far beyond the risk level in the plan they had agreed. Khadija tried to warn her away through force of will, but that is all she could do.

Betty put on a big smile and descended the stairs holding the tray just below shoulder level. There were about eight men sitting around the large, low round table, some smoking from shishas and some not. Still approaching the table she could see that they were all known and wanted men, and that one of them was Hani Nesralla's bodyguard from the poetry reading in Paris. Her heartrate began pounding in her ears and her anxiety level rose to near panic. The bodyguard looked at her and held his gaze.

"What the hell do you have on your feet?" he said out loud in English. She tried to smile and stand and turn for the stairs. She forgot that she had the sandals of the cleaners on. She hadn't even tried to find footwear in the women's quarters. That could have been a fatal mistake, she realised.

"Stop!" he said in English again. He seemed to have an American accent. *"I know you from somewhere!"*

She turned fully and carried on up the same stairs she had just come down, increasing her pace as she went. The man stood and shouted loudly, *"Stop her!"*

Khadija heard that over the list of names Betty was spitting out loudly and breathy enough for her earring to pick it while she was ascending stairs. Several men stood from the booths she was approaching and moved toward her. She kept a brisk pace and headed back toward the door through which she arrived, as the way to the opposite door was blocked by the rising men. As she crossed the empty floor her sandals slapped faster and faster against the soles of her feet and men rose from wherever they were. The other serving women receded to the walls along the side and stood rigid with their arms crossed, like they did whenever they expected violence. Betty was set upon and held fast, and she had to think fast to come up with tactics for a game where she was caught by the Islamists.

In the kitchen below, Khadija's heart sank. She hoped it wouldn't come to this. She hid Betty's abaya under her own when the alarms and the flurry of activity began. The two armed men nearby took up their weapons and headed up the stairs. Khadija started a general cry from the small group of covered women, keening in the local language, *"Take us out of here, take us home before it gets dangerous! We won't let these unholy men near us!"* directed at the cleaning crew boss. He put up his hands to try to calm the encroaching circle of women, but he too got swept up in the panic and said they were leaving immediately. Khadija encouraged this and intentionally goaded the most fearful of the women to keep them moving frantically. They exited the bulkhead door and flew into the van without carrying any equipment, and they drove off into the Sahel, staying well away from the fields of fire of the gun towers on the corners of the front gate. They were halfway to the village that was halfway to La Lance's camp when the crew boss realised that the new lady was not with them. He wasn't looking for her on their exit because he wasn't used to her. Now when he asked Khadija where she was as he put the van in neutral and coasted to a stop, throwing his arm over the back of the driver's seat to stretch his neck to look at Khadija. She was in a very tight spot too, she knew, and now was the time to do some active tradecraft of her own. She reached out to the crew boss, crying in anguish saying that her cousin was abducted, cradling each side of his head in her hands. There was a small syringe attached to a thimble on her thumb and it sunk into his neck and the plunger depressed. He reared back and she held his head as he fought to break free, until he slumped motionless in very short order. The women lost their cool again and chattered loudly at Khadija, screaming at her. Khadija reached into her abaya and felt under the left cup of her brassiere. She had velcroed a very small, mostly plastic handgun the size of a child's toy. It was plastic and white metal and it held seven short rounds of twenty-two calibre. This was not a powerful weapon, but psychologically the women would recognise it as a gun and hopefully it would bestow authority on her. She produced the small handgun and showed it to them, then fired a round through the van's roof. The bullet barely made it through the sheet metal but the report of the round in the enclosed space was quite loud. They all stopped and were stock still. Khadija ordered them all out of the van, and they complied. She ordered them to remove the van driver and lay him out in the floor of the van in the back. She assured them that he would make a full recovery within twelve hours. There was no need to bind him because he was immobile and would remain that way for hours yet to come, she explained to the women in the back. Then, she ordered the one woman who said she could drive to take them back to the outskirts of the village, and while they drove she called Rene on the satellite phone on the frequency reserved for Emirati intelligence. She reported everything to Rene who relayed it to Carl Horton, who was in the office with him.

On the other end of the line Carl Horton's mind was racing. Since he learned about the ultimate, nuclear terror attack he couldn't stop picturing it playing out somewhere in his beloved Midwest. He knew, intellectually, that the attack could happen anywhere in the western world, but he now had this pathology where he couldn't stop imagining it causing his own family to waste away. In his mind, his own self-interest and the greater good were perfectly aligned, and he had to do whatever was in his power to stop it. According to the field report coming across now, there was no way to rule out the possibility that Al Sudeiri was still in the compound, and the roster of bad men verified as present was a huge windfall. He couldn't take the chance that any of them should get away. He had to call in the bombing run now and call it a massive win. There would be some hand-wringing and pearl clutching in Washington because his asset and the innocents were still there, but he could easily make the case that the scales were tipped in their favour. He knew that young lady held an American passport, but was she really a real American? She was born in Africa and raised in France so you couldn't really consider her an American like the corn-fed, Christian God-fearing folks born in rural Michigan. Maybe with this he was striking a blow to win the war at home as well. He told Rene to recall Khadija and he asked him to advise his government that he, Horton, would be calling in a bombing run from a base in Europe, and that within six hours the compound would be removed from the map.

Khadija spoke to Rene in the local tribal language so there would be no chance of being overheard by Horton.

"You have to tell Mohammed Batu and the British mercenary. She is his daughter, did you know that? And it isn't right to leave them all there to die. Let me talk to them."

"Stay on the line. Stay with me as I cross the camp."

Rene walked to Batu's tent, called out and walked in without hearing the response. Batu was lying on his bed trying to stay still against the heat.

"Mohammed. I have Khadija on the satellite phone. Listen to what she has to say," Rene offered without drawing a breath.

Batu sat up on the bed and Rene put the phone on speaker.

"Go ahead, Khadija," Rene said, *"tell him what you told me."* And she did, and Mohammed Batu listened.

When she was finished, Rene said to Batu, *"He's your guy. What do you want to do?"*

Batu had questions for Khadija. Where was she now? What was the disposition of the women in her company? If they decided on some independent action then would she be willing to support them?

She answered all his logistical questions and said that she would do whatever it took, because she knew Betty would not leave her like that. Batu asked Rene if he would support independent action, and Rene said that the Americans had already decided and acted independently without properly consulting the Caliph. Between now and whenever the bombs dropped, anything went.

The Price of Freedom

Harry was sitting on his bed next to his packed rucksack looking at pictures of his children on his phone when Rene and Mohammed Batu approached his tent at a double-time march. They came right in, since they could see him through the screen of the rolled up wall, and Batu started talking briskly, insistently, right away.

"Harry," he said, *"Khadija is on the line and she has some very distressing news. Please listen to her and let me know what you're thinking."*

Harry could tell that something was horribly wrong immediately, and as Khadija unrolled her tale, Harry's mind was already planning what to do and how to do it. He had just found his daughter and he had to admit that he loved her as unconditionally as the two children he had raised personally. Elena had asked him one time in jest, *"What wouldn't you do for your kids?"* in an attempt to get him to pick up food from their favourite restaurant that didn't deliver. But the question remained with him. What wouldn't you do for your child? Where would you draw the line? He thought he had killed for his younger siblings when they were his charges, and he had essentially killed his own persona for the good of the younger ones. He had seen glimpses of himself in Fanta's profile and he saw Mariam's mannerisms and level headedness in how she carried herself. There was no way on earth he was leaving her to that fate. If need be, he would battle his way to her if only to end her suffering, even at his own expense.

"I have some ideas," he said, *"try to stay with me and see if this holds up."* They agreed to hear him out, and he went on.

"Khadija takes the abayas from the women in the van and sends them into the village on foot. We come to meet at the van and go straight back to the kitchen door covered up as the cleaning crew again. Khadija calls the contact on the manager's phone and explains that the manager had a heart attack on the way back, so we turned around to get the only help available out there. If they open the kitchen door then we can do the rest."

Batu spoke up. *"N'Djamena style,"* he said, referring to a hostage rescue that he and Harry had done in a dense urban environment in the capital of Chad. They went in with silencers on their Glocks and carrying only stun grenades. That way if they heard the report of any other weapon they would know that it was an adversary.

"That's good," Khadija said once it was explained, *"sidearms are all we'd need that close in and stun grenades will incapacitate but not kill. When we find her we just stun everybody there and sort her out later."*

"That's the idea," Batu said.

"Right," Khadija said, *"There has to be six of us. Who else can you get?"*

"I'll sort that out," Batu said.

"Mohammed," Harry said, *"anybody who comes has to fully understand the risks. This definitely won't be a walk in the park."*

"You get the vehicle ready, and bring extra fuel for the van," Batu said, *"I'll get the guys."*

Khadija parked the van two hours walk from the village and told the women to leave their abayas in the van and walk back. She said that her friends were coming to get her, and that in four hours the crew leader would come around and bring the van back to the village.

Back in the camp Batu showed up at the vehicle with Limier and two other guys. One of them was one of the team leaders who went by Jaguar. Early in his life in the Legion he had a bullet strike near his cheekbone at an angle and follow its curvature, leaving a deep scar that made him look like a big cat. He was joined by The Professor, one of the tech engineers. Harry nodded solemnly to both, knowing that they were aware of the situation and of the risks, and that they were volunteering to go anyway.

"Saddle up," Batu said. *"We'll get you fully briefed on the way."*

They set out in an armoured transport vehicle that had bulletproof flanks. They were able to carry enough fuel for the transport and the van to both make it back to camp. They had enough ammunition for a full-scale battle and they had bulletproof vests. Inside the back of the vehicle they continued to study the blueprint of the compound they had created with their measurements and scans. Harry couldn't remember ever having so much precise intel on a project before. The newfangled technology being deployed now really changed the level of effectiveness of small teams. Here they had six men who would try to do a precision extraction where time was more important than brute force. They knew how to get into the compound, they knew almost precisely where a prisoner would be held in the second level below ground, and they knew how many men would be present and how they would be armed.

Crucially, they also knew that nobody would be expecting them. The tactics they used in Chad were crude, but effective. Once they had breached they raced to the hostage, shooting anyone they encountered, anyone at all, who was not the hostage. This was very quick and it worked like a charm for them, but there were at least two unarmed people killed. They may not have had any real hand in the hostage taking and this time Harry didn't want to harm anyone unnecessarily. There were no true innocents anywhere inside that compound though. The element of time also factored right into the morality equation. From now, Harry estimated, there was a small chance that a Russian survivor of the ambush could stumble back to the compound with some distressing stories to tell. And there was the small matter of a sortie of American bombers racing to turn the compound into a smoking hole. Stopping at nothing to get his daughter out of there as soon as possible had its appeal too.

They followed the little blue ping on the electronic map until they eventually saw the van parked on the horizon. They drove up to it and it looked completely empty. As they were getting out of the truck Harry could see Khadija in the fading light, rising from an unseen depression in the ground just twenty feet from the road, behind them. She knew the van would draw the eye from whatever approach, and she used knowledge of the lay of the land and shadow and silhouette to stay perfectly hidden on an open plain. She approached the group and greetings were exchanged where she was introduced to Jaguar and The Professor. She showed them the cleaning crew leader, on the floor of the van in the back, in a drugged and incapacitated state. She distributed the abayas and the men took a few minutes to figure out which fit best on whom, and they fueled up the van and started toward the compound.

They went over the plan with Khadija in person, and they included the new step where Khadija doesn't wait with the van, but rather goes straight to the serving women's quarters to warn them, and then returns to the van. Though the plan was simple in design, execution could get complicated. They had to get the people inside to open the bulkhead or they had to use the mechanical separator to open it. The difference in time budget there could be the difference between success and failure. Then they had to move through the kitchen and secure the stairwell where Khadija could go up and the rest of the team go down, except for The Professor, who would be overwatch on the ground floor, keeping the stairwell clear. Batu and Harry would take the lead on the staircase down and Jaguar would stay at the bottom of the stairs until they had set the charge on the door's lock. Then they would throw stun grenades at angles and try to cover as much of the interior as they could. Then into the dungeon, set a charge to free Betty if necessary and beat a hasty retreat. Job done.

Once the plan was clear in their minds they fell silent and rocked through the rutted terrain listening to the hum of the engine. None of them were kids facing live fire for the first time, they knew the experience and they knew the consequences. They were a team of professional operators who could trust each other in a fluid and ambiguous situation. They were like a string quartet playing a complicated piece at the very edge of its register; their acuity and alertness were elevated and they were prepared to take the next action.

By the time they were closing in on the compound daylight was fading. Batu looked at Khadija and told her it was time to make the call. Khadija hit the button on the cleaning crew leader's phone and she very soon heard ringing on the other end. The five men in the van held their breath and stared at Khadija. Their lives could end up depending on this call. Khadija, knowing that, looked down at the van floor only. The men saw her face jump into animated coercion matching the speed and ferocity of urgent words rushing out of her mouth, none of which anyone understood.

Into the phone she shouted, *"He's having a heart attack! Help you have to help us please! He's unconscious and you are the only ones who can help!"*

A rush of shouting came from the other side of the phone, extolling her to calm down, asking who she was talking about and asking where she was.

The men in the van could see that Khadija had become a desperate and helpless woman, whose only chance was to hope that a man could save her. She knew which buttons to push on the local male psyche and ego to get them to open the door, and she was playing her role flawlessly.

"Please!" she shouted into the phone, "He's my cousin's husband and he's going to die. I know you have the thing on the wall. The thing that shocks the heart. Please just bring it and use it to save him."

"Right. Where are you exactly?" came out of the phone, to which she replied that they were approaching the work door now.

They pulled up to the bulkhead without seeming to draw the attention of the front gate. No one was around and all they could see was the blank concrete wall and the open desert. They all piled out frantically and laid the crew leader in front of the bulkhead door. Khadija banged lightly on the door with the flat of her palm and shouted for them to bring out the defibrillator. Two men stood inside the bulkhead trying to decide what to do. One of them opened the door a tiny bit by lifting it. Peering out into the fading light, the sliver of vision he had was taken up by the prone body of the crew leader, unmoving and unconscious. Khadija closed in on the creaking metal door while crouching deeply to peer directly into the crack. The man inside suddenly saw a large woman's head take up his view and her continued frantic pleas deafened him. It was one of the cleaning ladies. He knew her voice and he felt bad. He started to lift the door fully and told his colleague, who had been standing by with the defibrillator, to go out.

The door flapped open with a metallic clang and a man rushed out with a medical device in his hands and immediately crouched near the crew leader to check his vital signs. Khadija was crouched on the other side of the body. The other man came out of the bulkhead door and looked at the nearest woman and asked how long the man had been like this. Jaguar stood still and silent under the woman's covering garment. He had no idea what was said, and he had no chance of coming up with a viable reply, so he stayed silent. The man stopped and looked from one to the other, with eyes that landed on three sets of men's combat boots. He then looked back to Khadija and his comrade and slowly pulled a cell phone out of his pocket.

A sound like the ring of a steel hammer connecting solidly with a large nail rang out over and over. Jaguar and Batu both had shot the man with silenced pistols, and as he fell backwards and into the bulkhead, Khadija shot the other man. There was no other choice, and it had begun.

They poured into the bulkhead, dragging the body off the stairs. The kitchen was empty. They recognised the room from the descriptions and they moved quickly and silently when Khadija pointed to the doorway that led both up and down. They approached the door in two sets; The Professor directly in front with Khadija just to his side and Jaguar, Harry and Batu behind. The Professor tried the handle and the door opened. He peered in and then opened it wide to show an empty short hallway with stairs directly in front heading up and a wooden interior door at the far end. He went in and took a position at the end of the hallway with his back against the wall, holding the silenced pistol muzzle down with two hands. Khadija ascended the stairs as quietly as she could. Jaguar could see that she had an assault rifle under her abaya. Harry and Batu went to the door by The Professor's left shoulder and Harry gently tried the handle. To his surprise it turned. He looked at Batu and with the fingers of his left hand counted down from three to one, then swung the door wide open and trained his pistol's muzzle down the stairwell. It was dark and there was no one there. Without hesitation they went down the stairs and landed in a corridor, perpendicular to and directly across from the stairs. According to their intel and imaging the cells should be right through that door. Batu pointed to his exterior cargo pocket where the plastic explosive charge sat and then turned his palm to the sky, asking whether or not to blow the door open. Harry waved it off and pulled out a stun grenade and put his other hand on the door handle. Batu held one in each hand. It would be a ludicrous lapse of security protocol if the door to the holding cells were left unlocked, but Harry had to at least try. The handle turned and the door opened, and Harry heard music from inside. He threw the stun grenade in and to his right and Batu threw his two to his left, to the front and rear. Harry let go of the door and it swung shut on its own as they switched to their silenced pistols. The stun grenades were far from silent. Three of them going off in an enclosed area in rapid succession had a percussive wave as well as sound, and they all knew that this was the starting gun for active pursuit. They opened the door again and entered to see a very large open room with two cells built against the far wall. There were a couple of large desks set up and there was a sofa along the back wall. Betty was in one of the cells. There were five men who were in various positions around the room when the grenades went off. Three of them were prone and one was recovering his footing, from being thrown against a desk. The final man, furthest in the far corner was standing and he was drawing a weapon. Batu was the first through the door so he was closest to the active combatant. Batu moved directly to engage him and since his weapon was already drawn and directed he got off the first shots and hit the man's centre of mass. Harry followed, engaging two of the others and dispatching them before they had the chance to present a threat. Jaguar shot the man by the desk and immediately began looking for keys. The man Batu shot was wearing a vest, so the two rounds from the Glock at close range knocked him off his feet but didn't penetrate the armour. Batu closed with him and kept shooting until it was clear that he was gone. The spitting of the silenced weapon and the whining of the ricochets sounded like a nest of angry bees, and then it was over.

Upstairs, The Professor had heard how loud the engagement was, and he got quite nervous with nothing to do but stand there and keep watch. He listened closely for any noises coming from either side of the hallway and the bottom of the stairs. He could hear other ambient activity but he couldn't be sure of its direction. Then he definitely heard movement from further up, where Khadija went.

Below, Harry and Jaguar searched the desks while Mohammed Batu fixed the charge on the cell's locking mechanism. As he went about it he looked at Betty when he could, so he could assess her status. She was still wearing the server's clothes and she was conscious but out of it, like she had been drugged. She did not appear to have been physically damaged in any way. He had a timed detonator for the material which looked like two golf pencils connecting a high tech pocket watch. He held it up to Jaguar and Harry to indicate that it was time to blow the cell's mechanism apart. Neither Jaguar nor Harry could figure out how to get the cell door open otherwise. There appeared to be both mechanical and electronic keys required, so Harry gave Batu a thumb's up and got under one of the desks. Jaguar got under the other desk and Batu set the timer and ran to hunker down next to Harry. The explosion was quite loud and yet another shockwave went through the men. There was also a loud metal clanging, that Harry saw to be the brittle weld of the latch housing and the locking mechanism giving way and falling completely off. The cell door could now be slid open, and Harry ran to slide it far enough to get inside. He ran directly to Betty's side. Her eyes were open and her head was moving but she was not cognizant of what was happening. She would need to be carried. He holstered his weapon and began to sit Betty up, and he could hear that Jaguar and Batu had opened the door wide. Betty responded when he sat her up by putting her hand on his shoulder and looking him in the eye. OK, maybe she could manage to be upright from here to the van, Harry thought. He stood and drew her forearms along with him, and she rose through leverage as her feet landed on the floor and still directed her weight upward. Jaguar was right there, so Harry placed Betty's arm around his shoulder and when Batu came around the other side he put her other arm around his shoulder. Jaguar and Batu now followed Harry out of the cell and across the room holding Betty between them. The Professor saw them encumbered with the captive and trying to get through the door and across the hallway safely. He ran down the stairs and looked up and down the hallway. The electric light petered out a few feet in each direction and there was definitely ambient noise from activity somewhere nearby. The Professor told them it was clear and, seeing Harry just behind them ready to take the rear, he led them up the stairs. They couldn't fit three across in the stairwell so Mohammed Batu put Betty's arms over both his shoulders and carried her up the stairs on his back. At the top of the stairs Jaguar helped him again. The Professor had the door back into the kitchen open and they could hear Harry's silenced pistol going off at the bottom of the stairs. The Professor hurried through and made sure the kitchen was clear of adversaries. Then Batu and Jaguar came through with Betty and they could hear running feet from the stairwell. Then they heard more feet running together up the stairs as Harry burst through the door. Whoever was behind Harry was right behind him. Harry slammed the door shut and shouted in English over his shoulder, *"Run. Get her out of here!"* as he braced against the door to hold it shut.

▪▪▪

As soon as they had gotten through the kitchen Khadija split from the main group and ascended the stairs to where the servers' quarters were. She remembered Betty's voice in her ear, telling her how many stairs, the unlocked status of the door. Every syllable of it was critical now, and Betty's descriptions had been focused on what was important and the information had been accurate. Khadija went up the stairs deftly, but quietly, holding the assault rifle close against her side. She didn't stop at the landing. In fact, she turned the doorhandle abruptly and stepped through quickly. She could see a large rectangular dormitory room, as Betty had described. Two young women lay in different beds across the room from each other and one sat braiding another's hair in the open, living area of the room, nearer the opposite door. Khadija knew them by sight and they recognised her as one of the new local cleaning women. They all looked up at her and seemed to be waiting expectantly. Khadija had never spoken to them and she only ever spoke the local language in their presence, so they were surprised when she spoke in English.

"We have to leave here," she said to them, moving further into the room. *"Quietly, and immediately. Let's stand up and go right now,"* she said.

The two braiding stopped and the other two rose from the beds. They made hesitant perfunctory movements but didn't do anything purposeful. Then the one whose hair was being braided spoke.

"I don't know what's happening, but we should ask Mr. Bin," she said, standing. *"I'll go ask him now."*

"No," Khadija said. *"Stop there now,"* and she pushed the handle of the rifle so it lifted against the sling over her shoulder, revealing the weapon.

The woman with half a braid had been looking away in the direction toward the door, where she was headed. There was an audible gasp from the three who saw the weapon and Khadija stepped quickly and bounded toward the door. Khadija had put herself in the woman's space and in her field of vision and held the top of the door with her left palm. The woman's progress put her and Khadija's faces a mere foot apart.

"Don't!" Khadija hissed with the most emphatic quietness. The woman lifted her hands palms out and stepped back. The other three were all standing now, looking expectantly at Khadija and the other moved closer back toward her friend who had been braiding.

"We have to go right now," she said calmly without shouting. *"This place isn't safe. We have to get as far away from the building as we can, and now."* They then heard three loud and distinct thumps, like the deepest bass with the sound system on its highest setting. The woman with half a braid was spooked, and she ran for the door behind Khadija. Khadija knew from Betty's description that the muffrage and the foreign fighters would be right behind that door or the next one, and she couldn't let anyone through it in either direction. Khadija kept her right hand on the assault rifle. With her left hand she drew her silenced pistol and extended her arm fully, just as the woman was passing. She put the muzzle parallel to the woman's head so there would be no chance of hitting her, and pulled the trigger. The mechanical clank of the action

and the pneumatic hiss and spit of the muzzle coincided with the small cloud of wood splinters that erupted from the door frame directly in front of her left eye. She shuddered to a halt, shocked. They all then heard the louder explosion, not harmless and not very far away. They all felt it through the bottoms of their feet.

"We need to get out of here now," Khadija said and looked at each of them in turn. *"I'm going down those stairs and out. Follow me if you want to live."* Then, without stopping to check if they followed, she racked the assault rifle and took the safety off. The cartridges in the magazine were high velocity, with copper jacketed bullets. She walked back to the entrance door and heard movement and running feet, a slammed door, then a lull. Khadija opened the door and stepped out onto the landing. Unexpectedly, a group of four men entered the hallway below from the other end, through the door she knew led to the dungeon. Wordlessly they ran to the interior door just below her and threw their body weight against the door wherever they could get purchase. The thin panelled door bent and began to splinter, then slammed straight in the doorframe for a split second before they reared back to heave against it once more. Khadija took the safety off and descended two stairs so she had a direct and short line of fire. She braced against the kick and fired on fully automatic, maintaining constant fire until the magazine was exhausted, walking down the few stairs to maintain progress of the flow of fire. In the enclosed concrete block box of the hallway, ricochet buzzed all around, and her abaya but not her body was bitten twice. The front two men were pushed bodily through the door which now swung open. The other two had tried to writhe away into the lee of the staircase and that is where Khadija now stood. There was one second of roaring silence following the deafening roar of the gun, and then the women's screams began. They were terrified and shocked, and they ran for their lives through the carnage at the bottom of the stairs. Khadija kept her eyes on the doorway to the stairwell at the far end of the corridor as she loaded a fresh magazine into the gun.

Khadija was the last to come through the door into the kitchen where she saw The Professor pulling Harry by the neckline of his vest as Harry's feet stepped backward frantically trying to keep up. They went out through the open bulkhead. Khadija told the serving women to pick up any weapons they could find, and to her surprise they did. They were horrified by the bodies in the kitchen and by the vehicle, but they kept their wits long enough to follow directions.

Out by the van she could see that Betty was lying in the centre of the van on the floor, and that Harry was lying beside her. The van was running but the lights were off. Inside, the remaining team were working on the two on the floor. The Professor stepped down from the cab and came around the van to talk to Khadija. Everyone was holding a weapon and scanning the area alertly.

"I'm sorry that the van can't take anyone else. What do you want to do?" he asked.

"I'll take the ladies and head due south and wait for the bombs to hit. Exactly three hours after the bombing we'll come back to the road. Send La Lance to pick us up then."

They all nodded to each other in agreement. The women disappeared into the darkness and the van drove away before anyone came.

Nobody had noticed how seriously Harry had been injured until they got him into the van. When he redoubled his efforts to hold the thin door shut, he pushed his elbows against it and had his hands at the very top where it was bowing. When Khadija began her descent she was shooting down at a very sever angle. One of the copper jacketed rounds entered under Harry's right arm, severing the subscapular artery and entering vital organs. In the dark no one had seen the blood pooling at the bottom of his vest or discerned that his responses were fading. Once the van was moving, working by dim interior light only, they tried to figure out how to help him. Once his vest was off all became businesslike but frenzied in pace. Batu called out calmly for medical devices and materiel and Jaguar provided a staccato series of 'no's in response. All of that was in La Lance's vehicle back at the rendez vous. Batu packed the wound with the bandages they had with their operations' kits and tried to keep Harry engaged with him so he wouldn't lose focus.

Harry felt like he had been hit harder than he had ever been hit in his life. It knocked the wind out of him, and it took all of his energy and will with it. At first he was bewildered and he didn't understand why he had to pinwheel his legs under him backwards. At the van Batu had sat him down on the opening and he couldn't keep himself upright. There was no strength in any of his muscles, but the right side couldn't mechanically function. He hadn't drawn a breath since the rush of the door and on the floor of the van he started to founder and his body reacted badly.

Throughout his life Harry had a notion that inside him, and probably inside everyone, was a quiet listener atop whom the chattering mind rode. When the listener spoke, it was with feelings and not ideas. Right now he could feel these two very different aspects of who he was split, and communicate with each other directly. The quiet listener who Harry now thought of as his spirit was giving his intellect the very same advice that he had given on too many occasions. You are dying – there is nothing that can change that. Harry's mind went to Elena and to each of his children. He was so very proud of each of them and he thought of each of them in turn. He was overwhelmed with his love for them. His head rolled to the side and faced Betty's unseeing face just inches away. He was amazed that he was able to find an unknown daughter. He could see Batu and Jaguar below working on him, and he rode those feelings of pride, love and wonder right into the next world.

Retribution

A Shoulder for the Burden

Betty was coming around again, resurfacing from the depths of nowhere. Information came to her in fragmented slivers, cutting across all of her senses, each seeming to have equal importance. Her right shoulder was cold. She knew that now, but for a second that was all she knew. There was no ready-made ego to pick up the consciousness like flipping a switch and turning on a robot. She heard the loud hum of an engine. Now she knew two sensory facts. Other slivers came jabbing in, like the agonising headache, like her friends and her mission. As more and more of her life and self filled in, her panic rose. She opened her eyes and tried to move and found she was restrained. She was terrified.

The last thing Betty remembered was struggling against the crowd who held her fast in the muffrage. She had been dragged through the far door where one of the grey-bearded men dressed in western clothes jabbed her with a needle and she lost consciousness. Now she saw a woman about her age sitting across a small space from her. The woman wore a US Air Force coverall uniform and she was looking concernedly at Betty. Betty was lying flat with her chin and right shoulder aligned so she could see the woman.

"Good," she said, *"you're awake. You're safe. You're safe. I know you had a tough time but you're on a flight to Ramstein airbase in Germany, where you'll get an ambulance to Landstuhl medical centre."*

Betty felt the tension go out of her body. Her dry mouth worked against itself in preparation to talk. She weakly croaked out something that was lost in the whine of the engine.

"You're OK. You're going to be fine," the woman went on, *"We're about three hours out. Try to rest and we'll talk once we're on the ground."*

The plane was about the size of a small commercial jetliner but it was fitted out for medical care. It was dimly lit but Betty could see there were no chevrons on the woman's uniform, so she was an officer. Betty took a minute to keep her eyes open and assess her surroundings. The restraint she felt was from safety straps belting her into the narrow medical bed. She could see they operated the same as seat belts in cars, so she could easily undo it herself if she wanted to. Her arms were outside of the lap belt and there was nothing stopping her from getting up, except that she had IVs dripping into a port in the back of her right hand. Though she had just regained consciousness, she was exhausted. She lay back and slept until they arrived.

They approached and landed very quickly compared to commercial flights. Once they were on the ground and the noise level dropped, the woman who Betty assumed was a doctor leaned in and raised her voice to be heard over the taxi engine.

"A Malitani woman was with the team that handed you over," she said. *"She said this was important to you and you'd want to have it."*

The woman pressed a locket on a thin-chained steel necklace into her hand. It was a mundane steel clasp that Betty had never seen before. Without trying to hide anything, Betty opened the locket and could see there was a sim card clipped into either side. They were the two from Betty's phone. Betty felt for a pocket but she was in a hospital gown.

"I'll put that in with your other things," the doctor said, and took it and put it in a small Ziploc baggie with Betty's incidentals. *"You'll get everything when you settle in at the hospital."*

∙ ∙

The medical staff told Betty that she was there to focus on her recovery. They had filtered her blood outside of her body and they had given her nutrients and electrolytes to aid in her recovery. Her liver had been so overtaxed by the toxins that her body needed the help. Betty had been insisting that she talk to someone from her job, and the doctors kept saying that someone would come by soon enough. It was the end of the second day in the hospital before the man from the embassy came.

He was a middle-aged white man wearing business casual and carrying a laptop bag. He knocked, came in when asked, and introduced himself as being from "the office" and shook her hand.

"First off," he said, *"I'd like to thank you for your service to the nation. You can't get public recognition, but those of us who know are extremely grateful."*

That sounded too heavily rehearsed, she thought cynically.

"What happened back there and when do I debrief with the team?" she asked.

"We have to get you into a reintroduction therapy regime, according to protocol," he said. *"I know you want to stay in the field, but we have to be sure you're processing these recent ... events... well enough before you can get off the bench."*

Betty knew the rulebook, she read it cover to cover and was cursed not to be able to forget it. It was true that an operative who was near to loss of life in the field had to undergo a certain number of therapy sessions. She also knew that some crises took precedent over all else, even the well being of the agents assigned. She had a feeling that something more was going on but she didn't know what it was. Why had Horton decided to follow this rule now? Was he looking out for her or was he taking her off the gameboard? She didn't have enough information and it frustrated her.

She agreed to the sessions and signed some paperwork on his laptop saying she recognised that she was inactive for a minimum of one week. He told her the psychiatrist would come the following day and he bid her farewell.

Betty put on the sweatpants and jumper provided by the hospital and stepped out to walk the halls. Her head was clear and she had her feet under her. No one had given her any information about the operation and no one had even attempted to debrief her. She had been offered no way to contact the outside world; no one asked if she wanted to call her mother. They couched it in concern, but she was being cut out and kept quiet at the same time. She was on the fourth floor of a wing of the hospital where the layout was just two long hallways. She shuffled up one and down the other, noting that every room appeared occupied. At one end of the corridors was a nurse's station that had a counter with desks and office and medical machines behind it. Betty heard movement from behind where she couldn't see, but no one was sitting at the counter. She shuffled over to it, not trying to be inconspicuous and leaned heavily on the counter with her elbows, hanging her head as if in exhaustion. On the other side of the counter she saw clipboards and papers, and in the corner, a small clutch of personal material. There was a pack of gum, hand sanitiser, a car key and a cell phone. Betty still couldn't see anybody so she reached over and took the cell phone and slipped it into the pocket of her sweatpants and shuffled on.

She had a private room with its own bathroom so she went back and went into the bathroom, where she saw that the door could not be locked. She took out a tweezers and a small prying tool and removed the sim card from the phone and replaced it with her UAE sim card. The phone was well charged and it was loaded with all of the common applications. She was prepared to try a couple of different things to get the phone open, but as soon as she tapped to enter anything in the pin code it opened. She thanked God for small favours and turned it on to see messages from Khadija. Betty knew she had limited time, so she just tapped the number and the phone began to ring. Betty put it to her ear and waited while the tones rang off. It seemed like forever before someone spoke.

"Hello?" It was Khadija. Betty was both anxious and relieved. She audibly sighed but was too caught up in the moment to say anything else.

"I don't know this number," Khadija said from the other end of the line, "so I'm hanging up unless there is something to say."

"No, wait," Betty said into the phone, "it's me and I don't have much time. This phone is 'borrowed'"

"Fanta is that you?" Khadija asked.

"Yes. Are you okay?"

"Fanta I have some terrible news. Should I carry on?" Khadija asked. If only she knew how that increased Betty's anxiety; now she must know.

"Please," she said, "And I have questions too."

"I'm sure you do. Listen, Harry didn't make it out. He's gone Fanta," Khadija paused there to wait until Betty broke the silence.

Khadija knew the relationship between Betty and Harry. Unlike her own relationship to Harry, Betty's was more complicated but not entirely brand new.

"Oh God," Betty said, *"Didn't make it out of where?"* Betty asked but she could only think of one reasonable answer.

"Has no one told you anything?" Khadija asked.

"Listen Khadija I've been kept in the dark like a prisoner here. What happened?"

"After you got caught Horton ordered an airstrike to level the compound before any of the surviving mercenaries made it back. Me and Harry and a team from La Lance went back to get you and the servers out. We caught them by surprise but there was a firefight. Harry was our only casualty. I ran and hid with the girls in the hills while a couple vehicles came looking for us. The Yankees hit the compound with about four jdams and left nothing but a smoking hole. Those vehicles ran and La Lance picked us up. By the time I got back to the base Horton already had you on prepped for travel to Germany. It was all I could do to get you the sim cards," she concluded.

"So everybody from the compound is dead?" Betty asked.

"Everybody that matters," Khadija replied. "A few of the Russian mercenaries made it out and whoever came after us in those vehicles had a chance."

"We never confirmed Al Sudeiri. Why did Carl order the strike right then?" Betty heard workers speaking in raised tones, evidently far away from each other, speaking in German which Betty could not understand.

"Listen I have to go," she said. *"I don't think this is over though. I'll call you when I can."*

"Fanta," Khadija said, *"I'm sorry for your loss."*

• •

Sudeiri and Nesralla were on another call, and again Nesralla was not alone. His minders now spoke every language he did, so there was no point in trying to conceal anything that could not be alluded to cryptically.

"We have to assume Ahmed is dead," Zuz told Nesralla. *"There was an ambush in the desert and we lost our gold, and then the compound was destroyed and everyone inside was killed. If Ahmed made it to the compound then he wouldn't have been there long. This is a loss to the cause as well as a personal tragedy."*

They reminisced for some time about times they had with Ahmed. They shared a big part of their lives, not just the cause, and they both felt his absence. After a long time Nesralla brought the conversation back to the efforts supporting the cause.

"In Ahmed's name we must carry on," he said. *"This is the final step to force the world to leave us to order our modern society the way that best suits an Islamic world. This is the most extreme but Ahmed's loss has renewed my resolve to do it, and to finish it."*

"Yes," Zuz picked up his line of reasoning. *"Our resources are more limited now, but luckily we have already committed the investment to get this last thing done. And now for me too there is no hesitation."*

"You will have to be the one to go there," Nesralla said, *"there are no other options."*

"I know," Zuz replied," and *God willing there will be no problems along the way."*

They agreed to set the final wheels in motion and their leave taking for this call was especially poignant, as each considered if they should never speak with the other again.

■■■

Carl Horton had been back in Washington for a week and he was still being called in to different bigwigs' offices to explain and fill in details at the drop of a hat. Agency management was debriefed and they were happy about the results from the bombing in the Caliphate of Malitania. They had better results than they had in years, and there were press conferences by the State Department and by the office of the President showing the number of face cards by suit that were removed from the terrorism landscape in Malitania.

Behind the scenes they wanted to know how many civilian casualties there were, and how was it that he let Sudeiri get away? Where the inquirer had no influence over his budget or his career he communicated professionally that during fluid engagements some decisions had to be made and that he couldn't lose the bird in the hand. Where his superiors or congressional subcommittees with authority inquired, he provided evidence and minutes from the operation's logs. He never provided any testimony from the agent in the field though, because she was under medical orders to undergo emergency psychiatric care post-trauma.

The real reason was that he didn't trust her. She knew that he had ordered her into that compound only to decide to drop bombs on it while she was still in there. She knew that it was her biological father, newly discovered, who was the British mercenary who died during her rescue. Horton hadn't known their relationship at the time and he didn't know that La Lance would try something so foolhardy, or that the Emirati team on the ground would get involved. Horton had misread it, and now that he had more information, he wasn't sure she wouldn't be looking for some kind of revenge or what that might even look like. It was better for her to be shunted off in a comfortable gulag somewhere for as long as he could get. This would give him time to figure out how to get her off this operation altogether. Management would say that she knows the players and the background better than any other available asset, but Horton didn't want her to know anything about the threat from nuclear power.

To make things worse, he had reports of facial recognition hits for nuclear scientists and technicians from the Iranian and Pakistani nuclear programmes crossing the US border. The disconcerting thing about the reports was that there were multiple sightings of the same person crossing in different states at the same time. That meant disguises good enough to trip false positives for facial recognition and a coordinated effort to confuse where the real scientist crossed the border. This was all happening while cyber attacks on American civilian nuclear power plants increased four-fold in frequency and doubled in complexity. Over the last week there was a huge spike in incidents where low-grade physical security controls were tested across the American plants. More than his gut told him that Al Sudeiri had something very bad planned for the homeland.

And still. Still, there was not much to go on other than a grand scheme and a broad base of possibilities. Activity in all of the associated accounts had stopped completely. They couldn't track the movements of the two known principals and they didn't have any leads on specific threats to the nuclear plants aside from what they considered red herrings. He needed something to break his way. He needed to find Al Sudeiri and take him alive if possible. The resources available to law enforcement, the FBI and intelligence services was very limited now, since the country was in a state of high paranoia and threats from homegrown militias were extremely high. Watching and waiting weren't going to get the job done, but he was running out of ideas. He sat down at his desk again and wrote out an email to a contact at the Saudi embassy. Now was the time to call in all the chits and exhaust every trick in his book. There was too much to lose for him, his family and his country.

∎∎∎

It had now been a week at the medical facility for Betty. At first she felt that she had to be straight back into the fray, for her father's memory and to get closer to Carl Horton. But she had therapy sessions every morning, and sessions with a psychiatrist every evening. She knew that she was stuck there, so she thought she might as well try to get something out of it. They immediately addressed the fear and trauma, and then moved on to allow Betty to talk about some unresolved points from her childhood and young adulthood that caused her, in her own estimation, to have an overdeveloped sense of justice and equity. Betty felt better for talking these things out in a safe place and she did indulge in the mood enhancing meds they gave her, allowing herself to lower her guard and take the edge off for a couple days.

Also, she had spoken with Khadija two more times over the course of the week. They agreed to stay quiet about the location of the gold, buried under an empty ammunition barrel in a trebuchet pit so metal detectors would appear to have picked up a barrel half filled with empty shell casings. Khadija told her that Horton seemed very secretive before he left, clearly preoccupied with something besides debriefing from the operation. The Emirati military joined the operation with La Lance Fournie to clear and secure the compound site and the CIA sent a forensics team to analyse the site and obtain DNA samples. She had overheard Horton on calls with Curtis Chase twice before he was recalled to the States. Not only is something about the operation still going on, but it is also ramping up in some way somewhere else.

The agency's psychiatrist told Betty that she would be put on medical leave with full pay and benefits for the next six weeks to allow herself to readjust after her experiences. Betty would just have to check in with the therapist twice a week for question and answer sessions to gauge progress. Then she asked Betty what she would do with her time and Betty told her that she would spend some of it traveling Europe, since she was already there.

Two days later she was in Marseilles for Harry's memorial service by La Lance. She spent a very long night drinking with Mohammed Batu and hearing stories of the old days in the Legion and shattering glasses. Three days after that she was in Fort Wayne, Indiana at the headquarters of Curtis Chase's investment group. Before they had set out for Sombokto Chase told Betty that she could call him and he would answer. She was calling in that favour now. Chase sent the private jet and put her up in the accommodation reserved for Board members, so she had a three bedroom serviced home with car service and private security near the office. Chase said he could give her a long lunch and then dinner the next day, if she could stay that long. She agreed and he had them added to his diary.

She was young and strong and it had been a couple days, but she still felt hungover from going shot for shot with Mohammed Batu. To her eye, coming from the Sahel by way of Marseilles, Fort Wayne was dismal and cold when the plane touched down. To her surprise, he met her at the airport, taking the limousine right out onto the tarmac. He was standing next to the car when she came down the stairs, and his man opened the trunk.

"I'm flattered," she said. *"I have billionaires coming to greet me and carry my bags."*

"I wish that were why I'm here," he shouted over the sound of the engine winding down. "I have a late meeting in San Jose and I have to take the plane. I swear I'll be back for lunch tomorrow."

"Your loss," she said, "this was your big chance to take me out and show me the bright lights of Fort Wayne."

"Don't get down on Fort Wayne," he said. "This is my hometown and there's way more going on here than meets the eye."

His valet took his luggage out of the trunk and loaded hers in.

"Too bad you didn't give me more of a heads up. I'd love to show you around. Get with my PA to book it in."

He then stood back to look her in the eye. "I heard that the casualty in the field was your biological father. I'm so sorry Fanta."

She didn't expect to be affected by his sympathies, but she felt herself tearing up.

"Thank you," she said, "that's very kind."

He went to give her a Midwestern man one-shoulder embrace and she went in for the French double cheek kiss. This moment exemplified their differences in culture. It was very awkward until Betty grabbed his face and kissed his cheek very deliberately.

"Go and get more treasure for your horde, dragon," she said, "I'll be here when you get back."

They took their leave and he boarded the plane. He could see the limousine pulling away as they taxied to the runway to ascend. For the rest of the night he negotiated intellectual property rights to proprietary software products across Asia, and he kept rubbing his cheek.
■■■

On the tarmac Chase's man took Betty's suitcase and was putting it in the trunk when a nearby pallet jack operator hit the pneumatic release button instead of the drive forward button by mistake. A jumbo jet's worth of meals in a large metal container fell a foot and a half to the asphalt only twenty feet away from the limousine. It made a sound very much like a detonation, unexpected and close.

"It's alright," Chase's man said, squatting on his haunches to get close enough for Betty to hear.

Her right cheek was on the pavement and she was looking across under the limousine. She hadn't even realised that she had 'hit the deck'.

"That'll start to go away soon, hopefully," he said, "I still flinch though."

Betty got up and brushed off her jeans. She looked at the driver, unembarrassed. He was a large and well built man in early middle age. Some brown hair still showed through the grey and he had a salt and pepper moustache. He wore jeans with an oxford shirt and sneakers that looked like dress shoes on top.

"You served?" she asked him.

"Yeah," he replied but didn't add anything further.

Betty got into the back seat and he drove away, off the edge of the runway and onto a feeder road that led away from the airport. The airport in Fort Wayne was just out of the city, as is common. They drove for some time until Betty could see the lights of the tall buildings in the distance. The driver took an exit away from the main road into the city centre and they were on a major surface road, but running through neighbourhoods. It was fairly dark but she could see small retail strip malls here and there with commercial buildings dotting the three story rowhouse cityscape. This was the beating heart of Americana, and it didn't look like it was doing very well. Betty wondered what they were doing in a limousine creeping through this part of town.

"Where are we going?" Betty asked through the small window that separated the front seat from the passenger area.

"We're heading to Poplar. Mr. Chase asked me to show you where he grew up and give you the tour of "his" Fort Wayne."

"My name's Betty. What's yours?" she asked him.

"I'm Jim," he said.

"Well, Jim," she said, "if we're having a humble beginnings contest I'm very sure I win."

Out the window she saw a bar with a full parking lot and more than a few motorcycles. It had irresistible kerb appeal for a certain kind of Midwesterner, and Betty pointed it out to Jim.

"Let's stop here. I'm still keyed up and I could use a cold beer," she said.

"I'm supposed to hit the highlights and bring you to the accommodation," Jim said.

"You're supposed to show me the real Fort Wayne, right? Well I'd say that this is the place," she said, pointing to the bar with her thumb over her shoulder.

"I guess we could stop for one," he said, turning on his indicator. They had to get off the main road and circle the block to approach the bar again. The bar was a two story building that sat on a corner quarter acre lot, entirely paved, on its own. The sign in the corner of the parking lot near the street said "Shorty's" and it had an Indianapolis Colts horseshoe and a shamrock. Work trucks and old sedans took up the spaces that weren't motorcycles and the limousine looked very out of place. Jim parked it along the back fence away from the parking area where another car could get past if it needed to, but there was a clearly marked sign not to park there.

They made small talk as they walked around to the front of the bar, with Jim commenting on her outfit and her explaining that she was in mourning. She was wearing black jeans with a black turtleneck and heavy black engineer boots. He expressed condolences but didn't inquire any further. They walked up the ramp to the double doors of the entrance and they could see a pool table through the glass. Jim opened the door for her and she stepped into a typical local watering hole for the working class of the Midwest. Aside from a pool table there were dart boards and gambling machines. There was a long bar and an expanse of hardwood floor that had tables. The place was fairly well occupied, with people playing pool and darts. The long bar was lined with men watching a football game on the big screen, and the tables were about half full. There were a couple servers running back and forth through a swinging door and to and from the bar. Betty headed to an empty table and Jim followed. On the way she noticed there were only two other people of colour in the whole place, and that roughly a third of the patrons were women.

There was piped in music that could barely be heard over the clack of pool balls and inebriated conversations competing with each other, punctuated by a loud groan from the crowd when the Colts flubbed a crucial third and long. One of the hurried servers, a young man, stopped in front of them and faced them to get their attention. He asked if they needed menus and Jim told him they'd start with a couple drafts. By the time they were done taking off coats and hanging handbags, etc. the beers came. Jim paid with a card and said that they didn't need a tab. Jim had ordered them a knock off of a Trappist ale. They clinked glasses and she took a sip. It was a full-bodied and nutritious ale with an aftertaste that warned of the alcohol content. She really liked it but this would be her only one.

She hadn't been to the Midwest in a while. Global news had been reporting on what they were calling the American Troubles. If you listened to the reports you would think the country was on its very last leg, and that opposing camps were facing off everywhere. What Betty had seen since coming back, and especially here in this bar in this city, was the average citizen getting on with his life. America was a heterogeneous society now, and even cities with a population of a quarter million, like Fort Wayne, had communities of people from elsewhere. Though plenty of people had been radicalised, most people just wanted to provide for their families and live undisturbed. In Betty's mind that wasn't so different from places she had been in the Sahel, where all that people wanted was to be left alone, but fringe elements dragged the whole society to the extreme. They needed a purposeful, unified campaign from political and social leadership to tackle this societal problem head on, but the leadership were the ones with the most to gain from the division.

Technically, Betty hadn't been an American very long, but she felt as though she had been American her whole life. For naturalised citizenship Americans took a test and an oath that reinforced the values written between the lines of the Constitution; a sense of justice, equity and decency in public behaviour. Lately these expectations, and the conventions they travelled on, were breaking down. It was one thing to lose American hegemony in terms of machtpolitik, it was another to lose the example of the expectation of humanism and morality. Betty was determined to put America right and the world right, and she would do it on her watch.

"I went to high school with him," Jim interjected into her line of thought. *"I mean, we travelled in different circles, but I knew him."*

Betty knew he must be talking about Curtis Chase. She nodded and Jim went on.

"I was a jock and he was a nerd. He went to CalTech and I went to Fallujah. We both wound up back here. He has properties all over the world, sure, but his home is still in Fort Wayne."

He raised his hand to call the server and Betty saw the spiderweb tattoo on the back of his hand. She could see the tattoos on the side of his neck under the oxford collar too. Unexpectedly, she found a real need to know what Jim thought of the future of the country.

"Fallujah?" she said. *"That means you were ready to give it all for the Republic."*

"Anybody who signs the paper is ready, I know you know that," he said.

"So do you like it? You know, the way it is? The Republic?" she asked.

He sighed and took a pull off his beer.

"Yeah," he said, *"I know what you mean. But you know what? When you've seen the sky fall then you know when it isn't. And right now the sky isn't falling. One way or the other, I think we'll be okay."*

And that, to Betty, was the problem. Either way, the average American's life would go on as it was. But true isolationism in America would leave the good people of the non-aligned and developing worlds without a benchmark to strive for or a helping hand in an existential crisis. No, she couldn't leave the fate of the world to Carl Horton; he had already proven his analysis obtuse and his decision-making poor. No, she'd have to find Al Sudeiri and she needed Curtis Chase to help her.

They ordered pub meals which came in large portions and they finished their beers. Jim dropped her at the accommodation and she called her mother before going to bed.

■■■

Jim picked her up at eleven the next morning and walked her into the office where he requested a security guard escort Betty to the top floor, where the Board room and the Board's dining room were. At the top floor the security guard left her at the reception desk, where the young man in attendance showed her to her set place in the dining room. She sat and was approached by a server who handed her a menu and said that Mr. Chase would be with her shortly, and asked what she would like to drink. Betty asked for green tea and sparkling water with lemon, and she read the menu until Curtis Chase arrived.

He came in wearing casual clothes, with two people trailing him while he hastily scribbled his signature on tablets with his finger. He sighed heavily and took his place, set across from hers at one end of the massive table.

"I'm glad to see you made it back," she said, *"Did everything go your way?"*

"Always," he said. *"I lead a charmed life."*

He pulled out his chair and picked up the menu from the centre of his place setting. As he sat he said in an offhand manner, *"Horton must have you working overtime, with the Millenium Horizon thing and all."*

He sat and pulled his chair back in and unfolded the napkin over his thigh. His settling himself gave Betty a beat to onboard this information and decide how to deal with it. She had heard nothing, but this revelation in itself was very telling. Betty recognised the name right away, and she remembered working on the project right after she got to the States. The think tank exercise set the bar for tabletop scenario exercises. How did it fit in with all of this, and how did it connect with Horton? She had to decide whether she was going to play along and pretend like she knew what he was talking about, hoping that he would reveal enough information for her to uncover what she didn't know, or to tell him the truth about her situation.

"Well it's funny that you mention that," she said. "I haven't even spoken with Carl since the desert."

Curtis had been dipping a torn piece of bread into very high-quality olive oil and he looked up and raised his eyebrows.

"I see," he said.

"And that's really why I'm here," she said. "I've been put on medical leave and I've had no communication from the company."

"And that's a problem?" he asked.

"Al Sudeiri got away. I know the effort to apprehend him is still going strong and I know Horton is being super secretive all of a sudden," she said.

The server had approached her and she pointed to the Waldorf salad on the menu. She looked back to Chase and went on.

"I know his motivations are good but lately I've had call to question his judgment and his skill in analysing gathered intelligence. Can I let you in on a secret?" she asked.

"Of course," he said, "I'll keep whatever you tell me in confidence."

"What I'm going to share could have ramifications for me, so I'm showing you that I trust you. I have "fuck you" money too, squirreled away somewhere."

She paused for a second.

"I don't have to be here and I sure don't have to be putting my life on the line for the good of the country. But I am," she said.

"I don't know what you told Jim, but he's duly impressed and he says I should listen to you," he said.

"I need your help. I need information. I don't trust Horton to get this right and if we don't get Sudeiri then I think something bad will happen."

"So what are you going to do," he asked, "go rogue – is that what they say?"

"I want to use the available information to do my own analysis. If Horton is following the right leads and doing the right thing then I don't have to do anything more. No harm no foul. But if I find a thread he missed then we may avoid a disaster."

"Would you be doing anything illegal?" he asked.

"No," she lied, "as a private citizen I can analyse information and come to conclusions. But I have to give anything I find to authorities – I couldn't act on my analysis independently."

Now it was his turn to stall for time, pushing his own salad around the plate.

"A few weeks back," he started, looking up to catch her reaction, "Horton called me, saying that the events in the real world reminded him of one of the fail scenarios that we both worked on for Millenium Horizon. I looked into it and he was right. It was one of the fails that led to American isolationism and fortress Europe. The events and the timing were right all the way down the line. Only a nuclear disaster somewhere in the West is missing."

Betty remembered working on the project but her part in it was just number crunching for her professor. She never got actively involved. She just filled out data sets and coded a few things. But what Chase just said sent chills down her spine. They were expecting a nuclear disaster somewhere in the West. Horton probably had sidelined her because he was ashamed of what he did at the compound, or because he didn't trust her with the information. Either way, she had to go around him to stop the terrorists and then she would have to kill him for what he did.

"Oh my God," she said.

"I know," he replied. "I know you want me to give you all that I know right now but leave it with me and let me think about it until we have dinner tomorrow. Either I'll give you a dossier with everything I have or I'll give you a first class ticket to stay at the ranch on the Big Island until this all blows over."

"That's fair," she said. "Whichever option it is, I'm going to take you up on it."
∎∙∙∎

After lunch Betty asked for Jim again, and he took her shopping for incidentals. Then they swung by his house where he parked the limousine and introduced Betty to his wife; both of their kids were away at college. They all piled into the family Bronco and went out to a nice steakhouse for dinner and then they stepped out line dancing for the evening. They had a lovely time and Betty got back to the accommodation to watch the evening news and wind down with a cup of herbal tea. She took a shower and washed her hair, taking advantage of the high-end toiletries and top of the line hair dryer. Lying in bed in the quiet, peaceful, comfortable space she felt what it felt like – the freedom from want, deprivation, anxiety. This is what she wanted for little girls in the Sahel and beyond. But nobody was going to hand it to them. If the cabal had its way then there would be thousands and maybe hundreds of thousands dead, followed by a period where the black flag would run with impunity over the impoverished and outmatched peoples of Chad, Sudan, Libya, Niger and all across the lands of her origin. No, she herself, Betty would put a stop to it and correct the course of near history. Otherwise, what was it all for? Why did her newly discovered father have to die? He, who was never present throughout her life but was the one thing that kept her alive, in the end. She would stop Al Sudeiri to honour Harry and she would kill Carl Horton to reset the scales for herself. These were the thoughts with which she drifted off to sleep.

She slept very late and woke the next morning at ten o'clock local time. She had given up on having a base time zone, and she slept when she could for as long as she could. She had a message from Jim saying he was available if she needed anything, but she thought it best to leave him and his wife alone for today. She walked around the house and saw a retro landline phone on a small table in a hallway with menus from local restaurants next to it. There was a note explaining that all one needed to do was to call and say what they wanted and it would be delivered with no hassle or charge. She had no obligations until dinner that evening, and it was rare that she had a whole day for herself to do nothing but recharge. She decided that she would spend the day inside. She checked some of the names online and found that one restaurant was hosting a Michelin starred chef from Paris for a short residency. She ordered a fine dining feast for brunch and settled in to watch French language movies all day.

Around three o'clock Jim texted, saying that he would be there to pick her up for dinner with Curtis at six. She dressed for dinner this time, wearing a stylish black dress that kept to her mourning conventions but would not be out of place in the most exclusive establishments. At five to six she stood outside to take the air and Jim pulled up in the Bronco. He was wearing jeans and a Colts sweatshirt.

"Ah," he said when she got in, *"I should have told you. Curtis told me to bring you to the office. He ordered pizza and said you would be having a working dinner."*

Betty knew that Chase had agreed to assist.

"Do you want to run back in and change?" Jim asked.

"If you don't mind," she said. Jim parked and walked her back in. He sat on the sofa in the near sitting room and told her to take her time. She trotted upstairs and after a short while came back down in new black jeans and a black hoodie. She had her bag with her laptop over her shoulder.

They drove to the deserted tower in the centre of the city and Jim parked in VIP parking under the building. He used his access card from the private parking deck to activate the elevator directly to the executive suite. They got off the elevator one floor below the Board room. There was a reception desk across from the elevator bay and there was a young lady manning it, even though it was long past working hours. She greeted Jim and led them behind the desk and into Curtis's office, which took up most of the floor.

Chase's office had a sitting area with coffee tables surrounded by sofas, it had a meeting area with a large working table just like the one in the Boardroom and it had a dedicated area for his desk and traditional office furniture and the floor to ceiling monitor display; each was the size of a large room. He also had a backboard set up with a parquet lane in front of it. At the top of the key there was a large wire barrel filled with basketballs. When Betty came in she could see Chase at the working table, speaking with an older woman in a white chef's coat. He looked up when she came in and he waved her over. It took Betty nearly a minute to walk from the entrance to the workspace. He asked her to sit and he introduced the woman as his personal chef who would be taking her order for anything that she might want. He said he was having pizza. Betty thought that hand-stretched sourdough crust pizza would be delicious, and she placed an order for a vegetarian option. The chef took her leave.

"Do you know how my mind works?" he asked without preamble.

"Well, that's a bit out of the blue, but I wouldn't dare to know what goes on inside your head," she replied.

"I have a million things going on in my head at the same time. Some are big ideas, some are projects, business acquisitions, my mother's birthday, whatever. I can't stop myself from getting into the weeds on things and demanding perfection about every detail. The thing is, I became so successful that I now have to spend all my time keeping the plates spinning and I can't focus on detail."

She nodded. She had been unpacking her laptop, plugging it in and turning it on while trying to be a present, active listener.

"Now I have to have people for that. I have people who run projects, I have people who look after investments, I have people to manage my corporate relationship with governments – I have people for everything. The only things I do still get into detail about are things that can't be trusted to anyone else to do. When I pulled together information for your company I had people gather it but I did the initial analysis myself."

Her machine beeped to life and she went to the sideboard to make herself a tea, always maintaining active listening behaviours. Curtis Chase went on.

"I've always been an engineer at heart, but I had to turn into a business numbers guy. I had to turn into a people person too, to get everything done through all of those people I have running things. So if I bring all of these points of view to bear on the problem your company is working on then I'm left with some questions. Let's take this from the top and talk it through."

She sat with her tea, crossed her legs and leaned back in the swivel chair and said, "That is a great idea. We can fill in blanks for the other as we go and maybe we'll get a break."

"Great," he said. "You were the first person I spoke to in your company, so there's no need to rehash what we've both lived. I started communicating with Horton directly maybe a week or so after Hoover Dam."

"Sounds about right," she said.

"I had consistent requests for information and assistance from him, mostly for monitoring and analysing data for financial flows and forensic accounting requests. I set up a working group to respond to these requests, but everything still went through me."

"Okay."

"Carl started reaching out to me directly whenever he had some kind of breakthrough that fed into our analyses or opened a new line of inquiry. I put up with it, but it was starting to eat into my business focus – what I call my real life."

"This would have been while we were in the field in Malitania. We were gathering intelligence briskly and the situation expanded rapidly on the ground," Betty said.

"So when he called me in the middle of the night I was just about to start telling him off. That's when he gives me his thoughts about Millenium Horizon. He asked me to go back into the data and the parameters of the scenarios, to put the real life sequence of events in and see what happens."

"That's a great find," Betty said. "If we do crack this thing it's likely we'll have had Carl Horton to thank for it."

"It was. And he was right. We found any scenarios with these events in this sequence ended with and isolated America and fortress Europe. Critically, they all had one other event in common. The nuclear event."

"A shocking revelation to me yesterday," she added.

"Yes, unthinkable. But anyway, ever since then the company's requests have been focused solely on the U.S. Even when the origin of the data is outside the U.S., there's some connection to nuclear power in America," he said.

She looked at him intently now, her piqued interest real.

"When I add in the concerns you voiced over the past couple days, I get the picture that Horton may be scared or something, and he's losing sight of the scope of this problem. As far as I can tell there's nobody across this at your company except for Horton, so the fate of the free world could literally be in his hands."

"I think you're exactly right," she said, "and that's exactly what I'm afraid of. Horton could be losing his grip. My academic and professional expertise leads me to believe he has been too close to the radicalised nationalist movement here too. I'm not sure it's safe to leave it to him."

Across the office, one of the panels of the wall behind Chase's desk sprung out and slid along the adjacent panel, revealing the inside of a hidden elevator, from which the chef emerged pushing a steel trolley carrying a gourmet meal centred around hand stretched pizza. There was a break in the discussion while they helped the chef to spread a cloth and set the meal. She then took her leave, bringing the trolley back through the hidden elevator. Chase picked up the conversation again, and filled her in on the kinds of requests Horton had been making and the kind of information that was being reported to him.

"Assuming Horton focused on American facilities and American weapons, what could he have missed?" Chase asked.

"Well," she said. "I've been giving this some thought since you told me about this yesterday. If you are Al Sudeiri or Nesralla you need something to happen soon. Sending technicians from the axis of resistance isn't going to do anything for you in that time frame. As an analyst I'd de-prioritise this as a credible threat. Also, generally, American sites are harder targets than sites in Europe. This is particularly true for civilian sites."

"Right," he said, "go with that. What next?"

"I hate to say this bit, but it's true. If you need this event to drive Europe into hardening its borders and closing its ears to the Islamic world then it would need to happen in a major European country, like Germany or France."

"This all makes sense," he said.

"And think back to what their behaviours have been in setting up the financial networks and communication to and from all the different organisations," she said.

"At some point there is always someone from their personal past that makes the connection," he said.

"Exactly," she replied. "I'd want to know if there was anyone from their pasts that is connected in some meaningful way to civilian nuclear power in a major European country. How long would it take for us to have a definitive answer on something like that?"

"Here's the beauty part of being a billionaire. I'm going to make a few calls and in two hours we're going to have people in the room and around the world on screen working with us to solve this from first principles in real time," he said. "While I'm on the phone you keep working that magic and come up with the next four things we need to know by daylight."

This is what communication must feel like for his employees, she thought. She was happy to leverage all of the support he could provide, but she was not one of his employees and she never would be. What would be the point of having all of that 'fuck you' money otherwise? She nibbled on a crust of cold pizza and took out a looseleaf notebook and her favourite pen and started listing facts from her eidetic memory to get herself started while Chase told the wall to call and display certain people. They gathered a team of people and spent most of the night brainstorming, gathering data, analysing and concluding. There was frequent well informed challenge around the table and nobody's pride was hurt when something didn't go their way. Everybody was focused on discovering new information and connections, and because there wasn't much time the process got to be choppy. In the end though, after the sun had come up, they had a couple of viable scenarios and a significant amount of what she called 'actionable intelligence'.

Omar Gastineau had attended Trinity college, the nearest to Balliol physically, while the cabal was at Oxford. He is French, but his mother was born in Algeria, and he was a listed member of the Middle Eastern Studies Society. He is currently an executive director at EDF for all of Hauts-de-France, which includes responsibility for the largest powerplant in France, at Gravelines. Gravelines is among the oldest set of reactors and there is so much radioactive material that a serious accident would deny access to the English Channel, destroy a major server farm nearby and have life-threatening implications for populations downwind in the weather pattern, such as Calais, Lille and into the low countries. If they needed something big enough then an accident at Gravelines would probably do the trick.

There were four other pieces of actionable intelligence gleaned that night, and other people would be running those down to fill in detail and produce a threat assessment for Betty within twenty-four hours. The lead in Hauts-de-France was the only one that warranted her personal attention on-site, and she prepared to leave for France that day. She would travel using her own French passport and Chase would cover everything through a consulting retainer. She would have a team putting together every discoverable piece of information on Omar Gastineau and curating AI insights for her while she was in the air. She felt like this was an excellent lead, and now it was up to her not to botch the tradecraft.

The Final Gambit

One of her support team had contacted La Lance Fournie and rushed a contract with Chase's security consulting firm. They would provide whatever kind of support was required on the ground in France and Chase had agreed not to refuse 'any reasonable invoice', which meant that they had a blank check. La Lance and the support team in the U.S. began communicating and coordinating immediately; Limier was the project lead for La Lance.

While Betty was in the air the support team sent the research dossier to Limier to read and to provide a copy to Betty. Based on what was in the dossier Limier had dispatched trusted observers to Gravelines and the surrounding area and had retained a French law firm to officially request public records such as planning requests, licences and criminal histories. Also based on what Limier found in the dossier he prepared communications for the French police and for the ASN, the French nuclear safety authority.

Limier picked Betty up from Orly airport in Paris and after an extended greeting they got into the large black SUV and started their journey north. La Lance had reserved rooms and a meeting space at a mid-range hotel in the far eastern part of Calais and the rest of the team had taken the lead to prepare.

Limier sat in the back with Betty and it was someone else's turn to drive. The SUV had the centre row of seats configured so there was a small, recessed table between the passengers, with chargers and connectors. Limier set down and opened an accordion file with notes and documents that already included handwritten notes in margins and stuck on coloured flags and memos. Betty's phone and tablet pinged continuously for three minutes as the notifications accrued while she was in the air sounded off. They expected to be on the road for about four hours where Betty would get caught up on all of the research before the jet lag took hold and she had to power down. Limier would debrief her on the new intelligence before she started reading, and while she was at her most alert.

"There's a lot to know about our friend Omar, and a lot to know about where he works," Limier said to Betty.

Betty minimised her message window and made a show of putting her phone down, focusing on what Limier was telling her.

"After he graduated from Oxford he got his masters in engineering from the École Polytechnique in Paris and then spent most of his career at EDF. He had been climbing the corporate ladder and about four years ago he started actively pursuing his current role,

which gives him the most authority over what happens at Gravelines. He got the job three years ago when his predecessor retired at age fifty-one."

Betty interjected, *"So somebody could have paid off his boss to step down and open the seat for him?"*

"That could be plausible," Limier said. Betty gave a small nod, indicating that she had stored that information. Limier went on.

"I know you are a Parisian city girl, so I'll remind you that Gravelines is right on the coast, between Calais and Dunkirk. Bourbourg is a hamlet just inland from Gravelines on the river Aa. It was forgotten for a long time until the eighties when Gravelines was built, but now a lot of electricity executives and nuclear scientists live there. Omar bought an old mill on the Aa and converted it to his family home. He even restored and repurposed the millwheel to produce electricity."

Betty interjected with a question this time, *"So there's likely a massive stone building air gapped and off grid?"*

"There's more that supports that hypothesis. Planning permission applications show enclosed interior areas that are inaccessible and unused."

"So secret storage maybe?" she said.

"You're so cynical. Why do you want to think the worst of our friend Omar?" he joked, then went on.

"We'll have to get real eyes on the place and see what we can observe. If he has the place fortified then we'll be able to tell. Big stone building with fencing walls and its back to the river? A place like that could be impregnable."

"This is already feeling like planning an assault," Betty said. *"I'm not in the goddamn mood. If he's got an armed and fortified position in northern France then we tell the French authorities and let them deal with it."*

"That's always the best option, but we don't always seem to have play available," Limier said. He changed the subject and carried on.

"That was Omar at home. Here's what you need to know about Omar's daily work. Safety inspections used to be done by an independent division at EDF's head office, but they were outsourced to a London-based consulting firm owned, ultimately, by Hani Nesralla. Safety reports can be filed only after a partner at the firm and Omar Gastineau sign them."

"So they easily could have colluded and lied, since this conflict got under the radar, and we could be on our way to a meltdown now," Betty sighed.

"Unfortunately, yes," Limier said. "We wouldn't have known half of this or been able to make any connections without your friends in the States. They're able to learn whatever you need to know, in a very short turnaround time."

He tilted his water bottle straight up to avoid spilling as they went over a speedbump joining a slip road.

"Anyway, the lawyers have drafted communications to the nuclear watchdog and to the French police," he said, turning papers over until he found them in the folders. He took them out and laid them in the recessed table between them.

"If I were calling the shots on this one I'd ask them to move forward with the watchdog letter now, since that's based on facts that won't change and wait on the letter to the police until we've gotten eyes on the place tomorrow," Limier said.

"Right," Betty agreed, "please do that now, if you don't mind."

He took out his phone and made a call. Betty got sucked in to the folders and read for the remainder of the journey. They only talked intermittently and during their one comfort break. It was midafternoon when they got to the hotel in Calais. Their were three members of La Lance there already, with a passenger vehicle and a work van. They all had rooms on the top floor with balconies overlooking the parking lot. They checked in, met briefly in the conference room where Limier gave a short briefing and introduced Betty; after the memorial service in Marseilles she recognised all the faces but the only other person she knew was The Professor. Limier gave the team members their assignments and sent them off.

He stayed to monitor their communications and coordinate movements. He did that with his phone and a tablet, so he could meet Betty for dinner before she retired, exhausted.

She woke up after sleeping eleven hours uninterrupted and went down to the hotel's restaurant; it was four-thirty in the morning. She used the kettle and tea service to make herself a tea and she sat at a table and turned on her devices. After a few minutes Limier came down the elevator and walked through the dim lobby to the restaurant, looking for Betty as his eyes adjusted to the lighting.

"Good morning," she said to him, *"I'm flattered that you would set an alarm for me."* He must have planted a motion sensing camera linked and instructed it to ring his alarm when her face was recognised.

"Good morning," he said. *"Yesterday was a productive day for the team and I wanted to get you up to speed so we can hit today running."*

He put down his file folder on her table and went to get a coffee for himself. Over his shoulder he said, *"You can have a look at that whenever the sleep is out of your eyes."*

There was a stack of eight by ten black and white photos which she took out and looked at first. They were different angles and vantage points of the property. She laid them out over the whole table so they could see every one. Limier came back holding a coffee and put it on an adjacent table. Betty started pointing out features of the property and Limier added commentary or explanation where he could. There was no other sound in the restaurant so there were pauses of silence punctuated by Limier's staccato declarations.

Her finger landed on the two feet of barbed wire added onto the five foot tall stone wall that surrounded the property.

"All the way around, including the iron entrance gate. The planning application said they wanted to keep sheep and goats out of the grounds. Is there a goat that can jump twenty feet over the entrance gate?"

Her finger landed on and encircled two newer outbuildings within the wall, still made out of stone. They were built with only a small walkway between them and they were quite close to the main building that now served as the residence.

"Kennels," he said. "Not part of the planning application. Buildings this size should have been reported but haven't. They have four bully dogs who are definitely guarding the place."

Her hand pointed out crenelations at every corner of the roof.

"Definitely positions for concealed cover."

She pointed out several other points of interest but it was clear. The old mill had been 'hardened' defensively and there was no way to know what awaited them inside. She leaned back in her chair and crossed her arms and sighed.

"Everything points to us being right about this," she said. Limier nodded in agreement.

"This is just on the edge of being enough to report to French authorities," she went on. He nodded again.

"When it gets full light I want to go there myself and have a look," she said. "I think I'll deliver a package or something. If I get the hair standing up on the back of my neck then I'm going to report it straight away."

"I think that's the way to go," Limier said.

They dropped into planning the day since they were both up. They would send the team to pose as an arborist crew just around the bend from the old mill and they would surveil the property with drones and provide Betty information in real time. Once they had it clear in their minds Limier went back to bed while Betty went back to studying until the restaurant opened.

▪▪▪

By eight-thirty the team provided her with an old Citroen Picasso completely filled with cardboard boxes and bagged parcels. Driving that she would look like a private delivery contractor who are so common these days. They had added stencils and lettering to their work van, marking it with advertisements for a local tree service, including an active local telephone number. They checked all their communication devices to be sure they were all functioning well. They double checked the concealment of their weaponry and the operation of the thermal imaging readings from the device on one of the drones. Everything appeared to be in good order, and they quickly went over the morning sequence once more to make sure the actions and the timing were clear. First, Betty would drive out to the rural route the mill was on and make a couple of deliveries for good measure. While she was doing this, the team would get in position and send up the drones. Then, Betty would approach the property and fake being lost so she could go around the property in her car. If there were no surprises from the drone scans then she would approach the front gate and try to gain access. This set of actions should trigger several recognisable defensive activities, and if they did then Betty would get back in the car and drive on, giving Limier the signal to contact the authorities and maintain watch until the French police arrived. It was all set.

As they completed the final touches before setting out she thought how exhausted she was with all of this. She had to do all she could because the gravity of the situation required it, but if she lived through this she was going to take a very long time and disappear. Maybe she would take her mother somewhere far away; maybe Mauritius. It would be familiar enough and exotic enough so she could enjoy it without being shocked. Maybe they would go to the Seychelles. After that, Betty could talk to Miriam about moving out of Bamako. Her mother's safety relied on Betty's anonymity and Betty was less confident that she would never be identified as an asset. Maybe on their holidays they could discuss going away and not returning; it might be time to cash in on the 'retirement fund'.

She stayed in this kind of rumination after she set the satellite navigation system and headed out for the half hour drive to Bourbourg. The van set out at the right time and they checked in with each other to see that the comms were still working. She settled into driving the packed sedan and listening to the navigation system giving robotic instructions with a Parisian accent not unlike her own. She tried to calm her mind but she kept going back to taking her mother away to a French speaking island in the Indian Ocean, where they could figure out how to spend their days finally getting to know one another as mother and daughter. She would like to chance to make some kind of gesture that would show her forgiveness for her mother's sending her away so young. She would like to…

What the hell was that?

In her reverie she hadn't been fully observant, and when she passed the entrance to the filling station on her left she barely registered the blond man gassing up the s-class Benz. She was only traveling the speed limit, so to get a better look she turned her head in a very obvious way, which also drew his attention. She caught a glimpse of him going from profile to facing, and with that one second of view she thought it could well have been Abdul Aziz Al Sudeiri. She immediately pushed the clutch to the floor and depressed the brake to glide to a stop. Her deceleration was still fast, and some of the packages from the back seat tumbled into the front and fell onto her lap and some packages loaded in the front washed up against the windshield like a breaking wave. Could that possibly be him? And if it was, did he see her? If he saw her in that glimpse would he be able to recognise her? She had to at least get a better look, and she turned her hard stop into an abrupt three point turn. She threw on her right turn signal and started back into the petrol station's fueling lot, only to have the grey Benz pull around her and proceed in the direction she came from. Each driver was not expecting the other and they instinctively flinched to avoid collision. The two hundred and seventy degree passing occurred as if in slow motion and each had a chance to look fully in the others' face. Betty's face was nearly as closed to Al Sudeiri's as it was at The Little Frog.

She had to turn hard to avoid hitting the petrol pumps and she could see that the hose lay across the pavement. She could see the attendant running hard out of the shop only to have to stop short to avoid being hit by Betty's car. So, he had recognised her and dropped the hose to flee immediately. She had to decelerate hard again and manipulate the clutch, brake and gears only to resort to the handbrake to negotiate the tight exit. The satnav in the Picasso was bleating out recalibrated instructions to the mill and packages were flying freely around the inside of the vehicle. She made it to the road again and could see the rear of the Benz as Sudeiri tried to make distance between them. She immediately followed, accelerating as fast as the machine could. The Benz handled like a sports car and had hit speeds like a racecar. The Picasso was an unwieldy people carrier that was ladened down with what Betty now knew were real packages for delivery. They were on an A-road, what would be a state highway in America, and it had exits that were marked and controlled. Between flash shifting and batting away packages, she keyed the comms and shouted,

*"M'aidez! M'aidez! I have spotted Sudeiri and am in pursuit. Repeat. Have spotted **Sudeiri** and I am trying to maintain visual contact!"*

So it was Gravelines. There was no need to obtain further confirmation. The whole plan was off now that she had been spotted though. If Sudeiri got away then by the time the police were involved and up to speed there would be no chance of catching him, and perhaps little chance of reversing a nuclear meltdown. Betty knew that triggering a nuclear disaster wasn't like flicking a light switch. Gastineau must have had a process to break it down over time, likely ramping up the temperature and timing when the infrastructure would start to fail. But where were they in the process and would it be possible to reverse it – whatever it was? No, letting Sudeiri get away was not an option.

"Oh my God," came Limier's reply over the road noise, *"where are you?"*

"I'm on the same road as you, just much further behind. He's in a grey S-class Benz and I can't keep up. I'm going to lose him."

"OK," Limier said, *"We haven't been passed by a Benz. Let me think,"* he said, but he was already thinking like a Parisian cop. *"We'll stop and prepare to disable him and you make sure he doesn't take an exit."*

"Alright, I'll do that as long as I can maintain visual contact," she replied.

Limier pulled the van over to the side and turned on his hazard lights. He told one of the guys to prepare the extendable mats for puncturing tires, and he told another to set up the sniper rifle. He instructed a third man to launch the drones as soon as they came to a full stop. Limier went around the van on the side away from traffic and set up the reflective triangle to show the vehicle was broken down. As soon as they had confirmation they could open the rear door and the sniper, lying on the floor of the van, would have a clear shot at the Benz's engine block. A well placed high-calibre round or two could easily disable a car engine and if the Benz reached them, they could deploy the tool to puncture its tires. They waited.

Betty carried on up the road at the top speed of the Picasso. About ninety seconds after she lost visual contact she saw a road sign for an exit only a mile away and showing the following exit was not for another eleven miles. If she didn't take this exit then she wouldn't be able to get off until long after the Benz should have passed Limier and the van. It took her a mile to slow down enough to take the exit safely. She keyed the comms and told them what she was doing.

"I'm at an exit and I'm taking it. I'll look around down here; there isn't much I'd be able to do for you anyway when he passes. You should see him in the next few minutes, I would think," she said.

"Copy that," Limier replied, *"we'll send the drones in your direction in case he took that exit."*

The Picasso's tires squealed all throughout the tightly angled descent to street level. The load of packages was now moving around the cab fluidly and through the sharp turn cardboard had built up in a bank against her left shoulder and the Citroen looked like a snow globe left on its side. She arrived at a small strip mall trying to take advantage of customers from the A-road. She scanned the parking area and drove in behind the long building to see if there was a Benz parked behind there. She pulled back out and carried on toward what looked like a residential area. She wasn't speeding and she wasn't frantic. She used her cover as a delivery driver to prowl the roads and avenues, squinting into the distance. She got through the whole development and turned back to explore the other direction from the exit. She got the same result. The Benz should have passed Limier by now. She got back on the comms.

"I have no sign of him from here, and he would have passed you by now. You've seen nothing?"

"Nothing," came the immediate reply. "We've got the drones up and we are three miles from the next exit. Why don't we get off there and make our way back and you come up to meet us? If he's gotten off between us then we have a good chance of spotting something."

"Sounds good," she said. She shut off the satnav and turned on the map on her phone that showed where the tracker on Limier's phone was. Limier had the same thing on hers, so the could see where each vehicle was, generally. She found a fairly uninterrupted secondary road that headed west toward Bourbourg. If she were driving the Benz then this would be a good option for egress. She followed the road for a short way before she was driving through fields with hedgerows lining the shoulderless road.

The van soon found itself in similar landscape and their blue dots on the map crept toward each other little by little. Betty agonised at every country lane she passed but couldn't inspect. Sudeiri could have taken any one of these and gotten away. Sudeiri also must have known that many of these small access roads were for local farmers only, and they could peter out in a field or dead-end at a cliff face. They were relying heavily on the drones for a lead here. If he stopped moving then he may have a good chance of evading detection and waiting until dark. That's what Betty thought she would do. Now she had to decide where she would hide, and hope Sudeiri had the same idea.

They carried on doing this kind of grid search long enough for her to question all of her choices since recognising him. She started to think about what it would be like if he got away. How would she explain what had happened to her bosses at the company? She'd been trying to prevent the loss of thousands of lives; would her good intentions save her from falling afoul of the law?

"We think we have something here," Limier's voice came over the comms. "We've spotted a grey Benz south of your position. Looks like he got spooked by the drone and he's headed back to the A-road behind you."

"Good," she replied. "there's only one ramp on and one ramp off back there."

"We're going to do our best to stay with him," Limier said. "Remember, he doesn't know where you are and you're closer to the exit that he is."

"I got it," she said. "Hurry."

There was a rotary in the town road approaching the A-road, so traffic heading into town would come from the south and take the first exit eight o'clock, if the rotary were a clockface. The on ramp to the A-road was at two o'clock and the exit was sharp. She thought that this was her only chance. If she tried to stop him and he made it through then the Benz would disappear on the road as the Picasso had no chance of keeping up and the van was still meandering through semirural surface roads. She drove around the rotary and parked the Picasso across the rotary road the long way, where an oncoming car wouldn't have the chance to stop before they hit it.

Limier said they lost him under the canopy of trees in the town and she told him what she was doing, and that she had to abandon the vehicle because it was unsafe. She hopped over the berm that separated the rotary, on the far side where an oncoming motorist wouldn't see. She attached the silencer to her pistol, crouching in the dirt culvert ten feet away from the concrete separator for the rotary. No one else was about in the area. She took out her cell phone and called Limier's number. While it was still ringing she heard the screech of tires from the ramp and she came out to spring her trap. But it was a local contractor in a pickup truck that had come around the tight angle at too high a speed and had hit the Picasso in the rear passenger side, knocking it against the separator. Betty had approached at the quick, with the muzzle of the pistol pointing down and away from her to prevent a deadly accident if she tripped. When the contractor got out of his vehicle and filled the air with profanity, he only saw the top of Betty's head before she ducked back down. He was furious. Before he could let out his second stream of invective though, the loud whine of a high-performance engine drown everything out. This gave the contractor just enough time to jump clear as the Benz came into view and immediately veered away from the accident but still hit the Picasso and rode up the separator that was shaped like a Jersey barrier. It must have been travelling nearly forty miles per hour and all the airbags deployed. Glass shattered to small cubes and sprayed over the top of the separator like an insulted woman's drink. The contractor was standing in the middle of the road with his hands on his head, in shock an awash in adrenaline after nearly being killed. Smoke rose from the accident scene and vehicles ticked and hissed. Sudeiri hung from his seat restraint, dropping toward the ground. He appeared unharmed but he was unconscious. Betty hopped over the separator and approached the Benz. She produced her weapon and instructed the contractor to exit the scene immediately, which he did. Betty gave an update into the phone, saying that all vehicles were immobilised, but Al Sudeiri was trapped. She pulled at the door of the Benz but she couldn't get it open because it was bent out of shape and gravity was against her.

"This accident will get a lot of attention soon. You have to get here before the authorities do, or we'll have more explaining than we can do," she said.

"We're less than three minutes away," he said, and he was right. They arrived and pulled up beside the rotary. Three men hopped out with a long prybar used for tree roots and pried the door of the Benz open. They cut the restraints and lifted out the unconscious Sudeiri. While they carried him into the van Betty jumped in and desperately tried to gather up the documents and detritus from his briefcase and the glove compartment. The drone operator shouted to her from inside the van that the police were closing in and she had to leave now. Now they could hear a symphony of sirens in the distance, police, fire and ambulance. Betty wished she could flick a lit match and have the whole scene erupt in evidence-purifying flames like they did in the movies, but that was not possible. She scrambled into the back of the van just as the door was being slid shut and the van was pulling away. They landed the drone and drove as inconspicuously as possible back toward Calais and anonymity. Abdul Aziz Al Sudeiri was restrained and unconscious on the van floor, receiving medical attention. They had done it. Hopefully they still had the chance to avert a nuclear disaster in northern France.

Epilogue: Echoes Across the Desert

French authorities picked up Omar Gastineau from his house. Al Sudeiri and some hired thugs were staying there after kidnapping Gastineau's family, making sure that he carried through with the plan. Gastineau had rigged meters installed so the temperature readings would be misreported; half of the reactors at Gravelines would have melted down and caused a catastrophic disaster if they hadn't found out in time. The ASN took over the facility and is now running it directly through contractors; the French electricity company was sanctioned for its lack of oversight.

Betty and La Lance delivered Al Sudeiri to the company's station chief in Paris. Although they were grateful, they called Betty in for two weeks of debriefing in Washington, where Curtis Chase was also called in to answer some hard questions. Carl Horton was asked to retire and he took his family back out to Michigan where he now works for a private security firm. After Betty had a little distance from her loss she thought about her rage, and what her father would want, and she decided that Carl Horton wasn't worth a revenge killing. If she were to do it then she would leave no trace and not be able to be found guilty in court. The judgment wouldn't come from court though and the sentence would likely be permanent. Carl was free to live his shrinking life. She hoped he would become a better person.

Betty herself was instructed to retire from the service, which she readily did. She stayed out of court and she was free to live her life. Nobody asked her about any of her personal means, and she, Khadija and certain members of La Lance Fournie slowly and surreptitiously recovered the gold from the trebuchet pit and legitimised it or squirrelled it away. Betty went to Bamako and stayed with her mother for some time. During that time she told her mother what Harry was like and how he treated her. She told her mother that Harry had died saving her, and she gave her half of Harry's ashes and about ten pounds of gold fashioned into Tuareg jewelry. Betty told her mother that they were going to spend about three months together in Mauritius, living well and getting to know each other better. Right after one final errand.

Which brought her here. She came back to London over the water at night to meet Elena and give her the news. She handed off the ashes and helped Elena with the paperwork to get the insurance payout for the identity Harry held at La Lance. She gave Elena ingots of gold which Elena was scared to keep. Betty told her that she would help exchange it if she ever chose to do so, and Elena accepted it.

Elena gave Betty a watch that Harry received from his father. Harry kept it and Elena assumed it was a memento of a man Harry loved, but Betty doubted that. The watch was very nice, expensive and old. Betty didn't want to keep it but she didn't want to be rude to Elena either, so she accepted it and was going to deliver it to Harry's uncle Simon, who was in full time care in Dartford. During the few days staying at Curtis's place in Covent Garden, Betty dug a little into Simon's life, happy to get to know her brand new great uncle. She was moved by his history, coming from the same home as Harry's father, and by his commitment to 'being good'. Betty set up a trust for uncle Simon's care and from now on he would want for nothing and his private care would be of the very highest quality. There was a carer that Simon was very attached to, apparently, and the carer would be put on a full time high paying retainer.

It had been a period of highly charged transformation for Betty and she felt a heavy exhaustion as she exited the train onto platform two at Dartford station. There was almost no rail traffic at this hour and she sat alone on the bench just outside the closing train doors. The sun was high, the weather was dry and the smell of roasting coffee from the nearby factory permeated the air. A murmuration of starlings had taken up position in the branches of the trees separating the rail lines from the housing development behind it. The distant bird conversation lay melody over the droning of the jets of water from the fountain in the small pond under the tower of balconies. She would just tell uncle Simon who she was to Harry and say clearly and unequivocally that she was happy to have him as an uncle. She felt this was going to be a very good day. She yawned and stretched and headed for the exit.

Bonus Feature

Dartford Interlude

In the plexiglass backwall of the bus stop shelter across the street he could see the image of a young black man, muscular and lean with sharp features. Beside him stood a white man in late middle age, a head taller than the black man, clothed in whatever had come off the clearance rack. Cars seemed to pass through them and a meandering terrier behind them lackadaisically sniffed at litter that had caught itself in the shelter's stanchion, pinioned by the wind. The white man wore an olive drab knitted hat pulled down over his ears. The hat was pulled down a bit too far, and the clearance rack clothing was worn without consideration of presentation; the jeans pulled high over the waist, sweatshirt tucked in and belt fastened at the navel. The white man shifted his weight nervously and rhythmically from foot to foot, giving him the overall air of an overgrown toddler, unaware of the source of his own impatience.

He looked at the black man's face. It was the face on the identification tethered to the end of the lanyard around his neck. The name on the identification was Alfred Birima. So Alfred Birima was the person hovering there across the busy street, being but not being, defined by his proximity to the white man and his distance from himself.

A hill rose behind the bus stop with a steep set of stairs leading to the Dartford Borough Council offices and the shimmering edifice of Dartford station. Alfred was on the sidewalk with the Orchard Theatre behind him. The lights did not allow pedestrians to cross and the white man's agitation had grown severe. His side-to-side motion had been supplemented with forward and backward shifting approximating a step. In the reflection Alfred's hand instinctively moved over and held the white man's hand, instantly calming him and rooting him at the foot of the zebra crossing.

At that moment a cloud of teenage schoolboys on bicycles went whizzing by in a flutter of blazer tails and neckties, peddling hard to the roundabout and ignoring all rules of the highway code and of civility. Shouting over traffic to each other and flushed with the effort they appeared as a band of barbarians swooping down from Temple Hill. The one in the lead looked down at the two men's hands and shouted at the top of his lungs, "Why don't you grab him by the cock, you poofy n*****!!"

In that small blur they had shattered the reflection. There were some shouts in response from people at the bus stop and on the sidewalk opposite, but the biggest reaction came from Simon Holloway, who pulled his hand so the black man was looking directly at him.

"He said a bad thing to you Alfred. He said a bad thing for everyone to hear. He's a bad boy and you know what bad boys get."

"Don't you mind him Si," came the response, "It's only attention he's after and we shan't give him that." This is the thing that Alfred Birima would say, so it is what he says. Ignoring the insult of the petulant, entitled, perverse offender is what Alfred Birima would do, so it is what he does. Not put a sight picture centre of mass below his shoulder blades, leading minimally because of the vertical retreat of the target. Not pull the trigger of an assault weapon. Not kill another child.

The light changed, displaying the pictogram of the little green walking man. Alfred led Simon by the hand across the street where they passed the stairs to the rail station and headed left toward the set of shops below and behind it. Every Saturday Alfred picked Simon up at his care home and took him to browse the aisles of the B&Q where they would spend about an hour going up and down each section. Simon had to take the pamphlet from the greeter at the door and locate each of the largest sale items in the racks. He also had to handle each of the contractor's tools and get a feel for them by weight and balance, and explain the proper way to get the best effect from the tool with minimal exertion by the user. This is what his father had instructed him to do decades prior and he had never forgotten. Where there were bargains in the pamphlet that were not displayed or were not in stock, Simon had to confer with Customer Service to verify that they were indeed available and that they could be provided readily should anyone care to make a purchase.

Today there was an inflatable hot tub on offer but there wasn't one set up in the right area, nor were there boxed kits anywhere on the floor. Simon marched directly and purposefully the considerable length of the warehouse store to put the pamphlet on the Customer Service counter open to the page, and he began to smooth out the picture of the hot tub over and over. Today it was Anne who was stood at the counter in her black uniform coveralls and trademark orange apron. She was expecting Simon and she greeted them heartily as she approached.

"Hello my Lovelies. How are you and what can I help with on this beautiful Saturday?"

Alfred knew Anne now. Indeed he knew most of the employees by sight, but he knew best those employees who manned the Customer Service desk. Manned may not have been the most appropriate term. Most of the employees at the Customer Service desk were older and female – most of the younger and male employees were tethered to lifts or leading palate jacks with loads of paint or strapped loads of lumber. Alfred would see them and sometimes exchange greetings or pleasantries, but Simon seemed not to want to talk to them or to make eye contact. At the Customer Service desk, where discussion was required, it was safe to engage with others, and by design the employees there were not threatening.

As far as Alfred knew, Simon could not pick up on the nuanced emotions of others. Alfred had grown to learn that Simon was empathic and compassionate and that he cared deeply about the feelings and well being of others around him. He could not, however, seem to be able to project these to people who were not present or in his line of vision. For example, he wouldn't be bothered by the suffering of East Africans in a drought or famine because he couldn't comprehend their suffering. They were apparently out of his empathic range. Similarly, he was unequipped to pick up on the pity that was poured out to him by many. Alfred thought this was a good thing because he may well be drowned in it. Pity did not get his shoes tied, pity did not get him properly wiped after public toilet and pity did not make sure he was well nourished in a timely fashion. Alfred did these things for him because it was his job and he got paid for it. This saccharine gush of pity that Anne always turned on was wasted on Simon and Alfred considered it an insult – so who did it serve?

"This hot tub," he said, "somebody will be needing this. It's nowhere in the seasonal displays and it isn't in with the bathroom fittings. Surely if it were staged somewhere on the floor for later dispatch then the inventory would be marked. Can you lead me to it?"

Anne was effusive in her apologies. She was aware that this would be an item of interest and it was her intention to display management's instructions in the seasonal area by Garden, because this item is only available for immediate pickup in Bexley. It could be ordered for delivery to Dartford though, so he'd have to make do with the photo for now. Would that be OK?

To Alfred, her over-attention to the minutiae of the mundane was her perceived contribution to the greater good, and he found it condescending and self-congratulatory. He quietly resented her for it but he was aware that it could only come from a place of genuine emotion. She had engaged a primal connection. Alfred was jealous of her ability to access this instinct which he had excised from himself as an act of self-preservation. He now felt he needed to resuscitate it, as an act of self-preservation born of his new circumstances. Although Alfred wanted to, he could not pity Simon.

When they left B&Q they would walk back across the London Road and cross in front of the Orchard Theatre. To do that, they would have to pass the row of shops and the parking lot with the Pizza Hut. Every Saturday their little pantomime would play out, and every Saturday Alfred would play his part perfectly.

"What's that that smells nice?" Simon would ask. "That smells lovely, doesn't it?"

"That's pizza," Alfred would say.

"I'd like a bit of pizza. Wouldn't you?"

"We will get lunch at the park cafe, Simon. You know that."

"It's just that a bit of pizza would be lovely, don't you think? Can we go?"

"We're not allowed pizza, Si. You know that. Pizza Hut will be a special day for you and your Mum at your birthday."

"Pizza Hut? Can we go?"

"No, Si. I couldn't spoil it for your Mum. You wouldn't want that, would you?"

All the while Alfred would be leading Simon, past the Marks and Spencer food shop, past the Asda Home Goods, past TK Maxx and finally across where the smell of pizza abated. Once the immediate stimulus was removed the focus and obsession passed, and Simon became fixated on the next scheduled entry in the Saturday rounds. They crossed in front of the theatre where Simon took in all the advertisements for running and upcoming shows. This theatre ran legitimate West End shows and some lower end pantomimes and revues. Sometimes Simon could take half an hour asking a battery of questions about what he saw on the bills. Today there was a billing for a Cher tribute show by a drag artist and Simon was both confused by and obsessed with it. He asked if this were a man or a woman and Alfred decided to answer as truthfully and as briefly as possible. Alfred prepared himself for a long back and forth, but Simon just listened and stood quiet for a minute before finally saying, "Ah, so he's in drag, then, is he?" Alfred was curious as to where Simon's knowledge of drag artistry came from but he knew better than to ask about it and open a new can of worms.

They were on their way to the library, one of Simon's normal stops and one of Alfred's favourite on the tour. They walked through Bullace Lane just behind the millennium old church by the river, past the whitewashed tavern named for Wat Tyler, where he was supposed to have fomented revolution in the misty annals of history. Alfred never understood why the English paid so much attention to their history. They seemed to give a lot of weight to the fact that kings had oppressed people on this spot for a thousand years and killed them when they rose up. This happened everywhere from time immemorial as far as he knew. There was a large plaque on the outside wall explaining the history but they never stopped long enough to read it, because Bullace Lane always smells like piss and Simon wants to get away from bad smells.

They emerged onto the market street, parallel to London Road but blocked with bollards so only pedestrians could pass. The thoroughfare is paved with bright paving stones, and although Thursday is designated as market day many of the sellers set up on a Saturday as well. The publicans and the restaurants put tables out on the pavement and patrons take the air and enjoy a coffee and pastry or a cheeky pint in good weather. Today there is a busker playing an acoustic guitar and singing American folk tunes, giving the square the air of being 'good busy'. Central Park lies just outside the square, a good Kentish greenspace, manicured and arranged by local horticultural societies, and at the edge of the park stands the library. The building of the library is a grand Victorian stone public building originally endowed by Andrew Carnegie and now it has tasteful statuary situated nearby and it houses the local museum as well as the library. They head toward the library, making their way through the busy market. Simon is oblivious to the stares they get, as well as to the looks of pity. Several times during the busy transit Alfred levels a hard stare at a young man whose gaze lingers on Simon too long; Alfred makes it clear that his charge is not a target for predation. As they pass the Cool Beanz Café Alfred sees a young woman with severe Down's Syndrome having a cup of tea and a scone, sitting across from a young African man. Alfred recognises him from the agency. He is a Kenyan student in the eighth year of his three-year degree programme. He speaks no Swahili and he does not look at all east African.

They pass to the front of the library and they are caught in a traffic jam of young mothers pushing strollers and holding the hands of toddlers. Elderly couples walk tiny dogs in and out of the gate to the park under the iron eye of the statue of remembrance of the Great War. They walk the steps and go through the ornate double wooden door. Immediately inside there are welcoming tables and low couches amid low book racks. Some older patrons are deposited around that area, flipping through magazines and tasting through piles of books pulled discerningly from the stacks. Around to the left there are carrels with computers along the wall leading to a large room with a massive table. It is exam season and each carrel and each seat around the table is filled with mostly black and brown students, actively toiling over books and note cards, lips moving as they recite mnemonics. The opposite wing to the right was the children's library, with beanbag chairs and soft play toys. There were some low tables and bright, cartoonish, welcoming book covers lined the walls. Directly across from the library's entrance is an internal foyer with a step down and an open doorway marked as the North Kent Cultural Museum.

Simon always halts in the entranceway and takes a beat, ostensibly taking in the atmosphere and the sounds and smells of the library. He seems energised and purposeful in the library and his sense of belonging eases his ever-present anxiety. He then always walks to the museum entrance, saying, "Let's go to the museum first Alfred," as if things might somehow have been different this time. No one is ever in the museum, neither patrons nor workers, so they have the several rooms to themselves. The displays are arranged in date order and the two men stroll through the past from the neolithic period to the Celts, through Roman Britain and the Saxons to the Viking invasion and Norman conquest. The displays are sparse in the beginning, with neanderthal hand tools from nearby Swanscombe and then torcs and finely worked broach pins. The displays become more and more rich with artifacts as time progresses, and there is a full skeleton of a Saxon man on display. Simon always tells Alfred that this warrior-farmer is very likely one of his great grandfathers, though he has also told Alfred that his people all come from the north, and that he is probably a Viking from York, under it all.

They then go back into the library and approach the desk where two workers sit and where there is always a line of people inquiring into services or failing to communicate their needs in their mother tongues. Behind the desk is the bookshelf with the reserved books, which were requested by cardholders online and were brought to this branch from around the Kent County system. Simon approaches the desk from the side, queue jumping as the English say, and demands the worker's attention with comically inappropriate throat clearing. The tall, lean gentleman on that side of the desk turns his head and looks at Simon over his glasses. He is someone Alfred easily recognises now too. He seems to work every Saturday at the library. His features look to Alfred like he is a mix of Asian and European descent. His accent is educated southern England and his unassuming politeness gives the impression of longstanding familiarity.

Hands still on the desk while rising, he looks up at Simon and wrinkles his nose to adjust his glasses. "Can I help?" he asks.

"I believe I have some books on reserve," Simon says. His voice is the same as always, just a bit too quiet, face pointed on the oblique to the listener, as if he is speaking secrets into a rising wind. Here in the library it is perfect.

"Right, then, Holloway, is it?" Simon doesn't have a library card and he has no means of communicating his reserves to the staff. This man who Alfred recognises but does not know must go through the books and periodicals and personally select an offering for Simon each week. He turns and goes to the Reserve Shelf and looks through each of the clutches of reserves, segregated by named receipt and sometimes bound with rubber bands. He flips through, passes it, and comes back to it, as he must do for every other patron. Today he has two magazines and two books. Unexpectedly, there is also a CD in a case marked Do Not Remove From Library.

He turns back to Simon, handing him the material. "There you go sir. I've booked you an hour on Computer 14 in case you'd like to view your disc. There are headphones on 14 already. Do enjoy and please return the material before you exit."

As far as Alfred can tell, this man has just carried on a normal work transaction, servicing a customer who is no different than any other. In so doing, he has afforded Simon dignity and earned Alfred's respect.

Simon thanks him and he takes the material and looks at Alfred. Alfred looks around and locates Computer 14, set on a low table. There is a small namecard marked reserved in front of the keyboard. They take seats at the table and Simon begins to unpack his magazines and books fastidiously. He is rapt in his attention to these and Alfred gets the impression of a child on Christmas morning unwrapping presents. He has a glossy National Geographic magazine with a pull out map of Machu Picchu and a pictorial exploration of Peru. He also has a scholastic periodical for young learners which has an extensive spread of high quality photographs of baby animals. His two books are coffee table picture books. One recounts the adventures of a Victorian traveller on the Continent and one is on the history of lighter than air travel. His disc is a copy of the popular show Inside the Factory and this edition is a tour through a factory in the north of England where breakfast cereal is made. After careful deliberation Simon decides that he wants to start by watching the show and Alfred cues it up and gets it running for him, testing the headphones and adjusting the volume.

Simon begins watching the show intently, and Alfred lets the calm and the ambience sink in. This is why the library is his favourite part of Saturday. There is a hum of activity and it is a busy public space, but there is an attention to quiet where people are mindful not to draw attention. Without him knowing it, it put his senses into heightened awareness, and this time his mind followed.

****

They had been in the bush for over two months, dealing with booby traps and ambushes. Only occasionally did they encounter the rebels, but there was always bloodshed when they did. Now they were entering Monrovia, at long last. They were on foot and they had no mechanised support, no supply line, no artillery besides mortar tubes they carried themselves. There were just over a hundred of them walking into the rubble of the suburb, about half as many as had left Ghana six months prior. They were almost all Ashanti, led by an Igbo Nigerian commander who hated them and did not care a whit for their lives. They were in their now normal state of exhaustion and near starvation.

Even though the scouts reported no enemy presence, they moved quickly and were absolutely silent. They stayed at least twenty feet away from each other and in the early evening gloom they were hard to see. There were buildings along a high street that could at one time have been churches and shops and the haciendas of the wealthy. Behind them were more streets and more buildings and a whole city unplugged from any kind of infrastructure. They could immediately smell woodsmoke and human waste and it became more pungent when they got within the shadow and cover of the shattered walls.

His AR-15 was slung on his back and he held a cutlass in his right hand. It was a long steel machete with an overweighted bulbous curve on the end, for lopping and digging. A typical African farming tool, he had taken to sharpening this one obsessively to fill the dull hours. This was his normal posture for foraging. Coming into this once well inhabited place, they hoped to find any kind of food or something useful that may have been abandoned when the population fled. He had arrived at what appeared to be a compound house and along a shadowy far wall he found a low window where the wooden louvres had been burned out. He crouched and stepped through and was in a large furnished room. His eyes had no time to adjust to the near total darkness before he detected movement very close.

There was a figure that was semi-crouched and had been rooting at the base of an overturned table. Rising and turning left toward him, the figure was raising an AK-47 that was on a sling across his shoulders. As a reflex he brought the machete down on the rising figure, and this caused him to have to hop to retain his footing. The contact he felt through the tool was the same as if he had been sectioning a goat. There was meaty give, but also the ring of steel on bone. He caught himself from falling and was fully in the room now. He saw the figure for who he was. The face rising with the gun's muzzle had been an enemy combatant but the face now stopped in shock and horror was that of a child. A boy no more than eleven years old looked at him with betrayal and hurt. The cocaine and gunpowder fueled murderous zealot drained away and the boy remained. His left hand had been severed halfway up the forearm and nothing was stopping the arterial flow.

An unbearable pang of pity and remorse clenched onto Owusu's soul and clung to it like the smell of rotting bodies. The disgust that came with this savage and detestable act burned through him and resolved in an instant, out of necessity, an orgasm of self-loathing. The boy let out very high pitched keening as if there were no air in his lungs. Before he could fully cry out, Owusu had to silence him. He knew without thinking that the boy could possibly live through the day but would not survive this wound. He did what he thought most humane.

He threw the head through the opposite window, into the courtyard, heard the cries of shock and alarm and after one second threw the grenade to the same spot. He crouched against the inside of the cement block wall away from the window, setting his gun to three round bursts as the explosion deafened him and violently shook his internal organs. His body became a fluid with every cell buzzing and he became an observer watching what his body did on autopilot. He stepped through the window and began firing bursts before he could really acquire any meaningful targets, beginning with the far left of his field of vision. As people became visible, stunned by the blast or scrambling for weapons, he levelled bursts at them, only aware that he'd pulled the trigger when he heard the report. The click of the empty chamber return told him that his thirty rounds were out, and he pulled his sidearm and walked quickly and purposefully from body to body, dispatching the wounded. When his gun fell silent he heard small arms fire up and down the street and he knew his entire unit was similarly engaged.

****

Simon still had his headphones on, pulled tight against the pc's tower which had been dragged to the edge of the table by the cord. He was staring closely and concernedly into Alfred's face.

"You've done it again Alfred. Are you alright?"

Alfred had a full body spasm, like a head-to-toe charlie horse. Simon told him that his eyes moved like he was dreaming but they were open, then he convulsed once violently.

"That only means that I need to stretch my legs," he said, "Put the computer back on the table properly before it falls off. I'm fine, Si."

Alfred looked around the library and made sure he hadn't attracted attention. He stood slowly and gave an elaborate full body stretch to make it look like the paroxysm and the stretch were parts of the same dance. He checked that Simon was focused on the conveyor belt filled with frosted flakes and then walked slowly to the water fountain and took a slow, deliberate drink. He went back to

Computer 14 and sat at the table again, picking up one of Simon's books and opening it for show. He was alive, and he would stay alive today. Whether or not there was a tomorrow was in the hands of Onyame, but if one was granted then he would find a way through it.

These episodes were becoming less frequent but he worried that Simon would tell the carers at the home. He worried that somehow someone would become concerned about his fitness to be the responsible individual. He couldn't afford to have anyone revisit his vetting. The provenance of Alfred Birima's documentation was shaky at best and his relative anonymity relied on the fact that he was willingly doing a job that no Brit would take for the pittance it afforded. The truth was, though, that an inquiry into his true identity could result in his return to Ghana, which would be a return to certain death. He had cultivated his persona and presence as Alfred Birima out of necessity but it became crucial to him to leave Owusu Charles and to be reborn as Alfred Birima. Owusu Charles had killed children. Owusu Charles had used sexual violence as a weapon of war. Owusu Charles had tortured innocents knowing it was his own fear that drove him to comply. Alfred Birima had a degree from a technical college in Kumasi. Alfred Birima was supported by his family when he emigrated in search of a better life. Alfred Birima goes to church every Sunday and says the prayers and puts pennies in the collection plate. Owusu Charles has fled from a position of privilege as a member of the dictator's bodyguard. After faking his own death he can never return – his family's lives depend on it. If he is discovered then his little brother, both sisters and father and mother will all pay the ultimate price. He has to get these fits under control.

The morning has already grown long and drifted into afternoon. Now, once the books have been returned, they venture into the park itself. They do a lazy circuit of the walking path around the periphery, which goes from the library in the city past the playing fields, meanders through the fishing spots near the small ponds and then through the tunnel under Prince's Street and back. It is a good stretch of the legs and it gives Simon exercise he may not get throughout the week and it gives him the opportunity to greet small dogs and other walkers, giving him human interaction he may otherwise lack. Throughout the walk he tells Alfred facts about the dragonflies and squirrels they encounter, and he points out which landmarks and points of interest lie further afield from the crossings and fences they pass. It is as if he is exercising his memory as he exercises his legs. Once they have reached the flowerbed and the bandstand their talk turned to lunch. There is a very good café within the park, located at the children's play area. It is a small building with a wraparound porch on three sides, with full kitchen amenities and a large public toilet. Simon and Alfred usually order lunch and take it on the porch side facing the skate park and zip line. The café was busy today, and rather than dawdle while ordering, Alfred cajoled Simon into ordering their usual without their normal palaver over what Simon could and could not have.

This one day a week Alfred got lunch paid by the council. He tried to take full advantage of it by ordering as much as he could get within the allotted expense. Simon got an egg salad sandwich with a side salad and a cup of tea and Alfred got two orders of chips, which made for a good mound of steak fries, and half of whichever sandwich was the weekend special with a paper cup of tap water. After they ordered they went directly to one of their favourite tables and laid claim to it by Alfred hanging his pack on the back of a chair and Simon placing his handkerchief on his side of the table, weighed down by the condiment tray. Alfred would first take Simon into the bathroom to wash his hands and then they would take in the busy park scene while they waited for their food.

They sat quietly at first in the pleasant air. It was a cool day but clear, with high clouds scudding overhead. Some parents had set out blankets on the grass and were watching their children on the swing sets and climbing wall while clots of teens rode skateboards through the paved course that wound its way through the common play area. The zip line was a long cable set up between two posts, with a footstand hanging down from a pulley, so children could stand on it and launch themselves for the downhill ride of twenty yards or so. This was a popular feature and there was a queue of children waiting to board.

When Alfred was first assigned to Simon there was a period where Simon had to get used to him. Actually, they had to get used to each other. During that time Simon was always alert and visibly anxious. Simon never let a silence go for more than twenty seconds back then, but over time they became accustomed to each other's presence and Simon became calm around Alfred. Alfred knew Simon was comfortable with him when he noticed that he would allow a silence to grow. Now they had gotten to the point where they could sit together without talking, so the time together wasn't about accomplishing something or hashing something out – it was just time spent together.

They had spent about ten minutes listening to children play, the jingling of dog collars and the hum of conversation and shouted orders rise and fall whenever the café door would swing open and closed at the speed of pneumatics. Alfred saw Simon's face change and he leaned forward and half stood and then sat and half stood again, muttering aloud, "Oh dear, oh my. Oh dear oh dear."

"What is it, Si? Are you alright?" Alfred asked him.

"She must surely be hurt, the poor thing. Should we help?"

Alfred realised Simon must be talking about the girl who fell off of the zip line. He had seen it and taken it in, as he had observed all the activity around him and flagged anything that posed danger. A girl too young to be expected to hold onto the cable, whose legs did not have the strength to bear against the force and motion had fallen, at the height of the zip line's speed and landed hard on her side in the sand that lined the way. Her head had bounced off the ground quite clearly and after struggling on her back with the wind knocked out of her she eventually let out as horrendous a howl as her small body could muster. She managed to reach a sitting position, and there were no adults apparently coming to her aid. She was about thirty yards from where they sat and Simon was unsure of whether he should rise to her aid or not. Eventually they could see a young woman holding an infant making a bee line to the girl at as fast a walk as she could safely achieve, and Simon sat fully again.

Here was another stark example of what had become Alfred's crucial dilemma. He saw as clearly and heard as loudly this vulnerable child in danger and distress, but it did not at all register with him as point of concern. Now when he looked around the park he could see that every adult within earshot had actively taken interest in the girl's fall. All heads were turned that way, some had half risen, as Simon had, and several had stood to take action before the young mother appeared. His own lack of concern for the girl was worrying him for himself.

Through his own research at the library and through anonymous contact through the NHS he had been treating his own post-traumatic stress. The system in England is so alert and focused on providing help and care that he had to take extraordinary precautions not to get pulled into some kind of programme that would identify him and raise an inquiry into his occupation. He eventually found a therapist at one of the care homes in whom he could confide – he thinks she may be falling in love with him – and she provides guided cognitive behavioural therapy sessions before they inevitably fall into bed. It's working. The common symptoms of PTSD are abating over time, but this lack of compassion and inability to empathise, he fears, are symptomatic of an entirely different pathology. His stress from combat is understandable if not easily treatable, but this numbing of the emotion and purposeful disconnection from other humans could be the result of his experience as a torturer. This information he dares not share with anyone at any time. Though he is actually indifferent to 'correcting' himself, he fears that this discernible difference will eventually give him away, so he is committed to reversing this change in himself but he is absolutely at a loss as to how to proceed or even where to begin.

"Are you embarrassed by me, Alfred?" Simon's question pulls Alfred out of his reverie.

"What do you mean, Si? Why are you asking me this?"

"Sometimes when we're walking by people you go quiet and look at your feet. Sometimes when I do things like just now you go blank and leave me all alone."

"I often have a lot on my mind, Si," he quickly responded, looking back up and rejoining the conversation. "I'm never embarrassed of you. You are my job and I am proud of you."

"Mum was embarrassed by me around people. Dad would never go outside with me and he would scare me and Mum, but Mum would 'die a thousand deaths' whenever I had accidents outside," Simon went on.

"Speaking of that," Alfred said, "we should get you to the toilet before we catch the bus for home."

Alfred steered the focus back to the here and now, to the mundane. As he popped the last couple of chips in his mouth he thought how Simon's confession of his mother's embarrassment, especially coming from someone who looked and acted like Simon, would make a healthy person sad. And though the title of his occupation was Carer, Alfred Birima honestly, truly, did not care.

****

On the bus Alfred saw the drizzle blurring the windshield until the world beyond was an impressionist view of the stylised feeling of Dartford. The windshield on the bus's upper tier had no wiper, and the view continued to blur so nothing could be seen but Dartford's memory, until the tears streaked down allowing slivers of clarity through the cracks. It stopped at the bottom of East Hill and he got out. He came down the stairs and had to wait briefly in a line of patrons putting hoods up, adjusting earphones and preparing umbrellas to unfold while wrangling toddlers with no free hands. On the pavement he was the only one to turn up the hill. East Hill is steep and the bus goes up, so anyone heading that way stayed on the bus while everyone else moved off in every other direction.

He put up his own hood against the now light rain and began to trudge up the hill. With the steep grade it was like walking a set of stairs without steps. It reminded him of walking the hills of Mampong as a small boy. A short way up the hill there is a pedestrian layby on the left, with a cement paved circle about ten feet across and a bench with its back against the hill, facing outward and looking over the grounds of the veteran's association. In the cold and wet this bench offers some respite against the wind and there is almost always someone with no other accommodation trying hard to eke out some comfort there.

Alfred passed him or her now, walking to the back of the layby where there is a steep set of stairs, almost like a ladder, climbing the hillside behind. This is the pedestrian passageway to St. Edmund's Pleasance, the burial ground adjacent to where Alfred lives. He'd actually learned about this place in his conversational English classes shortly after his arrival. St. Edmund was martyred in 870 A.D. and his burial place was supposedly consecrated that year. The spire erected there was in the Domesday Book and several high-profile Protestant martyrs of Bloody Mary's short reign were also buried there. Again, a handful of dead from a distant past remembered for what purpose?

Atop the set of stairs he has arrived at the back of a warren of knotted roads trodden before there was an England, but populated with razor thin terraced houses in the Victorian era. The community had been purpose built in the 1850s to house families of working people but as the economy modernised its relevance dwindled and now it was just a hard to reach, left behind council estate. Alfred passed empty cider bottles clogging the grates causing flooding at each crossing. He heard the couples fighting within the walls only one layer of brick thin. He passed foxes, out in broad daylight foraging from the polystyrene takeaway packages overflowing the dumpsters incongruously left in parking spaces and painted with the council logo. Then he arrived at number eight Hare's Run. Home sweet home.

Hare's Run was a terrace of twelve houses with no green between the road and the doors. Each is twice as wide as Alfred is tall, and each has a downstairs made up of a galley kitchen and a sitting room. Upstairs there are two very small bedrooms and a bath. There is really no storage, and out behind the galley kitchen there is a small garden area that is completely full of the detritus of former lodgers and useful things that have no space indoors. The sitting room has an iron grate and fireplace that once served as the only source of heat for the home, but now the chimney has been pressed into use for the gas fired central heating and its prepaid meter.

A Sri Lankan couple are the official residents of number eight, and they have a toddler who is now nearing two years old. They occupy the front bedroom and they have two shelves in the small fridge and half of the cabinets in the kitchen. The other bedroom is occupied by their three 'unofficial' lodgers, including Alfred and two Nigerian men around his age. There was a bunkbed in their room that took up most of the space and the Nigerians used them. Alfred had a foam mattress that he stored under the bunkbed but as often as not he'd go down to the sitting room after bedtime and sleep on the sofa. The house was so small that no matter where you slept you were woken during the night by the crying of the small boy, Hemantha and the ministrations of his hyperattentive mother. Each of the lodgers paid the couple sixty pounds sterling per week rent, even though they knew the couple lived rent free.

Alfred used his key and came through the door and could see through to the end of the house. Noise from the TV in the sitting room droned out into the hallway and he heard heavy footsteps from up the stairs. In the kitchen he could see Nuvina, Hemantha's mother, holding Hemantha on her hip and pouring boiling water from a kettle into a small bowl.

"Hello, Nuvina," Alfred said.

"Good affnun," she replied. "Tea?"

"No, thank you," he said. He took off his wet coat and hung it on the peg by the door and put his backpack in the small open space below the stairs. He trudged into the sitting room, which had one couch and one oversized chair and a coffee table. Across from the table a small TV set sat on a packing crate. No one was in the sitting room and it still felt overcrowded. A soap opera droned out of the set with no one watching it.

Alfred sat heavily on the couch and shut his eyes, which immediately stung from lack of sleep. His mind powered down and in short order he was deeply, nutritiously asleep. He came to twenty minutes later when one of the Nigerian men shook his knee and called to him to wake up. Alfred was sitting on one end of the couch and one of the Nigerian housemates was sitting on the other end of the couch and the other was in the big chair. They both wore fluorescent yellow 'hi-viz' vests and they were already wearing their clunky steel toed boots. One of the men was holding a third hi-viz vest and Alfred saw his pair of boots on the floor next to the couch.

"Time for Alfred to become Ade," the housemate who woke Alfred said. "Come, eat before we go."

Alfred drew in a long yawning breath through his nose and stretched back against the couch and the wall behind it, lifting is hands and breaking into a full yawn. The smell of food came in from the kitchen, and it was Nuvina who had been cooking. The lodgers had a new arrangement with her such that, for a few pounds, she would cook something for them before they left for their afternoon shift, and Alfred had agreed to participate. He had thought that after returning from the Liberian war that he could eat absolutely anything if it would keep him alive. This was true, but he also found that living in a place where food was so prevalent and readily available that preferences impacted his diet more than he expected. And, being honest with himself, he just didn't like the spices Nuvina used and the smell put him off – he just didn't like Sri Lankan food.

He leaned forward and put on the vest and slipped his feet into the boots.

"I belly full on chips," he said. "You go chop. I wait you outside."

His Nigerian housemates had found him a job at the fruit packing plant they worked at in the docklands, and more importantly they had found him a person to be when he was there. They had a persona, a Nigerian named Ade Babalola, whose paperwork was processed but who was not there to take the job, for whatever reason. They brought Alfred in and took a portion of his earnings as a finder's fee and an administration fee for providing papers. Ade paid taxes and national insurance but he would never draw on public benefits; regardless of the legal status it was a good arrangement for the native English.

These young Nigerian men were nice enough and aside from good natured ribbing about jollof rice and national soccer teams, they didn't make a big deal out of his being Ghanaian. In truth, Asians and Eastern Europeans generally couldn't tell the difference between West Africans and called them all Nigerians anyway. Alfred had work that required him to communicate in a manner recognisable as fluent to native English, but these men did not. They were not of the class of monied Nigerians whose focus was on education, wealth and power. These were people from a developing community who were desperate for subsistence first and a better life second. They never needed to alter their speech to take advantage of an opportunity, so they spoke here in the manner they had brought with them. And to fit in and be more easily understood, Alfred dipped into the pidgin of his childhood when speaking with them and the others at the plant.

Without zipping the vest or tying the boots Alfred stood and stretched again and the extra inches of the soles of the boots made him feel ready to work. His housemates went into the kitchen and Alfred stepped out the front door to get away from the odours of Sri Lankan cuisine and Hemantha's nappy. Outside the drizzle had kept up and the sun was well on its way down even though it was early afternoon. He looked down the row of houses of Hare's Run and saw some of the front lights coming on. Each house had an eaves built over the doorway, giving the impression of a gable halfway up the face of the house. Outside of number ten he could see one of the neighbours and smell her second-hand smoke.

She was an Eastern European woman in an oversized winter coat bundled up around her neck though her legs were essentially bare. She was heavily made up and she smoked greedily against the discomfort of the cold. She was close enough that he could not ignore her, and she called him over. He took the few steps to the cover of their eaves and tried to remember her name. It was either Eva or Anna. They changed every couple of months. When he got to the front of her house the blinds on the front windows lifted and stayed up long enough for someone to assess that he was neither an opportunity nor a threat.

"Khello my khandsome neighbour," she said. "You are want a cigarette?"

Now that he was near enough he could smell fresh smoke and the smell of stale smoke at the same time. Her English was quite good, compared to the others who had come before her. He tried to remember if they had met before or if it had been her predecessor.

"No, thank you," Alfred said, "I don't smoke."

She stepped back a step and took him in, looking from his workboots to his hi-viz vest.

"We are all preparing for the work," she said.

He knew what she meant. Her garish makeup was not artistically done but it was visually impactful. She wore fishnets over bare legs and she wore spiked heels. He could guess what she had on under the winter coat. When he first moved in with Nuvina's family he noticed the comings and goings of strange men at odd hours, and once when he was taking out the rubbish the 'man' of the house came out to confront him, not knowing who he was or why he was there. Alfred made sure they were properly introduced, and since then he had become acquainted with each of the service providers who came into residence there.

He took a guess. "Eva, is it?"

"Anna," she said, "we met…" she stumbled looking for words, "…before."

He remembered now. She had met him on the footpath between the cemetery and the residential road, recognised him as a neighbour and tried to get him to advertise her services among the West African diaspora, which he explained he was unable to do. She seemed to take it all in stride.

He thought to ask her something, then thought better of it. Maybe it was because he was about to go off and pretend to be someone he was not, and someone he did not care to be. She saw him lost in thought and touched his shoulder.

"What?" she asked. "What is it?"

"Let me ask you," he said, "if it's OK."

"OK, OK," she said, gesticulating expansively as if to indicate that everything is OK to ask.

"How do you love someone when you don't know them?" he asked. As soon as he asked he wished he could take it back; he was sure there was no way she could actually know what he was trying to ask, and even if she did, the question was overly intrusive. She seemed to read his discomfort on his face.

"OK, OK," she said, "It's OK. I am like movie star. I am acting with mens. My job is actor."

While that landed with him and he was reflecting on it his two housemates came out of the door of number eight and called to him. It was time to start the journey to the plant.

"I have to go," he said, "have a safe night at work."

She reached out and squeezed his upper arm. "You are good man," she said, "You will having your dream."

He joined his housemates and they walked back down the Pleasance to East Hill and on to the bus stop outside the rail station where they caught the first bus of the two bus journey to the plant. Throughout the journey they engaged in light hearted banter and vehement complaints about the job.

Alfred found himself lost in his thoughts. Whether loving or aggressive, he always found the intimacy of the act demanded authenticity. He couldn't imagine eliciting a powerful emotional reaction while remaining so aloof. And yet here he was, spending so many of his waking hours cajoling, protecting, cleaning those who could not do for themselves. Wasn't wiping another person's ass undeniably intimate? But somehow he neither loved nor despised his charges – what did that say about him as a functional person?

It had been a very long time since anyone had told him out loud that he was a good man. He wanted to believe it, but what evidence did she have that he was good? The fact that he had asked that question and all that it meant, or maybe that he had asked permission? The question was, at its core, about separating the dancer from the dance. Can a good person perform an evil act and remain a good person? He had asked how she could love a person she didn't know. He may as easily have asked how could you kill a person you don't hate. He had put so many memories and feelings about those memories in a tightly closed box, but he could feel the hinges loosening. And he could feel the disquiet undoing the ceasefire with his own guilt. But he was a good man. She said as much punctuated by a touch, an off-centre smile around exhaled smoke, an earnest and unbroken stare. He felt that they had connected in that moment. Then the bus stopped outside the fruit packing plant and her words came back to him - I am acting with mens.

****

They had arrived at Gravesend, so named because this was the point in the Thames where the ocean tides drew everything back out to sea. Here the Thames had a deep enough anchorage and a strong enough draught to accommodate some oceangoing ships. This was a natural hub for controlling and moving goods and cargo into and out of the London metropolis and had been so for centuries. Huge warehouses were laid out in industrial complexes to funnel in cargo from the ports in the Northfleet and Rotherhithe areas and from the 'new' motorways connected to the tunnel under the English Channel not far away in Dover. The men were deposited outside of one such warehouse and the bus pulled away.

They joined a stream of workers coming from different buses and from the large parking lot and filed through the gate in the fence and through the door of the main entrance. All wore hi-viz vests and steel toed boots, and all wore warming headgear as they would be in a refrigerated environment for their whole shift. Inside the building they passed directly into the common area with access to the breakroom. On the other side of the breakroom the corridor was cordoned off by a waist high metal corral that fed the workers past the timeclock where they would punch in. At these times between shifts there were workers from both shifts milling about in the common area and the breakroom was packed. As far as anyone knew, there were no British workers there. Half of the workers were Eastern European, about a third were African and Caribbean and the remainder were South Asian. They clumped together in their communities in the breakroom and filed through the corral together and self-segregated on the lines.

Alfred and his housemates assumed all the white workers were Polish. The work was physical and required a high degree of fitness. The Polish have a national service requirement so all of the young men do at least nine months of military service at age eighteen. Fresh out of the Polish army and without marital or home ownership commitments many young men leave Poland straightaway and find manual labour in England. The minimum wage in sterling puts enough zloty in their pockets to begin their lives as university students, tradesmen or shopkeepers back home. So there are a lot of young, military-minded men who are on their own for the first time and encountering people from different backgrounds for the first time. To avoid conflict they stick to their own and keep their minds on their jobs.

The building is a typical space building, constructed out of corrugated metal and gypsum board and though it is three stories high there are no floors separating the space. There are offices, common areas and engineer's rooms at each level, built only against the walls. The vast interior space is taken up by a monstrous set of conveyors and sorting stations, so it looked like a massive child's toy set, fully constructed. There were receiving docks where product came in and was unloaded from tractor trailers using pallet jacks. The fruit was then unpacked by workers and loaded onto conveyors by type, where it went to clearing and washing stations to separate the product from the debris and mini-wildlife at its point of origin. From there it went to sorting stations where it was portioned out according to set procedures for produce type and customer, and then to packing stations where it was wrapped and labelled. Alfred's station was at the final stop. It was where someone stopped and ever so briefly inspected the final package for consistency in weight, packaging and quality before sending it to be loaded onto a pallet and shipped for fulfilment. Alfred had been assigned this job because he had been so good at all of the other jobs before them. Heavy lifting at unloading does not prepare someone to inspect the quality of fruit, nor does accuracy with a sprayer or speed in wrapping portions. Alfred soon learned that his rejection of portions led to poor metrics for those lines that sent them, and he found that he quickly became unpopular among his peers. Regardless, Alfred preferred this job because it required both his body and his mind. When he was unloading trucks or operating the sprayer only, his body would go on autopilot and his mind would wander places he did not want it to go.

A loud klaxon blared three times and echoed across the empty space while spinning red lights positioned around the entire facility flashed dark and warning. Overhead doors in receiving and shipping went up with rattling roars and the system of belts, sprayers and warehouse vehicles all clambered to life together, raising a dull roar that would persist for the next eight hours, broken only by break time. All the men made their ways to their stations while trying to finish off cups of tea and donning their ear protection. Alfred had to make his way close to the fulfilment station and climb up one tier of bolted metal scaffolding; it was a five-minute walk. Once he was ensconced in his place he would get a minute or two before the first products of the shift began to advance down the belt and he would find out what product he was working with. He settled in and prepared himself to focus because his role was both mentally and physically taxing. He had four rolls of stickers on a dowel hanging to the right of his head; green for good, red for failed on quality, yellow for failed on weight, quantity or packaging and black for failed on presence of foreign matter. Each package got a single sticker and was 'split' to the left for failed or the right for fulfilment.

After only about two minutes the first products came around the corner on the belt and he could see that he would be working with bananas tonight. He liked working with bananas because the quality was fairly easy to judge and the portions were often based on piece count rather than weight. Since they were in transparent bags he often did not even have to lift them and could put the correct sticker and split them quickly. But he also hated working with bananas because it gave the white workers a built in vehicle for racist tropes. Owusu Charles grew up in a country that had different tribes and cultures that were different in stark ways. Northern Muslims came down from the Sahel every year seeking refuge and respite from the hungry season. Every year their infants, elderly and infirmed fell victim to want and many families became seasonal refugees in the areas around Sunyani and Kumasi. The local Akans took the 'othering' shortcuts of populations presented with refugee flows. They called them 'twins' because they all looked alike to Akan eyes. They took advantage of their despair to engage them in labour that exhausted them physically and left them just barely above the subsistence line, or in worse cases robbed them of their dignity without consideration for their common humanity. In Liberia there were enemies and there were comrades; the well being of comrades was often placed above that of self, but enemies were dehumanised out of necessity. Neither Owusu nor Alfred had ever been a Black man in the way that Alfred was now. He couldn't have imagined how pervasive race is in every aspect of his life in this culture. As far as he could tell, to a great degree race determined opportunity and living standard. Even for wealthy upper class, 'posh' Black people race permeated every conversation and impacted every business dealing. Owusu Charles had been Akan, had been an enemy, had been 'other', but Alfred Birima was Black. He disliked it, but he had no illusion that things were any different in Barcelona, Marseilles or New York.

Alfred's station was one of the only entrances to the tunnels and walkways built into the maze of belts and machinery for engineers to access key points for tuning and repair. Because of this, the shift engineer came through Alfred's station an average of three times per shift. He was, of course, a white man, whom Alfred got to know fairly well. He was about Alfred's age and although he wore the same vest and boots his sweatshirts and other clothes were clearly low cost. He didn't have the Polish military haircut nor did he have the Polish military body type. In fact, he looked as if mosquitoes had been harassing and biting him all night. His eyes were sunken and brown-rimmed but his skin was a waxy milk white. He had black hair that he dyed even blacker, and his bearing was generally indifferent. He rounded the corner now and started walking up the gangway that led to Alfred's station. Alfred looked up and saw him just as he was edging over to pass by. He gave Alfred the middle finger, which Alfred readily returned. Since no one could hear each other they had devolved to simple gestures of greeting and this was theirs alone. There was no enmity in it but they used it to recognise that each was an outsider in his tribe. Although the engineer was white, he was older than the average Polish worker and he was a member of the Roma community from Romania. They did not allow him a sense of belonging and his defence was not to care. Through the few times they communicated verbally Alfred learned this and grew to like him. He must have exited from a different point of egress because Alfred did not see him for the rest of the shift but after about an hour he could see that the banana line had been adjusted and slowed slightly so the quality of product coming to Alfred was better and his shift was easier.

At breaktime he saw that he had a voicemail from Sunita and he called her back. He couldn't leave the break area and even though the machinery was all shut down he still had to shout to be heard over the lively banter. He shouted 'hello' into the phone when she picked up.

"Are you out at the normal time, Freddy? I'll come collect you, love," came whispering out. Alfred was straining to hear and he was again, as always, surprised by Sunita's speech. Sunita Rajkumar was born in Yorkshire and though her grandparents had arrived from Kenya with nothing but old clothes, they had become prominent shopkeepers. Their son, Sunita's father, became an important barrister in the city of York and he established one of the most successful practices in the northeast. He and his wife insisted that their children, including their daughter Sunita, go to the best private schools and receive the best tuition that money could buy. All four of them were made to understand they were expected to excel academically and become successful in whichever profession they chose. One son and one daughter joined the family practice and Sunita and her other brother both became medical doctors. Sunita was completing her practicals to qualify as a psychiatrist and had been posted to the London area by the NHS. Whenever she spoke with colleagues at the care homes she spoke in private school English, and the few times Alfred heard her on the phone with her parents he could tell her Hindi was fluent. Whenever she spoke to Alfred or other friends though, she spoke what she called Yorkshire, which at first was very hard for Alfred to understand. There were more glottal stops and word choice was different than for other native English speakers. Idioms were at first unintelligible but he learned from context and over time what each meant to her. For example, if she were wildly enthusiastic about something then she would say 'that'll do'.

Shortly after Alfred began at the care home Sunita saw him carrying his conversational English book and offered to help him study. He took her up on it because he needed the help, and because he found her attractive. He liked her almond eyes and straight black hair and he liked that her body wasn't hard or sharp or flat like so many idealised representations of women in English media. In fact, some of the other men told Alfred that they found her overweight and a bit plain. Alfred had always kept his own counsel on his preferences and ignored them. For his part, Alfred did not pursue women. If he found a woman attractive then he simply remained near her long enough to receive her advances and then did not reject them. He and Sunita became very familiar very quickly, and in short order she was facilitating sessions to help him in all areas of 'adjustment to the U.K.' as she called it.

"I get out at 11:00," he said, "Is this your time for the 'therapy' you do?"

"No, Love. This is a booty call. Don't you have those in Ghana?" the tinny laughter on the other end of the phone was drowned out by the racket of industry coming back to life.

****

Alfred told his housemates that he would be staying with Sunita and that they should go on without him. After the shift change he crossed the street, passed the bus stop and ducked into the dark parking lot of a warehouse that did not run shifts around the clock. This was the only place Sunita could safely park during the comings and goings of the shift change. Alfred walked through the opening in the fence and saw the sleek grey Mercedes idling quietly with its running lights on. As he approached she turned on the headlights and unlocked the doors. He opened the passenger door and greeted her. He insisted on spreading newspapers on the passenger seat before he sat, although she didn't care. He spread out the newspaper, sat down and was buckling his seatbelt . He could see that she was impatiently waiting to kiss her greeting. She started driving and he sunk down into the comfort of the bucket seat. The car was far more luxurious than he was used to and he always felt undeserving when he rode in it. He didn't want to distract her while she drove so he only spoke when she initiated conversation and took care not to block her view at corners. She followed her satnav's directions and went a different way than the bus route. They wound up getting on the A2 and taking the M25 for a couple of exits. This is where Alfred got a real appreciation for the quality of the vehicle's engineering. Sunita had a bit of a heavy foot. The M25 is the largest highway in the country, and these exits around the border between Essex and Kent were the best maintained and the best engineered. It was almost completely empty and when they hit a straightaway she said aloud, "Alright baby, show me what Daddy paid for!" She punched the gas and Alfred felt himself pushed back into the seat hard, as if he were in a rocket. In no time they were slowing to cross the Queen Elizabeth II bridge at the Dartford Crossing and Alfred took the opportunity to register the view. On his left were the major shipping vessels traversing the Thames Estuary with their lights illuminating the shimmering water below, showing just enough of the wake in the twinkling buoy lights to suggest motion. Alfred thought of it as a visual song. To his right there was the brash outline of Canary Wharf at night; the iconic London skyline lit up in opposition to the night, an actual bar chart of humanity's hubris.

Immediately across the bridge they exited the highway through a series of rotaries and found themselves deposited on the London Road just south of Greenhithe and they took the left toward Swanscombe. Even though it was full night Alfred could tell by the darkness that they were out of the city. They were on their way to Sunita's home at Ingress Park in Greenhithe. It was a development built around the original site of Ingress Abbey, a fortified religious site commissioned by Edward III in 1307 to complement the nunnery at Dartford Priory. In the early 1800s an Elizabethan mansion was constructed on the site and this mansion is now the centrepiece of the upper-class development of semidetached and detached homes and two- and three-bedroom flats built into terraced rows. Sunita's parents had purchased her two-bedroom flat as an investment, they said, when they found out she would be spending at least three years in the Dartford area. Ingress Park has manicured lawns, well-lit wide roads, crews for private sanitation and tree maintenance and secure covered parking. The buildings all have security and each tenant has a unique code for access to the common areas. In Sunita's flat the kitchen and bath fittings have a sleek industrial design and the kitchen is as large as the entire footprint of eight Hare's Run. The first time Alfred had stayed the night he estimated that he could reach Hare's Run at an alert march in roughly fifty minutes. He was dumbfounded that this place existed while less than an hour's walk away there were people eating from trash bins and pissing where they slept in the underpass.

Sunita had nightclothes for Alfred and the first thing he did was to shower while she made him a plate from what she had cooked earlier; she laid out a side salad, a salmon filet with rice pilaf and a sparkling water with lime. By the time she had done that and changed into her nightclothes she was able to sit at the table and pour herself a glass of wine just in time to join him. After a bit of light banter she transitioned into the topic she wanted to discuss before they retired for the night.

"Freddy, I want to talk to you about something," she said.

"OK," he replied.

"You remember our deal, right? You will always tell me the truth and I will stop asking about something if you tell me you can't say any more about a subject," she said. "You're still OK to stick with that?"

"Yes," he replied, wondering where this was heading.

"I really think our sessions – not our time 'together' but our sessions – have really been going well and you've been making a lot of progress."

She was referring to the cognitive behavioural therapy sessions, he knew. She had started with simple mechanics, like getting him to follow her finger with his eyes as he remembered experiences that were scary. At first she guided him away from the most traumatic experiences and strengthened the capability of dispassionate self-reflection by focusing only on the scary, knowing that the things he was likely to have been most traumatised by were things he did to others. She introduced the metronome and over time he became adept at observing the facts and understanding the circumstances of his memories. She had 'prescribed' him a five-mile jog three times a week, where he was to employ the same tactics using the sound of his feet hitting the pavement and the sound and cadence of his own breath. Alfred was still 'match fit' and he could run five miles quite fast if he were so inclined, but she told him to pace it to an hour to complete the circuit. To an observer he looked like a young man out running the London Road, but in his own head he was unpacking and then flattening and smoothing memories and returning them to their boxes ready to be put to better use or ignored if possible. She had described it to him as doing laundry, taking something rumpled and unclean and imposing order on it, and making it wearable in his life. He undertook the exercise mainly for her but he was soon amazed to find that the benefits were very real. He had gotten through a fair bit of the catalogue, through the most trying events of scorching the earth in Liberia, to 'fragging' their Brigadier, to the dread of being 'invited' to join the dictator's bodyguard. There he hit a roadblock. He could run from Dartford to Truro and back and he would not be able to finish laundering the last chapter of his time in uniform.

"In honesty I can tell there are things worrying you that we haven't really talked about. Not really," she went on. "I get the sense that you are concerned about empathic deficit and maybe you're worried about dissociative disorder," she saw that she had done it again, rattled off something a colleague would get but a layperson would not. She hurried to explain further, "I think you're worried that you don't care enough about people, Freddy. And I think you're worried that the old you in Africa and the new you in the U.K. aren't enough of the same person." Her Yorkshire accent dragged U.K. out to four syllables.

She lived in a bubble of luxury, he thought, but there was a reason she was considered such a good doctor. She was very perceptive and didn't delay in addressing issues once she had diagnosed them. He expected there would be more to this than a simple observation. He was a man's man, a Ghanaian soldier and an Ashanti warrior. His first instinct was to deny any problem as it was a sign of weakness. He had learned though that this woman's medicine worked if you followed the motions and the intentions of the spells. Her juju was stronger than any he saw fail in the warzone.

"That's probably true," he said.

"There's something I want you to do for me," she said.

He broke the building tension by glancing conspicuously into the bedroom. She broke into a brief burst of laughter.

"No," she said, "no, not no – yes. But that's not what I mean. Actually, when you think about it, that could help to describe it. A lot of what we do in there, you do for me." She paused to see if he understood.

"There are things you do to make me alone feel good," he nodded his understanding. "If your brain or psyche were broken then you wouldn't be capable of doing that without getting something out of it for you alone." She paused to check his understanding again. "So, clinically speaking, if it works in there than it can be made to work everywhere in your life."

He did understand, and he hadn't thought about it like that before. He did do things because it felt right to make her feel good. For Sunita Rajkumar, he cared. And it sounded like she said that if he cared for her then he could care for others again. He knew her fairly well now, he thought, and she would not shy away from lancing a pustulated infection to allow the healing to begin. She often said that her oath to do no harm did not mean to cause no pain. She had said that many times the only way to lasting health was through a painful treatment regimen.

He realised he had been staring at his plate and looked up at her. She had been watching him think.

"OK, so what do you want me to do?" he asked.

"Tomorrow is Sunday. I want you to go to confession," she said.

****

In the morning, after staying in bed late and having a big breakfast, they drove to Our Lady of Assumption in Gravesend. They parked a block away at a small park where the road to Northfleet split from the road to Gravesend's downtown. They walked back to the church, which was a large building that looked like miniature version of a powerstation from the Victorian era. It was a very boxy brick building with a tower in the front that did not taper nor did it hold any kind of iconography in lieu of a spire. There were no windows along the outside and an ordinary person would not identify it as a religious building at all. Sunita had timed it so they would miss the service and arrive in time for the sacrament of Reconciliation. She herself had never been inside the church and she did not expect to see anyone except for old white people coming out of the church and she was surprised to see young white people coming out of the church, along with small groups of brown people who were clearly immigrants. As they approached Alfred recognised several of the people from the fruit packing plant and he greeted them with a nod. He turned his head to see where they were going and he saw a gathering place like a pub or restaurant across the street with signage in a foreign language.

The outside of the building belied the formality of the space arranged inside. There were rows of pews in the nave sectioned off from the stations of the cross and the chancel, behind a carved partition, had the raised pulpit to the left. Along the walls where the nave met the chancel there were two rows of pews roped off and a confessional on each side. The confessional to the right had a velvet rope across both doors and handles, indicating there was no one inside. Sunita led Alfred by the hand to the pew near the confessional and they sat. No one else was in the church now and after the last parishioners had left the building fell silent. They both sat looking around the church, taking in the unfamiliar Catholic iconography and unsure of what to do next. After a minute or two a priest in vestments emerged from the sanctuary and walked purposefully to the confessional, not looking anywhere or at anyone. He went inside and closed the door. To Alfred he seemed to be a rather old white man who didn't appear very engaged.

Sunita took Alfred's hand and told him to go through the other door into the adjacent box. He whispered a question about what would happen and how to proceed and she reminded him that she was a Hindu and pushed at his shoulder until he left.

He went into the confessional and noticed first that it was backlit somewhere, so it wasn't full dark. There was a triangular seat built into the far corner with a frugal cushion upholstered on. There was a kneeler close to the wall abutting the other box, which he could now see was actually quite a dark screen.

Outside in her pew Sunita could hear the two men begin a conversation that would carry on for over an hour. At least twice she heard the staccato sobs of a grown man crying, and she could tell it wasn't Alfred.

The conversation began with an awkward and eerily long silence until the priest said, "Begin your Act of Contrition, son."

"I don't know what that is," Alfred replied.

"Are you a Catholic, son?" the priest asked. Alfred could tell he was a native English speaker but he wasn't an Englishman. He thought maybe he was from Australia or South Africa.

"No, sir, I'm a Baptist," Alfred said.

"Ah, I see," said the priest, "Catholic priests are called 'father'."

"What?"

"Priests are called father. You should refer to me as father."

"Oh. Yes, OK," Alfred said. He remembered his Catholic comrades telling him that long ago. He thought it odd that a man who could have no children should be called father.

"So you're not a Catholic but you've come here for your sins to be forgiven. Why?" the priest went on.

"Egya, I'm not sure. My doctor brought me here because something is stopping my healing that I can't get past."

"Eh-jaah? What is that?" the priest asked.

"I said that? I didn't realise. It means 'father' in my language," Alfred said.

"What language? Where are you from?"

"I speak Twi. I'm from Mampong-Esoro, the land of high hills. Where are you from?" Alfred's curiosity had gotten the better of him.

"I'm from Cloch na Coillte, the land of the stone in the woods," said the priest. "You're Ghanaian. You're in your late twenties. Were you in the Liberian war?"

This old man was more aware of the wider world than Alfred had expected. Alfred considered what to tell him or not to tell him. He was wary of disclosing his past to anyone. The pause grew long enough to sidetrack the conversation.

The priest continued, "This is a place of sanctuary and confidence. Anything you tell me here I cannot share with anyone. I am acting as the representative of God, who is the only one who can forgive. No government department or law enforcement agency can ever learn what is said here. This is the place for you to give voice to your sins, in order for them to be forgiven by Almighty God, forever." There was a short pause while the priest thought, and then he quickly added, "I should tell you that I would be bound to tell authorities if something you disclose has someone in danger now – were any of your sins against the law?"

Alfred contemplated that for a second, then said, "I was in Liberia. And as for my sins being against the law, where I was there was no law. There was no justice, there were no human rights. Where there is no law there can be no crimes, correct? Where there is no humanity can there be no sin?"

"Do you believe in God, son?" the priest asked.

"Of course I do father," Alfred said, "but I know there are places God has turned away from, places on earth empty of God."

"I know how it can feel like that sometimes," the priest replied, "I felt that way about El Salvador when I was young. But God is in the people. Each of us carries His divine light within us. Wherever there are humans expressing free will there is humanity."

"Soldiers follow orders," Alfred said, "soldiers do as they are commanded."

The priest heard a change in Alfred's voice. He knew not to fill the silence that followed. He waited for Alfred to continue.

"Even if the commands are to harm the helpless, it must be done. There is no free will."

The priest chose his words carefully. "What would have happened if you refused to carry out your orders?"

"Refusing an order in a war zone is not just insubordination. It is treason. Refusing an order will bring death."

"It is human to be afraid," the priest said, "it is divine to know in your heart what is right and what is wrong. But the world isn't black or white. There are choices you must make and things you must do that will damage your soul, no matter what."

The priest paused to let Alfred reflect. He went on, "You have to say out loud the choices you made, how they hurt people, and that you are truly sorry. If you bring your sins out, confront your conscience and ask for God's forgiveness out loud then it will certainly and finally be granted. I promise you."

He paused again to let Alfred decide whether or not to continue. Alfred had the old feeling that came over him when he knew he would be going into combat. He was ready to open that box, take everything out and examine it under the eye of God himself.

"I can tell you everything and nobody else will know. Then in the end you give me God's forgiveness for all I have done. Then nothing else?" Alfred asked.

"Not nothing," the priest said, "Your soul is more free from sin than the day you were born. Then you take your life into the future you choose without the burden of the past."

"Alright," Alfred said, "I'll tell you."

He started by explaining how it felt to be a teenager away from home for the first time, filled with enthusiasm and purpose at the prospect of returning peace and the benefits of a well-ordered civil society to the people of Liberia. Then he explained what it was like being in a minority unit in an essentially Nigerian army. He explained how they were sent to the worst of the fighting in the worst conditions, how they were not supported and how they were told they must provide for themselves deep in the bush. Foraging in some villages became looting, really. They told the local people they required their support to protect them from the rebels, who often were their own family. Alfred told the priest how they were harassed by snipers and ambushed whenever they ranged anywhere on operations. How it became clear in one village where the people had to have known of an upcoming ambush and didn't provide any warning. Of venting their frustration and their grief for their dead by extracting revenge in the form of reprisal killings.

The priest could hear Alfred's voice and demeanour change as the story went on. He started with enthusiasm in his voice when he talked of helping the people of Liberia, then it became angry with the realisation of their own victimhood. His vivid descriptions of the deaths of his comrades was chilling. His voice became shrouded in grief and shame when he told of the killing of unarmed civilians. He told it as a thing that had happened, in passive voice. The priest interrupted him here, saying it was important that he say explicitly what he himself had done in order to receive absolution. It brought Alfred out of his cadence and refocused him on his own role and his own actions. He wished he could say that he was not affected by those feelings and that he had acted only honourably and at the very least had done no harm himself. But he told of the very personal, very intimate acts of swinging the cutlass, of pulling the trigger. There, in the West African jungle with no one to judge, with no accountability, he had not lost his humanity but rather had freely given it away. And to whom? He had given it over to the devil within; to rage, to hatred, to the limitless frustration at their own impotence.

His rumination stopped when he heard the priest softly crying. Alfred asked why he was crying, and the priest said that he cried not only for the souls of the lost, but also for Alfred's. The priest told him that the suffering he inflicted is suffering that he too has inflicted upon himself, and that he has borne it even until now. He quoted Mark 8:36 and bade Alfred to go on.

Alfred explained that once they had crossed this Rubicon they were never again the young soldiers who left Ghana. They knew they had to kill their leader in order to save their own lives, and now that there were no prohibitions of anything, they did. They would fight their way to Monrovia and join the Ghanaian unit that was positioned in a static position between two warlords' forces. The further they got into the bush the further they got away from their own humanity. Out there, Taylor had no forces, just allied warlords he had granted rights of pillage in return for fealty. These animals had kidnapped and brainwashed children into becoming murderers. After first contact with these groups they realised they had killed children. They were horrified but could not figure how to pass through the territory without having to fight, without having to carry on killing child soldiers.

Alfred then described the psychotic breaks that led to unconscious acts of violence back in Ghana after their return, and how these incidents were now crimes. These brought him to the attention of those who recruited for the dictator's bodyguard, and he rejoined some comrades in the service of this one man's paranoia. He described being party to kidnappings, torture and extrajudicial killings. He described the atmosphere of fear and paranoia and how the lives of their loved ones were held in escrow should they falter in their gruesome duties. He explained how he didn't fear death at all, but how having the lives of his family held at the whim of a paranoid and capricious dictator was unbearable. Even if he were to kill himself then that would lead to enough suspicion to doom his family.

Finally, he described how he had been given a target in a rival politician's security detail who had the same age and build profile as he himself had. He explained how he broke into the man's house alone, killed him and changed clothes with him, took his belongings and his identification and put his body in the government vehicle he had staked outside his home in Tema. He doused the body in gasoline and let it burn for a long time before detonating the bomb underneath. Then, using the dead man's passport and valuables to dash, he conspicuously crossed the border into the Ivory Coast. From there he became another nameless, stateless refugee migrating towards Europe. Sometimes he was Liberian, sometimes from Sierra Leone. Eventually through connections in the camps he came to England and was 'papered' as Alfred Birima at a cost of twenty thousand dollars cash. The name he did not disclose to the priest.

He had now done it. He had given voice to the deeds that he could not expunge from his soul. He asked the priest aloud how he could be allowed to carry on living after all of this. He asked what was waiting for him in the afterlife if he got what he deserved. The priest told him that as a child of God seeking absolution what he deserved was forgiveness. The priest forgave his sins in the name of almighty God and told him that his penance was to carry on. He must, from now on, live a life of peace and wherever possible he must undo hurts and remove fear and want from the lives of others. This he could understand. Indeed, it was how he was already trying to atone and carry on. This was the only time he had sat and told of his life all the way through in one sitting. Even as he was telling it some of it seemed too farfetched to be believable, but there it was. Now that it was all out and wasn't his alone to bear, he felt relieved of its weight. There was at least another human being who had knowledge of it and had not only declared him worthy of forgiveness, but he had also bestowed forgiveness as a divine sacrament.

When he came out of the confessional Sunita had her head on her arms leaning on the pew in front of her as if she were asleep. She looked over and him and sat up and yawned.

"Done?" she asked.

He didn't answer. He needed a minute to sit and gather himself. He had just relived so much psychological trauma that he needed to let it process. He wanted to sit quietly and in safety until he felt he could function again. He sat next to her in the pew and reached out and held her hand. The other confessional door opened and the priest came out, wiping his eyes with a handkerchief and walked on by, pausing for the briefest moment to lay a hand on Alfred's shoulder. He made eye contact with Sunita and nodded before carrying on.

****

There is a Turkish barbershop halfway up East Hill. Dark wood and mirrors are features of the interior décor and there are overstuffed, leather upholstered benches for patrons waiting for haircuts and shaves. There was an old man who was puttering around filling the receptacles that held the combs with germicide and sweeping up hair. A TV hung high in the corner was tuned rather loudly to music videos for the benefit of customers in the barber chairs and those waiting for haircuts. Although the shop was busy, the three working barbers were working slowly and engaging the customers and each other in spirited banter.

This was part of what they thought they offered as a community service. All three of the barbers were born in Turkey but they spoke English with an exaggerated South London accent which they must have worked on affecting, since they lived in Essex and were working in Kent. They must have been trying to create an atmosphere like they saw portrayed in barbershops in urban American films, but the banter was more antagonistic than collegial. They had been talking about a soccer match but then somehow got on the topic of one of their colleagues virility and manhood, and detailed barbs about what happened at a club called Atik the night before were thrown around.

This shop happened to be a preferred provider for the Dartford Burrough Council, and they had a standing order for services for recipients of council benefits. This is the reason Simon Holloway sat in one of the chairs with the barber cape velcroed around his neck, staring at himself in the mirror. Simon's carer sat in the bench against the wall, apparently lost in thought and not paying attention.

Alfred sat on the bench not lost in thought but actively engaging his memories and trying dispassionately to observe his feelings. Since he had actively confessed aloud he had felt liberated to apply Sunita's strategies to the full complement of his memories. And since then, too, he had been experiencing more powerful, impactful emotions about them. He felt this was, for his spirit, like the twinge of a knitting bone, the itch of reconnecting flesh. He had tilted fully into the anguish and the fear, and he had felt safe enough to do it because Sunita was with him, armed with her education and fortified with the knowledge of centuries of medical science behind her. She had encouraged him to employ her tactics and to normalise the process, but to remember to stay in control. He had done it so far. Now he felt like there was one final truth to encounter, one last accountability he had to own up to in order for that guileless young boy in Mampong to return, bonded to the present through the unification of the lives of Owusu Charles and Alfred Birima. He had, in this barbershop, lifted the lid on the final box.

Loud commotion, shouting and howls rose up and commanded the attention of all in the shop. The young man whose virility was questioned had made some horrible remark about a young woman passing by the shop window and the response was loud enough inside that she turned her head to see, could imagine the commentary and scowled a grimace through the window as she continued down the hill. Simon was obviously hurt by all of it. He was completely uncomfortable with the loud, inappropriate banter and when this vile, unspeakable thing was said about the nice young lady he couldn't contain his anxiety. He started to shake, his eyes turned down and his lip quivered. The barber was still engaged in the hooting afterburn of the insult when he caught Simon's reaction in the mirror, and without stopping to make one thing about something else he raised his voice again so the whole shop would hear and declared in his bad accent, "Are you some kind of a bloody simp, mate? Are you gonna fookheng croy?" He then looked around for approval from his compatriots.

Alfred had snapped back to the moment and caught Simon's reflection in the mirror. In Simon's face he could see the anxiety, the fear, the uncertainty. He could see how the sum total of his anguish was more than someone who could not understand should be expected to bear. More than that, when he looked in Simon's face he could feel the fear and uncertainty; the anguish shaking him like a ragdoll had become Alfred's too. The faces from his memory presented themselves and demanded to be felt as well, finally illuminated by the flickering light of the burning huts after these long years.

The carer got off the couch and approached the barber. The laughter died down instantly and the barber stood still, holding his scissors low. Tears were rolling down the African's face but there were no sobs, no changes to his focused and intense breathing. He made no attempt to wipe away the tears. He walked straight up to the barber and leaned forward, pushing his own face toward the barber's face, rigid, every muscle of his body tense, his jaw flexing wildly.

"I killed them all," he said, the last word bitten off into a brutal exhalation.

"Wot? You wot?" the barber was shocked and confused.

"I hacked them all to death. They were terrified. There was nothing they could do."

Simon let out a kind of a sob which led into him fairly shouting, "I don't want to stay here, Alfred!"

"No, of course not Si. Come on, we'll get your haircut somewhere nice." Alfred unfastened the barber cape and led Simon out by the hand.

****

Dr. Rajkumar sat across the table from Simon Holloway as he stared out the window.

"Are you alright Simon?" she asked in a calming voice.

"Yes, Doctor," he replied.

"What are you thinking about?" she asked.

"I'm thinking about the smell," he replied.

"The smell?" she asked, somewhat surprised.

"Yes," he said, "I always pass by here with Alfred but we never get to come inside."

Alfred approached the table walking briskly from the counter, focusing intently. He carried a tray that held a large pizza and three precariously balanced drinks.

"We're here now, Si," he said, "Pretend it's your birthday but I'm not your Mum."

"Oh that smells wonderful, doesn't it?" he asked, "A bit of pizza would be nice."

Alfred put the tray in the middle of the table, slid in next to Sunita and surreptitiously squeezed her hand.

Printed in Great Britain
by Amazon